A Dr. Eustis Mystery

Uncommon
Murder

I0634118

Tamsen Evans George

Riverhaven

Books

Uncommon Murder is a work of historical fiction. Historical names, locations, and events are accurate and intertwined with fictional situations and conversations. The Historical Notes at the end of this book provide further clarification.

Published in the United States of America by Riverhaven Books
www.RiverhavenBooks.com

Edited by Bob Haskell and Christopher E. Blackman

Paperback ISBN: 978-1-951854-47-8

Credit for front cover: Brent Goodman
Cover photo: Tamsen Evans George
Author photo by Lisa Jo Rudy
Book design by Stephanie Lynn Blackman of Whitman, MA

Also by Tamsen Evans George

Allegience: The Life and Times of William Eustis

and

Revolutionary Murder

In memory of George H. Trim

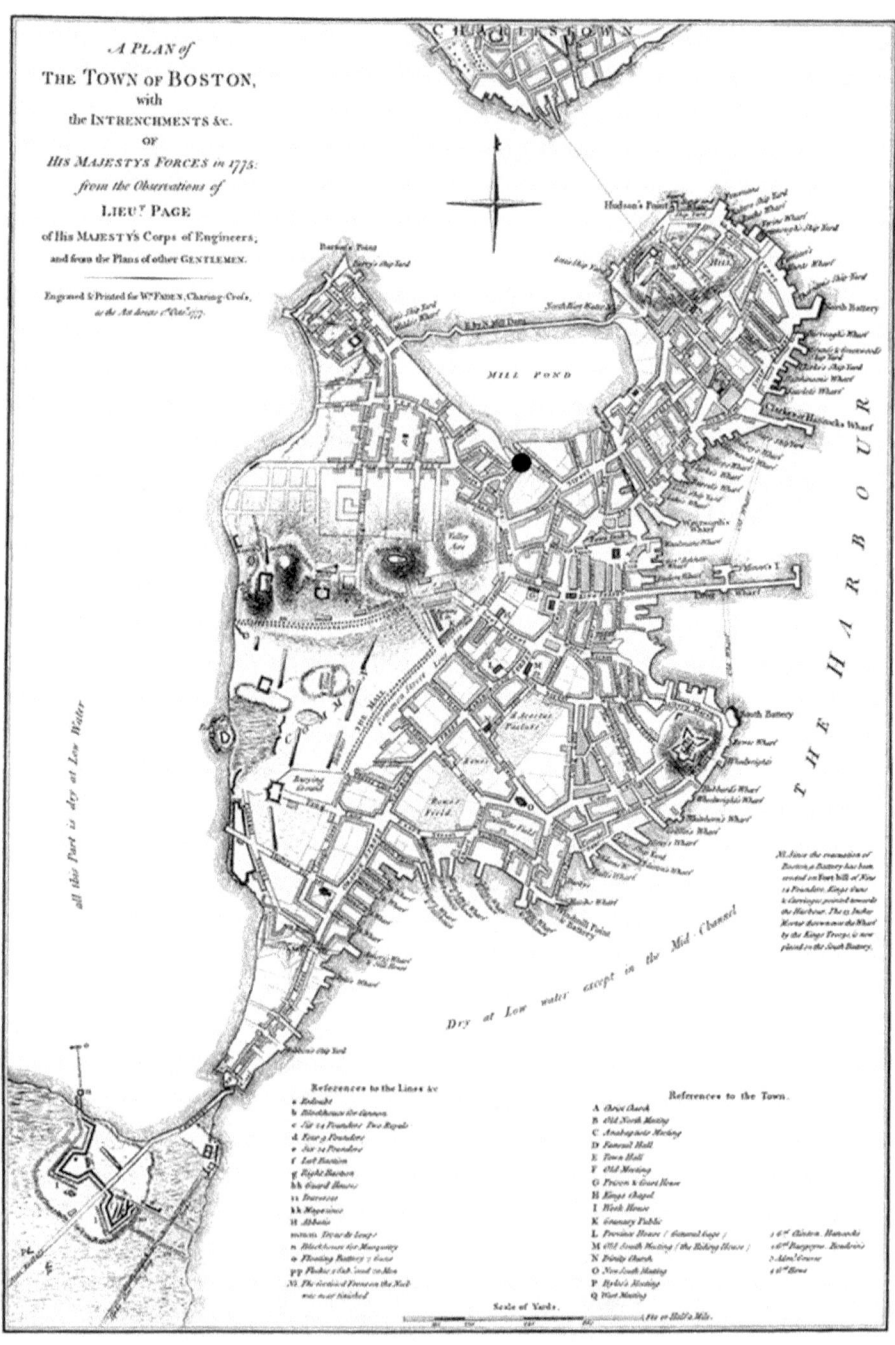

The black dot on this map shows the location of the Eustis household.

CHAPTER 1

The wind tore furiously at his coat tails, and he clapped a hand on his tricorn hat. It was what the locals called a nice, brisk day. Dr. William Eustis tried to steady the telescope he was holding in one hand as he looked out over Boston Harbor. A ship had made her way between the islands and anchored a distance out. He knew the crew was supposed to await permission before approaching one of the wharves. A yellow flag unfurled into the wind from a back stay was waving wildly. The required quarantine flag. It was usually flown on first arrival in a harbor followed by an inspection for smallpox.

He scanned the superstructure and saw very few crew members. Mayhap they were sick below? If so, that was a bad sign. He steadied the telescope once again and surveyed the length of the ship. He saw a small figure of a man work his way toward the stern and then climb to the top of the side where the ratlines attached. Going up to check the sails, Eustis thought. But then the man jumped into the harbor.

Eustis hoped the probable crew member could swim. Most sailors could not. The man's action spoke of desperation. The doctor looked around him. There appeared to be no rescue activity or any indication that the man's action had been seen.

One old man was sitting on a barrel on a wharf and gazing toward the south over the other wharves. Was he the only other one who had seen the man jump? Eustis raised his scope again and looked. Although there was plenty of small-boat activity within the harbor, there still remained no activity on deck of the now-anchored ship.

Was he running from something? God's teeth! If that man gets into the town, it defeats the idea of quarantine. Not good at all. But what might be good is to consult with his brother, Jacob, a ship broker dealing in imports and exports, in his office on the wharf. He had to return the telescope to him anyway.

"Good morning, Jacob. Brought back your telescope." Dr. Eustis greeted a few minutes later. "Could I come along with you? I was just going to take a walk along the wharves. I am curious about today's catch. And what ships are in. Which is the one that just arrived?"

"Captain Augustus Bonham's, a trading schooner, probably up from the Carolinas. Let me show you the latest one here, Bill. I've got this possibility of working with a new shipping firm to set up a route to Saint Petersburg on the Baltic. Across the Northern Atlantic. Come see their latest ship. There is only a breeze blowing."

Jacob's "breeze" just about blew them off the large wharf. The smell of the sea, salt air, and fish rode on the wind. Fish were being cleaned for market, and some of the cod were laid out on racks to dry under protective netting. Excited gulls shouted about their discoveries. Men repaired nets and unloaded the day's catch. Several cats were loitering, hoping for handouts or perhaps a bird distracted enough to be caught.

Eustis enjoyed the noisy excitement of the morning's successful bounty. He and Jacob walked out on the wharf, passing mysterious cargoes in bags, barrels, and boxes piled up for stowing or removal for delivery. Eustis wondered what was in them. What was shipped in from Empress Catherine's Russia, and what would be sent back? He could see why it fascinated Jacob. The active energy and noise stimulated the senses from nose to imagination.

As they walked along, he looked down into the harbor water on one side, saw the huge pilings that held everything above the tidal ebb and flow. Seaweed, barnacles, crabs, harbor fish, and schools of minnows. Wooden ladders let men get down to small rowboats that served the ships anchored farther out. A captain – or at least someone important – was climbing up onto the wharf from what looked like a whaleboat. A secondary officer carrying a portfolio followed the man up the ladder. The launch crew remained behind to coil lines and make the boat ready for his return.

"Captain! Sir! Please stop!" called out a man who seemed in charge of the launch that had put its passengers ashore. The captain waited for his secondary officer at the top of the ladder. He glared back down with a noticeably irritated gesture.

"What now, Mr. Fletcher?" he barked.

"There's something here in the water, sir."

"Well, I am busy as you can see, and I am not surprised. It is a harbor. There are things in the water, including fish! You can at least take care of it, can't you?" He turned and strode purposefully away followed by the man with the portfolio.

Both Eustis and Jacob paused, curiosity dominating the moment. Should they offer assistance?

"Is there a problem?" Jacob called down. "Can we help?"

The man in the launch gestured toward the wharf. "Seems to be something big floating, bumping on the barnacles and in the seaweed." He peered under the wharf. "Could even be a person."

Jacob immediately went down the ladder followed by Eustis. Clinging to the base, he looked into the shadowy dim area beneath the wharf. "You are right. It does look like a body!"

Eustis also wanted to take a look, but Jacob blocked him on the ladder.

"Jacob," he reminded him, "I'm the doctor."

"Right you are, brother," said Jacob and moved farther into the launch, freeing up the base of the ladder. Then, turning to the man who seemed to be in charge, he asked, "Do you have a boathook? Or something like a grappling hook?"

Eustis looked into the murky swirling depths under the wharf. Slivers of light fell through the cracks of the planking above. Jacob was right, he thought. And they needed to get whatever it was, and it did look fearsomely like a person, out into the light.

The man, perhaps the coxswain, at the rear of the launch gave an order, and one of the crew near the bow pulled a long pole from under the seats. It had a substantial hook on the end. He leaned far out over the side and attempted to hook onto the floating object. It took several tries and a move to the most forward of seats, but he managed to grapple onto the body, for that is what it turned out to be.

Silence, concern, mumbles of what to do among the crew in the boat

3

and then Eustis's voice. "Let me introduce myself. I am Dr. William Eustis. Can we get him to shore so I can examine him? I'm a surgeon and knowledgeable about bodies from the war years."

The stunned silence was broken. The crew moved into action, pulling the body close to the launch. Casting off, the men quickly rowed toward the muddy shore, hauling the corpse alongside. Two of the crew then jumped out and dragged it up onto the beach.

Eustis had climbed back up the ladder and hurried down the wharf to meet them, circling to the shore through weeds, tall grass, and debris, both marine and domestic. Gingerly, he walked across the mud toward the body, giving a momentary thought to his shoes. Drat it. The second pair that would need serious cleaning.

Jacob had hailed the watchman, and they awaited his arrival and the reveal of the drowned man. Looking it over with his professional eye, Eustis saw that the man had been in the water long enough for rigor mortis to have come and gone. The head and gray face were somewhat damaged from contact with the rocks and pilings under the wharf.

Gently closing his eyes, he noticed how young the man was – in his twenties. His clothing was soaked, of course, and it was hard to tell what had killed him, or even if he had drowned. He was dressed in what Eustis thought of as sailor's garb – homespun linen shirt, canvas pants, and bare feet. Rubbing against the sides of the pilings had not helped. The face was not in good shape which might make it difficult to identify the deceased. Luckily, neither crabs nor fish seemed to have gotten to it.

His hair lay in tangles plastered across his forehead. After a cursory look, Eustis said, "We'll have to find out who he was." But there seemed to be nothing in his single pocket. The crew looked around, unsure of what they had gotten into, knowing their captain might return at any moment.

Jacob stepped forward, relieving them of further duties. "I know the people here. We will wait for the watchman. You can go back to your post. Thank you for what you have done."

The crew was clearly relieved, and the coxswain expressed his appreciation. "We are with the ship, *Reliable*, just in from Halifax. If we

4

can be of further assistance, just let us know."

Eustis could tell the man was being polite and certainly hoped that neither he nor his crew would be further involved. They pulled back to their position at the foot of the ladder.

Eustis crouched by the body, and Jacob hurried to get more help. Eustis thought immediately of the man he saw jumping from the ship flying the quarantine flag that had entered the harbor. Could this be that fellow? No, not enough time for the rigor to have gone, however.

It was not more than ten minutes before Jacob returned with several dock workers who brought a large barrow used to carry goods off a ship. They efficiently loaded the man's body into the barrow and started to trundle it back toward the slope that accessed the wharf. They suddenly stopped, and one called back to Jacob and Eustis left standing on the beach. "Where shall we take 'em?"

"Can you just pause a bit?" Jacob asked. "I sent a boy for the watchman, and the constable may have to be involved as well." The men seemed happy to take a break, and one called to the gathering crowd. "Hey, you lot. Anyone got somethin' to drink? Beer or anythin'?"

Eustis stepped close to Jacob and muttered, "We'll have to get an identification. I wonder if he was known on the docks."

Jacob went over to the men, asking them, then checked with some of the bystanders. "Does anyone know this fellow?"

"Yeah, I do," said one wearing a faded red headscarf and the full trousers usually affected by seamen.

"Me too," said another. " 'E's the one wot fills in when we need 'nother to make up a crew. Lives somewhere here 'bouts."

"Boardin' 'ouse, prob'ly" said the first.

"You got a name for him?" asked Jacob.

"'E said 'is name was Monty somethin'. Thurman mebbe, or somethin' like that."

"Did he work around here? Or for anyone?"

"Aye. 'E did small jobs for Captain Bonham. Deliveries an' such."

At that point there was a commotion on the wharf. The watchman had arrived. He climbed down to look over the situation and was told about the man being found under the wharf. Then he introduced himself to Eustis and Jacob on the beach. "John McAllister. My watch house is just up that road. If I need anything, I'll get a hold of you at some point, doctor. Meanwhile, I'll get this body tucked away." And immediately he was off to deal with the men and the barrow.

Eustis was not sure where they would trundle the body but assumed he'd find out when the watchman returned to talk to him. He had not taken their names and addresses. Probably he would expect them to wait there. But for how long? He and Jacob waited, watching, but then the watchman left followed by the two men with the body in the barrow. Well, he was the man in charge, thought Eustis. The beach and wharf emptied out of spectators, so they left as well.

They walked up to the street, passing the crowd that had gathered and was now enjoying talking about what they had seen. Eustis noticed a young woman with a small child, perhaps two years old, clinging to her skirts. She looked familiar, something about her reddish blonde hair under her mob cap. He turned to Jacob, indicating he was going over to talk to her. Jacob was amused, noting how attractive she looked.

As Eustis approached, he was startled by the reaction of the woman. "Dr. Eustis? Really! Is it you?"

He thought he had recognized Norah Lindholm from the women's settlement near West Point. She did not look terribly different, similar dress, no apron, but she did look tired, probably because of the young child. How had she come to be here in Boston?

"Mistress Lindholm!"

She extended her hand, and he took it, turning to introduce his brother. "We live here, but how did you come to be here?"

Norah explained that she and her husband had moved to town about six months ago, and her husband worked in shipping and receiving for one of the businesses on the wharf.

"How amazing! I live with my brother here and am beginning to get back into medicine. I took a couple of years off to recover, and now here

6

I am, meeting you."

He got the address of her boarding house and promised to come see her sometime. He wanted to hear about what she had been doing in the intervening years and was glad she seemed cheerful and well.

He made a mental note to take a look at where she lived and bring a gift for her daughter. Perhaps *The History of Goody Two Shoes*. He had heard it was the latest in educational books for girls. And girls should be educated too, or as much as they could be.

The two brothers walked back home, cutting through Cold Lane to arrive at their end of Sudbury Street, all the while thinking of getting their dinner. Jacob, interested in women as usual, asked questions about Norah. Bill explained that she had been a patient of his at West Point, then he asked what Jacob knew about their own Boston constable.

"My personal opinion?" asked Jacob. "Enoch Cobb? I think he is in over his head, but it is a lucrative appointed position that he will not give up. He and the other constables supervise all the watchmen in town. Keep track of what they are doing. His wife is very pleased with both the money and the title."

"Hmmm. I know the body is the town's business," said Eustis, thinking back to his experiences just a few years ago at West Point. "I expect I'll have lots to distract me elsewhere. But I can't help it. I am curious how this drowning will be handled. It has been the most surprising day."

"Not to worry," said Jacob. "Things are moving here all the time, and the constables or the watchmen will come up with something. We've done our part."

"But no one asked for our names. What about that?"

"I guess they may not be concerned. Besides, we introduced ourselves to that watchman."

"No gathering of information?"

"Not likely. Too much trouble. They will say it is a drowning. He certainly came out of the harbor. We've had several like that in recent months."

"But I have not heard anything about it."

"No. Doesn't make the *Gazette*. Might as well let it go. And now we need to get our shoes cleaned."

They walked down the narrow driveway to the back wing of their house and the small workshop once used by their father. They carefully stomped all of the mud they could off their shoes. There was a well-used iron boot scraper to help finish the job before entering the backdoor.

The kitchen smelled enticing as always. Clearly their sisters had been busy. Bread, pie, onions in meat stew, everything to make the mouth water. Dinner was waiting, and they eagerly sat at the table in the kitchen. Catherine privately thought they were losing their proper manners by always eating in the kitchen and hoped to go the extra step of at least moving dinner back to the dining area where it should be. The only problem was that they often needed that room as a bedroom. Hard to combine the two.

CHAPTER 2

Later that afternoon, sitting by the fire, Eustis mused about their departure from West Point. He remembered turning the iron key in the lock on the hospital door, putting his hand on the rough planking, and leaning in, his forehead against the wood. Was it memories, pain, a combination? Leaving after so much had happened there. Eight years. The war ended in November of '83. General Washington left for New York and then went on to Philadelphia to hand over his sword to Congress, symbolically ending his command of the Continental Army. Drs. Eustis and Sam Adams Jr. were ordered by the general to shut down the hospital, get the invalids off to their homes, and disperse the remaining hospital materials from cots to pots. Then they, too, could go home.

The Revolutionary War had more or less simply ended. There had been no celebration, recognition, or appreciation for the men's eight years of service. No salute by a grateful populace. Once the peace treaty had been signed and confirmed by the Congress, it was just over. The men were mustered out and could leave. So they packed their haversacks and did just that.

The two of them, Drs. Adams and Eustis, had closed the last hospital and headed home. "Well, that's it," Adams had said. "We are off – homeward bound – at last."

Everyone else had already left. Some officers, probably ten or so, had ridden down to New York with General Washington to see him off. Others just faded into the landscape.

The two doctors slowly headed north. Adams may have contracted some weakening disease. He did not look well, wheezing and coughing often. Eustis strongly suspected consumption, although they had avoided any direct discussion about it.

Now it was 1786, more than three years since the men had arrived back home in Boston where each had settled into the warm chaos of crowded family life: Sam in his father's house and Eustis in his second-floor room in the back ell of the house where he had grown up. His brother Jacob had raised the roof and put in a window so that he could look out over Mill Pond and even see the masts in Boston Harbor off to the right.

Eldest sister Catherine had become the lady of the house, having married Ebenezer Wells about three years before at the end of the war. Their father, Benjamin, took advantage of Catherine's marriage to move out of the house and into his new wife Elizabeth Lazenby's house nearby.

Eustis's other siblings were also in residence: brothers Jacob and Nathaniel and sisters Prudence and Anne. And baby Benjamin Wells, now a year old. Welcoming their brother back, the family saw a thin, careworn man just under six feet tall, face drawn, looking distinctly older than when they last saw him. The war years had not been easy on their brother nor on anyone else. He was quieter now, but his kind, hazel eyes were the same, looking with caring concern on everyone.

* * *

Eustis had barely finished his midday dinner when his friend, Sam Adams Jr., wrapped in coat, hat, and knitted scarf, knocked on their door. Welcoming him in, the young women fluttered around Sam.

"Good day to you all," he greeted them. He could not smoothly remove his tricorn from under his scarf, so with some humor he graciously saluted and bowed. "I hope everyone is in good health? Bill, would you be interested in taking a walk around the town?"

"Sam! You are looking fine this afternoon, wrapped up well. How are you feeling? And the cough? Are you drinking that milk I advised?"

"Yes, doctor," mocked Sam meekly. "But let's go out. I want to talk."

"And I have news for you too."

Both trained doctors, the men looked out for each other. They had needed recovery time following their years in the war. At the least, frequent walks afforded them the chance to talk about politics, the governing or lack thereof of their state, without having to explain anything to the Eustis sisters.

Nearly ten years ago, in 1777, well before the war ended, the states had signed the Articles of Confederation, an alliance of sorts. Its main concern was coordinating the new states in defense if they were attacked. Other than that, the states, acting as their own mini-republics, were on their own to decide how they would govern themselves, even writing their own constitutions. Some began to mint their own coinage, establish import taxes on goods even from other states, and enact their own laws. Now, differing opinions of how the new republic as a whole should be run emerged as a common topic in taverns and homes.

"You'd best dress well. 'Tis a mighty cold wind coming down from the north," Sam cautioned.

Eustis's youngest sister, Anne, moved forward to wrap a muffler around his neck. She wore her hair in a long braid hanging over her shoulder when at home.

"I realize, little sister, that if it were not for these superior mittens that you made for me, my fingers would surely drop off," he praised. Half his age, she laughed and hugged him.

Eustis and Sam headed out for the large central open space in Boston, the Common, followed by Aggie, a mixed-breed dog who had adopted the family about eight years before. She had been foraging on her own while Boston was under siege during the Revolution and had followed Anne home, thrilled to find a new family. She had become Anne's special companion but would go along with anyone who seemed to offer entertainment of the dog variety. It was hard to tell where she had come from, perhaps that pack that scavenged around the waterfront.

To their right as they walked, John Hancock's grand house nearly topped the hill with several others along Beacon Street. Much of the open area, no longer a British campground, was used for what it was intended – pasturage for the town's cows. Owners ushered them out in the morning and called them back at milking time later in the day. Meanwhile, they thrived on the company of other cows and the grass.

Life seemed good. A cemetery in the far southern corner of the Common held the grave markers for the poor British souls lost during a winter of occupation, various skirmishes, and the 1775 retreat from Concord and Lexington. Another area of the Common closer to the town's business center was used for public gatherings and an occasional hanging.

As soon as he got the chance, Eustis told Sam about the surprising discovery of the drowned man and the lack of identification. "Furthermore," he added, "no one seems to be concerned about his identity. I am not sure what to do, but I think I should do something."

"Surely they will give you a chance to look the body over," Sam predicted. "Can you get a decent post-mortem? Any idea how long he had been in the water? How about rigor mortis?"

"There was not much interest," said Eustis. "I will have to go to find the chief constable."

He looked across the vast open space filled with trees sporting the bronze, red, and orange of fall colors, browning grass, and drying stalks of milkweed. There were not many cows in view. Aggie was interested in several spots along their path indicating the presence of past friends.

"You know, Sam, I also worry about this other business of the farmers' revolt in the west. The sad part is that the farmers have a real problem. It just worries me that they are unable to pay cash toward their basic property tax, and the state has no money to let it ride, just as you said."

"Well, you best start on the corpse," Sam offered. "Somehow, dead persons seem to be a more immediate concern to me. Although they do not pay taxes either. I would be concerned with that rather than with the farmers."

Eustis watched a red-tailed hawk circling and also kicked at a rock on the path. "Yes, but I admire the farmers. The farmers have got to come to some other agreement or arrangement with the state. They can't all be bankrupted for lack of hard cash."

Sam shook his head. "Until they do something, I say again, you best pay attention to the dead man."

"Yes. I intend to go to the Town House tomorrow to see what I can find out. As for the farmers, 'twas a bad year for crops, and that means a bad year for them. I read in the newspaper about how that farmer Daniel Shays sold the sword Lafayette gave him. Can you imagine how desperate he was? But he is probably not murdering anyone. And I know that we have to get both of these issues resolved."

Sam paused, coughed. It took him a while to stop. He spit on the path then dug in his pocket for his handkerchief. "I appreciate what my father says about the farmers' situation more and more. But much as I enjoy talking, I find that I have to head back now and hope you will let me know what you find out. I am exhausted. I need what energy I have left to get home. But it's so good to get out."

So saying, they turned back toward the North End, walking more slowly to accommodate Sam's lagging energy. After calling Aggie, Eustis took Sam's arm. This hasty return to home is not a good sign, he thought. I know I am also still in recovery, but he is progressing so much more slowly, if at all. I had hoped he would get better with home care and rest. That was supposed to work.

"Can we check out the Bell in Hand or the Green Dragon tonight – once I have rested?" asked Sam. "Would you want to do that? I can warn you that my honored father may be at the Dragon, and he still wants to get you into politics."

"Indeed. He is a marvelous old gentleman," Eustis said, smiling. "And he has always been very good to me. You knew he had already talked to me? But I am far from sure about any politics yet."

CHAPTER 3

They met as arranged later that evening to walk to the nearby Green Dragon Tavern, a favorite place. The tavern did its main business on the first floor and saved second-floor rooms for private meetings such as Sons of Liberty gatherings. They approached late that afternoon as the sun was beginning its early retreat, adding dappled reflections to the metal dragon silhouette

suspended above the door. The lighted candles inside turned the tavern's windows into a glowing gold.

Sam secured a small round table near one of the windows in the already noisy room, stowing their unlit lanterns on the floor. Eustis, once unwrapped from his outer clothing, went to the publican at the rear bar. He brought back two tankards of cider. Several men stopped by their table, offering their wishes for the full recovery of both men. The large, smoldering hearth made the whole atmosphere congenial, exuding fellowship and friendship – until there was a disturbance in the back corner.

Two men, one bewigged and dressed finely in waistcoat, jacket, and silver buckled shoes, and the other, a laborer still in his working clothes, bandana around his neck, stood and glared at each other.

"I fought for my freedoms in this country. I starved," charged the laborer. "You didn't come out! You stayed here and made money. Who do you think has more right to state his opinions? I'll tell you. I do!"

"Now just a minute, my good man," said the well-dressed one, trying to speak in a soothing voice. Unfortunately, it all came out as condescending. "Without my efforts, you would never have managed to even get to New York! I have my rights too, and that includes a right to make a living."

The confrontation soon swelled into a large group of contentious customers. As the pushing and shoving began, Eustis felt he could sit silent no longer. How could this devolve into an argument about who did more for the country? It was absurd. He arose angrily, calling out, "Just a minute here. What's going on? Do you realize how you are undermining just what you all fought for? That many of our friends died for? You are destroying everything we worked for. Are you falling for that idea of personal gain over community good? It will soon be yuletide. We'll have an egg grog or a rum toddy and be in a cheerful mood celebrating a good year just ending. For now, just let it go."

Several of the men looked at him. They knew he had been away for the war effort during the entire eight years and could not challenge those credentials. Several moved away, muttering. Eustis called out again and moved toward the angry group.

"We can talk this out, my friends. No need to fight over it. We may have a disagreement, but that does not mean you will get anywhere by fighting over it. We won't get ahead by going back over old upsets. We can be better, do better."

The publican stepped from behind his counter with the handle of an ax in one hand, lightly smacking it against the other hand. "I'll have you just move on outdoors now, gents." Another very large man joined him. That ended the discourse, and Eustis went back to Sam.

"By God, Sam. 'Tis been getting more and more problematic. Why can we not just get along? We ought to be able to talk about it."

"We fought for a democracy, my friend, and we got it," Sam answered. "We'll be fighting over everything from now on. No strong kings or rulers for us. Everyone has a right to their ideas, and we'll settle our differences by arguing in Congress or by the vote. As long as we agree to be bound by the vote, we'll be fine."

"Hmmm," muttered Eustis. "Some people think they can get their own way if they yell the loudest. And others seem to admire that. They do not seem to see it for the cowardice it is, that of making accusatory noise to 'win' arguments and not use creative discussion. I do not understand why the loudest is supposed to be the best."

"One thing I had wanted to talk to you about was just this," said Sam. He gestured at the room. "I heard that some of this upset could be

15

influenced by broadsides, posted or delivered to various people. They are extremely insulting and imply all kinds of impropriety or bad behavior either on the part of people we know or the recipients. There is no way to tell who is sending them or why. I think they stir up even more animosity."

"What do you mean 'delivered?' By the mail? Or through the door?"

"Indeed, both. And they are posted on the streets. Surely you've seen them?"

Several men at the adjoining table began to gesture and talk loudly, each one asserting that he knew the best shops at which to do business, citing the leanings of one proprietor. " 'E's a good conservative thinker, 'e is!"

As the argument began to dominate, Eustis signaled to Sam that they might want to leave. He didn't want Sam to get caught in a brawl. He picked up his tricorn and lighted the lanterns while Sam struggled into his coat. The argument grew louder as they made their way to the door.

Walking slowly back to the Adams house, Eustis was glad it was not far. The seasons were changing, and it was getting cold. At Sam's house, Eustis assured him that he would investigate the dead man as well as the broadsides and the farmers. He suddenly had more than enough to do.

Walking back home, he thought about the general upset he had seen around the town. Of course, there were many things that the town or state could or should do. People knew that. But it would take time.

Maybe Sam's father, the venerable patriot Sam Adams Sr., was right. He might affect more improvements by being in politics than in medicine. He might even work toward lighting the streets. Benjamin Franklin certainly thought it was a good idea. Eustis carried his lantern to see and be seen because the streets were lighted only by faint candlelight from household windows. Many talked about lighting as the way of the future and something the town should consider.

There were other problems too. It didn't help to have radicals trying to stir up unrest – likely for their own gain. He vaguely remembered seeing the posters but had ignored them as obviously false and of little

16

interest to him. He would have to be more aware. If people's opinions could be influenced in this way, they should all be aware of it.

* * *

Streaks of the emerging sun woke Eustis. Going downstairs, he entered the family's warm kitchen that was redolent with the beginnings of a stew in a pot over the coals. The smell of onions? Sausages? Bread just out of the bake oven. And coffee! He pulled a stool up to the large central and thoroughly-scrubbed table. Coming into the room, Jacob thumped his brother's shoulder, saying he was off again to meet with customers down at the pier. As a shipbroker, he dealt with anything he could trade or move on ships.

Eustis drank his coffee and thought over the day ahead as he watched his sister Catherine prepare the oven. Married and the eldest sister, she really ran the household. She had one child, and it looked to Eustis's experienced eye that another Wells would be joining them.

He asked her about the idea of lighting the streets at night, saying, "New York has some lighting at night along their major streets. What do you think? Should we have that too?"

Catherine smiled at him. "I can see that you are getting your mind as well as your energy back. And I see the changes coming. But I am not sure Bostonians are ready for anything as new as lighting. People take care of it themselves."

Bostonians thought they did as well if not better than New Yorkers because they had higher standards and values and were not sure about possibly inappropriate liberal ideas. They certainly did not want theaters. The behavior both on stage and off was highly questionable and unsuitable for much of their population. They were sensible, and it was more economical if walkers after dark just carried their own lanterns.

Eustis thought there were a great number of things that could be done to improve the town, and he was beginning to come around to old Sam Adams's way of thinking. Mayhap government was indeed the way to go. Then he could really affect what was happening for residents. As it was, he depended on someone needing his help when they were sick. He wasn't doing anything that was not reactive. He wanted to try being proactive, perhaps fixing things earlier. Not just waiting for a call.

He had a meeting at Faneuil Hall Marketplace that morning. After finishing his breakfast oatmeal, he donned his coat and stepped into the chilly morning. He thought of the last months of the war when they were all at West Point anticipating closing the hospital and the New Windsor encampment.

Back then, Eustis had talked with General Henry Knox about what it would be like, wondering what they all might do after the war. The officers realized it was unlikely they would see each other after peace was declared. They came from all thirteen states and did not live near each other in one place. Soon the close bonds of friendship with their fellow warriors would be broken – a devastating loss. Years of hardship together had made them brothers. When the men talked over their concerns, an idea floated into the conversation. Possibly they could form some kind of association so they could all remain connected. And with the encouragement of Baron von Steuben and Henry Knox, they had done just that.

Eustis heard hoofbeats and paused, pressing his back against a brick wall to let a wagon pulled by a large draft horse roll past. The roads were narrow, and there was just not room for everyone all the time.

General Knox had prepared the proposal for a new organization to be named for the Roman general Cincinnatus. In the Roman story, that general had taken up arms, resolved the fighting, won the war, and then retired to his farm. It seemed their general was doing the same by returning to his Virginia estate, Mount Vernon. The new organization's name honored Washington. Scarcely a month had passed before the officers met and officially birthed the Society of the Cincinnati. It would be a heritage organization for the descendants of the officers. An announcement was sent to every officer who had served in the war.

Within a year, the officers in each state had formed their own organizations and selected officers. The national chapter selected General Washington as president and Henry Knox as secretary. The

Massachusetts contingent named General Benjamin Lincoln to its presidency and Dr. William Eustis as vice president.

Today, the Massachusetts Society of the Cincinnati was meeting in Faneuil Hall, a large building built by and given to the town by Peter Faneuil. It served many purposes, not the least being a covered area for a large market. A columned meeting hall filled most of the second floor. The society usually met in a smaller room on that floor. Removing his tricorn, Eustis headed upstairs.

Sitting to General Lincoln's right, he looked around the room. They were all good men and even better friends. Lincoln tapped the table and immediately called the meeting to order. He wanted to discuss the issues facing their organization and state. First on his list was upsetting news just received from their Congress in New York about the uprising of the farmers in the western part of Massachusetts. Just days ago, in mid-October, Secretary of War Henry Knox had urged action and wanted to call on former President Washington to reactivate the army.

Indeed, Congress could call out the militia but realistically could not pay anyone. Then the desperate federal government finally arrived at another decision, a brilliant solution they thought, one that would cost them nothing. They would pass the problem back to the state that had the trouble – Massachusetts. The residents should solve it because it was in their own state and it was about the state taxes they had imposed, not federal taxes.

General Lincoln asked the assembled officers for their thoughts. There were ideas, opinions, and objections. The farmers had attacked a federal courthouse, so surely that made it a federal matter, and the problem of any uprising should be resolved by the Congress. And Massachusetts, just like Congress, had no ready money to pay soldiers. Lincoln felt there must be a resolution or they would have anarchy in the state if not the country. This was the first test of the new republic. What would or could they do? He offered his opinion.

"We have to be realistic," he said. "Congress can do nothing and have passed it on to us. If we were smart, we would solve it. That would end all this stupid criticism of us as a private, elite group.

"I suggest you let me talk to a friend in the militia, gentlemen. Perhaps we can work out something. I believe that if I can come up with some funds, we might arrive at a plan. Let me see what I can do. If we can get back together in two days, I should be able to have an idea if it is even possible. I can talk with Governor Bowdoin also."

The meeting adjourned, the men to seek what information they could before coming back together again.

CHAPTER 4

Eustis decided to walk down by the harbor on his way home, heading toward the masts and nets hanging to dry. Being near the water always helped his thinking. There was a great deal of distraction. Actually, it was probably not what he truly needed for clear thinking, but somehow water helped. He wondered if anything had come of the man he had seen jumping overboard. Who was he? Had he survived? And he needed to locate the constable.

The wharves were in their normal busy state of activity; mild, though, compared to years past. Unfortunately, since the war, they had not yet managed to achieve the shipping frenzy that prosperous shipyards and trade bring. They were, however, in an exciting state of growth and hopeful efforts. Many merchants were casting around for new markets, new ports. Some were looking seriously into possibilities across the Pacific Ocean in China.

Eustis happily anticipated warmth and good food once he got back to Sudbury Street. Cath could create every meal that her mother had made, and her sisters had also learned their skills at their mother's knee. They ran an excellent household, and there was growing evidence in the kitchen that storing and preserving food for the winter was uppermost in their minds. They talked of their arrangement to share a pig with a neighbor who had adequate room to raise it. It would be slaughtered soon. Apple slices, herbs, and ropes of onions were already hanging to dry from pegs in the ceiling beams.

"There is mail for you, Bill," said Prudence. "I picked it up at the Green Dragon when Anne and I went this morning."

"Anything interesting?"

"I have no idea. But it is addressed to you, and I was not going to leave it there for just anyone to open."

"Thank you, Prue. You look out for us so well. I am anxious that you might decide to go off and make your own household with some unworthy man."

The sisters giggled.

"Alas and alack! If she does that, I'll have to marry," said Jacob, pretending to be shocked, then laughing. "Unless you beat me to it, Bill."

"No worries there," said Eustis. "I am not even healthy enough yet."

Changing the subject, he said, "But I have all kinds of news. I can tell you about the Society meeting this morning. And have you heard what was found under Jacob's wharf?"

That quickly shifted their conversation away from matchmaking.

"What is the Society up to?" asked Catherine who had just entered the room and eagerly sat down. Her back was achy, and she needed a brief rest. If their father came by that evening with his wife, she would be ready. They knew he would want to talk about all the news as well as their siblings in Virginia who were anchoring the southern end of their trading business.

Answering her question, Eustis said, "We talked about how the farmers out in the west cannot pay their taxes and are having their farms confiscated for lack of cash. The worst part is that they are so desperate that they have taken to arms and closed several of the courthouses. I do not think that is right. Congress cannot do anything and instead has turned it over to us here in Boston. The Society is trying to think of ways to solve this mess."

"But what can be done?" asked Jacob. "This is not the way this country is supposed to work. Those poor farmers are losing their property, and then how do they make a living? Do you think Congress will make up an army and go out there?"

Catherine watched her brothers, listening. She had ideas, but they had not asked her.

"I don't know," said Eustis. "But if they do, I want to be involved. This kind of thing just should not have happened here. It probably points out a flaw in the states' agreement that needs correction. The basic problem is that there is no money, so the federal government can do nothing. Nobody can function. Not the people, not the states. Nothing can happen without money."

"You wouldn't really go, Bill, would you?" asked Anne. "I mean, if there was an expedition? What about your health?" She sounded worried.

Eustis looked at her. She was younger than the two sisters who organized most of the homemaking, and she got worried more easily. He remembered her best when she was barely learning to read back before he went off to the war. She grew up while he was away during those eight long years.

"It is not immediate, little sister. Do not worry. We have another meeting in two days. Then the general may have an idea. He knows a great deal and will talk with other people. But where is this mail?"

Anne indicated the pie safe against the wall at the back of the room. Important items were placed on top and, of course, any baked goods were inside behind closed doors. Eustis went over and picked up his mail, finding two letters of great interest.

"By Jove," he said. "One from Elijah and Noah, and one from my dear old friend Bill North. Excellent! Just who I wanted to hear from."

Bill North had moved to Duanesburg, New York, bought a farm and was recently married to a local girl. Back about two years ago, several of Eustis's friends, including North, had gathered for several months in the New York countryside. Following Thomas Jefferson's ideas for developing a republic, North had said to Eustis that at least one of them ought to marry and become a proper householder. They should give up their present life and act as more responsible citizens. They must work with Jefferson to bring the ideal into being. North wanted to help create the image of a responsible and respected citizen of this republic. When he left them, he was a man on a mission.

Although he admired women, appreciated their wit, dress, and style, Eustis was not ready for marriage. It appeared, however, that eligible young women around town thought this attractive single man certainly ought to be. They swarmed around him everywhere. Even his friend Aaron Burr had recently written, asking if he had met Miss Susan Binney, saying he had heard she was remarkable. But enough of that. A lot of memories lived in the letter from North, and he would read it many more times.

23

Eustis unfolded the other letter. Elijah's news was, as usual, both interesting and concerning. Eli did the writing because Noah was still learning. He was embarrassed that his handwriting did not yet look like Elijah's. But their news!

They were traveling back toward the Northeast, Eli wrote, and still had both the horse, Belle, and the mule, Sally, who would surely send their regards to Eustis if they could. After stopping in West Point at the settlement and visiting with Elijah's grandmother, the young men intended to come to Boston to see the doctor. They had encountered no problems lately except for some flooded rivers and heavy rain as they were working their way through Pennsylvania. If Eli mentioned it at all, Eustis thought, it must have been wretched.

He had worried all the time that the young men were away in the west. He had become heavily involved in their lives and keeping them safe during the war. When he thought about the dangers, he was nearly frantic knowing he had no way of saving them or even knowing where they were when they were off in remote places – such as in the wilderness of Ohio. He tried to laugh it off as being a mother hen. Both young men were over twenty now, but he knew the reality of their safe return was still not assured. Most likely, Elijah's grandmother, the indefatigable Mrs. Eldredge, was equally concerned.

Then he wondered, when was this letter sent? Could they be approaching even as he read it? He looked over the outside carefully. It was well worn and had obviously had several adventures of its own. There were no indicators of date or where or when it had been sent. God's teeth! Well, they would show up whenever they did. I don't think I ever told them an address. They could probably ask directions from people on the way. But he surely would like to know more than he did right now.

He could feel a little excitement growing, thinking of seeing them again. If they stopped at West Point, he would get all the news about the good people in the settlement there. And he could tell them about Norah being in Boston. He wondered about Noah agreeing to return to

24

Massachusetts where he had been enslaved. But that was before the war, at least ten years ago. Massachusetts had ruled against slavery in a court case in 1783. But there were still slave catchers sneaking around to kidnap and take young Black men and women back to the South to sell. Maybe Noah would decide to go whaling. Those crews were recruited based on their skills, not their color.

CHAPTER 5

When the sun dipped toward the horizon, Anne went to collect their two cows. It was time for milking, and the cows would be wandering toward home from the huge grassy Common. They were kept in the barn or in the tiny, fenced space behind the barn they called a pasture. On good weather days their cows, Hattie and Hazel, went out to graze with many of the town's livestock. Daylight was quickly fading when Anne approached to usher them back from the Common.

But where were they? Both cows were usually right by the gate waiting. She walked into the Common's large pasture. Where had they wandered? The silly cows. And then she saw them by a clump of ragged bushes about halfway along the walking path that led to the Hancock property.

"Come along, girls," she called out. It seemed strange. They didn't move from the shelter of the shrubbery. And they usually came when she called. "Come, Hattie, come, come," she called and continued to walk toward them. It looked like someone had hobbled their feet together. Who would do a thing like that?

Hazel was just behind Hattie and both looked at her with their sorrowful brown eyes and lowed softly. They seemed pleased she had come to rescue them and take them home. She looked around carefully and down at their feet to discover they had indeed been trapped. A snarl of old fencing – mostly sticks, rope, and wire – was wrapped around both cows' legs. Anne would have to unravel it to get them out, and it would be getting dark soon. She bent to her work hoping the family would not get too anxious. As she unwound the rope, she had to move around or back into the bush somewhat.

"Ahh!" What was that? Oh, no. A person's arm? In the common grazing area?

Anne hurried to finish freeing the cows and usher them homeward. She would speak with Prudence who was very much like her name. A careful thinker and unlikely to panic. Prue would know what to do.

* * *

Eustis was in the sitting room frowning over his reading, an explanation about a medical

procedure that seemed more wishful thinking than practical, when Prudence burst through the

door. She seemed uncharacteristically alarmed.

"Oh, come quickly, Bill," she gasped. "Quickly! Run! It's Anne. She's in the kitchen."

"But what's the matter, Prue? Is she all right?"

"We must go to the Common, and we should probably bring Jacob too. Is he home? Please, please. Come now. Quickly!"

She grabbed his hand and pulled him out the back door and toward the barn. Anne was inside closing the cows in their stalls.

"What's happening, Anne," he called.

"I found the cows. Just go with Prue, or she'll never let it go. I'll catch up."

Eustis decided he had better walk to the Common and grabbed a lantern from a peg.

Determined and with a narrow focus, Prue led him purposefully along the cobbled road, never quite explaining why they needed to go back. It took about ten minutes to reach the Common. She pointed toward the bushes uphill to the right and tugged at his arm.

"Anne found something up there. She will be along soon."

"But what, Prue? Found what?"

"She said it looked like an arm, maybe a hand," not wanting to give in to her fears. Then, through clenched teeth, "Please come. Hurry."

Approaching, he absentmindedly noted the large houses along the top of the hill with their windows glowing. Despite the failing light, he could see that, indeed, there was a snarl of rope and trash halfway under the bushes. They needed more light to see better so he lit the lantern. Holding it out, he peered at the ground in front and then at the rope,

27

seeing nothing alarming. It would have to be cleared away regardless, or it could snarl another animal.

A stray dog joined them, sniffing around the bushes. Suddenly it pulled back and ran. Perhaps it heard its master calling, but neither Prudence nor Eustis heard a voice. Eustis bent low and looked again. As the branches were disturbed, it seemed like a hand or arm was indeed protruding from under a bush. "God's teeth! This could be a mess." He looked around him.

What to do about Prudence? About Anne? She was on her way. It would not be good if the young sisters were exposed to a dead body. If an animal had not disturbed it so far, it ought to last through the night. He had better get this sister home and stop the other from coming.

Prudence, on the other hand, was smart and clever, wise to her big brothers and their ways. She thought they always wanted to stifle her, although they called it protection. She knew immediately she was right when Bill casually said there was nothing to see and that they might as well go home. After all, it was growing dark, and they could not see well anyway.

Some upper-class ladies might have described Prudence Eustis as bad mannered. And she probably was. But it made no difference to Prue what high-class ladies might think at this moment. She knew she was right. Someone was under that shrubbery.

Eustis realized he had a big problem. How to get Prue away. Bribery? It had worked when she was a pesky girl of eight. But she was now seventeen. "Prue," he said, "perhaps you can carry the lantern and guide us home. Then we'll come back early tomorrow when we can search properly. Can you not agree to that?"

She frowned. "Do not treat me like a baby."

Fortunately, the growing darkness helped, and she began to look around them and how far they were from the street. Soon they would not even be able to locate the street except by the lights in the houses.

"Oh, Bill. Could you just look underneath?" Prue pressed him. "Then I promise we can come back tomorrow."

What could he say? "All right, I will. But you best go over by the road first. It may not be good or anything you want to look at. Then I'll look under."

Prue realized that to get her brother to do what she wanted would require a bargain. She agreed to move back, but only if he looked now. He first watched her carefully then leaned over and lifted the branches. He could see an arm, but there also seemed to be a body behind it – and it moved. There was a faint groan. It was alive!

"Oh, no," gasped Prue who had crept closer. "Uh-oh! You have to help!"

Eustis got down on his knees and crawled forward to see that a person of uncertain size and gender had indeed hidden under the bushes. There was debris and what looked like a wool horse blanket pulled on top. A boy?

If he was going to get whoever it was out, he would need help. He could not leave Prudence there, nor should he send her alone back to get the brothers. He crawled in farther and managed to locate the person's head and shoulders. He got a grip on the shoulders and started to shift the body out from underneath. Branches scraped at him and his burden. Prue got down on her knees and helped tug on an arm.

Eustis knew he needed Jacob and Nathaniel to help if the person was unable to move as he suspected. They needed their wagon. Someone would have to get help.

Once they got the person out of the snarl of underbrush, Eustis stood and looked around. Where were the people who walked on the Common when you needed them? He could see a person and a dog but at a distance.

"Prue, how brave are you feeling? Could you run as fast as you can back home and get Jacob and the wagon? I cannot go and leave you alone here. I fear I must stay and try to do what I can for this person. It is far too cold for him to be out here. He seems terribly weak and close to death."

Prue was nothing if not brave, and she immediately took off, running back across the empty dark pasture toward the house lights along

Tremont Street. This was her discovery, and she was not going to give up. She arrived panting at the back door on Sudbury Street, calling out for her brothers.

Catherine, relieved to see Prue, was puzzled by her appearance, her soiled skirt and state of alarm. She had been very close to calling in help from the neighborhood to search for both of them. Bill lost on Boston Common. With his sister. Indeed! She was glad she'd stopped Anne from following them.

But then Prue called out. "Jacob! You have to help! Bring the wagon. We found a near-dead person on the Common. Please! You have to be quick! And where's Nat?"

She grabbed her shawl from its peg, left the kitchen, and headed back to the barn. Her brothers hurried after her to find her starting to harness their horse, Nelson.

"What is it? What's happening?" Jacob demanded.

She explained as much as she could while still urging Nelson to take the bit in his mouth. Jacob moved to help her. "Bill is down there now?" On hearing this, Nathaniel left them and headed down the driveway toward the Common. A few minutes later, the wagon with Prue and Jacob caught up to him just as he entered the large field. Prue directed them to where they could see a figure crouched over something on the ground.

As they drove up, Eustis stood and said, "By God, am I glad to see you! Here. If you can help me, we can get this young fellow into the wagon and back home quickly. I need to get off all these covers and look him over. But it is too cold here."

He threw the person's blanket and an old hat with a rounded crown into the wagon.

Their kitchen was warm and smelled of their earlier midday dinner when they returned to their home. Their bedraggled find, wrapped in rags and the blanket, was carried in by Jacob and Bill. Catherine hurried to prepare a place in the downstairs bedroom. It took two to carry him to the bed.

They left Bill to undo some of the coverings. He was surprised by some objections and moans escaping from his patient and paused to assume the role of reassuring physician. Prudence came to assist and discovered, to her surprise, that the patient did not rebuff her like her brother.

Unwrapping the head revealed a dirty young face with greasy, light brown hair poking out from a scarf or bandanna.

"If we can get off the outer coverings, perhaps we can give him a rest and let him warm up," Prue suggested. "He looks very young, and mayhap he is lost. Does he look confused to you?"

Her oldest brother agreed. "We can take turns sitting with him until he is warmed and fully conscious. I may need to bleed him later, just to get him stable."

They left the young man huddled under more covers, telling him they would return with warm milk and something for him to eat. Catherine would not be happy that they had failed to get all the dirty clothes off, but their patient seemed grateful to be warm and protected. They were not sure he understood completely. Perhaps he did not speak English and was from a ship in the harbor, maybe a recent arrival or indentured escapee.

Their quick supper of bread and cheese with apples was spent discussing all of Prudence's suspicions and concerns. Ebenezer, Catherine's husband, with little Ben on his lap, seemed more entranced with playing with his son than the problems of the new discovery, giving Ben bits of bread soaked in milk. The women all expressed concerned about their patient's lack of speech. Within half an hour, Prue had milk, several slices of bread, and a hot water bottle and was prepared to sit with the young visitor.

Catherine insisted she had better accompany the next morning's expedition back to the Common. She suspected they might need her direction. At the very least, they needed to make the Common safer for the cows, and they would require the men's strength to unsnarl all that mess.

31

Anne still argued that they should all go. It was finally agreed that it was not realistic for all six of them to do so. Nathaniel and Bill would investigate in the morning. Jacob had a business appointment at his office on the wharf, and he did not want to risk losing a possible shipment.

Eustis went to check on his patient, finding him asleep and curled up under several quilts. His face was visible, and his color was better. Rather than disturb the fellow, Eustis decided rest was best, and if Nathaniel shared the room, any nighttime upset could be dealt with if and when it occurred.

CHAPTER 6

Dawn brought ribbons of glowing pink and yellow along the horizon. Maple trees were beginning to display their seasonal colors. It would be sunny and get a little warmer, the crisp kind of October day they all enjoyed. It reminded Eustis of those early morning hours at West Point and reminded Catherine of all that still had to be done before winter arrived. And they would need to plan for possible guests – Bill's former aides. And Bill would need more clothes if he went on the expedition to stop the farmers' rebellion. And more stockings. There was just too much. The only good thing was that their father had not visited last night.

They gathered in the kitchen and breakfasted on coffee and Catherine's corn cakes with butter and cheese. Somehow, Eustis had to admit as he sipped his coffee, he was feeling better. With all the odd concerns coming to him and the addition of a puzzling patient, he realized he was closer to good health than he had been in several years. Not the usual morning doldrums, not as drawn to solitary wandering, not as anxious, not as tired. Maybe he was starting to recover. That people needed his attention seemed to be helping. Added to that was the realization he actually was interested in helping them.

Happily, he had several things to look into that morning, not the least of which was his patient. They had heard no sound during the night. He needed to get that situation cleared up. He also had his Society meeting and then wanted to check with the constable about that body found floating under the wharf. He had several ideas to suggest.

After saying he'd speak to the watchman about their discovery the previous night on the Common, Jacob waved farewell and headed for the wharf and to find that man. The others could walk to the Common, and Prue could lead them to the right shrubbery. Anne would stay and help Cath get started on the chores. But first the patient needed attention.

They dispersed. Cath tied little Ben with his leading strings to a table leg and began to organize the laundry with Anne. Cath feared her determined little son would crawl into the hearth. Nathaniel and Prudence started for the front room. Realizing they could easily overwhelm his patient, Eustis asked everyone to wait a bit so he could talk to him first. He carried a clean shirt and breeches with him.

Slowly opening the door so as not to be startling, Eustis peered around into the room. His patient was sitting in the bed, covers drawn to his chin, eyes large. He looked terrified. As the doctor approached, he cringed and clutched the quilt more tightly.

Eustis placed the clothing on the bed and spoke gently and quietly. "Good morning. My name is Dr. William Eustis, and my family found you on the Common last evening. We brought you here. How are you feeling?"

Hazel eyes blinked, and a soft childlike voice answered. "Thank you, yer honor, sor. I'm most grateful to ye for allowin' me to get warm. I 'uz so cold last night."

Thinking this person was more of a child than he had supposed, Eustis asked, "Would you be able to eat some bread and milk, if we brought it to you?"

"Pray do na go to any trouble, sor. I be gone as soon as I get meself t'gether. I do na want to bother ye any longer."

"Let me assure you, my friend, 'tis no trouble. I have cared for many people throughout the war. I am a doctor, and part of my calling is to help people. I'll talk to my sisters about a tub and bath for you too. Then, after a bath, put on these clothes and we will find you a jacket and shoes."

Turning to go, he said, "When you are ready, come join us. We can have dinner together later. Unless you want assistance in getting out of your present garb? Do you need help washing? My sister Prudence will be bringing hot water."

The child looked confused and doubtful. Eustis wondered what he had done to confuse him or if he had ever felt any adult kindness.

"No, no, sor," he said, "No need 'tall. Thank ye for the hot water. I c'n take care of all that. Be right there soon's I can."

Clearly he wanted privacy. Eustis went to the kitchen to ask if a tub and water could be taken in and left so their patient could wash. Prudence was happy to do it. She had seen the condition the boy was in and his clothing.

"Just leave it with him inside the door, Prue. He seems very nervous about his appearance or any of us helping. Probably embarrassed and wants to attend to it himself."

Prue brought the tin bathtub to the door, and Nathaniel fetched several buckets of water. Another trip brought two kettles of boiling water to warm the bath. Eustis knocked at the door and, without looking much at the patient, they deposited a linen towel and slid the tub and water just inside the room.

The men realized they needed to get to the Common quickly to meet the watchman Jacob was sending. Cath and Anne were to be at home if anything happened or if their patient came out earlier than expected. Prue would go with them.

Prudence and Nathaniel arrived with Eustis at the Common to see the watchman standing by the gate. They thanked him and told him about the snarled rope they had found and the danger to the other cows. They held off alerting him to the presence of the young man they had found. They would deal with one thing at a time, and all their sympathies were with their guest. They did not want him in jail.

Eustis needed to get back to the meeting of the Society at Faneuil Hall, scheduled for ten o'clock. Leaving Nathaniel and Prudence to more or less supervise the watchman's search for more potential traps, he hurried back to Faneuil Hall and the same second-floor room.

Beginning the meeting, General Lincoln asked for their news and then gave his update. He had succeeded in acquiring some financial backing, enough to start their planning to ride to Worcester and parts beyond, likely Springfield. It would depend on where the farmers were camping. Somewhere out there to the west. Based on what he had raised, they could start to advertise for and enlist militia.

Lincoln thought they would need a substantial group to impress the farmers who were extremely angry. Desperate people might not respond to soft persuasion. He planned for the militia to leave within two months if possible, probably during the yuletide in December. And it might take as much as two weeks to get there with their gear. Especially if they took cannons. This would become clearer as the plans came together. He ended by asking who would join him in recruitment and in the expedition.

"I'll be there, general," said Eustis. "You will need a doctor or several if there is an engagement. I also wondered if General Knox is in Boston? I have not heard from him yet, and he usually is here for the winter. He might have some influence or could help us."

"Thank you, doctor. As the new secretary for war, he has only a clerk and secretary for staff and, of course, no money. He would have to recruit just as we are doing. Perhaps we can gain his support. It would be reassuring to some, and I'll send out word to all the towns. And to the general as well. If the recruiting news gets out as it should – if we have some slight monetary offering, and Knox backs the project, we may well succeed. Let's see if we can get some enthusiasm going. And shall we continue to meet on a weekly basis?"

There was further discussion on recruitment and who to notify before they all dispersed, some excited by the prospect of joining former comrades again. Eustis needed to hurry back to Sudbury Street to see his patient, or whatever he might call the boy, who should be bathed or back in his bed by now.

His sisters were determined women, and it had been several hours. He noticed that clothes had been hung out to dry in the backyard. Entering the kitchen, he found Anne braiding and weaving onions together so they could hang in clusters. The two others were discussing certain construction options for a shirt spread over the top of the table. Catherine seemed particularly pleased as she looked over at him.

"Greetings all you hard workers," he said. "How did everything go?"

"There is a surprise for you," said Catherine, smiling. Eustis thought she must be relieved to have gotten all the washing done. Or maybe little Ben was sleeping. "Go and see our guest," she added.

He knocked on the bedroom door before entering. Then he stopped, stunned. There appeared to be a very young girl sitting on the bed, scrubbed and pink in one of his sister's shifts, and looking terrified at his entrance.

"Excuse me, miss. I was not expecting this. I am sorry for intruding."

"I'm the one sorry, sor," she said. "I dinna want to be a problem, but the other ladies said that I stay and put me back to bed."

Although baffled, Eustis knew how determined his sisters could be. "But what happened to the boy?" he asked, frowning. "I am confused." Then, as he began to get over his shock and really look, he saw her hair was quite short, unlike his sisters.

"'Twas me," she said. "I hadda cover meself to escape. A wicked man bought me to work for 'im, but when I got bigger I 'scaped. I just be goin' now and be outta your way." And she started to get up.

"No. Wait!" Eustis gestured for her to stop. "Can we just talk for a minute?"

He moved toward the foot of the bed. She dove back under the covers. And Prudence came into the room.

"So, brother. What do you think of our guest now? And wait until you hear her story."

Eustis sat at the end of the bed, and the girl pulled her feet back as close to herself as she could. He did not want to scare her, but he felt he needed to know what was going on.

Prudence moved forward and said, "Do not worry, Sally. You are safe here. Tell my brother what you told me."

Eustis asked as gently as he could, "That is your name?"

"Aye. 'Tis Sally, sor," she whispered, almost cowering away from him.

He realized she must be very afraid of men. Perhaps she had been mistreated?

"Can you tell me?" he asked.

Prudence moved closer to the head of the bed, taking the girl's hand. It came out that the child was sold into an indenture when she was four years old. She was taken by a gruff old man in his wagon to his farm somewhere and put to work in the kitchen supervised by an old woman who hit her. As her abilities and body grew, Sally had been worked even harder.

Eustis glanced at his sister. "Do you remember where you came from?" He asked as gently as he could.

"I dinna know, sor. Seems 'twas always with 'em, but they said something about sendin' me back to a place if I was bad. I think it was like deadman or diddaton, somethin' like that. Mayhap it was so I'd be punished. I dinna know."

"But, child, how did you get here from someplace out in the country?"

"I useta watch the river. An' one day, there was a man w' a flat boat goin' by. I saw 'im, and I jus' ast for a ride. It took more 'an a day, mayhap three, and 'e let me sleep inna boat. But he pu' me out by the harbor. He was meetin' with some folk there. Could ya tell me, sor, where I am?" She looked up at him with big, bright eyes that were between hazel and green in color.

Eustis looked at her and observed her arms. Scrawny was the only word for them. They were almost too thin to do anything. He bet the rest of her looked the same way, wondering how she had survived.

"You are in Boston town safe with the Eustis family," he said. "I'll leave you alone now. And my good sister will bring you more to eat. You have to get your strength back, my dear, and then we can talk more."

After they left the room, he looked at Prudence and said, "Unbelievable. How did she make it? She is so undersized, just bones. I'll bet she has not had a decent meal in her life."

"Certainly looks that way," agreed Prue, stepping ahead of him into the kitchen.

As Prue and Anne prepared their dinner, he talked more with Catherine. "How old do you suppose she is? Oh, Cath, what can we do? It seems like a desperate situation for her. Poor child. Reminds me of what Shakespeare said: 'Though she be but little, she is fierce.'"

Catherine was as determined as she always was. "I've told Eben about her, and he agrees. We'll keep her here, get her in better health, and try to find out more. Those people who treated her like that need to be prosecuted and locked up. Although I don't know if in truth there are any legal protections for her. I'll at least find out. Meanwhile, you have not had your dinner either."

She gestured at the kitchen table and at his place that was already set. "It's pease porridge and bread. We put carrots, potatoes, onions, and everything else from the end of the garden in it. Even bits from the ham bone. Should fill you up. Anne is taking a bowl right now to our guest.

"And Bill," she went on. "I will be having a friend for coffee later in the day. Perhaps you will join us?

"Happy to, Cath," he said. "Who is it?"

"Do you remember that nice woman with the child near where you found that drowned man? I think you said you had met her before. I wrote a note and invited her to come by. I hope you can at least come to greet her."

"Certainly. It will be my pleasure to become reacquainted."

He sat at the table. The bowl of pease porridge was marvelous as was the fresh baked bread. He ate heartily, happily thinking about what he wanted to do with the rest of his day until he looked at his sister and suddenly had a suspicious thought.

"Matchmaking again, Cath?" he grinned. "Because she is married. And I delivered her first child under dreadful circumstances. That baby died."

"Do not be ridiculous, Bill. I know all about that! I just want to welcome her to the neighborhood. They moved here only about six months ago. Now I better check the laundry. See how dry it is. Come along, Prue."

And she went to the yard with her basket.

CHAPTER 7

Eustis visited and quickly tended to a patient not far from their home. His small, hopefully-growing medical practice so far consisted of caring for friends and neighbors. This visit involved removing sutures he had put into a youngster's leg a week ago. Soon he was back home ensconced in the sitting room, his feet up on a stool, reading a book while he waited for their afternoon visitor.

A rap on their front door brought Catherine running to open it and welcome Norah and her child. She ushered them into the parlor where Eustis quickly rose to greet her. A cheerful, two-year-old daughter was introduced as Annie, named in honor of Mrs. Nan Eldredge, an old friend of Eustis's from West Point and Elijah's grandmother.

Eustis was charmed by Norah's little girl who was very observant, commenting on all she saw around her. She was particularly excited when Aggie came in to inspect the new arrivals. Norah had a challenge containing Annie in her arms.

When Anne came in, and found a little girl named almost like her, she asked to show Annie around the house to give the adults some time to talk. Aggie padded along, perhaps because the two seemed much more interesting than the adults left in the parlor.

Norah told how her husband, Albert, had wanted to get into the shipping trade and came to Boston to work, it being a busy port. It seemed he needed a new focus and change. He was lucky, she said, to have found the work, evidently just what he had been seeking. Eustis noticed she spoke of her husband in a removed, matter-of-fact way. It was almost as if he was an acquaintance rather than a husband. Eustis then wondered if he was being too much the romantic, admitting he may have some misunderstanding of all this.

The visit was short and congenial, ending with Norah saying she needed to hurry back to get Albert's supper underway and Annie fed. They walked her and Annie to the door and spoke of further occasions to meet.

Norah turned on the doorstep to again express her appreciation. "Thank you so much for inviting me into your home. It is lovely to see how happy it is here. I only hope I can achieve this in time."

* * *

Taking advantage of every hour of sunlight the next morning, Cath hung out her washing. A baby in the house created so much more to scrub. And they had a great deal of laundry anyway with a household of nine. A neighbor equally engaged in her laundry passed on the news that the fishing fleet had come in.

Prudence and Anne caught up a basket and hurried to the market to bring home fresh fish for their midday dinner. By late morning, all three women were making pies and had started the fire for the bake oven. Baby Ben, again attached to the table leg, occupied himself by alternatively trying to untie his leading strings and banging a spoon against an iron pot. Aggie watched, keeping her distance. Ben could be a hazard.

To everyone's excitement, the market visit provided mail as well as a nice codfish for a pie. Someone at the Green Dragon would have brought their mail to Sudbury Street whenever convenient, but getting it now was better. The letter looked to be from the south, near West Point as indeed it turned out to be. Eustis felt a rush just opening it, remembering his years there. Nan Eldredge, that delightful friend, had written! The old midwife wanted to share news of her grandson Elijah and his friend Noah. They had arrived safely back from their travels.

"They are there! In West Point," exclaimed Eustis.

"Who are you talking about?" asked Prudence, curious at the joy in her brother's voice. "Some people you knew there?"

"By Jove! Those boys made it all the way into Ohio and the wilderness and now they have come back here. And she says Noah has a wife! How astounding."

"Read it to us," said Anne. She could tell by her brother's face that the letter was intensely personal. She probably should have given him a minute. But she wanted to know what was so interesting too.

It would seem the boys, for that is how Eustis continued to think of them, had arrived several weeks ago, had settled in with Mrs. Eldredge, and she was caring for them with lots of good food to get them ready to continue their explorations. They would come north to see Eustis, bringing all the news, and should arrive within a week or so.

"But she did not say anything about Noah's wife," exclaimed Anne. She had heard all the stories over the past three years of her brother's young friends. Their travels seemed as good as a novel even though she had not yet read one. Novels were considered inappropriate for young women and difficult to find in Boston.

More practical, Prudence asked, "Where will we put them?"

"I am not too worried," said Eustis. "We don't know what their preferences are. They might want an inn. Or they could be fine with a shared bedroom here, or the barn."

"We do have the small room," offered Catherine.

"But that is not sufficient," exclaimed Prudence. "We need to be ready."

"Well, we should probably talk it over and see what ideas there are," said Eustis. "But I don't see any problems. And there may be friends who will help."

"I know that none of this is your concern, Bill, but we will need to know. What do we do about dinners? What do we do about bedding? You do not understand!" Prue came close to stamping her foot. Eustis, realizing his best move was to retreat, did.

"I am off to find Sam," he announced, rising and making for the door, grabbing his outside coat off the peg. Aggie jumped up, tail wagging, apparently also of a mind that outside would be a good place to go.

Donning his tricorn and wrapping his scarf around his neck, Eustis started down the cobbled road toward the Adams house on Winter Street with Aggie following closely behind. The sky did not look particularly threatening, so they likely had a fine day ahead.

The Adamses' housekeeper, Surry, directed him into the parlor. She was an interesting woman, thought Eustis. She had arrived in Boston years ago as a slave, was bought by the Adams family and immediately freed, then continued to live with them as their housekeeper. She had cared for the senior Adams and now his son for decades.

He found Sam reading a medical journal. He was wrapped in a shawl and looked comfortable in a large padded armchair.

"Good day, Bill. You look pleased. What news?"

"No excitement on the street today, my friend. But in the mail." He pulled a chair near Sam. "Do you remember the women's settlement near West Point? I have heard from Mrs. Eldredge."

"I remember her! Was she not a midwife, and you helped her in a difficult situation?"

"Indeed. And she sent news of our two favorite young men. Remember Robinson House? Elijah and Noah? They are on their way here right now, traveling through Connecticut but staying outside of Rhode Island. It is not quite safe there yet for Noah."

"Well, that is something to celebrate. I hope we will have some time to spend with them?"

"I think so. Mrs. Eldredge seemed to think that we may have to care for them through the winter if the weather turns."

"Hoo boy! I hope that is the case! Well, not really. But you know what I mean."

"I surely do. My sisters are all excited, talking about dinner menus and where we can lodge them. They do have a certain point to their concern in that we are a full house and no extra rooms. And Noah is married!"

"How interesting. And we do here," said Sam. "Have rooms I mean. It might work, and we can help."

"That is very generous of you. I knew you would help us if you could. But you need to check with your father. Let's wait and see what the situation is."

"Oh, you know him. My honored parent is at his happiest meeting new folk and being helpful. He loves the challenge of straightening out any situation involving betterment of life for anyone. He will be intrigued with Noah – and a new wife!"

"Yes, I know, Sam. But I still say 'let's prepare.' " And he almost laughed hearing himself echoing his sisters. "You could talk with him, but we best wait before committing too much. I always think caution is best before rushing in.

"Oh, and Mrs. Eldredge wrote something that I did not share with my sisters, a warning about Norah's husband. It was not much, but I am surprised that she would actually write it. I am not sure if she was implying anything or not. When Norah came by for tea at our house yesterday, she said very little about him. And one more thing. What do you know about Captain Bonham? I have heard that his wife has locked herself in her room with the curtains drawn. Must be deeply depressed or upset about something."

"Hey, Bill, you are at your best when you are trying to find out answers. I remember how all that went. I will ask around about the Bonhams. He has quite a fleet of ships, and they have that plantation down in Barbados too. I thought he was beginning to take his business to Bristol rather than Boston. He was transporting slaves, and it is a more accepting port."

"Thanks, Sam. I have been thinking about them since I saw one of their ships come into the harbor the other day. I thought I saw a crewmember jump overboard."

"Whoa, Bill. You never mentioned that! I'll listen around. Mayhap my father has heard something there. I do know that their son was reported missing. Something about him going overboard in a storm off Connecticut. That could be the problem for his mother."

* * *

As Eustis walked back home, Aggie trailing him, he worried about Sam's pallor and lack of active movement. He seemed so lethargic, tired all the time. His exhaustion should not have continued this long. Seems he would have to speak to him again and ask if he might listen to his chest. They had talked of consumption although even that had been

44

difficult. They probably would have been better consulting with a separate doctor and not each other.

Entering the kitchen, he was struck first by the smell of drying apples and then with how well his sisters ran the house. I hope they do not leave to get married, he thought. Then we'd be in a real mess. But they may want their own homes. When Catherine married Ebenezer Wells, Eben had moved in with them and continued his own outside work. Then Eustis's father moved into his bride's house nearby. He likely thought that with Cath in charge and Eben there, everything could continue as it should. After all, by marrying Catherine, Eben had acquired her share of the house.

Eustis checked in with his sisters about their patient, and hearing that she had eaten her breakfast went to see her himself. He tapped on the door and entered to find her sitting up in the bed, wrapped in an extra blanket, and writing on a slate. One of his sisters must have brought it to her, and he could see she was trying to copy letters of the alphabet. He hoped she had some schooling. She certainly should have learned to write her name by now, or at least as much as she knew of it. But it looked like she was struggling. He asked how she was sleeping. She was not waking as much, she replied, and was beginning to feel more secure and warm. He next asked what she remembered.

"I dunno, sor," she said. "It seems I mostly 'member the bad things. The woman who told me what to do. Said I could sleep in the kitchen near the fire if I was good. If I was bad, I had to go into the back shed, and it was cold there. She let me eat off their plates after they were finished, or I got bread ends. But it was better than outdoors."

"Yes," said Eustis. "You could sleep in the kitchen most of the time?"

"Mostly."

"Did you go to a church or school?"

She looked puzzled. "I dunno. Church? But I do know what a school is. I saw some other small people go in the door of a school once. I mostly did work in the kitchen or barn."

"And what was your name, my girl?"

"I tol' you. 'Tis Sally."

"But any more names? Do you have a family name?

"I dunno what you mean, sor. I got no family but those folks who kept me."

"I understand. Is there anything else you remember outside of the kitchen or barn? Did a cow live there? Or what did your house look like?"

"Oh, yes, sor." She grinned, "We 'ad a cow 'cause I took care of 'er. Every mornin' I hadda go to pull her milk out. Sometimes I was bad and drank some of it. But I was hungry, and then I hadda stay in the shed. Cows were my bes' friends."

Eustis decided he would have to go over her life many more times and would ask the girls to try too. At midday dinner with the family, he found that Anne had decided to begin Sally's schooling. She had discovered that the child knew nothing about writing or reading and took it upon herself to become her teacher. It would make her future survival possible. But they did need to find out more about her and where she came from and her name. Actually, they needed to discover her whole identity, where she had lived, the people who owned her indenture.

Eustis, again wrapped up against the afternoon chill, went out to a medical call in the neighborhood. He had time to think as he walked. He had not considered opening a medical office due to his health concerns but responded to calls from those who knew him. He had wild thoughts of what Elijah might decide to do with the rest of his life. Maybe they could even work together. What if they could go back to the way it had been at Robinson House with the three of them? He could open an office. But he was way ahead of himself.

He remembered he had not sent a note to Norah Lindholm about the letter from Mrs. Eldredge and her news of the arrival of the young men. He would like to let her know, and Prudence knew where she lived. He also meant to bring a gift for her daughter, sort of a friendly welcome to Boston. But was it proper? Hmmm. He would ask Catherine.

He had many more items on his list to attend to. First was finding the constable and asking about the drowned man. No one had contacted him, and he thought he should have been. If this medical visit was short, he would go over to the law enforcement office afterwards. They had said the man's name might be Monty Thurman, and they could have found out more by now.

CHAPTER 8

Constable Enoch Cobb's office was in the Town House where all manner of the town's business was handled. After locating the right room, Eustis discovered Mr. McAllister, the same watchman he had met at the wharf, sitting at a desk with papers strewn across the top. He was trying to sort them into piles, clearly not his favorite activity.

"Mr. McAllister, may I ask you a few more questions? Could you identify him? The drowned man? Was he indeed Monty somebody, or another name? Monty Thurman perhaps? And where did he live?"

McAllister happily put aside his paperwork.

"Nah, Dr. Eustis. We have not pursued it. No interest. No one came askin', an' we usually just wrap 'em up and take 'em over to that holding tomb at the Granary Burial Ground. Then we wait 'til there are several to tend to and bury a bunch of 'em. And he's still there, not tucked in yet."

"But could you tell me anything about him? Where did he come from?"

"The constable was not interested. Said it was probably someone who fell off a ship. So we didna do anything. An' no one came to ask about 'im. My guess is that he was on a ship that came into the harbor, an' he fell overboard or was pushed. And the water is really getting cold now. The shock would have killed him. Not our problem, doctor. We guard the shore and the town."

"But if violent men come off the ships into the town, should you not be interested? There is a coroner for Boston, I collect. What does he say?" Eustis also remembered the man he had seen jump overboard. He should ask about that too. They might well be the same person.

"As I said," McAllister went on, "'tis not our problem long's they do not break the law. Only if they get to disturbin' the peace around here. Then I lock 'em up.

"The coroner usually decides it is an accidental death when someone dies. And then before we bury 'em, I can show the dead one to people who are curious. You want to see 'im? See if you know 'im?"

"Would that be a help to the coroner or the constable if I look him over? I can examine him. I've done this in the past."

"Well, I'll ask. Back in a few minutes." And he went into the office behind him and closed the door.

It wasn't long before Constable Cobb, the same man who Eustis had seen in the distance when the body was trundled away in the barrow, came out.

"Who are you, sir? Newspaper or curiosity? The coroner has taken a look and says it does not look like murder to him. I already gave information for the newspapers just so the town folk are not worried. Are you trying to stir up a situation? Because that is not acceptable. You understand me?"

"Indeed, I do, Constable. I am Dr. William Eustis. I happen to have experience in identifying a corpse from my time in the war in the Hudson Highlands so thought to offer myself to help. And when I saw him in the water under the wharf, I thought he looked to be badly disfigured by time in the water, striking barnacles, that sort of thing. But he could have been in a fight. What if he was not from a ship? Has anyone come to draw his picture to circulate for identification?"

The constable seemed to relax a bit and seconded the watchman's offer of a look at the body. They seemed to think that would take care of the entire episode. Eustis wondered if others had also had the opportunity to view the body.

It was a short walk to Tremont Street and the Granary Burial Ground where the watchman had a key to open the door of the partially underground storage crypt. Eustis ducked his head and entered, stepping down, followed by McAllister. The strong odor should have warned him, but he was surprised to see four unburied corpses wrapped in linen sheeting and waiting on shelves on either side. Fortunately, McAllister seemed to know which one they should look at.

"We will be gettin' these into the ground soon, before it freezes. After that it will be too late. You want me to unwrap the whole thing?" he asked with what seemed like some anticipation. Maybe he liked impressing his audience.

"Is there a table where I can examine him?"

"No, sir. We just use the shelf. Never had any other request like that," he explained as he moved to remove some of the linen wrapped around the head.

Eustis stepped closer, again noting the familiar smell. This one better get into the ground soon. How long has it been? Three days? Long enough, especially given the time previously spent drifting in the ocean. This man may have been dead for some time.

As he looked at the face and head, he noted severe bruising, a split lip as well as cuts and scratches perhaps caused by repeated contacts with the pilings. But some bruises were lower down on the back of the head, not where they should be from hitting the pier. One in particular stood out at the nape of the neck. It looked like the man had been hit with a heavy bat or something thicker than a cane. The handle of a tool perhaps? A bosun carried that sort of baton. He had also seen bartenders and publicans with appropriate bats stored behind their bars to subdue unruly or drunken patrons. This death could be the result of a brawl or accidental drowning.

Eustis asked McAllister if they had stopped into the various public houses to see what anyone knew or if anyone had seen a fight only to find that no one had been interested enough to inquire. The authorities preferred to operate on their initial assumption that it was a drowned man from a foreign ship.

"But have you examined his clothing for clues?"

"Not worth it, doctor. The coroner did not think it was important enough, and we do not have the time or interest."

"Hmmm. You have given me a lot to think about, Mr. McAllister. Let me see what I find, and I will get back to you at some point."

"Happy to do this for you, doctor. Any time you want to see more, just let me know."

Eustis left, hearing the watchman lock the door behind him. He walked slowly back to the North End. He then thought of the child Sally and several questions that he might put to her. She had done an amazing job of keeping herself alive, and he wanted to know how. And he wanted to get back to talk with Sam. It might be that his father had the connections they needed.

Entering the kitchen, he was greeted by Aggie, wiggling and waving her tail, and a smiling Anne, both pleased to see him. Asking about Sally, he took off his scarf and coat and hung them from a wall peg. Prudence said he had enough time before their supper to see Sally. They hoped she would be able to join them.

Eustis discovered Sally fully dressed and sitting on the bed with her slate. She seemed less scared of him, and he sat on a stool to ask her more questions.

"You have had an amazing time and I want to know more about how you lived. How long have you been living on the Common, under those bushes? Were you there one night or many?"

"I don't know 'zackly how many, but lots. I 'as watching all the time."

"Watching what? Were you looking for something?"

"Well, ye see. I think that if my ma left from back there, she might come to this big town, and now I can find her. I jus' don't believe she could go off and leave me, so mayhap she was coming here to work and make money to get me back."

"I understand. I wonder also if you saw anyone that looked right to you?"

"I am not sure what she looked like. But I was watching the big houses. If I went to the back doors, sometimes they would give me food. An' she could be in one of those kitchens."

"Did you see anything else around the big houses?"

"No, sor. There was a lot happenin' at some of 'em. People goin' in and out, but I did not see my mother. I saw some ladies though. 'Nother house, the big red one, was all men. They were busy and had wagons. I think they got some things an' sent other things to the harbor. Mostly at night."

"I understand, Sally." He thought that must be the Tolliver house. Interesting. They could be smuggling. "We'll think about this some more. Maybe you and I can go walking there sometime." He paused again, thinking, frowning. "And you hid under the bushes?"

"Uh-huh. I could wrap up and stay warm there. It was my safe spot. But it began to get real cold."

"Well, come with me and we will have something to eat. We may be able to talk more later."

Interesting, he thought. A determined child searching for her mother, thinking she could find her after all these years. If she was indentured when she was four, that must have been more than six years ago. And although she did not look any older than ten, she probably was.

She got off the bed and willingly came with him. The three sisters were there as was Ebenezer and little Ben. Jacob let in a burst of cold air when coming inside with Nathaniel. Sally hesitated then seemed to brace herself. She didn't run back to the bedroom, although it appeared as if she wanted to. Brave girl.

They gathered for leftover fish stew, even better the second day. Prudence brought a loaf of cornbread to the table. Perfect for the beginning of the fall season. Later, the women washed the pots and bowls, and Sally was shown how they liked to dry their utensils and tableware and put it all in the cupboard. She said they did not do that where she had been. Or at least she had not seen it. She had her own bowl and spoon. That was all.

The sisters pursed their lips, looking at one another. Anne offered to help Sally with the alphabet after they were finished, and Prudence said she and Cath had their knitting to get to. They were starting to prepare for winter and had a long list of items that would be needed, especially if Bill went on that expedition and with yuletide coming just when Cath's baby might arrive. It was going to get complicated. They hoped they could develop Sally's domestic abilities and teach her to be useful, and she would need warm clothing as well.

* * *

Ushering the cows to the Common the next morning, Anne noticed the changing colors on the trees. They might be getting close to a frost or there may have been one last night, she thought. After all, it was mid-October and mighty lucky they had found Sally before she attempted to survive through the winter under those bushes.

The day had warmed by late morning, and Eustis planned to go look over the Common again. Anne was taken up with teaching Sally, and the older sisters were cutting fabric, anticipating an afternoon of sewing. Jacob was down at the wharf with Nathaniel. Eustis thought he might circle around to the harbor to see them later.

Standing by the now familiar bushes, he looked around him. The area seemed raked over; tidied up with no debris or anything else around to indicate who had been there. Sally would have had a clear view of all the big houses along the ridge of Beacon Hill. Even now, he could see the activity of carriages and visitors in front of John Hancock's house. Next to that, slightly smaller but clearly an important residence, was Abbott Tolliver's substantial brick house. That obvious wealth, the variety of activities, and many visitors might attract poorer people hoping to make money. He then mused about how those obviously well-to-do owners had made that money. By owning privateers, people had made a great deal during the war. Their ships captured and looted British ships and sold it all – vessels and cargoes alike. Remembering Sally's remark, he suspected the Tollivers were smuggling, or had been during the war.

What else or who else Sally had seen remained a puzzle. Eustis decided he would talk it over with Sam. Surry let him in. Sitting in the sun by the front window, Sam was watching the street. "Saw you coming. Looks like you have things to talk about. I can tell by the way you walk. Here, sit and tell me everything."

"Well, good day to you, Sam. I do want your opinion," said Eustis. "I went to talk with the constable about what they knew about that dead fellow we found floating in the harbor. Can you believe it? He was not interested in inquiring about it or identifying the man at all. That is just shocking to me. I am not sure where to go with it. But the watchman showed me where they temporarily store bodies until they get a burial detail together."

"What do you want to do about it?" Sam asked. "Do you want to get involved again in some investigation?"

"No, not at this point. But it is making me so curious, and annoyed too. And I feel some sense of obligation, having been there when he was found. There has got to be more to it than a sailor falling off a boat. They don't do that. And how could the crew not notice? This one had a substantial bruise indicating being hit at the back of his neck, not from just bumping into a piling."

Sam frowned. "I can see your point. If this was a suspicious death, or a murder, or something like that, the constable should be interested. There might be a murderer walking around in our – or his – town. He seems to be avoiding part of his job. Perhaps it will occur to him. And I thought the coroner was involved in this. Does the watchman seem interested?"

"Not that I could tell. Perhaps I should ask questions to see if I can find out more, something that might get his interest," Eustis reasoned. "If we could get a drawing of the man, I could show it around on the wharves. I can get back into the crypt where he is laid out. Do you know anyone who can draw well enough or anyone who would know?"

"I'll find out. There has to be someone available. Your brothers should know about harbor life and who is around down on the wharves. There has to be talk somewhere, and I'll bet Jacob knows where."

Later, as Eustis walked home, he thought he would ask Jacob for help. Perhaps he should come look at the man. He might even recognize him.

As they gathered near the hearth that evening, the women brought out their sewing baskets, Anne hoping to teach Sally some basic stitches. She had not even heard about the basic rite of passage for a young girl of making a sampler to show that she knew the alphabet and fancy stitches.

The women also wanted their brother to tell them what had helped him to keep warm during the West Point winters. Prudence showed them a vest of wool she had knitted and laid it out on the table. Maybe she should add sleeves?

"Looks excellent, but how do I get my coat over it with sleeves?" asked Eustis. "My coat is fairly tight in the sleeves. It is more stylish that way. Perhaps more wool stockings? Or a knit hat?".

Eustis, Jacob, and Nathaniel huddled together and discussed the dilemma of identifying the drowned man. Jacob knew of a possible artist to make a drawing, a student skilled at sketching a likeness. He would send the student a note that evening. And disagreeable as it was, he would even look at the body himself.

Eustis was particularly concerned to discover if the man had actually drowned or was put into the water after he died. He could have been unconscious. Either the shock of the very cold water or actual drowning could kill him. And it was too late to use rigor mortis as any indication. He remembered another situation like this at West Point where he found that a man was definitely dead before he entered the water, and he wondered if this was the same. The mark at the back of his skull did not seem at all like an accidental bump into a piling – especially if it had barnacles. They would have made scratches. If he was beaten before going into the water, it could involve dockworkers or others.

Eustis knew he should find out if the man had water in his lungs. That would require a full autopsy. Without that evidence, drowning might be difficult to prove.

CHAPTER 9

Upsetting news arrived the next morning in a note from John McAllister, the watchman. The collection of bodies in the vault was scheduled to be interred within two days. Best move quickly if they want to get a drawing. Jacob agreed to meet that afternoon and would accompany the student artist to bolster his bravery. Eustis would first have to talk to the watchman and implore him to let them back into the crypt.

McAllister was waiting at the vault entrance as arranged when they arrived at the Granary Burial Ground. The accompanying artist had his drawing pad and charcoal and worked quickly. He wore a handkerchief over his nose, not to conceal his identity, he assured them, but to diminish the odor. Meanwhile, Eustis kept trying to peek under the wrappings without disturbing the drawing in progress. Finally, it seemed finished to everyone's satisfaction, or at least the artist's. Eager to leave, he promised a finished copy, bid his farewells, and vanished.

As it happened, Jacob was not that thrilled by his experience with the body either and also wanted to leave. But Bill Eustis was disappointed that he could not have more time. He had more questions. Was it definite the man had been beaten? Were there other marks? And what about the lungs?

Eustis spoke to McAllister. "Is there any way for me to see him totally unwrapped? Naked? I want to look at his body."

McAllister looked askance at him. "What are you? Some kind of catamite?"

"No, no, no, Mr. McAllister! I am a doctor interested in this man's anatomy for a murder investigation. I want to know if he drowned or was killed. Please! Talk to the constable. Or perhaps I should. There is a way to prove he drowned."

McAllister still seemed suspicious and indicated they should leave right now. He was not unwrapping anything. He ushered them out and turned to lock the vault.

Jacob was trying to maintain his dignity rather than taunt his brother who clearly did not want to leave. Eustis just scowled and began walking away. They were out of time and could not wait another day.

Fuming about McAllister, watching his brother as he steamed away, Jacob spoke: "You do know that he was a physician in the war for eight years running a hospital for General Washington. He worked with all those famous military folk you have heard of, and he knew them personally. He kept more people alive than you ever did, and you do owe him an apology." Then he too turned and strode away. McAllister was left in front of the crypt feeling confused and defensive.

As they walked back toward the North End, Eustis said, "I just want some information, and they are not interested at all. They don't understand what we can discover that could help inform our decisions. What can I do?"

Jacob wanted to be soothing. "I understand, Bill. Let's think of who can speak to the constable. How about Mr. Hancock? Or the elder Adams?"

"Hmmm. I'll talk to Sam I guess. Hate to do it," he shrugged, sighed, "but it seems I must."

He saw Jacob off at their house and continued on to the Adamses' house. Admitted by Surry, he found Sam, handkerchief in his hand, wrapped up by the window. It seemed as if this was his favorite place now.

"A good day to you, Sam! I need your help – your father's help really. I must be allowed to examine the body of the man found under the wharves, and the constable and watchman do not understand nor are they interested whether he was murdered or not."

"Hold on, old chap. Is this a new fixation? Let me understand. My honored father will be arriving shortly for his midday meal. You can talk to him then. Actually, perhaps you will join us."

"That would be very kind of you. I would like to discuss my disagreement with the constable. That man called me a catamite because I wanted to see the body naked."

57

Sam broke into laughter to the point where he had to struggle for breath to speak. "I can imagine it." He wheezed. "You are going to have an interesting reputation! Oh, my! Young men better watch out." And he dissolved into laughter again, ending in a difficult coughing attack.

Their visit continued for another fifteen minutes until the senior Sam Adams came into the room. He affectionately patted his son on the shoulder and greeted Eustis. "Welcome, Bill. I have not had a chance to talk with you in days." He indicated Sam. "And I am so glad you can keep this lazy fellow on his toes. I hear you are having some difficulty with our constable." Then, holding up his hand, "Now, don't be surprised. Surry keeps me informed."

Eustis felt relieved and settled in for a few minutes to explain his dilemma and desire to discover who the dead man was and the way he died. Then he might be able to find out who the murderer was, if there was one. Could it really be someone off a ship as they all seemed to want to think?

On Surry's invitation, they went in to dinner where their discussion continued. By the end of a substantial meal, the senior Adams said he would follow up and talk to some people who might be of assistance.

"Revere might be of help too. He knows a lot about what happens in the harbor. I'll check in with him."

Eustis went home feeling a lot more successful and told his sisters about it as all three sat knitting and coaching Sally on her sampler stitches. Little Ben was in a child-size seat with wooden wheels that he could move by pushing with his feet. It had large fenders to keep him confined to the room and out of the hearth. Unable to do more than bump into objects, he crowed happily and slammed into a bench.

When the sisters went to the kitchen to see about their supper, Sally came shyly to the doctor to say how happy she was with them, how much she was learning, and how she hoped she could stay always and forever. He was touched and remembered he was going to try to solve her problem of identity as well.

"Sit with me for a minute."

"Yes, sor. But shouldn't I go help?"

"It will be fine if it is just for a few minutes. They have enough help for the moment. Here, come sit in that big chair. The one with wings. You will feel safe as if you were in your own fort."

Sally did as she was told and settled in, looking quite comfortable as she looked around at her "wings." Eustis sat on a nearby wooden stool. He looked at her.

"If you agree, I would like to try another way to find out something about where you came from." At her look of alarm, he hastened to add, "It does not mean we will send you away. Not at all. It's just my curiosity. I think you probably have an even greater adventure story than we even know. Please. Will you try it?"

She shyly nodded.

"First you need to relax. I am not going to bite you." At that bit of humor, she sat more snugly in the chair and settled her hands in her lap.

"I just want to try something. What we will look for is some memory of the time before you went away in the wagon. Please. Just close your eyes and listen to me. And do try to relax."

He used his most soothing voice. "What do you remember when you think of your home when you were very little? Perhaps when you were two or three years old? Way, way back."

At his gentle urging, she settled deeper into the soft chair and, eyes closed, thought for several minutes. "I think," she said, "that I 'member a big house with lots of rooms and lots of nice people in 'em."

"Very good. Did those people always stay in their rooms? Did they have closed doors?"

"Oh, no. They came out and went down the stairs. Sometimes they went away and sometimes they came back but after a long time. I could watch 'em from the railin'."

"Where was this railing?'

"At the top o' the stairs."

"What was at the bottom of the stairs? Can you see that?"

"No, nothin' more. Mayhap a big room? Jus' nice voices. Nothin' else." She opened her eyes, looking at Eustis, pleased with her memory. "Did I do it right? I wonder if I lived there. In the big space. Can you tell me? We can find it, an' my mother could be there."

"You did very well, Sally. An excellent job of memory. And if you can try it again, you may find even more. Perhaps just as you are falling asleep you could try thinking back."

"Ooh! I will, I will!" Then she hopped up and hurried into the kitchen, calling out that she had remembered something. The sisters immediately said how proud of her they were.

* * *

The following day, after his morning coffee, Eustis intended to go promptly to the Town House to find the constable. But first he wanted to see McAllister. It was easier to talk with the watchman than the constable who got defensive whenever he was questioned. McAllister was much more accessible in his small watch house, and when asked for a few minutes of his time he gestured toward a stool. "Please, doctor, take a seat."

"Thank you, Mr. McAllister. I apologize for being so difficult. I am interested if there is any more information on the drowned man – any identity yet? – or if you have heard about other activities or situations like that."

McAllister appeared amused. "You lookin' for more dead bodies, doc?"

"Not unless you have any extra ones lying around," Eustis laughed. "But I am very interested in anything new or unusual that has happened on the waterfront in the last few days or weeks. Any angry protests or fighting?"

"How did you hear about that?" asked McAllister.

"I have not heard anything specific. I was concerned that any other drownings might be related and mayhap started some kind of a reaction."

The watchman sighed. "It's not good now. Generally, the wharves are filled with good, hard workers, just wantin' to get their jobs done and collect their pay. Sometimes there is a little rough housin', but lately there has been more upset than usual, arguments and even bullyin'. The men seem on edge. Some eejit will shove another and it sets off a fight. I have nae seen this much reactivity and anger in a while. Now men are carryin' heavy sticks or bats. I saw Al Lindholm with one."

"Now that is a problem," Eustis said. "Do you suppose our dead man might have set off a fight? And it caused others to get into it?"

"Could be. They get rowdy when money is involved. There is always more tension. They all are watchful, practically twitching, either about to run away or attack."

"What or who can be causing it? Are there rumors out there?"

"There are groups coming together and talking in the taverns about armaments. Men are hauling out old uniforms too. I hear that there is an army gathering. Do ye know of any kinda rebellion, doc? That could be it. We don't want to get caught with our breeches down if the French are coming. They could come in here, you know, and we got no defense planned. Nothin' is ready around the harbor."

"I understand the anxiety, Mr. McAllister. And the concern about the French. But some of that activity people have seen or may be concerned about involve the preparations for the Cincinnati's expedition heading out to Springfield to stop those rebelling farmers. I am going with them as a doctor. I don't know how long it will be, but we will leave within weeks – certainly by mid-December."

"Might be it. I can try to pass the word and see if that calms 'em down."

"That would be helpful. But I'm also concerned with the identification of the dead man."

"Still after it, are ye, doc?"

"Yes, of course. I should think all of you would be. Does your constable not talk about it? How can you just let someone get killed in your jurisdiction and on your watch?"

"I can tell ye this much. We've had no questions or discussions. Though it seems strange now that ye mention it. I'll keep a lookout for ye. Mebbe ask around."

"I appreciate that. I only hope we can find out something more before I head out there to the western snows!" Eustis rose from his seat.

"Me too, doc. Me too. It is just that if there is no family around or interest, we kinda let it drop."

"Perhaps you can review it once more? If you do not know his name, how can you search? Ship schedules or something like that? He needs to be identified."

The wind was rising and pushing in fog accompanied by a rank smell as the tide turned and began to come back in to cover the outlying mud flats. He thought about Sally while walking back home and pondered her story.

She had talked about a large house with rooms and happy people who came and went. He would think it over, and something might float to the surface. But it was a good attempt to recover her memories, and she might be willing to try again when another clue could be discovered. He might try Sally on names.

Later that afternoon, a neighborhood boy brought a message for him from the elder Sam Adams. He had made it possible for Eustis to unwrap and spend more time with that corpse, but it would have to be immediate. The sheriff intended to have the burials tomorrow. McAllister had said nothing about that earlier! May not have been told then. Now he only had the afternoon. Telling his sisters, grabbing his medical kit, coat, and hat, he quickly went out, not stopping to answer questions about any midday dinner. "I'll be back for supper."

* * *

Several hours later, walking home in the growing dark, he enjoyed the brisk fresh air unscented by any ancient tomb effluvia and mused over what he had learned. The dead man was better dressed than the usual workers around the harbor, so he was probably not a crewman. His battered body displayed several signs of a beating. He had gotten the worst in a fight with the major damage being a severe blow to the back of the head. The use of a bat or bludgeon? Perhaps a fist fight had started, but it had ended in a severe beating.

A scarf or kerchief, caught up in the wrappings, turned out to be a nice, blue color. Eustis seemed to remember his sisters calling it indigo and saying it came from the South where they grew the dye plant. If he was off a ship, this man must have sailed down there to trade – perhaps Massachusetts apples and salted cod for Carolina rice. He had tucked the blue cloth into his pocket thinking it might help with the identity process.

Eustis wondered why he had not heard of a row on the docks from Jacob, but it was a huge complex of docks and wharves that surrounded the peninsula of Boston. He seemed to remember hearing there were fifty or more of them.

A brawl should have attracted attention, but it was a noisy place around the harbor with the taverns open, and a silent ambush would not be noticed. His brother was number one on his list for a discussion. Jacob would certainly know who to contact with questions about any fighting if he had not already heard about it.

Entering the kitchen, Eustis found the women enjoying tea in front of the kitchen hearth before they got supper ready, sewing, and listening to Sally tell about her former miserable life. They appreciated their tea, having boycotted it during the Revolution. Catherine reassured Sally that she would remain with the Eustis family, that they needed her.

Jacob joined him in the keeping room with two tankards of cider so they could talk. Drinking it down by half, he placed his mug on the table beside him.

"Ah, that is good. Thank you, Jacob. You sure know how to help a weary man. Now, let me ask. Could you search your brain for any story of a recent brawl on the docks. I was finally able to examine the dead man today. They will be interring those bodies tomorrow, and our man looks as though he went through a thorough beating, bones broken too. He was dressed in good clothes, not like a dockworker, but he had a blue scarf. He may have worn that scarf because it was tucked in the linen they had used wrapping his body. I've got his drawing too, the one we can use for identification. Could you help me show it around? I want to find out his name."

"I will not forget him," said Jacob with a grimace. "It's impressive that you've come this far. But I am not sure how recognizable our sailors are. They seem to come and go, and we do not always get their names. Some are crew or officers on ships. Some are workers hired by the day or could even be passengers. We can ask. And I'll go around with you tomorrow. What we should do is go early to where men gather looking for work. They hope to get selected for odd day jobs. A man in charge of loading cargo on a ship might come and pick out six or eight likely workers and hire them for the day. They might know if our man was from some particular ship. Of course, the whole process could have been some smuggling operation, and there would be no records or names at all."

"I would be truly grateful for your company, knowing where to go tomorrow. And early morning will work for you? I have another Cincinnati meeting with General Lincoln later in the morning."

"Yes indeed. Early morning is best, and I forgot that you are still involved with that farmers' revolt out in the western region. Those poor fellows. You are going out there? Do you know when you'll be off? 'Tis getting cold now, brother, if you haven't noticed."

"Believe me, I have. And I just hope I can come up with sufficient clothing and that we find suitable places to sleep at night. And stockings! Our sisters are working on it. It will take our company some time to even get there, but I think we will be off by mid-December, missing our yuletide here. Meanwhile," he sighed, "we can tend to this other problem."

Anne came to the door and suggested they come in for supper, already laid out on the kitchen table. Idle chatter over cheese, pickles, butter, and bread led to Sally again telling them proudly about her success in remembering a location. The entire family praised her and urged her to remember more. Unfortunately, this pressure heightened her defenses, and they realized it was of no help to demand results. It was far better to appreciate the warm apple pie placed on the table.

CHAPTER 10

The aroma of freshly-brewed coffee and Jacob's quick raps on his door brought Eustis downstairs. He had needed the reminder. Dawn had not yet arrived, but there were peeks and streaks of its beginning. Jacob was already seated with his coffee, cornbread, and butter courtesy of the family cows. This was the best and most delicious way to prepare for their investigations, Jacob suggested, grinning, when his brother sleepily staggered in.

Prudence joined them holding a squirming Ben on her lap. He seemed to think he should get on the floor.

"Are you two off to the harbor this morning?" she asked. "We'll be doing more preserving and getting the last of the potatoes and parsnips into the cold cellar. Sally has been a godsend to help with all this, and she is beginning to do some sewing. When do you actually think you'll be off westward, Bill?"

"Jacob was just asking. I think I'll know more after this morning's meeting. I hope I can tell you tonight. All depends on General Lincoln having sufficient men and money, and I know he has been out looking for both. The farmers' revolt continues, so we will probably leave by mid-December. I'll hate missing the yuletide and your specially mixed egg-grog punch though. It is as good as any I've had in a tavern. Better!"

Jacob interrupted. "But first we are headed for the harbor. The men gather for work early there. Ready, Bill? And Nat is intending to help you here, Prue."

They rose to get wrapped up in their outer wear, adding knitted mittens, hats, and scarves. Eustis pulled his boots over his woolen stockings. Heading out to the road, they left the later arrivals, Eben and Nathaniel, in the enviable position of not having to rush out, cheerfully wishing them a good morning. A cold November gust off the water immediately ensured they were both awake. Hurrying to the waterfront, the men grabbed their hats and bent into the wind.

Arriving at the shore end of Hancock's wharf, one of the gathering spots for unemployed dockworkers, Eustis circulated among the hopefuls. He took out his drawing and asked them to look at the picture. Could someone help with identification? Did they know who this fellow was? Many of the men tried to be helpful, but as many just wanted to watch for work. He persisted, helped by Jacob who many of the men recognized.

An hour later, Eustis looked at Jacob. They had little cause for celebration. No name for their man. Their venture seemed dismal and disappointing.

"Let's try another place, maybe a smaller wharf," Jacob suggested. "There is another spot for men looking for work."

They tried farther along the harbor until they could no longer feel their toes, and a stop in a tavern seemed a good idea. They were on Ann Street and went into the Bell in Hand where just being inside was a pleasure. Anything hot tempted them, particularly coffee.

It was not long before Eustis rose from their table. "Thanks for the coffee, Jacob. I have to head over to my meeting in Faneuil Hall. Do you suppose we can do this again? Maybe tomorrow?"

"I am happy to help you, brother. I'll see you at home. If you want gossip, you may also want to try around other taverns."

* * *

Eustis walked to the market and upstairs to his meeting. As he climbed the stairs, he realized how lucky he was to have three sisters and a youthful helper in Sally working around their home. He also recognized that without them he could not get out to do his explorations or even have the wool muffler that he wore. Sometimes it almost made him feel guilty that they were working so hard. But there were no other alternatives. It was the end of the harvest. Nat had gotten the potatoes up, but much of the food preservation involved women's work – by the sisters and Sally. And then the men could go out and bring home the additional funds they needed.

Once everyone was seated, General Lincoln opened the meeting and got several immediate questions about the plans.

"Yes, I understand. My good wife wants to know as well," he said. "We will leave with what we can gather by the middle of December. You should each bring a horse, all your cold-weather clothing and necessities including a musket, powder, and balls. Please tell me if there are difficulties. I am hoping the wagons will work out, but we will also need sleighs and sleds to carry most of our gear.

"I suggest that you stay near the supply wagon, Dr. Eustis. It will carry all the medical materials you will need. And thank you for that list. I presume you will assist in gathering these supplies?"

"Yes, general. I've already gotten my orders out so that I will have plenty of stock."

"Good, good. If there is anything that you believe we need to work out, let me know. And I suspect your wives are knitting up a storm." He chuckled, joined dutifully by everyone around the table.

"I plan that we officers will have inside accommodations although I am not sure about all of the men. There should be barns and churches available too. We are short on tents, and I would appreciate it if you know of any. We'll also have a wagon for some split dry wood to make sure we can get fires started. And for food supplies. Rice, flour, corn meal. The Society should avoid any repetition of the difficulties of the past war if it is possible. I've also talked with Revere about powder and ammunition."

Eustis was trying to keep track of his duties, making a mental list as the general wrapped up the meeting. "We'll continue meeting next week, and in six weeks we should be off. Anything else?"

With his to-do list spinning in his head, Eustis left the hall and started uphill toward the North End, intending to head home to Sudbury Street, walking carefully on the wet and slippery cobblestones. A loud yell rang out. "Doctor! Doctor Eustis, sir!"

He stopped, turned toward the sound, and stopped. There stood two young men, one dark, one light, grinning ear to ear. They had found him, and he had walked right past, concentrating so thoroughly on the road surface and his thoughts.

"Well-met, my friends, well-met! Huzzah!" Eustis reached out to shake hands, pat shoulders, first one than the other. "How did you find me?"

"Oho!" said Elijah Eldridge, "We have our ways. Don't we, Noah." He acknowledged the young man with him, jabbing his arm with an elbow. In a quick assessment, Eustis saw that they seemed healthy – and older as he probably did himself. Noah was doing well, still using the same wooden leg, he noted. It was not evident if he was worried about returning to the place of his enslavement. By God, it was good to see them.

"Come home with me," he said, and arm in arm they headed toward his house. He could not stop wanting to laugh or celebrate somehow, and he especially wanted to get them all safe in his home. If he was a boy of ten, Dr. Eustis would have been skipping.

It was not far before he relinquished his grip on them to lead them through the back door and into the kitchen. They found Prudence and Anne chopping vegetables to add to their midday dinner.

"Look who I have!" he exclaimed. "Noah and Elijah!"

"Yes, isn't it marvelous," said Anne, smiling. "We met them when they first came by looking for you. We've sent a note to Sam. Cath is upstairs working out the sleeping arrangements with Maria."

"Maria?"

"My wife," grinned Noah. "We do not want to cause any trouble, but your good sister, Mrs. Wells, says you knew we would be coming." There was a slight question in his statement.

"Well, yes, of course," said Eustis. "My brain is in a fog. Your grandmother wrote a letter to me, Eli. I still cannot believe you two have managed to get this far! You'll have lots to tell. Probably for weeks!"

Prudence waved them ahead of her. "Let me bring in some small beer and coffee, and you all go into the keeping room."

Eustis picked up the suggestion and ushered them into seats. He stood and looked. His boys. Right here. And looking very successful. He laughed and sat down. "Well, tell me all."

"But I do not know where to begin," said Elijah. "You want to start, Noah?"

"Me? Where do I start?" asked Noah.

"At the beginning and then go on until the end," said Eustis. "I am not in any rush."

It was then that a young woman stepped hesitantly into the room. Noah leaped up to go to her. "May I present my dear wife, Maria Royall," he said.

"I wish you joy on your wedding. Now here is a story," said Eustis, smiling. "Where did you two meet?"

Noah went to an armchair and Maria joined him, perching on its arm. The attractive young woman was a dark caramel shade. Her hair was black, tied back, and tightly curled under her mob cap. She looked at Noah with a slight smile, quietly waiting.

"It was quite an adventure," he said. "Eli and I arrived in Cincinnati and were going along the riverfront looking to see if we could pick up some work. They had several boats there to go across or up and down the river, but we did not know enough yet about them. Everyone was armed with knives, muskets, or pistols. Just in front of us was a group of people disembarking from one of those big flatboats. It was piled with pelts. Looked like deer and maybe fox to us. Probably would be traded for other goods and supplies. We did not see any women. Then we suddenly noticed that two of the people disembarking were women of color linked by chains with one man supervising."

"Uh-oh. Not so good," said Sam Adams as he came into the room. He greeted the young men, happily shaking hands and hugging all around. "But, pray, do not stop your story."

Noah continued after waiting for Sam to sit and everyone to settle in again. He smiled at Maria.

"We were not sure if slavery was allowed in Ohio, but we saw some very questionable things going on. The territory was not really settled although people were pouring in to try establishing a homestead. Anyway, there were few or nothing much for laws. It felt very wild and dangerous to us, about as far from Boston as anyone could get.

"There certainly was suspicion and anger between the settlers and the French and the Indians in the area. We heard enough to know that some white men went after escaped slaves or any people of color and took them to the South to sell. It was every man and woman for themselves – truly rough frontier living."

"We decided we would get supplies and stay outside the village, and we watched for anyone who looked at us too much," said Eli. "And Noah has papers that he carries all the time."

"I surely do," said Noah, looking down into his lap. "I know I am at risk of being taken and put up for sale at any time. But let me tell you the rest. We followed those women and saw that they were taken into a barn by the waterfront. They were either going to be sold down the river or put into a brothel right there." He paused and intently looked at the other men rather than explain in front of Sally.

"And then we came up with a plan," added Eli. "Actually, it was a memory of what you did those years ago at my gran's settlement that got us started."

"Uh-oh," said Eustis. He tried not to show his concern, masking it with amusement instead. What had they gotten into?

"Hmmm, yes," said Noah. "So – the front door of the barn was closed and barred. Thinking of you, we went very slowly and quietly around to the back to see what was possible. There was a small door and, even better, several loose boards. We took turns peeking in through the cracks. These two women were tied to a chain that was suspended from a big beam overhead. They were just sitting in the hay. It looked like they were waiting."

At this Maria smiled at Noah. "And we were," she said. "For you." He patted her knee and continued the story.

"We moved away from the barn and went to a place nearby where we could talk. Both of us were thinking the same thing, that when it got dark we would try to get them out. But then what? We had to come up with a story in case anyone questioned or stopped us. We had to be able to explain. You understand? We needed to appear perfectly innocent and to have the right and authority to do this."

"Come on, Noah. Don't keep us hanging! What did you do?" asked Sam. Noah's audience was intently focused.

"We reckoned we might have to change the story after we talked to the women, but our first idea was that we would have Eli act grand and be a southern gentleman. I would be his valet and be married to one of the women. Then to explain the other woman, we would say that as Eli was going to pick up his wife from visiting her relatives for the past three months, he had brought her maid for her trip home. But we soon realized that did not seem like it would work in Cincinnati. Where could we say the wife was? What estate? Where was she visiting, and where we were going back to, you know, where we lived? It took some time to figure out our story. And by then it was getting dark."

"We did go get some supplies and food to bring with us," said Eli. "And we'd bundled all our possessions together and had them packed, ready to go. We were all set."

Eustis and Sam were almost on the edge of their seats. How had they pulled it off?

"Yes? Well? What happened?" Eustis pressed. "Don't tease us, you wicked numpties!"

Noah grinned, took a sip of his small beer, and then got on with it.

"Because I was darker, I had a better chance of moving around without being seen, even though I had my wooden leg," he said, his eyes twinkling. "So we decided to give it a try. And I had my crutch too. The small rear door was secured, but one of those wide boards was really loose, and I could pry it over to the side. Eli waited, back a little, to keep watch and give an alarm if he saw anything.

"I squeezed through the gap. But I didn't want to alarm the women because they might scream and I crept up very carefully. But then I realized that this one," he squeezed Maria's hand, "had been alert all the time and had secretly let Juney know too. Because of their lives, their safety, they were very watchful.

"I tried to let Maria know with hand signals that I was there to help. I don't think she believed me at first. Not until I began cutting the rope that bound them to the chain. I just had a small skinning knife, but it did not take long."

"It surely seemed like it to us," added Maria. "We were saying our prayers."

"Once I got the rope cut through, I knew we would have to remove their chains. But we needed time for that, so we just hustled as quietly as we could out through the gap in the back wall. Eli was there with his horse and two mules. My Sally was one of them."

At that, their Sally giggled to think she had the same name as Noah's mule.

"We needed more horses but did not have the time to get them, so the women had to ride double. We snuck out of the town, and then, after about three hours on the trail, we found a hidden place to set up a camp. We worked on removing the shackles from the women, got our tents up, and tried to look like a prosperous organized team getting ready to get our mistress. We wished we had a carriage or wagon, but we went over our roles so we would know what to say, and we began to gain some confidence. We intended to say our carriage had been stolen. That worked until the sheriff rode into the campsite with two other armed men."

There were audible murmurs in the room.

"Eli stepped out to talk and acted just like a duke. He asked them who they were and why they thought they could just ride all over our site. Sort of took the wind away from 'em. But what really made it work was the appearance of about six Shawnee who seemed friendly to us. The sheriff and two other men realized they could not fight us and the Indians if it came to that and kind of backed down and left after warning us not to make trouble.

"We were all into our acting roles and hoped to convince the Shawnee that we were only traveling through. It was Maria's and Juney's cooking that helped there. They had two rabbits cooking in the pot and offered to share. In the end, we became quite social. The Shawnee shared some of their food, a sort of a bread, and then left to set up camp not too far away. I think they would defend anyone from the sheriff."

"I wish we could have seen your performances, Noah," said Eustis, grinning and shaking his head. "You got away?"

"Yes, sir. It seemed we had better move as soon as dawn came, and the women were ready. We pushed north and followed the river. Tried to leave no indication we'd been that way."

"And then the four of you turned northeast, homeward?" asked Eustis.

Eli took up the tale. "Well, as soon as it seemed safe. We traveled north along the edge of the Ohio and Indiana territories. But that is all Indian Territory, not a state. The land belongs to the Shawnee and the Miami people who have an alliance, and there are also random bunches of renegades and trappers. And traders. Totally lawless. We knew we'd be much better off, much safer if we could get into Pennsylvania, so we turned east. This whole country is beautiful in its own special way, but just not safe for us, especially with the women."

At that point, Anne came in and suggested they all come for their midday meal. She and Prudence had set up the dining room for the occasion, although the room was a bit crowded with a bed in the corner. But with the table leaves opened out, they all could sit together.

Sally was eager to hear more about Indians and to talk about the mule with the same name.

"I'll bet Noah's mule Sally has had more adventures in travel than you," kidded Sam. "She has certainly gone farther into the wild west. She probably has a guardian angel."

Sally peeked at him and giggled. She was not too sure about angels.

The three most recent arrivals, Eli, Noah, and Maria, appeared delighted by their immediate acceptance into the household.

"There is more to these stories," said Eustis. "Tell us how you became married."

"I can do that," offered Elijah, laughing, and glancing at Noah. "Sometimes he gets embarrassed over telling how he fell in love. It took me to tell him he was being such a lackwit, a total eejit."

"Well," said Prudence, smiling, "tell us!" Voices echoed her request. Anne took Ben, Cath brought in coffee and more small beer. Everyone settled in for another story.

"I think it all began when we finally managed to get a wagon at Fort Recovery on the border. Then it was all about how skilled Maria was in making camp," said Eli. "Anytime she looked at Noah, he was just barely able to function. He lost his crutch. He lost his shoes. He even lost his speech! If he didn't have a smart mule he would have lost his way altogether." Everyone chuckled. "It just took Maria to get his head straightened out."

"Well," said Noah, grinning. "At least I was smart enough to realize I needed help and that she was the one to do it."

"And I am sure glad that you did," said Eli. "It all turned out well, and the reason that Juney is not still with us is because she recognized old friends when we got into Pennsylvania and went through the very town where she had lived years before. She decided to stay there. Slavery is abolished in Pennsylvania, the first of all the states. It was safe and worked out well for her. She knew a minister in the town who would marry Noah and Maria, and all Juney's friends helped with a party. Actually, we hated to leave her behind and may go back to visit sometime."

"But you said you might plan to stay here awhile, didn't you?" asked Catharine. "We can always find work for people here in Boston. There are many jobs around."

Maria reached for Noah's hand, smiled gently. "We would want our own place to live, although we are very grateful for your invitation to stay here for now. But we will look at the whole town. Just what little I have seen makes me think it is very busy and does lots of business. Everyone seems to be working at something to make money. It might be that a smaller town would suit us better."

"Yes. That is Boston. Making money is important to everyone here," said Eustis. "But it was a difficult time right after the war when we lost all our trade. All of it! With England, of course – but with everywhere else too. We're in a massive recovery now. Just look at what has happened with the shipping in the past three years. The waterfront is coming alive, really jumping now. Our population is growing too. Just in the area of medicine or caring for sick people, there will be a need for more suppliers, transportation, and the people who can provide medicines and care. You would be needed here, Eli."

"I understand, but we have to find where it feels right to us."

The group gradually broke up. Cath took Ben away for his nap, the young women cleaned up the kitchen, and the men went into the keeping room to talk further. Then they decided to walk to the Green Dragon for cider and ale. Eustis also had an ulterior motive for the visit, looking for patrons who might know what had happened on the waterfront and recognize the deceased man's picture. He had told the others briefly about his quest for identification.

"Really, a body? You mean a dead person? Under the wharf? Are you sure?" the three had asked in awe.

Eustis laughed at the doubting travelers and reassured them that he knew what he was talking about.

They donned their winter coats, Eustis picked up his drawing, and they ventured into the chilly evening. Under a darkening sky, they walked down the road carrying their lanterns. Along the way, Eustis told them again of his wishes and sad lack of progress in identifying the man. Noah and Eli suggested that they had wanted to do some sightseeing and it could easily include prospective inquiry spots, like other taverns. They could start taking the drawing of the man with them to show around the next morning if Eustis had no luck at the tavern.

CHAPTER 11

The gambrel-roofed Green Dragon Tavern had a large taproom on one side of its central entrance. Opposite was a dining room. Private meeting rooms were on the second floor, a convenient place for the Sons of Liberty. The men ducked through the door under the hanging sign with its dragon silhouette.

It was still early enough that the tavern was not the dark and smoky place it would become by eight or nine o'clock that evening. By then, tendrils of smoke from the pipe smokers would add to the general aroma of whiskey, beer, wood smoke, and unwashed men.

Sam had gone ahead. When the other six men entered, they almost immediately saw him with his father at a table in conversation with Paul Revere. The senior Adams's dog lay under the table. Revere was waxing enthusiastic about his plans to build a foundry nearby on Lynn and Foster Streets. He hoped to get it started next spring.

Eustis, Jacob, and Nathaniel walked over and introduced Eli and Noah to the Adams group while Eben went to claim a large table. Eustis took advantage of the moment to show the two Adams men and Paul Revere the drawing of the man discovered under the wharf.

"I am sorry, Bill," the senior Adams said. "I wish I could help you, but I see so many men around the town and the waterfront that they begin to look alike. I will not admit 'tis due to age, but take a look, Sam. What do you think?"

The younger Adams looked at it carefully then handed it to Revere.

"Not one that I know," Sam offered, "but as we talked earlier, I'll keep asking around for anyone who is missing. We're about to set off now. Will I see you tomorrow?"

"Absolutely. I'll be calling and perhaps we can take a walk," Eustis replied. "I have other things to talk about with you. I would like to find a chart of the harbor or to find someone who might know about the tides and currents. I will also ask Jacob tonight. And I want to know where to find a good dame school for our new ward, Sally."

"Bring her along if your sisters can spare her. I would like to know this child better, and discover if she is really as clever as you think." suggested Sam.

Before he left, the elder Adams told Eustis that he also wanted to talk more with him about educating the young and would look forward to seeing him the next day.

They watched as the two Adams made their way to the door. Everyone they passed seemed to have something to say, some information or request to pass along. And for his part, the senior Adams remained gracious and cheerful during the long process of leaving, always being protective of his pale son.

Pushing stools and benches around a small table, Eustis spoke with the barmaid about their order. Jacob and Nathaniel went to get white clay pipes from the box by the hearth, filled and lit them with a twig from the fire, then returned to the table to sit.

Noah looked around, relieved to see two other men of color at a corner table. He noticed Eli doing the same thing. This was getting to be a congenial and possible place, he thought. Often he had been asked to sit in another room or to wait outside. In Massachusetts, abolition of slavery was barely two years old, not quite secure yet. It also might just be a practical business plan in Boston where everyone was welcome as long as they could pay.

Once drinks arrived and all were settled, Eustis rose to go show his drawing of the dead man to other patrons. No one seemed to recognize him. Perhaps the Green Dragon was not where this man had relaxed. Probably it was just not near enough to where he lived.

One of the men at a nearby table looked over. "Lemme see it." Eustis handed it over. "Huh. Looks sorta like Bertie Sommers. Didn't know he'd died." He showed it to the other man at the table. "What do you think?"

"Eh, could be." The man squinted as he looked at it.

Eustis took the drawing back. "Where could I find this fellow Bertie?

Does he live around here? And do you know anyone called Monty Thurman?"

"Dunno any Monty. Bert's got a family somewhere. I saw him down by the docks. But that was a while ago."

The doctor thanked the man and indicated he'd keep looking further. He was pleased that someone thought it was a recognizable drawing. Sommers, huh? Add that to the suggestion about Monty Thurman. He would also look into Sommers.

* * *

The next morning, bright skies and fall's frosty air seemed to inspire the entire household to get bustling about their tasks. Maria saw her two menfolk off with Jacob who was going to show them around on the way to his office at the wharf. She began her first washing, one of at least four she anticipated. She wanted to get the men's shirts scrubbed first and spread over backyard bushes to take full advantage of any possible bleaching from the sun. She planned to start on their stockings and small clothes next. That would require lye and boiling and scrubbing. She planned to talk more with the other women later. Perhaps they could answer her questions.

In particular, Maria wanted to find out how to locate Mrs. Phillis Wheatley. Maria had heard of her and listened to her poems when growing up. A Black woman poet! She was an inspiration, and Maria wanted to thank her in person. Because of Mrs. Wheatley, she had wanted to learn to read herself.

Although Sally was fascinated with Maria, she was happy to go along with the doctor to see his friend Sam. Then Eustis felt Maria's eyes on him and decided to invite her to come along to meet Surry as well. She hesitated but decided to go. Under the circumstances, perhaps the laundry could wait an hour or so. And Eustis would then have a backup person to get Sally home if need be. Grabbing his now-folded drawing to take with him, he was ready to go. Sally had watched him put it in his pocket.

"Doctor, sor? Can I see the pitcha'? I wonder what a person looks like."

"Have you never seen a drawing?" asked Eustis. "I'll take it out at Sam's house, and we can look it over there. Right now, I would like to get on our way."

He handed Sally her coat as Prudence approached with an extra shawl. She did not want their charge to get chilled while she was exploring with their brother. He might get forgetful and stay out too long, not having any experience with children. Again Maria would be a help. Neither Prudence nor Anne had yet been able to take Sally around the town as much as they wanted, being needed at home to prepare for their guests.

Any walk in Boston was contrary to a peaceful stroll in the country. Noisy neighborhood activity surrounded them as they worked their way along the road, from the clang of steel on an anvil at the blacksmith shop to the industrious hammering of a carpenter as he built coffins in his yard in front of a big open barn door. A cow, late on her walk to the Common, was being chased by small boys, and independent-minded pigs challenged clucking chickens, all seeking something to eat.

Eustis took unconscious delight in Sally shyly taking his hand as they walked down the cobbled road toward the Adams house. Maria followed quietly. They passed two women with market baskets who smiled pleasantly at the young girl. Suddenly embarrassed, he wondered if passersby would think she was his daughter. But then, that might not be so bad.

Surry welcomed them at the Adamses', as usual, and after introductions, knowing Eustis's proclivities, she immediately offered coffee. Then, inviting Maria to come to her kitchen, Surry took Sally's hand promising some other delight for her. Eustis went in to see Sam in his accustomed place, wrapped up by the window, book in hand. He took the drawing from his pocket as he approached. "Any idea how to discover who this fellow is? What do you really think of this search, Sam? Is it truly useless?"

"And good morning to you too," greeted Sam, chuckling. "You are on task this morning, my friend. To answer, I am not sure your search is useless, just that it will take time because of the roaming nature of our population. Men come and go on the waterfront. The shipping alone; they deliver things and leave, pick up other things and leave. People come in for short jobs, *et cetera*, and you know how it goes. Sometimes they are just here on Saturdays or for Sunday services."

"Are you advising me to give up?" asked Eustis.

"Indeed no. Just know that because most people are moving around, it necessitates time and a large amount of luck thrown into the mix. You remember how names changed during the war too."

"As I thought. But I do not want to give it up. I also have totally different ideas to share with you. And as you asked, I brought along Sally, the child added to our household more or less by default. You will remember her and you have heard of how she was found on the Common. She is charmingly intelligent, and I hope we can educate her, at least to know her letters and to read."

"She does not? I am very surprised. Most commonwealth children are literate. How did she get missed? Or is she one of those who are unteachable?"

"Oh, no," said Eustis. "Not at all. But I would like to remedy it. My sister Anne is starting to teach her the letters of the alphabet. So, do you know a particularly good dame school in the area?"

"I can talk to my father. He is very supportive of young women getting educated, and he may know of a particularly good spot for a bright girl. She is, isn't she?"

"I appreciate that, Sam. But you also should meet her. Let me call Surry."

But that was unnecessary as Surry led Sally into the room at that moment. Had she been listening? Introductions were made, and Sam settled in to chat with Sally. He wanted to know what schooling she had, only to discover, as Eustis already knew, that she had been deprived of any schooling or even basic instruction. Sam could see immediately why his friend wanted to remedy the situation.

The child was delightful. Her hair was a middle brown with a slight curl cut shorter than was stylish for girls. But it was her eyes that charmed. They were a greenish blue color, brighter than hazel. Striking. Bill had never mentioned her eyes, mused Sam. I thought he was observant. Does he not see them?

Sam could see how fascinating a project it would be to try educating this girl who had no family or mother to teach her. It seemed like a grand experiment. It might even prove just as his father believed, that all girls could be educated despite their family backgrounds.

Eustis showed Sally the picture that had been laid out for Sam before he folded it to put back in his pocket. She took it in her hand carefully, looked, and then studied it longer.

"I seen 'im," she said.

"What? Wait! Are you sure?" Eustis was startled. "Look again. And tell me where you could possibly have seen this man, Sally. You have been living with my sisters since I found you and before that under those bushes. I understand you would like to please me, but you do have to be accurate."

"'E was where the boatman put me off when I first came here," she said.

"At the wharf? You mean at the harbor? Can you show me where?"

"I think I can, doctor. But I dinna know how to get there from here."

"By God! I am amazed. You could be a tremendous help, Sally. We can walk down by the waterfront on our way back to Sudbury Street. It is a very large area so it may take us a few days, but we will find it."

Just before leaving, Eustis turned to Sam and asked, "Could you know the whereabouts of a woman named Phillis Wheatley? Maria was asking me about her. She wrote poetry."

"Of course. I am amazed you do not know her. That was the poet Phillis Wheatley Peters. She had been owned, enslaved really, by John Wheatly. You may remember General Washington even noted her abilities. But you are too late, Bill. She died practically penniless not two years ago. Her husband was in debtors prison at the time. They lived up by Copp's Hill."

81

"Ah, Sam. That is wretched news. I wanted to fulfill Maria's wish."

Sam was beginning to look tired, and they prepared to leave. Surry came in with shortbread cookies for Sally to take home, and Sally wondered at the munificence of the Eustis friends. She had never experienced anything like this generosity.

Outdoors, gray skies closed in and the wind rose. The doctor decided they should walk home first and venture out on their search immediately after their midday meal. Perhaps the sky would not carry through with its threats. Although billowing clouds had appeared, and the day had turned ominous, a wind change might possibly clear it up. In New England, the weather was not guaranteed, constantly changing, not unlike their own lives.

He led a disappointed Maria and a happy girl back up the road, Sally eager to show Anne the marvelous little shortcakes that Surry had given to her. Even Ben was given one to gnaw on with his four new teeth.

Lightning split the clouds during their meal in the warm kitchen. No walking along the waterfront with this approaching downpour. The women hurried out to get their laundry in. Afternoon kept them all to indoor tasks, each woman with her basket of threads and yarns, mending or knitting. Jacob and Eben, donning oilskin jackets, insisted on going back to their offices, and Nathaniel went with them. Eustis spent an hour rubbing wax and grease into the outside of his winter boots to condition them and prevent water seepage. As Sally watched and worked on her stitches, he asked her about her progress with letters.

"Are you learning their shapes and sounds? What is the sound of the letter with the big belly?"

"The big dee? Do you know, doctor? Is she gonna have a baby dee? Like Catherine?" Sally asked. He was delighted and had not realized how original the thoughts of children could be.

Standing and peering out the window, he noted that the road was already covered with puddles, rain now mixing with snow.

"How is our supply of wood?" he called out. "I can get more in now."

"Probably should," Anne called back. "I'll help."

They piled on outer clothing and went to the barnyard woodpile. After two trips, both carrying cut and split logs, their supply in the large kitchen box was renewed, and there was a good pile laid out by the keeping room fireplace, ready to add whenever needed. The parlor and its fireplace would soon be closed off for the coming winter. Growing up in the house, they had called that room the "good people's room," mostly reserved for ministerial calls or visits from important people. In the cold of winter, most people stayed close to their warmer kitchens and put visiting aside.

He thought about their postponed walk to the shipyard. "Sally," he said, turning to the girl. "Do you remember when you came ashore in the harbor? Were there shipyards around or just docks and large wharves? You know what I mean by a shipyard?"

"Mebbe. Is that where they build very big boats?" She gestured with her hands, spreading her arms.

"Just so. Were any boats being built around where you landed? I am asking to decide where we should look tomorrow. Many of our shipyards are located up here in the North End."

"Umm, there was something like that but more far away from me. They were on this side," she said, lifting her right arm. "We came in to land after them, by some big boats, but they were tied up, not loose."

"Thank you, Sally." She smiled with pleasure. "That gives me a good idea where we should go. I'll ask Jacob about it too."

CHAPTER 12

The weather had managed to clear even before coffee was made and he got out of bed. Eustis thought of the note received the evening before from General Lincoln. The expedition needed more sleighs. Had Eustis any idea where they could find them? Thinking back to how Henry Knox had moved all those cannons from Fort Ticonderoga, it made sense that moving the expedition's assorted gear to Springfield and beyond involved sleighs. Some wagons and carriages had removable wheels enabling their owners to attach runners for winter travel, but they were used more for people than weaponry or fodder and all the other necessities for winter expeditions.

Where to find sleighs? This was why sensible armies went into winter quarters, he thought, and here they were heading out instead. But we persist. And come December it will be one hundred miles or more of persistence. Out and back.

Climbing out of his warm bed, wrapped in a shawl, barefoot on the freezing cold floor. He looked out his window at the unexpected late October snow, all courtesy of the north wind. The roads were rapidly turning to mud and slush with wheel tracks from wagons and carriages. Boot prints staggered alongside close to the walls.

He hauled up his breeches, getting his usual long shirt tucked in so that it was more or less smooth in front before he came downstairs and hurried out to the privy in the special passage connecting the old carpentry shop to the barn. Sally had not known what to do there, so Anne had taken her in hand on privy etiquette. She did know about chamber pots and assisted in emptying and rinsing them, clearly a chore she'd done before.

Morning chores needed to be completed including milking Hazel and Hattie, and Eustis had to send a note back to General Lincoln before he and Sally ventured out on their quest. By ten that morning, the sun had come out and was actively melting everything it touched.

Eustis planned to walk along the waterfront, beginning with the wharf owned by John Hancock, the town's largest employer, then work farther south toward the pride of the harbor known as Long Wharf, largest of the lot at a staggering half mile in length, an open-armed welcome to the sea trade. Trying to avoid puddles, the two made their way down Fish then Ship Streets to the waterfront.

Hancock's wharf workers barely managed its chaos amid the trading ships and fishing boats tied alongside, loading and unloading cargo. Negotiations were loudly going on between owners' representatives, buyers, or sellers. Sightseers strolled by, getting in the way, and businessmen and traders looked for their merchandise to be delivered ashore.

Sally conducted herself bravely as they passed the mayhem, striding along but keeping very close to Eustis. He realized he had to stop thinking of her as a child. She was growing more assured in the care of his sisters. Definitely on her way to becoming a young woman.

Then she recognized where she was. With great excitement she pointed out where she had come ashore by the muddy sand flat at the side of the large wharf that was south of Hancock's called Wentworth's Wharf.

"Well, there it is and here we are," said Eustis. "Now, tell me all about it."

And so she did. Her adventure began in the summer when she hitched a ride on a boat going down the Charles River. The man in charge of the boat tied it to a piling and disembarked after furling his small, single sail. He had waved farewell and promptly climbed up on the pier. It seemed he had a business meeting with some traders. Sally wrapped herself in her cloak, took up her bundle, and climbed the ladder. She then looked around for a place of shelter. Where did people live in this place? She would be on her own now. But that was what she wanted, was it not? It seemed so different from what she had expected.

She had wandered away from the waterfront and up toward the town. It became confusing, so she decided to go back to the wharf and look for

85

the man who had brought her. She began to think it might be a good idea to see where he was going next and if she might go too.

It grew dark, and several of the sailors on the dock began to talk with her. One even gave her some bread. Happy about the bread, she was not sure what he wanted or why he stayed with her. When he tried to put his arm around her, she cowered, turning away in fright. He gave up, assuming she was too stupid to realize it was a way to make some money. She next spotted a place near the shore where cargo and shipments were assembled. She could get between several large, piled boxes and nestle down. When the sun disappeared, used to ignoring her hunger pangs, she felt safe there.

Noise woke and surrounded her when the dock came to life in the dark just before dawn. Crawling stiffly out of her shelter, she walked again toward the town, looking for food. The big buildings were made of brick and stone with fancy gentlemen walking along the street. Carriages, unlike anything she had seen before, rolled past with ladies in them. And no one noticed her. Some other children with books went past, and one girl saw her and asked if she wanted food. When she said yes, they laughed and told her to go to the nearby public house, pointing farther up the road. And indeed, she could see a sign, so she went there, then around back to the kitchen door. Lots of smelly barrels were piled around, mostly with rotting fish, food, and bread scraps. She thought she might sort through them when a woman came to the door and said, "You there, girl! You want to work?"

And she did. She also looked for the man who had given her the ride in the boat but without luck. The kind woman fed her and gave her a blanket of sorts, mayhap from a horse. It surely smelled that way. And she slept in the tavern's stable loft for the next few weeks, washing dishes and mugs in the kitchen during the day.

Eustis interrupted her explanation to ask, "But how did you get to the Common and into that shrubbery?"

"One day I walked over to the big green place. I really like cows. They are my favorite friends. Those made me think of 'em at my old house. I used to live with 'em a lot. I decided I'd live near the cows. But every night they went away, and I was still hungry. So sometimes I went back and worked at the tavern to get food."

Eustis noted that all the time she was talking she was looking around. They had circled around to another wharf area, closer to Jacob's office. He decided that before they went back, they would check with his brother. There were six or eight small sheds or houses lined up on the same wharf, each doing business, some with specific shipping companies and as many with individual agents.

Jacob was located in a tiny house a short distance along the wharf. This was his office, but he did not have much time to chat with them. A large coastal trading ship, sails furled, was being maneuvered alongside the wharf, and dockworkers and the ship's crew were working to secure it safely to the large pilings.

Eustis skirted around the activity and opened the door into Jacob's small office, waving Sally in with him. Despite it clearly being an interruption of business, he was counting on Jacob's sympathy and took the drawing from his pocket to show to his brother who had already seen it several times. He then passed it to the others at the counter. "Do you know this man? Got a name for him?" Sally hung back by the door.

"Could be Bert," said one peering at it. He turned to the man next to him seeking confirmation.

"Mebbe," said the fellow.

"What's Bert's last name? And where does he live?" asked Eustis, remembering he had been identified as Bert by that other fellow at the Green Dragon. "Do you know where I can find him? Please tell me, or if you need to check with someone, tell my brother."

"Dunno. Haven't seen him fer awhile. He sometimes went to sea on a job. Mayhap down the coast. Could be there."

"Well, as I said, can you let me or my brother here know if you see him? Also anyone named Monty Thurman. It's important."

Returning to their house and warming reddened hands by the kitchen hearth, Eustis reported to his sisters that he and Sally had a possible new lead on a man named Bert. His last name was not certain. Someone had guessed Sommers. And this Bert was said to be around the docks not far from Jacob's office.

"But, Bill," exclaimed Cath. "There is a Sommers family just down the road! I wonder if it is the same."

Later that afternoon before their supper, he asked Jacob about Bert and found that the only Bert that Jacob knew might also be the husband of Norah Lindholm. Albert Lindholm who worked for him had sometimes been called Al or Bert on the docks.

Interesting, thought Eustis. I certainly hope there is another Bert around. I surely don't want to be the one to tell Norah that her husband is dead. I'll do more scouting tomorrow, and if I find Norah, I can gently lead up to it, ask her if he is here, and show her the picture. Even better would be to find her husband. He is supposed to be working on the docks too. And I have just another month or so before we leave for Springfield. Meanwhile, I have got to get myself ready. He began to feel crowded by everything he had to get done, including securing his medical kit and supplies.

He believed that despite how much he agreed with the farmers that their property should not be foreclosed because they did not have cash to pay their taxes, there was still no call to get guns involved. Guns were not the answer here. There ought to be a way to resolve it, to reach a solution. But it proved that the Articles of Confederation allying the states, now little more than five years old, was not working as well as hoped or planned. Congress, without money, could not quell an uprising, had no army to call out, and could not prevent the farmers from taking over the courthouses. And defense of the country was supposed to be their job. It was a mess. They were just lucky that the French were distracted by their own problems or they could walk in and take over. They had their own revolution brewing in France.

CHAPTER 13

Norah and her husband Albert, with their daughter Annie, were renting a room in Mrs. Flanagan's boarding house on Salem Street near the burial ground on Copp's Hill. They had two windows, a big bed with a trundle that could be pulled out for Annie, a little table, a bench, one chair, and pegs on the wall for clothing. There was a stove for heat with a niche above it and shelves. Mrs. Flanagan cooked a midday meal for all her boarders.

Before Albert had angrily slammed out that morning, Norah had done her best to get everything the way he wanted, as neat and clean as possible. She had gotten his coffee ready and set it at the right place on the table and had laid out a clean shirt. But something had set him off. He told her how he was making such an effort to get ahead but insinuated she was not helping to do her part as a wife and mother, much less as a housekeeper. Why could she not get it right? She had let their child cry and wake him during the night. She should realize how he needed his sleep and better food. Perhaps she needed more discipline, he threatened. Maybe another day locked in. How would she like that? And she had to control the child or he would do something about that too.

Norah, tears in her eyes, sat on the edge of the bed and hugged little Annie. The child seemed to know her mother was in trouble and patted her arm. She was relieved her father had not hit her mother. That had happened once before at the end of one of these tirades. But what could a small, frightened child do? And Norah, sympathetic, understood that this was not the way Albert wanted to live. He was going through a hard time, she knew, and she was sure he really wanted a good life for them all. He just could not get steady enough to do it. Ever since the war, his anxieties and desires for order had overwhelmed him.

Perhaps she could take a walk with Annie by the Eustis home over on Sudbury Street. Norah envied the feeling it had of being a happy place even with all those people. If she was lucky they might see her and invite her in. But by the time she and her daughter arrived to slowly walk by, the women inside had settled into their chores and the men had gone to work. Should she approach the door? Maybe not. It might be seen that they were desperate for company. No one looked out the windows.

* * *

Midday dinner brought the men back to the house, one after the other, removing quantities of outside clothing, scarves, and coats.

Elijah and Noah had been walking around considering the possibility of setting up their apothecary in Boston. Was it a better location than in the Hudson Highlands? It was certainly less rural. Perhaps as a growing town, Boston could provide more business as Dr. Eustis had suggested.

Their meal was a noisy affair with opinions and news to be dissected and analyzed. Jacob suggested that Bill come back with him to lurk in his office and hope that this unknown Bert Sommers – or Albert Lindholm – or some other Bert came by and they could talk to him. And was there another possibility? What did Bill think of just sending a note to Albert?

The doctor, however, had received a note from a patient requesting a visit, so he could not commit to going to the wharf until later. His patients came first and brought in his contribution to the household funds.

Catherine stood by the table arching her back and rubbing it as her sisters got the basin to begin washing the dishes. Her back bothered her. She had made arrangements for a midwife, Betty Flint, to attend her. Mrs. Flint lived nearby and could be called at any time by just sending someone – a child or husband – to her. Cath did not consider asking her brother. Childbirth was not men's business and was usually handled by midwives unless there were some desperate circumstances. The midwives knew what they were doing and had fewer infections and more success compared to the doctors. Her sisters were also there, so she was not concerned that her brother would be leaving within a few weeks. And Maria had said she had experience in midwifery too.

As soon as he had seen to the house call, reassuring his patient that his rash was not smallpox, Eustis wanted some time to talk more with Sam. He found him ensconced in his customary place by the window overlooking the street. Sam greeted his friend, commenting that he could understand Bill's desire to escape his house when the women were in a flurry of planning for his departure.

"Aye, they do look after me," Eustis agreed. "But I wanted to talk over what your thoughts were on the harbor and on Sally. I think we found where she was put ashore." He sat in a chair. "What do you think of her?"

"Well, my friend," said Sam. "I have to wonder why you described her as you did but seemed to ignore her eyes. They are striking. Do they remind you of anyone?"

He could see Bill trying to think about what he remembered of Sally's eyes. "Shouldn't be that hard, Bill. Her eyes are beautiful and a brighter version of your own. Are you sure you know nothing about her family?"

"No. I hadn't thought about it. But now that you mention it, I wonder what we were doing about ten or twelve years ago."

Sam watched him. Bill looked like an abacus, moving the beads as he calculated.

"You were off on that surgical internship," Eustis said, "and I was still here working with Dr. Warren. Hmm, I miss him every day. But I do collect that the young woman was only about fourteen years old, too young to legally marry, and there was something about her having a connection with the Warren family. Was her father one of Warren's patients?"

"Not sure," said Sam. "I was away as you said. But I have since wondered if there was some difficult circumstance, something they would not talk about, maybe rape, in which she became pregnant."

"Well, I guess it did not interest me much at the time. I was so involved in everything happening around me, trying to be of help and learning about Dr. Warren's efforts to organize a state government. He was extraordinarily busy, making speeches and writing for the cause. But he was still aware of his patients. I completed my internship at just about that time, and he asked me to remain to keep his office open while he focused on the beginnings of the rebellion with your father. You remember. All through 1775 until that infamous day, that desperate day, April nineteenth, we'd cared for many patients. We were both away from Boston when the gates at the neck were locked down that evening. I was out in Lexington with my family."

"Ah, yes," said Sam. "I remember how sick your mother was by then. A delightful woman and always devoted to you, making sure you were as well educated as possible." Then he laughed. "Do you remember how mad you were when you had to stay in to practice your writing?"

"Yes," Eustis chuckled. "We had good times as children here, and my mother certainly wanted the best for us. When she died it was really dreadful." He looked down at his hands. "I still miss her. Neither of us, Dr. Warren nor I, could get back into the town in those days. The British had closed the gates. I am glad that I went to Lexington with Mr. Gill. I might have gotten stuck in town and not gotten to see her. I think I recall that you were off in Newbury or near there."

"I remember," said Sam. "But before that, what about that young pregnant girl that Dr. Warren sent out to Dedham for boarding with that other doctor?"

"By Jove! Sam! You are brilliant. That was Dr. Ames, Nathaniel Ames. He combined doctoring with running an inn in Dedham. He was a good friend to Dr. Warren. Did you know that David Townsend and I took up paying the bill for care of that child after Dr. Warren died? Warren had taken it on at the beginning, and we more or less inherited it. I do not remember why now. How interesting that you would think of that," he mused.

"What happened to the young mother?" asked Sam, watching him.

"I don't remember. Her name was Sally Edwards. People disappeared during the war. Just vanished into the surrounding countryside. I think it is likely that her family took her home to start her life over. Or they could have moved away and disappeared. But Dr. Ames regularly sent a bill for the care of the child. Right up until six years ago – 1780 – well before the war ended. Dr. Ames had agreed to keep her until she could be put out for indenture when she was four years old. He'd gotten some woman to care for her when she was very little. Wet nurse, I suppose. I do not know if that was an agreement with the mother or where she ended up. Strange how her family disappeared. Or that child for that matter. Maybe they were loyalists."

Sam looked at him carefully and waited. Eustis seemed to be contemplating speaking but did not.

"I have to wonder," said Sam after a pause. "What if this child is the same one that you were paying for? What if this Sally is that Sally? And how old would she be now?"

"By God, Sam. It never occurred to me." Eustis looked stunned. "I'll have to think about this for a while." He stood up and then sat down again.

"All I have to do now is speculate," said Sam. "It is just a thought I had after talking to her the other day. But what else is the news in your busy life?"

"Yes. Well, hmm. I am not sure. The sisters are working and teaching Sally her alphabet and how to sew properly. Do you really think she could be that same child?"

"As I said, I can do nothing but pass the time left to me in wondering about things in this world. Playing the game of 'what if.' You remember how it helped us down in the Hudson Highlands. And we still need to resolve that poor drowned man you found before you do any marching off with the Cincinnati."

This new possibility about Sally had stunned Eustis. He could not think of anything else, much less that business with the drowned man. He desperately wanted to leave and go walking so he could think it through. And Sam could see that.

"I understand, Bill." Sam chuckled. "Come by to see me tomorrow first thing and we can talk everything over again. Sleep on it. And you also understand, this Sally idea could be nothing. I don't even know where you would begin to prove it. Unless she remembers something relevant."

Eustis, remembering that Sally had said something about a name that sounded like denim, felt confused. He hated being baffled like this. Surgery or even another murder seemed so much easier.

"Thanks, Sam. I believe I will take you up on your suggestion. I do need to think it through, and perhaps you have a valid idea. I have no idea how she could be the same child. It's impossible! I do not even know how to check it."

"You will figure it out, and I'll be here waiting tomorrow. Pay attention walking home," he cautioned, smiling with amusement. "Watch out for walls, for horses, carriages, and dogs too!"

"Oh, um, yes. I will see you tomorrow, Sam." Eustis fumbled his way to the door and went out, more or less heading in the direction of his home. He walked slowly, trying to clear his mind.

CHAPTER 14

Jacob's suggestion that Eustis spend the morrow in his office and watch the activity on the wharf seemed a good one. But Sally. What could he say to her? Did he need to say anything? Might be best to discuss the whole situation with his sisters, especially Prudence and Anne first, before he went away. They would be responsible for Sally if he was not there. Cath would be planning, awaiting her new arrival, setting up the bedroom, and getting extra clothing made, linen sheets and towels ready. And that brought to mind what still needed doing. Had they brought the baby cradle out of the attic yet?

He was welcomed by Aggie, squirming in circles, her tail frantic, along with chickens wandering around the barnyard seeking choice bugs. How amazing if it were true about Sally. He had vaguely wondered about the child's future years ago after he had stopped paying for her care but quickly became distracted by his own patients and everything happening during and after the war.

He entered the house just as it began to rain, hoping to join Nathaniel in a cup of coffee before dinner, and eager to talk with Sally about her memories. But, thought Eustis, what is it about plans? Man proposes and God disposes. Cath pointed toward the keeping room.

Oddly, Elijah, Noah, and Maria were waiting for him, sitting together. Eli appeared to have been elected spokesman.

While they had enjoyed their visit to Boston, he said, they still had some concerns. They thought they liked rural areas more than the city life which was too close and noisy. Other small villages might benefit from their occupation and be where they could build a home and set up shop.

Depending on the weather, with a nod toward the rain pelting the window, they would be riding out again within a day or so to explore to the north of Boston and were considering going as far as South Reading or Lynnfield. They had heard those towns were prosperous with small businesses. It might suit them, and, if not, they would come back, perhaps head south again. None of it was sure. But the temperature was relatively mild at the moment so it seemed smart to take advantage of it.

The sisters were disturbed, protesting, asking if they could have done more. Eustis himself wondered if he had not paid enough attention. Was it the murder? He had believed they would settle in Boston, open a pharmacy.

Elijah hastened to reassure the family.

"No, no, doctor. Nothing you did. We are thankful that we know you are here and that we can come back. Indeed, it is a reassuring anchor for us. But we also need to know what our options are, and that requires going to see for ourselves. We have to explore the greater area while we can."

Noah added, "And we need to make sure any place we want to settle in would be safe for us, that they would accept us."

Eustis knew exactly what Noah meant. "You'll need to have Elijah with you. Have you the proper paperwork to ensure Maria will not be taken into captivity again?" he asked. "You know that slavery's only been illegal here a short time based on a single court case. The outer towns may not be as aware. I am going to see Sam tomorrow and can ask him. Or his father."

"Yes, good idea," said Catherine, overhearing. The others agreed, and Eustis put it on his mental list for the morrow. He was sure the senior Adams would have a suggestion or could come up with something quickly. He always seemed to.

"But, please, know that we do not want you to leave," implored Catherine. "You must write to us through the mail if nothing else."

As Eustis thought about it later, it began to seem like a good idea to have an outpost in a rural town. It might be just the thing if ever Boston became too crowded, although he doubted that would happen.

* * *

A day later, before midday dinner, a letter arrived as Eustis, going over his notes, was finishing a mug of coffee after returning from a patient visit. He had written to Dr. Ames in Dedham to ask about the disposition of the baby girl for whom he had once sent support money. He quickly unfolded Ames' letter and read.

My dear Dr. Eustis,

How pleasant to have a missive from you. I wondered if anyone was interested in that child's fate. She had been more or less deserted. If her mother is still alive, she has shown no interest. Indeed when the child reached four years old, the legal age for indenture, I submitted her name as an abandoned child to the town committee. They placed her with a family. I am not sure where she is located now, however, as the family left some years ago to create their own homestead in another town. The child went with them. I do not know what became of her mother. She left town shortly after her daughter's birth, leaving the baby in my care. As I collect, the girl's father came for her. This had happened before with young women who did not have the benefit of a husband. I am hopeful this, although inadequate, answers your concerns.

So, Eustis thought, it was indeed possible that their Sally was the same person. If he just had names! He planned to talk with her as soon as he could.

That evening, after their supper, Sally was happy to play their little game of memory. She sat in the big chair, her safe place, close to Eustis. He began by asking her to close her eyes, clear her thoughts, and take several deep breaths. Then he approached the subject of what she might see or remember. Did she remember names or traveling? Perhaps going in a wagon? And what did she see?

"Very likely. How long were you in the wagon, Sally?'

"I think mebbe for days. I only 'member being put down when I had to get to the grass to make water. I think I slept in it too. The big people went into a building, but I stayed in the wagon."

"You have done a wonderful job of remembering, Sally," Eustis said.

The girl beamed. She had so rarely experienced praise that it almost overwhelmed her.

"Is there anything else you can think of?"

She sat back, folded her arms, and almost cradled herself while she rocked slightly back and forth, thinking.

"I was real little. I know that, an' hungry. But I always was so that wasna dif'rent. I think we got to a place where we would live after that."

"And you grew up in this new house, did you?"

"I think so, but we might have moved again. I'm not sure. There was hay an' cows where I c'd sleep, an' a nice dog was there too."

* * *

Eustis looked for Prudence or Anne. Sally was trailing Anne who was beginning to look exasperated. She encouraged Sally to go talk with the doctor. "And thank you, Sally. You have been a good helper, but I have some things I must get done by myself."

Eustis could see that she was eager to have a few minutes alone. Welcome to a taste of future motherhood, he thought.

Picking up on this cue, he asked Sally if she would come walking with him as he was going to see Sam. The only person as interesting as Anne, although second best really, was the doctor, so Sally agreed. And she liked Surry and her cakes.

Once wrapped up and after calling Aggie, they walked toward the Adams house. Eustis studied her appearance as Sam had suggested. He had been primarily fascinated by her undeveloped intellect and was startled when he really noticed her eyes. Sam was right. They were extraordinary. The iris was darker on its rim and very light in the middle. Sally, on the other hand, chattered about her new learning experiences. Books had stories! Everything was new and fascinating to her.

"Did you try remembering more?" Eustis asked. They paused, watching out for remaining puddles and moving aside for a horse drawing a fine carriage with closed curtains.

"I have," she said after watching the horse and giving a little skip. "But I have na got anything yet. I think I am mostly happy just bein' here." Then noticing he seemed disappointed, she hastened to add she would keep trying to remember.

On arriving at Sam's house, Surry opened the door as usual. She directed him upstairs to Sam's bedroom and asked Sally if she would help her in the kitchen. They needed to serve the coffee to Mr. Adams and his visitor, and she could help set up the tray.

Sam was sitting by his bedroom window looking impatient. He turned eagerly when Eustis came in.

"I give you joy on this fine morning, Mr. Adams," said Eustis. "How are you finding this busy day?"

"Not too bad," said Sam. "But I am truly glad you came by. I'm bored, and there is nothing new outside the window. Do you have any books you could share with me?"

"You know, you stunned me when you asked about Sally. I had not thought of her appearance at all. I have not worked out yet whether to tell her she may have a family name. She is so anxious to find her mother. I'd hate to disappoint her if it ended up not being true. We can talk all we want and suppose anything from little bits we may know, but how do we get proof?"

"I know, Bill. But just do it. Let's be realistic. Her mother is not going to come claim her. Stop thinking like an academician and wanting to do research. We do not have to prove anything. It's all conjecture, and no proof will be forthcoming."

"But, Sam, I would prefer to have some proof. I know that I cannot be her father. I, at least, know enough about how that happens to know she is not my child. Even if she has those hazel eyes."

Immediately following a knock on the door, Surry and Sally entered with a tray of coffee. The men immediately dropped the subject, accepted the coffee, and, after Surry and Sally left, went on to discuss the educational system in the town. They agreed that it did need updating. Just educating the boys was not enough, and the dame schools could only do so much for girls. Both boys and girls attended the dame schools in the beginning and learned to read and write, but the boys went on in their educational system, and the girls went home to learn housekeeping. If there was not a family member to teach their daughters beyond a certain point, the child just did not get the opportunity. If some girls wanted to know more, how to read books for instance, they should not be prevented from it. Both men thought it might be interesting as an experiment, if nothing else, to see if girls were likely to want more.

The conversation then turned to the floating body. Eustis's notion of looking at maps or charts of the harbor appealed to Sam. He suggested getting someone, a sailor perhaps, to tell them about the currents. They may have grown up around the harbor, but that did not mean they knew how to interpret what was going on out in the water around the islands.

Noting the time, calling for Sally, Eustis hurried back up the road, arriving at home just in time to welcome his father and stepmother, Elizabeth, for dinner. They had arrived early and first sat in the parlor talking of their past week's events. Then, on Catherine's invitation, they went to two separate tables for their dinner. Cath had opened up the dining table and set it for the five men. She, her mother-in-law, her sisters, and Sally would eat at the kitchen table. It worked well because the women could talk about what they wanted – from the latest babies to projects, politics, or neighborhood gossip. All they needed to do was keep supplying the men with food and good cider or ale.

The men's conversation included an update on Eustis's attempts to identify the recently drowned man. Jacob offered news that he had located a chart of the harbor's currents. It had only taken a brief visit to the harbormaster's shack that morning, but he thought the chart would serve his brother's purpose. Perhaps they could go over it later that afternoon. One tiny bit of progress.

Their father was interested in his son's efforts to find the dockworker named Bert and suggested he, too, would keep an open ear for the name as well. He also wondered if the drowning had anything to do with the growing animosity he observed at the harbor, not just among the dockworkers but also among the shipowners.

His children were amused by his attention to every detail. As a skilled carpenter and proud builder, he could never resist checking over the house that he still owned for any needed repairs, looking at the windows, running his finger down the molding edges on the doorways when he passed through. He had done years of maintenance and remodeling and was proud of his accomplishments. He was not going to see it neglected.

* * *

After breakfast, when most of the family had begun performing various morning chores, Eustis asked Cath to pause and sit with him for a moment.

" 'Tis Sally, Cath. Sam and I think we may know who her mother was. There was a baby delivered by Dr. Ames in Dedham to a young woman in her early teens named Sally Edwards who had come to Dr. Warren for help when I was an apprentice. Dr. Warren sent her to Dr. Ames for room and board until she gave birth. Then I suspect she left the child with him to put out for indenture as soon as the babe was old enough. Dr. Warren had taken on the obligation of support. After he died, David Townsend and I helped pay for the child's board with Dr. Ames. I have written to him, and it all matches up with what bits Sally remembers. So, Cath, what do I do? Do I tell her of a desperate young woman who might have been her mother? Will that make her even more determined to find her?"

"Ah, so that's it," Catherine said. "I do not know how she would feel. Arrange it so that either Prudence, Anne, or I am there too if you do tell this to Sally. Anne would be good. But it is curious. Maybe the girl or the family abandoned that baby."

"Could be abandonment. I do not remember hearing anything," Eustis reasoned. "And Anne may ease the shock for Sally right now. She can reassure Sally that it will not change her stay with us." He looked at her, eyebrows raised with concern. "It would not, would it, Cath?"

"Not at all," Catherine replied. "But let me go talk to Anne now." She stood and squeezed his shoulder before going off to find her sister.

After dinner, the family's conspicuous gathering for a discussion made Sally anxious. What was happening? She was not sure if she had done anything wrong. The three sisters assured her that all was well. Once everyone was seated in the keeping room, Eustis, standing by the hearth, began his revelations. He went back over his days as an

101

apprentice with Dr. Joseph Warren, explaining that in the first year he was with him, a very young woman, likely about fourteen or fifteen years old, had come to the doctor's surgery for help. She may have lived in the area, but he did not know where. He thought her family knew Dr. Warren. As the story went on, he got to the point where Dr. Ames came from the town of Dedham in his carriage to pick up this girl and take her back to his inn where she would live until she delivered her baby. He tried not to stare at Sally, but he could tell she was fascinated by the story.

Then his revelation. He said that he had received a letter from Dr. Ames. Both Sam and he now believed that the young woman who came to Dr. Warren's surgery all those years ago was Sally's mother. Her name was Sally Edwards, so her baby was given the same name.

There was a pause as Sally stared at him. Her mouth opened in shock. The family sat in silence waiting for her reaction. Anne, who sat next to her, put an arm around her shoulders.

"My mother?" Sally said faintly. "Where is she?"

"I am sorry, but we don't know that at this time," said Eustis. "But we now have more information than ever before. She may be around Boston, but she probably is not. I think it is most likely that she has indeed moved away. The war made everything very mixed up and confusing. She left you safely with Dr. Ames to care for until he found a family to take you when you were four years old."

Nathaniel spoke up. "What now? Is there anything else we can do?"

"It will take more searching, Nat, and frankly I am not sure this woman wants to be found," Eustis speculated. "She has probably developed an entirely new life. I think we should just go on now as before but with the knowledge that Sally has her mother's name with the surname of Edwards."

Nat rose to the occasion and swept off an imaginary hat. "Good day, Miss Edwards. May I welcome you to our home?"

Sally smiled, and Eustis realized he was over the worst of it. He was sure there would be more to discuss later. But for now, Sally seemed to be accepting it. She would later have to deal with the thought of having been given away by her mother, and perhaps why. Now, being the center of attention was both worrisome and wonderful. The sisters came to her and gave her reassuring hugs.

"Just know you have a home with us, Sally. And now we need to get back to our chores," said Cath, setting an example by picking up her sewing basket. Even Aggie, tail wagging, busied herself – licking Sally.

CHAPTER 15

Nathaniel suggested to Eustis that they check out a tavern up by Copp's Hill. Armed with lanterns, they arrived at a public house called the White Horse just as the wintery light was failing. The tavern was wedged in among other businesses in a section of town that supported a thriving waterfront. On one side of the tavern was a millinery shop with living quarters above it and a neighboring general store. There were several buildings that looked like boarding houses down a short alley behind the tavern. The alley ended at a small barn and sheds.

They entered a friendly space filled with the usual small tables, benches, and stools, the noise of happy men talking, arguing, and playing cards. Aromas of whiskey, beer, and something recently out of an oven – bread or maybe pie? – added to the general impression of good will. The publican's long bar ran across the back of the room. Several tables were already occupied, one with a card game just beginning.

They selected a table near the others, and a thin, dark-haired young man wearing an apron approached to take their orders. "Ale, cider, or whiskey, gentlemen? We also have our own homebrew beer. And a supper selection if you are hungry."

Eustis glanced around. Their neighbors did not appear to be there for the food, but then it was not quite late enough for supper. Most cradled tankards of what he presumed was beer or cider.

"Do you live around here?" he asked the waiter.

"Yes, sir. I have a room above the market next door. Several of us do."

"We'll want two of your beers. And you may know of a fellow named Bert? I think his family lives near here."

"No. Sorry, sir. Many people live around here in the boarding houses, but I do not know anyone named Bert. I'll be right back with your order."

"Eh, don't be discouraged, Bill," said Nat, looking at Eustis. "We've only begun to look. And I am interested in all these possible places to live. With this many options, people probably move in and out all the time. No one is going to know everyone."

Eustis sighed. "You're right. I am trying not to be discouraged. It also occurred to me to tell Elijah about this neighborhood. He might like it here."

At that point, a short and very round woman came bouncing into the room carrying a large wicker basket. She wore her apron, mob cap, and cape but also seemed so wrapped in shawls that if she tipped over she might roll.

"Good day, gentlemen. Will you be needing any ribbons or pins?" she asked the patrons. She approached to talk with the Eustis party but was distracted by several men she seemed to know well at a neighboring table. Or at least when they called to her, she hurried over, laughing as she approached.

"What did they call her?" asked Nathaniel.

"Joyful, I think it was," said Eustis. "She does seem to be a congenial individual."

They could hear her chortles as she continued laughing with the men.

"You know, I would be smart if I took some pretty ribbon back to our sisters in appreciation for all they are doing to get the winter food supplies in," remarked Eustis.

Nathaniel winked and nodded. "Good idea. And a reward ribbon for me too?" He laughed. "I got the whole barn mucked out. And really, in truth, Bill, our sisters should not be doing heavy work out there."

As she was leaving the nearby table, Eustis called to the cheerful, rotund woman to come speak to them. "Mistress! May we see your sundries?"

She introduced herself as she approached their table. "Good day, gentlemen. I'm Mrs. Noyes. I'll be happy to show my wares. Are you interested in ribbons? A young lady to please, perhaps?" She twinkled at them.

Eustis bought several ribbons from her, believing his sisters would be pleased. In doing so, he was subjected to all sorts of questions including his identity as Dr. Eustis. So he felt it was only fair that when the transaction ended, he could also get some information.

"And you, Mrs. Noyes. Where is it that you live? Nearby?"

"Yes, doctor. Just behind the White Horse. That big house there."

"Boarding house? Many rooms?"

"Yes, sir. Do you need a place to stay? I would be happy to recommend you. We could use a doctor living around here with what goes on at all hours of the night. And there are families living here too."

Eustis thought he should try to get a little clarity but not have her assume he wanted to rent a room. "No, no, Mrs. Noyes. I am trying to find where Albert Lindholm lives."

"Ah yes, a troubled soul our Albert. It is Albert Lindholm, you said?"

"And do you know him? May I ask why you called him troubled?" asked Eustis.

"I am sorry, doctor. I thought you knew him. I apologize for thinking ahead."

"Not a problem, Mrs. Noyes. I was not being clear. I am looking into his family's welfare and in particular Norah, his wife."

"Oh my." She laughed. "Here I go jumping in again, but I'm glad you are doing that. It has not been a good time for them. Just kept going downhill after they arrived. I know he does not mean to be so angry, but he is. He was in the war I hear. That sometimes changes a man."

Nathaniel had kept quiet, just listening, not wanting to interrupt the flow. More customers had entered the tavern, and he could see that Mrs. Noyes wanted to get back to her sales. At the pause he could not resist asking, "Were they calling you 'joyful?' "

"Oh yes." She chuckled, her cheeks red, and then throwing her head back, she broke into a loud, cheerful laugh. "They call me joyful for my name, and rightly so. I did not fully introduce myself. I am Joyful Noyes. And my two sisters are named Hopeful and Glorious. We call them Hope and Glory." She laughed again.

Both Nathaniel and Eustis could understand why this warm soul was such an asset in the neighborhood. She was most likely a confidant to many neighbors. They would like to get more time with her.

"I will be right with you," she called to several tables who were calling and waving at her.

"You have business to attend to," said Eustis. "Perhaps we can talk more later."

Both men rose as she nodded and got up from her bench to begin moving among the tables.

"What a pleasant woman. I would be pleased if she lived near us, Bill," said Nathaniel as he sat down again. "But don't tell our father. He'll have me setting up a store here. And this is good beer. I wonder how they brew it."

They relaxed at their table and ordered more beer, thinking they would return to the White Horse often. Both men knew they had only begun to uncover the information that might be found there in the Lindholm's neighborhood.

Joyful Noyes returned to their table only to bid them farewell and say she had to get on to her next sales stop of the evening. She hoped, as they did, that she would see them again soon.

Finding their sources limited after Mrs. Noyes left, they decided to head home for supper. Just outside the main entrance, Eustis stopped to watch five men walk by, not coming into the tavern but going down to the main road that ran past Copp's Hill and its cemetery. The men seemed quite congenial as a group. But where did they come from? Maybe one of the boarding houses. They had not been in the tavern. To their right were the boarding houses and at the end of the alley what looked like a small barn and shed. Had they come from there or a house? It was tempting to go look. He looked at Nathaniel, raised his eyebrows, and nodded to the right.

Instead of turning left, they approached the barn. There was no noise. The front door was closed with a large hasp and lock. Odd. Who locks up their barn? Maybe it was used by a company for storage and the men were boarding house residents. Eustis rubbed his nose, thinking. Why was the barn locked? Too much crime in this neighborhood?

"C'mon home, Bill," said Nathaniel. "Don't waste your time. 'Tis nothing. Let us walk along. I am getting ready to sit by my own fire."

"What if Norah Lindholm lives along here?"

Nathaniel resisted. He wanted to go back home and knew his brother could easily get distracted by something new. "It's coming on dark soon. Even though we have these lanterns, let's plan on exploring this barn tomorrow. Come back in daylight and look around some more. We are likely going to run into some North and South parades. 'Tis the season, and they can get rowdy."

Indeed, early November usually brought brawling parades derived from the far earlier British celebrations of Guy Fawkes Day on November fifth. Those celebrations commemorated saving Parliament from fiery destruction. Now in New England it was called Pope's Day with neighborhood parades, burning effigies, bonfires, and rioting. Over the years, it had devolved into violence between two neighborhood gangs, one from south of town (the South End) and one from the north (the North End). Participants were all male – maritime and other working folk. It usually ended with bonfires on the Common. Although it had quieted down in recent years, Eustis was not eager to get into the middle of anything. They headed for home.

* * *

Eustis was sitting in the keeping room, his stockinged feet on an embroidered footstool, when there was knocking at their door. A small, terrified youngster, all pink knees and elbows with huge eyes, stood there. His family, just a few houses from theirs, needed a doctor. Now. His big brother had an accident while chopping kindling for the fire. It was a familiar story of missing the log and slicing deeply into his leg just below the knee.

"Pray, sir, could the doctor hurry? 'Tis Tommy. Please? There is a lot of blood. Can you come now? Please?"

Prudence mobilized to get his coat. Anne rushed for his hat and scarf while he pulled on his boots, glad at least for his brief rest. He had recognized the small boy as one of the neighboring children. He grabbed up his medical bag and headed out into the night with the boy. Any supper would come later.

The child's home was set back behind another, its door facing a short dirt lane. A woman opened the door, introducing herself as the boy's mother, Mrs. Tabitha Sommers. She immediately turned and beckoned Eustis into the kitchen where he found a very pale boy with tear-stained cheeks whimpering and clutching a large wad of linen against his leg. It looked like a piece of sheeting, possibly from a bed.

Eustis removed his hat and coat, put down his bag, and looked around for what he could use. He needed to quickly stabilize his wounded patient. The kitchen table seemed best. The woman quickly cleared the beginnings of their supper and wiped the table. He had not realized her name was Sommers and remembered seeing her many times in the roadway.

He hastened to both reassure her and the small boy who'd followed him in. "This will work out very well, Mrs. Sommers," he said. "Pray, do you have other towels or linens? And is your husband possibly at home?"

"No, doctor. 'Tis only me with the children. He's away for another month at least. Off down the coast to sell fish and bring back live oak for the shipyards. Mebbe get rice too. In this weather," she added, sighing. "I know they hope to bring back a lot of lumber. Can make winter money that way. Otherwise, they go after fish."

Eustis spoke to the boy with the injured leg, introduced as Tommy. With help from Mrs. Sommers, he lifted him to the table.

"Do not be worried, Tommy. I have been a doctor for a long time. Before I even look at your leg I am going to give you something to make you feel better." He took out his small vial of laudanum, giving the boy a half teaspoon, reminding himself how difficult it had been to get any laudanum during the war.

When the boy lay back on the table, a cushion of rolled up fabric could be put under his knee and the wrappings eased off. The axe had luckily cut his leg just below the kneecap and not into it. Although it had cut deeply to the side, the kneecap looked fine. When the coverings were removed and the compression lifted, the wound started bleeding again. Eustis worked quickly to apply a tourniquet before deciding whether to stitch the leg or cut more. He just might be able to save this boy's leg. It depended on the bone. As he took out his strap and buckle, he wished he had his cauterizing iron.

Just then, Nathaniel knocked at the door and let himself in, having heard the news and followed his brother.

"Am I glad to see you." greeted Eustis. "Pray, could you hurry back to our house and get my cauterizing tool?"

"Will do, brother." And Nat was back out the door, already running.

CHAPTER 16

When Nat returned, Tommy Sommers was asleep on the sheet-covered table. The laudanum combined with exhaustion and fear had done its work. His worried mother leaned over, clutching his hand and murmuring to him. She certainly did well by both the boys, Eustis thought. Their shirts, probably made by their mother, were a nice, blue fabric.

Eustis had explained that he would do exploratory surgery and, if nothing had been seriously severed or broken in her boy's leg, he could clean and stitch up the wound and possibly save his leg. It seemed worth the try. They just had to beware of infection. There always was some, but it was a matter of how much.

He took Nathaniel aside and explained the help he needed. "Can you hold him absolutely still even if he jumps and screams?"

Nathaniel had little to no experience in this. By God, Eustis wished Eli or Noah were there. They both knew the surgical routine. But he would have to pin his hopes on his brother to not let go.

He made all the preparations he could. Rum and more laudanum were available. They tied Tommy's legs to the table, put a strip of leather in between his teeth in case he woke. His knee breeches had been pushed up to clear the area and his long shirt moved out of the way. Nathaniel prepared to hold Tommy down, and Eustis started to loosen the tourniquet for a short time. He would need to look for any spurting arteries.

"Ready?" At the nods from those around the table, he began probing the wound. The boy jerked and cried out and Nathaniel leaned in, holding on. Mrs. Sommers clutched the boy's head to her bosom. It would be best if he indeed became unconscious.

One artery needed tying off, but everything looked repairable. It was just luck that the axe had missed cutting into the shin bone. When Tommy passed out again, Eustis finished quickly, then stitched the skin together. The internal stitches tying the artery would disintegrate inside over time.

As he tied off the last stitch, Eustis said, "Mrs. Sommers. You will have to keep this boy in bed for probably a week or more. I am not sure how long it will be before he can walk. What we are worried about is infection. I hope cauterizing will help with that."

Finishing that process, Eustis made sure the wound was bandaged tightly. It was not pretty, but it would hold. He picked up a rag to wipe his hands. "I'll be back tomorrow, but call me sooner if I am needed."

Nathaniel helped Mrs. Sommers move the boy up the steep staircase to a bedroom while Eustis packed up his surgical kit, wiped his tools on the rag, and prepared to leave.

Both hungry, he and Nathaniel had barely gotten settled back at home, seated for their supper, when there came another knock on the kitchen door.

Not again! God's teeth! Who can be there? Probably some bloody, misbegotten bog-rat of a messenger.

Ebenezer rose from his chair and opened the door to reveal the watchman, Mr. McAllister, scarf wrapped up to his ears against the cold night.

"Yes?" said Eben. Not disguising his lack of interest in their visitor.

"Dr. Eustis?"

"I am sorry. Not me. He is over there." He waved his hand.

McAllister saw and recognized the doctor and approached the kitchen table.

"Doctor?"

"Yes, Mr. McAllister. See here, I have just come in from a difficult surgery. I really need to eat something. Pray, go into the keeping room until I can talk with you. I won't be long. 'Tis not an emergency, is it?"

"No, doctor. The man is dead, so I guess we can wait a little." He left to go through to the small room where he warmed himself, sitting on the bench by the barely glowing hearth.

Within fifteen minutes, Eustis went into the next room to find the watchman staring into the dying fire. "I appreciate that you waited, Mr. McAllister. Now what can I do? What is happening?"

"I was glad to warm up, doctor. I thought you would be interested that we found another man floatin' in the harbor. Right near to where we found that first one. I just thought maybe you would like to take a look before we take 'im away."

"Yes, I would. Shall we go now?"

Back in the kitchen, he began to put on all his usual outerwear, pulling on his boots. McAllister followed and stood near the back door.

"Will you be late, Bill? I will make sure the latch string is left out," said Prudence as she handed him a lighted lantern.

"Thank you, Prue, I have no idea how late I'll be."

They ducked out the door and began the familiar trek down to the harbor. As they approached the same wharf as before, Eustis looked intently at McAllister. "Same as before?"

"Yes, sir. That is why I came to get you."

"There has been a gap of some days since the first body, more than a week, unless there was a body found that I do not know about."

"No, sir. I thought that mayhap the killer went somewhere or had something to take him away, another job – or he just did not come out in the cold! Could have sailed south to get warm." This last comment with a stifled chuckle.

"Let's see the body. Over there under that canvas?"

McAllister nodded. "Those men over there talking to Constable Cobb found him. They are usually around here and tend to different tasks – loading, unloading. You know the work."

Eustis walked over to the draped mound and lifted a corner of the canvas covering. The body of a dark-haired man, possibly in his thirties, was laid out, his hands crossed on his chest, seemingly arranged for burial. Hair and clothing, both in good repair and the current style, were soaking wet. His shirt was stained, possibly signs of blood, and it appeared that he had been in the harbor for a while and likely drowned. There were bruises around the head. It was hard to make an inspection

113

in the lantern light. The doctor wanted to get a better look, wondering where the blood came from, and realized he would again have to deal with the basic preferences of the constable. Get him buried. Now. He sighed and headed for the group of men including the constable.

As he approached, he noticed their levity and realized they had been waiting for him long enough to have started passing a bottle around. Probably came from a nearby tavern.

"Good evening, constable. I am sorry to have tarried, but I just completed a complicated surgery. Surely you can allow me a few extra minutes?"

"Evenin' Dr. Eustis. Is this going to take as long as the last one?"

"I cannot promise you otherwise. I hope that it can be handled efficiently. Will you also be storing this man's body in the Old Granary vault? And if so we can make the same arrangements to attempt an identity. Unless you have one?"

"No. I was just asking these, ah, gentlemen over there," said the constable. What was his name? Eustis was caught short. The men he indicated were much amused that the constable had called them "gentlemen."

"So, no name for the dead man?" asked Eustis. "Otherwise, I'll have to get a drawing and time with the body to examine it to determine the cause of death."

One of the men in the small group called over. "Are you the doc who looked over the last one? Mebbe Bert or Monty?"

Walking toward them, Eustis said, "I believe I was. Can you tell me Bert's surname and who this man is? It really is important if either of them had a family."

"Bert did. A wife. I know that. Don't know where she is. Nice enough lookin'. I saw her once."

"Aha. And where might you have seen her? Near here?"

"Naw, it was over in a tavern near where they lived, Salem Street. Up by the old fort there on Copp's Hill. But are you sure that Bert Sommers really is that other dead one? I thought I saw 'im just a few days or so ago, workin' on a ship at the wharf. And I have not heard he was dead."

Now this makes a puzzle, thought Eustis. We will have to confirm that whole identification process. But that first one is buried now. Ah, well. I at least still have that drawing. And rosters from the ships in the harbor might be important. He tried not to reveal his frustration. "I will try to check everything. You have been very helpful. Do you live somewhere near here? What is your name, and can I reach you again?"

"Abe Hanson, sir. Happy to help. I live near Salem Street too. A boarding house, Mrs. Anderson's. There are a good number of them around there. Good tavern too, the White Horse."

"Thank you, Mr. Hanson. I know the place. You've been very helpful."

The constable, thinking he was losing control, stepped in. "Thanks, doc. I'll take it from here." He waved to his helpers, possibly other watchmen or recruits. They approached with their barrow, loaded the dead man, and trundled him off.

"I will come to your office tomorrow morning," said Eustis. "If I may."

"Very good, doctor." The constable touched the brim of his hat and walked away. The group of men followed, probably headed to the nearest pub to talk about it all.

Left standing on the wharf, Eustis turned to McAllister. "What did you think about that? And what is the constable's name again?

"'Name is Cobb. Enoch Cobb. Seems fine to me, but you will have to keep pushing to get anything from 'im. Without you being a nuisance, they will just tuck him in with the other unknowns."

"But that man, Hanson, seemed to think the other body that was buried did not belong to Bert. That should count for something. Could be more than one Bert? Still don't have a clear identification really."

"We can always hope to get it, sir."

"It had occurred to me, Mr. McAllister, that a map showing currents in the harbor would help. My brother got one. We thought it would help figure out how the bodies washed up here, even if it only proved that most would on any incoming tide. Of course, this one may have been pushed in off the wharf too. But if there is a strong current, it is likely that everything adrift comes in here."

* * *

Eustis had been distracted by other matters besides emergency medical calls as the countdown for leaving with the Cincinnati expedition began. Still, the mysteries of the dead men weighed heavily. He went to confer with Sam about the harbor chart, taking Sally along.

Eustis spread out the chart with notations of the currents in the harbor on the table Sam used as a desk. Both men leaned over it trying to locate the wharves they were interested in, planning to backtrack from there.

"Arrgh!" muttered Sam. "I can't read this! We need help here."

"You're right. I cannot even locate where we are. Wait a minute! Is that the longest pier there, the long wharf?" He put his finger on a heavy extended line coming, it seemed, from the land into what must be the harbor. "And those lines must be the currents.

"Now, I have been told that the currents follow the tides and are strongest in the channels or deeper parts of the harbor. That means anyone going into the water over here would end up here." He indicated where the wharves protruded. "Huh! It seems anything that falls in here would wash into the wharves. So it could be from a ship, or not." He and Sam studied the lines on the chart.

"I think we have a better bet continuing to ask questions. Jacob can look up the tides, and I want to know when and which ships were in during those days also. I will go over it with him at home tonight."

He remembered how he at least had the backing of General Benedict Arnold during his last investigation at West Point. Here he had no authority. But now he just wanted to relax with some beer and not think about murder or dead men. Or the time left until his departure.

* * *

His first stop of the next day was to check on Tommy Sommers, his young patient of the day before. While walking to the Sommerses' house he thought over his next steps to get the identifications of this Bert, or whoever he was, as well as for the new body. Then check at the burial holding crypt or the Town House. Cath had told him that their father might be coming for midday dinner, and he wanted to put in some time with Sally. A busy day ahead.

Tommy lay wrapped up in his bed with his mother nervously hovering. Eustis unwrapped the dressing. The wound was red, swollen, and oozing. It was clear that the cauterizing had not totally prevented an infection. Eustis tried to think of ways to ease the pain for the boy and slow the infection. He needed Eli. He always had been a great help with his experience in medicinal herbs, but he had gone off. Drat! Those herbs would be the best bet, and he prescribed compresses of comfrey. If the boy had problems sleeping, a little laudanum would help. Leaving a small vial, the doctor said he would return the next day unless they needed him sooner.

* * *

As it happened, the visit to the Granary Burial Ground crypt yielded some answers but raised more questions. The odor brought him immediately into the present, and he set to work. Few of its shelves were occupied this time, and there was room to unwrap the newest occupant. It was a well-muscled man with his worn, less-than-stylish clothing in fairly good condition. He seemed to have had an injury to his nose at one time. Eustis could immediately see that these new injuries and the bruising were not the same as he had seen on the first victim. There was evidence of a knife wound entering on the left side under the ribs and pointing up toward the heart. The blade looked to be about five inches long and an inch wide. Much like a sailor's working knife. This man could have been stabbed in a fight or a brawl in a tavern and the knife might be traceable.

Less likely but possible was that the man was so drunk that he tripped, went into the harbor, and drowned. But the knife wound? Eustis wondered how much he might have been drinking before getting into the fight. There were no large bruises found at the back of his neck. But the question remained. Who was he?

117

Emptying out the man's waistcoat pockets, Eustis found a few coins, a pocketknife, a pipe, and a tobacco pouch. There was a surprisingly expensive watch with a smashed glass that had stopped at 12:13. Morning or night? Probably after midnight when it had been broken in the fight. There was also a folded piece of soggy newspaper. Eustis would take it home to dry it.

Nothing else would help with identity. Again, as he'd urged McAllister, they should get a drawing done and ask at all the ships and businesses around the harbor about someone who might be missing. He would wait to see if McAllister found anything else.

Back at home, he found a letter from Eli and the two Royalls, Noah and Maria. They had arrived in South Reading and reported that they were happy there for the moment. Nearby was a nice large lake, likely with fish. They still were unsure if it was the place to settle in permanently, but it might be. They would know before long but could still try another place. They had also heard the praises of New Bedford as being much less prejudiced and more welcoming to free people of color and natives. They might decide to go there. Seems that if a person could do an efficient job connected with anything in the whaling business, it made no difference what they looked like as long as they could do the work, from the rope walk to actually harpooning a whale at sea. The local natives, the Indians, were valued not only for labor but particularly for their skills with the harpoon.

CHAPTER 17

A heavy frost marked the turn of the seasons with decorative designs on windows and walls. The harvest and preservation of sufficient food to get the family through the winter was nearly finished, firewood cut and piled up, their cellar stocked, and the growing anticipation of yuletide and solstice seasons arriving. Always questioning, Bostonians took their religious activities seriously and did not believe that Christ's birthday could be that accurately determined. No date was in the Bible.

Boston in 1786 was shifting toward the Unitarian belief in a trinity-less God. Only a hundred years or so before, Puritans had been escaping from the domination of the Catholic and Anglican churches. And the year before, King's Chapel, renamed the Stone Church after the war ended, had reestablished itself as a Unitarian church.

Most Bostonians welcomed the approaching solstice and the change to a new year and longer days, cheerfully saluting the annual arrival of yuletide with revelry and drunkenness. But in each and every church service in late November and early December, additional prayers were offered for the safety of the men on the Springfield expedition expected to march any day for the western part of the state.

* * *

Eustis decided to find McAllister, the watchman. He wanted to tell him about the now dried and unfolded piece of newspaper found in the dead man's waistcoat pocket, and he should find out if anything had been done to get a drawing made of the most recent dead man. Moreover, he wanted to walk over the area near where the man had been found.

He thought of one good thing as he walked along. He had located Norah's husband, Albert Lindholm, efficiently supervising work on the docks with various gangs of men. Lindholm's obsessive desire to have everything work smoothly and his strict, unforgiving supervision had gotten the enterprise precisely organized but at a substantial human cost. Albert was far from popular with the dockworkers. And some would not

119

even take a job if he was in charge.

Something was not right. It was not necessary to be liked if the job worked well, and now with less confusion, it did. In fact, it seemed Albert spent extra-long days there, and then bought drinks at the nearest tavern to try to convince his workers that he was their friend. Indeed, efficiency brought quicker turn around and more income, but he had a reputation for a bad temper. The dockworkers could not forgive the punishment and abuse. It was not that easy to buy them off with beer as Lindholm seemed to think, making his gesture, if anything, more insulting.

McAllister was found in his little house, now his most likely location in the windy December weather. It was hardly much bigger than a backyard three-hole necessary and had a high desk, but there was space for two men to sit very closely inside on two stools.

Those damp northeast winds blew constantly across the cold harbor and right into the town. After wishing McAllister a good morning, Eustis gratefully took the other stool in the shelter of the workplace and took out his piece of newsprint. Carefully unfolding it, he pointed out to McAllister the possible vague letters hand printed along the margin of the scrap. They looked like numbers and letters done in charcoal or black chalk but were not clear enough to read. This discovery did not arouse any interest in McAllister, so Eustis then asked about the situation on the waterfront.

"Not bad now. It could be better if that cove Lindholm stopped buying beer for everyone on his work gangs. They hate him so much they just show up for the drink, toss it back, glare at 'im, and then leave, still in a rage. Sometimes, I've had to quiet 'em or lock 'em up." He frowned. "Have you checked on his family, doc? I 'member his wife."

"My sisters have seen her at the market and say she seems to be managing well. I am not concerned about it yet. What I am concerned about is the lack of progress we have made on discovering how those men were killed and by whom. And getting drawings shared around for identification."

"Just have to wait to see if something shows up, doc."

"I intend to take a quick walk down on the wharf before I go. I regret that I have not been poking around as much as I would like, but I'll get back to it once I return from this expedition. General Lincoln has required almost all of my time of late."

Eustis was somewhat embarrassed for not continuing to pursue possible clues in the death of the men. As he explained, he had been called in often by the general to assist with arrangements during the countdown to the departure.

"You will have lots of time to think and arrive at some ideas in your time away," offered McAllister. "We'll have time and more to discuss when you return. May God go with you, sir."

Eustis continued on down to the harbor area and out along the large wharf. There was not much activity, it being a windy, wintery day. He studied the planking and around the pilings as he strolled along. There were snail shells and other assorted broken shells. Dropping them from a height, the seagulls broke them to access the delights of the interior. Not far from the end there appeared to be stains on the gray weathered wood planking. He could not assume it was human blood because many men and boys fished from the pier and could have cleaned their fish. But it caused him to slow down and poke around. Oddly among other shell debris, there was a cigar stub stuck at the edge where piling met planking. He picked it out and sniffed. It smelled exotic. He pocketed it, intending to take it home to look over. Huh, he thought, the men on the docks did not smoke cigars. I wonder who or where this came from.

* * *

In mid-December, just a few days before Eustis was due to leave with the army, Cath summoned her sisters and sent Anne for Betty Flint, her midwife. The bedroom had been made ready for the anticipated delivery and subsequent lying-in for the few days Cath would stay there. Her sisters would try to enforce at least that much. They helped her back up the steep staircase and scolded her to not come down until they gave their permission.

The men were invited to remove themselves, and the house became an anticipatory waiting and delivery site. Sally had never seen anything like it. She was both entranced and scared, Anne taking the girl under her wing to explain what was happening. Dr. Eustis offered to stay but was firmly told by Catherine he would be called if anyone thought it was necessary.

But it was not. The men left for work. They were finally allowed to return that evening for a late supper following the arrival of a second son for Ebenezer and Catherine. The little bundle, to be named Ebenezer for his father and grandfather, was passed around for admiration, celebration, and toasts to both parents.

Eustis went back to visit with Sam one final time before the Cincinnati expedition rode out. He had gotten personally prepared and his gear packed and wanted to wrap up any loose ends, and now he had one day left. Surry opened the door as usual, and he found his way to the bedroom, pulling up a stool to sit beside Sam at the window.

"How are all the departure activities and expedition plans going in the Eustis household? And a new baby?" Sam sounded slightly depressed, possibly anticipating his friend's absence and weeks without his cheerful stories and adventures.

"As you said, I have another nephew, Sam. I am still relieved I was here in case of need, although, as you know, they threw me out of the house, banished me to the barn. And our household has certainly shifted in its nightly noise level.

"One interesting thing. That cigar stub I told you I had found. I had time to really look it over, and I took it to a man who imports and knows tobacco. It seems to have been a rare blend of tobacco from Barbados that is not imported here. Now you, my friend, can help puzzle this out while I am gone. Who smokes these fancy things around here? Must be a private supply. Certainly not smoked by the average cove down at the waterfront."

"Happy to ask around, Bill. I thought they were imported by wealthy gentlemen for their private use, probably from down South. Someone will know. It may not be related at all, you know. 'Tis sorry I am that you will be missing the first several months of your new nephew."

"You know, in all honesty I am not." Eustis said, "'I am fine to miss infant screams demanding attention. It is a good time to be away. Cath will need the sisters. And your situation here will be better than mine – weeks of over-tired, dirty, and cold men riding weary horses. Want a seat on one of the baggage wagons?"

"No thanks, my dear sir. I much prefer my window although I realize the sacrifice you are making just so that you can say you went on this thing – this expedition. My God, Bill," Sam paused. "You know 'tis going to be wretched. And I'll sorely miss you."

"Indeed, I know. But let's think of other things. I wanted to review with you the pathetically small bits we know about this issue of the dead men turning up in the harbor. When I finally got to look over the second body you remember I found in its wrapping an unusual blue scarf, dyed with a southern indigo color. Do not pass this on, Sam, but I kept it when they took him for burial. I thought it might help with identity. And now this man has seemingly drowned but with a knife wound. His pockets brought us a soaking wet newspaper scrap with vague lettering."

"Mighty thin on clues, Bill. Have you deciphered the numbers on the scrap of paper? A blue scarf, newspaper, and a cigar butt. It seems to me that you are assuming they might be connected to the same murderer."

"It seems to me that the murder took place on or near that spot. The first man who drowned came off a ship. The second man was lured to the spot for a meeting or assignation, probably by the gift of the exotic cigars. He was knifed and pushed into the harbor where he floated around before finally coming to rest on the beach several wharves north. It stands as a good working premise at the moment."

"Nothing is clear, Bill. That may all be wishful thinking. You need more time to even figure out who's who among the dockworkers and why they seem upset, much less who is smoking cigars on the pier."

"Then what can we do?" asked Eustis. "I thought they understood about our expedition. Could you find out if there is a leader?"

"My father does say there is an increasing flurry of complaints about Lindholm's brutality down at the wharves. He is not sure who is leading it, if anyone. By the way, have you been to see Norah lately?"

"Ah, yes. I also wanted to tell you that my sisters have seen Norah down at the market, and although she is exceedingly wrapped up in shawls, they say she looks well enough, as does little Annie. They did wonder, however, that Annie was hanging onto her mother's skirt as much as she was. I wonder if that is some childhood concern. But they said all seemed to be well from what they saw.

"I have had few chances to go talk to more people. I suppose I should be pleased with the increase in the number of patients needing my services, but I am conflicted about coming up with answers to these other puzzles. I've had no time recently due to General Lincoln's needs. Any new thoughts?"

They spent time going over all possibilities, providing Eustis more than enough of a review to send him off with a maze of hints or puzzles in the whole mystery of deaths on the docks.

"'Tis all good, Bill. Relax. You go on your expedition. I'll hold the fort for you here. I can ask questions through my father, and he may be able to find what is going on. Your job right now is to survive these next few months, help where you can, and come back. You know, my friend, you do have me worried. Truly, I am concerned about your safety."

"I do know." Eustis laughed. "I suppose it will give me something to think about as I ride along looking at horses' asses in front of me all day and wishing I was not in a saddle."

Eustis put out his hand, grasping Sam's tightly. He wanted to say more in appreciation or just laugh. But he could not. Nodding, he rose to wrap up again before leaving.

* * *

Chilled from his damp and muddy walk back from Sam's house, Eustis removed his boots, donned a shawl, and hastened to sit by the kitchen hearth, extending his stocking feet to get dry and warm. His sister Prudence laughed and teased him as she chopped ham from the bone for their dinner. "You should be used to all this weather. You are not allowed to complain! After all, big brother, are you not preparing for the Springfield expedition? And just to note, are you not leaving tomorrow?"

"Yes, yes," Eustis answered, focusing on the warmth returning to his toes and hoping he would not get a call to go out to treat someone.

* * *

During the morning of the grand departure, the Society's new army assembled near the Town House. With some commotion and a great deal of effort, the wagons, sleighs, horses, and riders found and lined up in their companies. Residents, families, and friends all gathered to watch and give a final sendoff cheer. Jacob, Nathaniel, Prudence, and Anne holding Sally's hand came to see their brother away. The young girl was terrified, convinced Eustis might never return. But the sisters reassured her that he would and wiped her tears. Newly reelected Governor John Hancock gave a short farewell speech and sent them off to repair the reputation of the commonwealth.

Drat it, Eustis thought as he rode Nelson toward the town gates. He missed them already, especially Noah's and Elijah's company. It was not the same riding out without the two of them. His gear and that of others was on a sleigh pulled by two very sturdy borrowed horses, available because there was no plowing in the fields for them until spring. They would be returned to the owners when others were borrowed as the army proceeded west. Boston's town gates stood open, and the men paraded through, down the road and over the wooden bridge into Cambridge, establishing their first camp a short distance beyond. It had begun.

As they moved west, scouts determined all possible camping sites, towns made their inns, public houses, and fields available, and homeowners opened their barns. For more than three weeks, led by General Lincoln, the wagons and marchers plodded westward to Springfield. Snow intervened as did rain and occasional hail, but they kept moving. There was a great feeling of showing Congress that Massachusetts could handle its own problems. They would do it right and well.

125

CHAPTER 18

In mid-January, Daniel Shays and nearly twelve hundred farmers rode to the Springfield Arsenal intending to capture some of its weapons. They were startled by an unexpected defense –the commonwealth's new army. On his arrival, General Benjamin Lincoln had immediately moved to surround and secure the arsenal.

Local enforcers did not run away as had happened before when the farmers succeeded in closing the courts. The unexpected size of this new army defending the courts and its obvious readiness stopped them. Two rounds of grapeshot were fired from the armory, wounding three of Shays's men, and the entire situation changed. For the first time, the farmers had come up against seasoned troops – veterans who were members of the Society of the Cincinnati and their experienced companies. Earlier, local militia, some of whom were friends, had looked the other way, secretly taking the farmers' side. It took everyone by surprise, and the farmers hesitated. It seemed they had better do something – or negotiate. Many ran.

* * *

On returning to Boston at the end of February, the Cincinnati troops, including Eustis, were welcomed as heroes. They had quashed the farmers' revolt, and toasts to their success were raised in all the taverns around town. It may have seemed bizarre to salute the fight to pay taxes in Boston after all of the earlier calls against it before and during the Revolution. But this was their country, not Great Britain's, and many took advantage of the occasion to celebrate. The people had agreed to run things this way, and unless the law was revised, everyone would have to contribute whether they lived in the eastern or western parts of the state. Some were coming around to the idea that they should print their own money as Shays's followers desired. It would be better than the Spanish dollar.

Shortly thereafter, Governor John Hancock, acknowledging the impossible situation the farmers were in, pardoned the remaining prisoners including Daniel Shays whose name had been attached to this whole uprising because he had authored or signed one of the petitions. Although the farmers' rebellion against paying Massachusetts taxes in cash ended, no one was fooled. People knew that Congress, in fact the entire experiment of the new republic, remained mired in problems of governance.

As had the other officers, Eustis came home with stories to tell. Because his participation in a mounted charge resulted in the capture of a fighting group, he was acknowledged as being an active fighter. Somehow this action seemed more exciting to the populace than his eight years as an army doctor.

Hearing that the returning army had arrived in Cambridge, the Eustis sisters set up the big table in the front room and started cooking. They prepared a feast, gathering the entire family to celebrate Bill's return. Their latest addition, at a little more than two months old, Ebenezer Junior was proudly presented to his uncle so he could see how this new nephew had grown during his absence. Happy to be back on Sudbury Street, Eustis eagerly sought news about the time he was away.

The family wanted to hear about their brother's adventures. Settled in with everyone in the keeping room with cider in hand, he related his most exciting moments. His company had arrived in Springfield three days after the first incident at the arsenal and was sent north to camp in Hadley. By then, Shays was negotiating with General Lincoln.

"The next afternoon, I was out riding with a patrol making sure the area around our encampment was clear. The surprise came as the day developed. We were just riding along when we suddenly stumbled onto a small group of farmers. They were likely from nearby but had not been given any task and must have been waiting for orders.

"Our patrol paused to figure out what to do, then we just turned and headed for them. All of us had the same mind to create an ambush. Someone had yelled 'Charge,' and we were off. We officers waved our swords and yelled and rode into their camp. The others came right behind us."

"But Bill, how could you just do that? How many were hurt?" asked Prudence.

"We had the major advantage of total surprise, and I think their reaction time was slowed by being so cold. They fled as fast as they could. Most left their supplies behind. Others, shivering, raised their hands and surrendered. Luckily, it happened so quickly that no one was killed or injured. Everything, the entire rebellion, ended in another two or three days."

After nearly six months, it had taken just one more encounter in a snow squall to bring the rebellion to a close. The militia captured about a hundred fifty farmers during the storm. Many of the escaping farmers hurried into Vermont, and some rebellion leaders were arrested including Shays. Two leaders were immediately hanged, but not Daniel Shays.

For his part, although he'd had no call to care for any serious injuries, Eustis returned feeling successful with new ideas and new enthusiasm and none of the old lingering lethargy. It had somehow been washed away in the snowy western hills.

While away, he had heard from Elijah, Noah, and Maria about their decision to move into a boardinghouse in South Reading and about their initial difficulties in finding anyone who would rent rooms to them. It was only after Eli spoke of opening an apothecary with Noah that they finally seemed legitimate enough. People were suspicious of the abilities of people of color, and Maria tried to overcome her uneasiness about settling in a hostile place. It remained to Eli to reassure them that all would be fine. And this was supposed to be one of the safer states for anyone of color. They would find out.

Eustis went to see Sam as soon as he could. After the two and a half months that Eustis had been away, he found Sam's appearance disturbing. It could be that he had become used to Sam's appearance, but it looked like he had lost ground and was thinner, paler, and coughing more. There was a reason why the disease was called consumption or the wasting disease. It did eat away at its host. In contrast, Eustis felt increasingly in good health while his loyal and closest friend seemed to be slipping further.

Served coffee by Surry, the men sat in Sam's room, and Eustis could report on his experiences. "You would have been amazed, Sam! They were all just huddled together, and when we rode in making all kinds of fearful noises, waving muskets, they just stood up and raised their hands. I think they were very cold, very hungry, and as tired of the rebellion as we were."

"I'm happy for you, Bill. You needed this interval to get started again. While you were away, I talked often with my father about resolving the country's problems. I agree with you. People cannot just start a rebellion if their lives are not working. There has to be another solution, some other options. Our residents should not be ruined, should not lose their farms, because they have no cash due to our state's own inept abilities in handling money. This whole problem is not resolved. It still exists. The commonwealth, and I think the country, is broke and broken. We could print our own money like other states do. But what about our revered revolutionary ideals, all those ideals we fought for?"

"Alas," replied Eustis in mock despair. "I leave for only about two months or so and look what has happened." He smiled. "Seriously, Sam, I do understand what you are saying. I also believe that we will get our government straightened out. But it will take more time – and argument, of course. And what about that conference being planned right now in Philadelphia in two months or so. May or June? The Congress is planning to put out a call for delegates from all the states for a giant meeting to revise our Articles of Confederation."

"We have been watching. You, however, have missed out on what has been going on here," said Sam. "Have you heard about the letter lawyer Adams's wife sent home? He is an ambassador now, and they are living in London. Mistress Adams writes that our country's reputation, if we ever had one, is ruined and becoming laughable overseas," he sighed. "And all I can do is just sit here!"

Sam was exasperated. "I worry about all those successful countries who might decide to move in on us. They certainly have an interest. Think of Spain or Holland. Or France, Bill. They are building to revolution now. If they can ever get over Bonaparte or he gets control, they will look at us. They invested substantial money in us, and we have no plan for defense. You know this is not good. We are more than ripe for the picking."

* * *

As Eustis walked home, ideas ran madly through his head. He had forgotten to ask Sam if they had discovered some leader of the disturbances around the harbor. There was so much to be done. It was still bothersome that he had no identity for the dead men either. He doubted the constables had done anything. Better go see McAllister immediately and start again, look for more recent information. He hurried along, cursing the wet snow, watching for puddles on the streets. A comforting smell of wood smoke rose from the hearths in the houses he passed.

Coming into the kitchen, Cath went to the pie safe and handed her brother a note from General Lincoln requesting his company with the other Society of the Cincinnati officers. Governor John Hancock wished to see them at eleven the next morning.

* * *

Two men in uniform, General Benjamin Lincoln and Dr. William Eustis as president and vice president of the Society, met on the Common on the way to their morning meeting. They were joined by several other officers. His sisters had overseen Eustis's dress before letting him leave. They had insisted that he wear his hair neatly clubbed rather than loose with Cath tying it up properly.

As they walked across the Common toward the Hancock house, Eustis could not help thinking of those Puritan ancestors who had determined that the area should be set aside as a common ground back in the 1630s to be used for grazing their livestock. Now more than a hundred years later, those more than forty acres were still being held in common. And cows were led or sent over daily.

Approaching the Hancock house atop Beacon Hill, Eustis noted the neighboring brick mansions, Tolliver's on one side and two more on the

130

other. They all looked appropriately busy with colorful carriages drawing up or leaving. Eustis thought of Dr. Warren who had been particularly proud of his own crimson carriage.

Built of cut granite in the Georgian style, the Hancock house was awe-inspiring sitting by itself near the summit of the hill. It stood out magnificently as one of the most impressive private residences in Boston, looking across Beacon Street onto the Common. Passersby could easily picture royalty waving from a balcony above the entrance door.

The men climbed the stone steps to a front door that swung open as soon as they arrived at the top step. Hancock's uniformed butler, a man of color, welcomed them and indicated they were to go to the front parlor where the governor awaited them. Hancock extended his hands in welcome and suggested a choice of wine, brandy, or coffee. Once they were seated with the other officers, the butler, assisted by a young footman, promptly served their selections.

The governor stood to give a brief speech thanking them and the Society of the Cincinnati for their service in settling the farmers' dispute in Springfield. General Lincoln graciously responded. Then, formalities over, they could relax, drink their coffee or brandy, and talk informally about what to do next.

"You all understand our country's situation," Hancock said. "I have hopes for this new conference to be held in Philadelphia."

"Is it definite then, sir?" asked Lincoln.

"That is my information. But I will await an official notice before announcing it."

"Have you heard if there is an agenda – what they intend to decide or deal with at the conference? Will they rewrite the Articles?" asked Eustis.

The governor looked amused. "I may have my sources," he smiled, "but they do not go quite that far. Wishful thinking I am afraid, doctor. And before you ask, it will be the legislature who will decide on our delegates. They should be taking that up shortly.

"In other developments," Hancock added, "you may be interested that the Charles River Bridge should be completed by June, and I believe we will have great enjoyment from celebrating that. We should have an opening parade, and the Society could be very helpful in planning that."

This set the men free to speculate about appropriate celebrations, a parade across the bridge perhaps, and the time passed easily. The governor's guests realized the reception was ending when Hancock stood and, with graceful bows of appreciation, they were ushered toward the entrance hall. By then, there was not much more they could say anyway. Heading home, most decided to walk across the Common and conversed in twosomes as they went.

"If that convention in Philadelphia can possibly straighten things out, it will have all been worth it. But I fear otherwise," noted Lincoln to Eustis.

As anticipating discussions of his latest news with his brothers, Eustis passed several elderly and some not-so-old cripples. There were remaining signs of the recent war all around in the men he saw, empty sleeves pinned across their chests and those with crutches and canes. But he could not be distracted now. Instead, with luck, perhaps he could wrap up some of the questions he had this week.

The sisters had created a marvelous puffy concoction of bread, cheese, and fresh eggs and removed it from the brick oven just as he entered the house. Eustis felt inspired but not to accomplish anything he realized. He wanted to relax, to quit worrying. How good it would be to have a day without worry. I could settle into my chair with some Shakespeare for the afternoon, he thought, and then go to the White Horse. It was hard to resist.

But another thought came to him, and he made a mental notation on his long list to visit Norah Lindholm, perhaps on the morrow. She may have as many answers for him as he might discover at the White Horse. And there was that oddly locked barn nearby. Just too many unanswered questions. And maybe that barn was no longer locked. I want to cross some of these things off my list, he mused. Perhaps Nathaniel will go to the White Horse with me while we still have daylight and we can look into that barn.

132

CHAPTER 19

Eustis and Nathaniel made it to the tavern by four that afternoon. They had first hovered around the still locked barn at the end of the road hoping to find some way they could look inside. Its windows were too high above the ground. Without a ladder, and unsure about walking around the sheds to access the rear, despite that being exactly what was needed, they decided they could get more information in the tavern.

"I'll stand you a pint inside," said Nat, and they wandered into the main room to look for a table. Eustis saw one near another small table surrounded by five men who looked vaguely familiar. At least they looked like the usual dockworkers or sailors who hung around the piers.

"Do they look ...?" He turned to Nat who was already heading in that direction.

They claimed two stools at a nearby table and sat down, looking for the waiter.

"Maybe I should just go over," said Eustis. "They look busy. Hold the fort." He rose and went to the corner bar where he interrupted the publican who was deep in conversation with another patron, asked for two tankards of their excellent beer, and turned to go back, catching sight of rotund Mrs. Noyes coming in the door. This definitely foretold a fruitful visit.

He joined his brother and indicated with a nod that Mrs. Noyes had come in. Nathaniel grinned, eyes sparkling with the idea they might get information. He was glad they were starting their quest again. Now all they needed was patience.

The discussion at the adjoining table got a little louder. "Ya know if they got any plans to celebrate anythin'?"

"Nah. The bombats prob'ly can't count. We're in 1786. It's been ten years. They've missed it." The speaker picked up his tankard, looking glumly into the remains.

"Yeah, but Abel, that's been more 'an ten years. I think we ought to do something, get more organized. You fought down there in New York."

"It's our governor who should," said another man at the table. "Was he not in Lexington in '75? Or someplace else 'portant. How 'bout we go see Sam Adams? He can get the Sons to pay attention."

"Nah. I'm not so sure about that. He's not been fighting – too old."

"Whaddaya mean? Without him, it woulda never happened."

Eustis and Nathaniel were intrigued. What were these fellows talking about? Then Eustis considered what was happening ten years ago. 1776? Those were the years when it all began, and he had been there – right at the beginning. There should be some recognition of the anniversary, but probably not enough to please this group. As veterans, they would want more.

The aproned young man who they had seen before came toward them with two brimming mugs, depositing them without ceremony on their table. This attracted a glance from their neighbors. Eustis looked, leaned over, and asked, "So you fought in the war? Were you in a company from Boston?"

Three men looked at him. One volunteered that they had joined up after the battle on Breed's Hill in June. They looked questioningly. "Were you ...?"

"Yes," said Eustis. "From day one. I got a look at Lexington just hours after the fight. My parents lived there, and I was worried about them, so I caught a ride out that afternoon and signed up with Parker's Company that evening."

"Well, that's pure amazing," said one of the men, the one with the long face and heavy eyebrows who reminded Eustis of Baron von Steuben. "You really were there."

"Uh-huh," said Eustis. "I am a surgeon, so I tended to people being carried off the hill, down in the Sun Tavern. Were any of you there?"

"Hey," said one of the men, the one addressed as Abe. "Mayhap you worked on my arm. 'Tis doin' just fine now." He flexed his arm to show how well it was functioning.

And then they were in accord, a brotherhood settling in for pleasant talk. Memories, stories of their hardships, the sound of cannon balls flying overhead, and the wrenching lack of food and clothing.

Eustis ventured to ask a question, not wanting to endanger their association but desiring to get back to his purpose for being there. "Have you noticed that the barn by those sheds at the end of the road is locked?" He waved his hand in the direction. "Do you know anything about it?"

Two of the men looked at him, frowning. Was he possibly getting out of line? Another happily informed him that some group had started meeting there. Mayhap they were the ones who locked it.

"Huh!" said Nat. "I wonder why."

It seemed none of the men at the table knew what went on at the gatherings. Just that they happened. "'Twas locked, you say?" asked one.

"Could it be storage?" offered another. The men stared at him.

Eustis wondered if they knew anything about those notices being spread around. "Do any of you know about those broadsides that people have been getting?" he asked.

"You mean the broadsides people been findin' in their pockets or posted on the walls?"

"Yes. I wondered if they might be connected to that group that uses the barn."

"Dunno. We could go see."

"Yeah, let's just go find out. I have to head home now anyway."

Three of the men got up and moved toward the door.

Feeling somewhat sidelined, Eustis noticed Mistress Joyful Noyes looking in their direction. He waved at her. He did not want to get the men questioning why he had a particular interest in the barn. He was just curious because it was not usual for a barn to be locked.

Mrs. Noyes, basket on her arm, rolled in their direction. Such a delightful woman, thought Eustis. She might be mistaken for a cider keg in the right light. She greeted them cheerfully, and Eustis asked her if she could tell them where Albert Lindholm lived.

At that, the other men listening in from the neighboring table looked at each other, shaking their heads.

"Aye, the war did an awful job on our Albert," one said. "He is real edgy and can get crazy angry in a minute's time if anything seems irregular. He wants absolute order. I think 'twas the war that done it."

"What do you want with 'im?" interrupted another. "He gets in 'ere and drinks his wages and then goes home to beat his wife. Ain't a good situation 'tall. He's been behavin' like a spoiled sausage all his life. Wants ever'thin' his way. An' there's a child too."

Nathaniel could see the shock on Eustis's face. He knew this was worse than his brother suspected.

"Is anyone helping them?" Eustis asked.

"What can anyone do?" said one of the men introduced earlier as Amos. "A man has a right to beat his wife – as long as he does not kill her. He's the head of the family."

Mrs. Noyes was still standing at Eustis's shoulder, listening. "Do you know anything we can do, Dr. Eustis? That little girl's in danger."

"To be honest, Mrs. Noyes, what Amos says is accurate as far as the law. Nothing can be done legally. But I will ask around. Perhaps I can talk with Mrs. Lindholm."

Walking home, he said to Nathaniel. "We've got people upset around the waterfront, a group storing unknown items in a locked barn, a man beating his wife, and it is just ten years since we went to war for a better country. Are men so damaged by fighting that they have lost their bearings? I'll go see Norah tomorrow. Perhaps bring a sister. We cannot let that go on."

Walking home, Eustis remembered he wanted some time to talk to Sally. He knew he could not stand it if she were threatened by an out-of-control man. He worried about Norah as another one who had been through too much already. She'd defended herself before, and he believed that if her child was in danger she would do it again.

* * *

A day later, the rising sun was welcomed as a change from the Bostonians' usual dreary March decor of overcast skies with storm clouds. Residents had hopes for continued clearing and a little warmth, and the Eustis sisters thought of washing clothes with the chance of drying outside.

Eustis knew he must attend to his patients. He would start by checking in with Mr. McAllister then move on to Norah. He strode down the driveway and the road. Suddenly, a bundle of anxious boy piled into him from behind. Turning, grabbing the small, wiry youngster, he saw that it was Tommy's little brother. What was his name?

"Whoa, young man! Tell me what the matter is."

"Dr. Eustis!

"But let's start at the beginning. Tell me your name."

Having to provide a basic answer seemed to settle the boy.

"I'm Eddie, Eddie Sommers, doctor. You 'member my brother, Tommy, right?"

"Yes, I certainly do. And you came to get me to help him. You were very brave as I remember it. Now tell me, is there a problem at your house?" Eustis put his hand on his shoulder to reassure him.

It seemed like a simple story. That morning Eddie and Tommy had been in their room getting dressed. He had heard someone bang on their door and his mother answered it. He heard her cry out, then slam the door. She ran upstairs and sent him for Mrs. Morse and went into her room and closed the door. And he went to get Mrs. Morse, the boy did not really know what the news was. Except his father had not come home in a long while.

"How long has your father been away?" he asked.

"Weeks 'n weeks," said the boy. And Eustis suddenly thought of the indigo scarf from the beaten and drowned man he had looked over. He looked at the boy's soft, deep blue shirt and reconsidered. Perhaps he had come back. Perhaps he had drowned.

He patted the boy's back and said that he would look into it and be back by the next day if he had any news. As he strode toward the watchman's shed, he wondered what could have happened to result in a man or a husband being gone for so long. Jacob would have news of the harbor trade. He needed to find out the name of the coastal trader Mr.

Sommers was said to be on. Which reminded him that he was not really sure of Mr. Sommers's first name.

Eustis apologized for the interruption, telling McAllister about the odd similarity between the indigo dyed clothing at the Sommers household and the scarf that he had found with the first body. What could they do? Seems someone could or should have notified Mrs. Sommers if it had been her husband's body.

McAllister said that indeed they would have notified her, particularly if he had fallen overboard. He could check on what records they had, but he was not sure that would provide the crew roster or names. And he had heard nothing further about any shipwrecks since the last storm. He thought the most pertinent information they needed would be identification. Did Eustis still have the drawing?

As he walked back to Sudbury Street, the doctor decided that his immediate next chore involved picking up a sister or two to go see Norah Lindholm. Her husband was being very heavy-handed with her – perhaps unnecessarily beating her. Later, he would go back to the White Horse because he had not shown the drawing there. And although it might be a shock, it should be shown to mothers and wives of any possibly missing men and Mrs. Sommers.

"How do we find out the names of the people on these coastal traders, and how can we track if someone died here or at sea?" he asked as soon as he got into the keeping room.

"You best try to talk with Mrs. Sommers when you can before we set off any alarms," cautioned Jacob. "She can do an identification of the drawing. Take a sister. Indeed, take Cath with you. She is good at this."

Eustis knew his brother was right.

CHAPTER 20

In his search for an identity, Eustis would show his drawing to Mrs. Sommers – the first stop on his list of house calls. Walking toward the Sommerses' house, Cath carried a small basket of baked goods. In Eustis's pockets were the two drawings, and he carried his small medical bag. Mrs. Sommers opened the door and ushered them toward the parlor, pleased to see Catherine.

"My dear Mrs. Sommers," said Catherine. "Perhaps we can sit for a minute. I hope we do not have bad news for you."

Catherine's suggestion upset her. She hurriedly sat as did Catherine followed by Eustis. "'Tis not my boy, is it?"

"No, no, Mrs. Sommers," hastened Eustis. "I believe he is coming along very well. We wanted to talk to you about your husband."

"Have you found out anything?" Her eyes began to tear up, and her hands clenched a handkerchief in her lap. It reminded him he should ask about the blue scarf he had found, but he could not get distracted from his main purpose.

Eustis held out the drawing of the first body they had found, several months ago now. Mrs. Sommers put her hand over her mouth. She glanced at the drawing then looked up in some confusion at the doctor.

"But this does not look like my husband. How did you get this? Where did it come from?"

Eustis explained that the body of a man had been pulled from the harbor, and in an effort to identify him, the drawing had been made. He asked if she had any other drawings of her husband. Has anyone ever made sketches of him? He paused, not wanting to rush her or appear to lack sympathy. "I found a scarf dyed with indigo with this man."

At the mention of the scarf, she collapsed into Cath's arms. "It doesna' look like him, but it must be Bert! I made a scarf for him. But that was months ago."

Afterwards, Eustis went on to his next visit, and Cath remained behind to settle Mrs. Sommers. She decided to wait until someone else arrived, just to make sure all was manageable before she left. She asked if there were other relatives who lived nearby, intending to go over it all with whoever came.

Walking back home to get Prudence to accompany him to Norah Lindholm's boardinghouse, Eustis wondered if indeed there could be a mistake in the identification. What if they were wrong and it was not Bert Sommers but someone else who had drowned? But that would mean he had to start over again. And then there was the blue scarf. He would take it to Mrs. Sommers to see if it was her work.

Meanwhile, another idea kept running through Eustis's head. Could a man do more in government than in medicine? He had discussed it several times with David Townsend who would probably not be back in Boston until late spring. Politicians served during the winter months, then left Philadelphia for home. Governing was not intended to interfere with other occupations, planting, and harvest times. He needed to get a letter off to Townsend. Thinking of his to-do list, he walked into his own driveway, startled by having arrived there so quickly.

All appeared organized at home. Anne was ready to remain with Sally, and they would work on various projects until Cath got back from the Sommers house. They were churning butter. Prue had brought several firkins into the kitchen for packing the butter, later to be stored in the cold cellar under the house.

Before leaving, Prue removed her apron and changed her dress into one more suitable for making calls, and brother and sister promptly headed toward Copp's Hill and Norah's boardinghouse. Prue carried a small cake in a basket. She was delighted to be the leader, having been there once before.

The boardinghouse was just two streets beyond the White Horse. They inquired of the landlady for Mrs. Lindholm and were directed to the third floor. Norah called out hesitantly when they knocked, asking who was at her door. Eustis indicated to Prue that she should answer, not being sure they would be let in otherwise. Norah's voice sounded nervous and apprehensive. She opened the door and peeked out then made an effort to close it, but Eustis pushed back.

"Please. Let us in, Norah," he asked.

She hesitated, then backed up and let them enter, limping to the bed in the corner where her small daughter, not quite three years old, lay curled into a ball. The small room was dark, its windows covered with shawls, light coming in only around the edges.

"By God," exclaimed Eustis. "Are you alright?" The skin high on her cheek had been split, likely from a harsh blow, and he could see bruising, new and old along her arms. Realizing the absurdity of his question, he went to her and sat beside her on the bed. "Let me look at your eye."

Prue rushed to Annie to see if she too was injured, why she seemed reluctant to move. Prue wondered if that meant something had been damaged in her insides. She turned back to look at her brother in shock. "Oh, Bill!"

Norah leaned forward and dissolved into tears, huddling against Eustis as he wrapped his arms around her. As she wept, Eustis tried to think of what they could do. If Norah came away with them, she could be pursued as a runaway. Albert Lindholm would want her back. But what if he did not. It would be best to assess Albert's situation. And how long had this beating been going on? Husbands had rights to discipline a spouse but not to injure them to this extent.

Prue had stirred up the fire and was heating some water over the hearth. She hoped to find coffee or tea among the scant food supplies, not wanting to impose herself on the child until Annie, watching intently, was ready. Her brother, as the doctor, as a man, might be more alarming to Annie, but to Norah, he was an old friend.

When she was able to talk, after much sniffling and repeated hiccups, Norah tried to assure them that she really was fine. As she spoke, both Eustises noticed a new speech pattern. Her sentences now ended in a questioning lilt. She said, "Really, I am fine?" She had been so censured or become so insecure that she could not even be sure about her condition, beliefs, or ideas.

Although Eustis wanted nothing more than to wrap up Norah and Annie and get them out of the room, he realized that until they had a clear plan he could not let their emotions take control. They couldn't just react. He looked at Prue. She had found coffee and was brewing a pot all the while keeping her eye on Annie.

"I am going out to get us some food," she said. "Would Annie be able to come along with me? We will not go far, and Annie can help me find the best things."

They could see that Annie was tempted and that her mother looked anxious. "That is all right, Norah. I will be right back," said Prue. "Do not worry. I think it might be a distraction for her."

Annie had slid off the bed and was standing next to her mother. She patted Norah and said, "Safe wit Miz Eustiff." Then she stepped forward and offered her hand to Prue. "I show you where ta go."

"Well, let me just get my bonnet and cloak and we'll be off on an adventure," Prue promised. "Have you got warm clothes?"

The child pointed to a pile at the end of the bed where Prue found a small coat, knitted hat, and mittens. Eustis looked gratefully at her as she prepared to leave with Annie. This would give him time to talk to Norah without Annie overhearing.

He rose and leaned over Norah to examine the fresh wound on her cheek. He hated the thought of a scar, and it would be necessary to pull the sides of the split together.

"I am sorry, but it seems you should have several small stitches to help this heal," he told her. "And it may cause questions when Albert comes home. Perhaps we should discuss how you want to handle this. I can hide it under a bandage, but even that would be noticeable."

Norah struggled to marshal her thoughts. She must keep Annie safe, somehow. She also realized she needed medical care and Dr. Eustis's help. Her voice quavered and she asked, "But what can I do?"

"Let us first have a little coffee, and then we can discuss all the options we have and make a plan," Eustis reasoned. "Albert will probably be dismayed at your appearance when he comes home. I cannot

142

predict if he will become angry or remorseful. Does he ever apologize?"

"I do not think he can." said Norah. "But he will buy me a present. If he apologized, it would mean he was not right in everything he did."

"And when might he get angry again?"

"I cannot tell. I just watch and try to have everything the way he wants it and not to attract his attention. It could be anything that might upset him. Lately it has been the amount of food, that there is not enough, or how it is cooked. He does not seem to realize that he gives me too little money for food, so I find what I can at the edge of the market and try to make it do. I think he spends most of his pay at the tavern before coming home."

"Could you tell him you do not have enough?"

"When I try, he thinks I am criticizing him, and it just upsets him?" She was back to questioning.

Eustis sipped his coffee. It was in a mug, and Norah had a teacup. He wondered if some had been broken. He was conscious of his complete inability to do anything other than give her medical care. He could not do what he really wanted – to take her away to a safe place. That would take further planning. He desperately needed to consult his brothers. Prue would have ideas when she came back after spending the time with Annie.

He carefully explained to Norah as he was attending to and then bandaging her cheek. He would develop a plan but not until after he consulted with his family. They may well have good suggestions. Meanwhile, she had to stay there and protect Annie. Prue would bring food so Norah could cook a decent supper to mollify Albert when he came home.

"Can you get through the night?" he asked. "I will get back here as soon as I can. Do you think he will become angry that you have received help?"

"I do not know," she answered. "I know I have to do the best I can, and it is so comforting that you have listened to me."

"But why would I not? Norah, we have a long history together, you and I. We're friends who can help each other."

"What if Albert decides you are trying to take me away?"

"Send him to speak to me if he has questions. I'll be ready." He tried to reassure her while realizing she could possibly have a truly difficult evening ahead. He could not help thinking that it would be good if Albert did not come home at all.

CHAPTER 21

Just then there was a knock, and the door opened to reveal Prue laden with produce and Annie clinging to her skirt.

"Mama, look what I got." The child ran to her mother showing off a cornhusk doll.

"That is a good market you have here," enthused Prue. "I found all sorts of fresh things for you."

The women sorted the food, discussed recipes, and both Eustises set off within the hour, leaving assurances of a rapid return the next day.

As they walked toward home, Prue relayed what she had learned, adding to Eustis's fears.

"By God, we have to remedy this as soon as we can," he said. "I wonder if I can still intercept him at the docks this afternoon. He may suspect her of contacting us and get angry."

Prue agreed with making the attempt but cautioned about sending Lindholm home in a rage.

"You could try your new friend the watchman, Mr. McAllister," she suggested.

Leaving Prue to walk the last short distance home, Eustis turned off toward the watchman's shed. He would find McAllister and ask him to accompany him to the wharf.

But where was the man when you needed him? The shed was empty, its door locked.

Eustis quickly headed down toward the harbor and Jacob's office. Perhaps his brother would know where he could find Lindholm. Bursting into the office, he interrupted Jacob's discussion with a captain to ask for his help. Even the captain became interested about the urgency of his behavior.

"I'm sorry to interrupt, Jacob. I'll explain later. Now I need to find Lindholm. It is critical!"

"I understand. Try Wickford's wharf. Two to the north. Can I help?"

"Getting me there would be a distinct help in this situation."

Jacob beckoned, and the two immediately went out, turned right and, followed by the captain, walked quickly toward the next wharf.

"Just along there," the captain called after them.

"He's supervising cargo loading on that coaster up there," said Jacob as they hurried toward the farther wharf. Eustis could see that the last few barrels were being loaded. Lindholm would probably dismiss the crew as soon as the task was finished.

That was exactly what was happening as they approached, walking out on the heavy, weathered planking. They could see Lindholm waving off the remaining few men who did not look happy about their experience, muttering to each other.

"Ahoy there, Lindholm," Jacob called out.

Lindholm paused and waited for the two men to approach.

"Can we have a word?" Jacob added.

Eustis decided to be direct and to accept all blame if any was given. "My sister and I went to call on your wife as my family had not seen her for several weeks. When we arrived, I found she needed my care."

He waited to see what Lindholm would say.

"What did she tell you?" he demanded. "She has recently been getting confused in her mind, and I am worried about the safety of my daughter. How did she seem to you, doctor?"

Uh-huh, thought Eustis. Concerned husband. Slightly crazy wife. So that was the way he would present it.

"I am worried, Mr. Lindholm. She had a serious wound on her cheek. You will see where I bandaged it. I will be checking in on her again tomorrow. I expect you will see that she gets no further injuries or upset again tonight."

"Thank you for telling me, doctor. I will make sure she rests. Is there anything else? My daughter?"

"Annie? She had a nice visit with my sister. They planned your supper. I believe both your wife and daughter are doing well just now."

And you had best keep it that way, Eustis thought. After a few more cautionary suggestions, he turned with Jacob to head back home. He had wanted to add I am watching you but thought he got the idea across. He had a sudden thought and turned back to say, "Mr. Lindholm, I would be pleased to spend time with you, should you care to talk. I know you have been under a great deal of pressure with all this work, and I may be able to be of some help." Then he added a further incentive. "Perhaps some medication?" There was no response.

When he left Jacob at his office to go directly home, he said in parting, "Our supper should be interesting. I want to discuss all the information we have learned and perhaps come up with a course of action."

The doctor directed his steps back toward the watchman's shed, hoping to have a word with McAllister before he locked up and went home for the day. When he saw the door still closed, he considered leaving a note but realized he had no paper. Heaving an annoyed sigh, he turned to head back to his own home. Doing so, he saw McAllister chatting with two women with baskets, likely on their way home to start cooking for their families.

He calmed his irritation, realizing this was also part of the watchman's job. Approaching, he called out a greeting. "Mr. McAllister, have you a few minutes?"

When McAllister waved the women off, he turned and approached Eustis.

"What can I do for you, doctor?"

"Seems I just bring you problems, Mr. McAllister. Is there a place where we might talk?"

"Indeed, doctor. We may attend to my office or to the nearest tavern. Your choice."

Eustis thought the tavern might be too public and elected, despite the lack of ale, to follow McAllister to his shed.

"Now, sir," said McAllister, "what is the latest?"

Eustis told of his afternoon tending to Mrs. Lindholm and of his worry that her husband may get angry again overnight. He also wanted any suggestions for a solution. Did the watchman have any experience with this sort of upset?

As they sat squeezed together in the little shed, McAllister went over the rights of the husband but added that he did not want any messy murder on his watch. It had happened once before, and he wanted to prevent anything like that again. He promised to stop by the wharf to chat with Mr. Lindholm as soon as he could the next day.

Eustis suddenly had a curious thought, probably the result of his visit to the Sommerses' house. "On another question. Can you tell me where that blue scarf was found, the one that I found wrapped with that first body, those weeks ago? Do you remember that?"

McAllister frowned, pursed his lips, and looked up at the ceiling of his little shed. "Yes, I do. When we hauled that fellow's body out of the water, he had it wrapped in his fist, sort of around his arm too. If you are asking if he was wearing it around his neck, he was not. Is it the scarf that has you worried?"

"Uh-huh. You understand, Mr. McAllister, if that scarf was not owned by the dead man, Bertram Sommers's poor wife could be upset without reason. Although we need to figure out why it was there. Do you see how it changes everything?"

"Yes. I do. Are you saying that we are at the beginning again and do not know who that dead man was?"

"It could be. The truth is that sadly I do think so. But I am going to discuss it with several people and see what I can prove. I am also on the trail of a person who smokes very expensive cigars."

With that, leaving the stunned watchman and clutching his hat, Eustis walked against the wind back toward his home, thinking he had to go over it all again. Who was this poor dead soul? And he would have to redo his lists of possibilities.

If it was not tied around the dead man's neck, could the blue scarf have been ripped from someone else? Were there other blue scarves? Or could it have indeed been on Bert Sommers and been pulled off by the dead man in a desperate struggle?

* * *

A clutch of Eustises sat around the kitchen table over supper with the futures of both Norah and Annie foremost on their minds. They agreed they needed to come up with a solution to Norah's untenable situation and kept hoping that one of them would produce the solution.

"We need a miracle," sighed Prue.

"I have several things I have to do tomorrow," said Eustis frowning, "and I must check on Norah first thing in the morning. When would be a good time for me to find Lindholm on the docks, Jacob? Oh, and McAllister said he'd also try to get to Lindholm in the morning. I am hoping that if we are more attentive we may be able to stop this behavior."

"But what about us?" asked Prue. "What can we do? Truly I am not sure any of this will stop. I want to somehow get them out of there."

"We need to know what others have tried, what might have succeeded in other cases," said Eustis. "Let's talk with caution to everyone we encounter and then compare notes tomorrow midday. And there's another thing. I am not sure any longer that the first dead man I looked at was Bert Sommers. He may still be missing, not dead. Mrs. Sommers said she did not recognize the drawing that I showed to her."

"Oh no, Bill." said Prue. "I thought you at least had that resolved. Again, what else can we do to help make this misery end for that family?"

"One of the things I realized," said Eustis, "is that we do not know exactly which ship Bert served on, or if there were several. That could be very important. Perhaps Jacob and Nat can see what they can find out about listings of crew members and what ships were in the harbor when he might have left – as far back as the end of the summer. And see what ships have returned from that group. And I'll ask Mrs. Sommers too. By the way, does anyone know her Christian name? I seem to have forgotten."

"She was introduced to me as Tabitha," said Prue.

"Thanks, Prue. And we'll get on with finding those other names."

149

The brothers agreed. Jacob thought the information might even be his office, or they could go over the back issues of the *Gazette* or the *Boston Centennial* to see what the sailing listings reveal.

"You look exhausted, Bill," said Cath. "You should retire with a cider or beer and relax. We'll finish here, and then I will prescribe an early night. We'll head out first thing in the morning."

* * *

My dear Elijah, Noah and Maria,

I am anxious to hear that you are doing well in that small village. I hold good thoughts for your success wherever you decide to settle, although I have to admit that I wish it were nearer to Boston. My brothers and I were investigating a tavern called the White Horse, hoping to find further information on the puzzling murders here in Boston Harbor. They are not resolved. While walking around the area near Copp's Hill we found a perfect area in which you could settle and find possibilities for a pharmacy. It is near where your old friend Mrs. Norah Lindholm found lodging. Should you decide you want to look further for your future location, please come back for a visit to us in Boston. We are eager to show you what we have found.

Yr.Obd.Svt,

W. Eustis

* * *

Somehow, and it may have just been the sun coming through the clouds and starting to clear the fog, the men felt upbeat and happier when donning coats, shawls, and mitts and heading off to find out what was possible on this new day. It was better to be actively working or on a mission than sitting and worrying.

The women first cleared away remnants of breakfast. Then with the cows milked, they wrapped up in coats and capes and left for the market taking Sally along. They thought she might be feeling abandoned, but she said she would have been fine staying with the cows. Prue looked at Anne and said, "No, you come along with us. You need to learn about the market."

Jacob headed for his office to determine Lindholm's whereabouts, and Nathaniel sought the watchman. After sending a note to Sam, Eustis walked toward the docks to catch up with Jacob and find Lindholm. Aggie was left in charge at home.

Eustis found Jacob pouring over his shipping ledgers. He greeted Bill. "If you want Lindholm, I expect you can find him supervising the loading of a coastal schooner just down this pier on the left." He smiled. "I'll come check on you in a few minutes, in case he goes off his head."

Eustis went as directed and soon came to a group of men rolling barrels up a ramp and into the hold of the vessel *Rising Tide*. They were supervised by Lindholm who carried what looked like a riding crop. He whacked it against his leg as he watched the men. "Hey, you there! Watch what you're doing! I want it packed in there very carefully. You know I'll be checking."

Looking critically at the loading crew, the doctor could see marks on sides of faces where the crop had struck. He was not even sure why they worked on this crew if they were treated this way. But he soon realized these were the men left after everyone else had secured a job for the day. More desperate, they took anything available.

"Hello there, Mr. Lindholm," he called out. "May I have a word with you?"

Albert Lindholm turned to see who had addressed him and then came forward, walking slowly so as to assert his own authority. "What do you want?"

"Remember me? Could I please have a word with you. It will only take a minute."

Lindholm considered, looked at the loading crew, and agreed. "Where do you want to talk?"

"Your choice. Would it be easier on board?"

Lindholm beckoned Eustis to follow him. They walked up a steep ramp from the pier to the deck of the ship. There Lindholm stopped and faced Eustis. "So? Again, what do you want this time?"

"I am checking to see how your evening at home worked out and how Norah is this morning. Would I be upset if I stopped by to check on her condition?"

"What right do you have to keep bothering me?" Lindholm shot back, beginning to breathe heavily, rapidly worked himself into a temper.

"As your wife's doctor, I feel responsible for preventing further injury to her. I will be checking on her often whether you are amenable to it or not."

"Just you wait a minute here, doctor. I have rights as her husband, and I will check with the watchman, perhaps even the constable."

"You do that, Mr. Lindholm. I am only warning you to be careful."

Eustis turned and walked back down the gangplank. Behind him he could hear Lindholm almost growling, beating his riding crop against the side of the vessel. He began to wonder if he had gone too far, if he had instigated more trouble for Norah.

CHAPTER 22

"You know, Bill," said Sam as he lay on his bed, propped on pillows, shoes off, not daring to brave Surry's scolding for putting his shoes on the counterpane. "We are going at this whole thing the wrong way." Copies of the *Gazette* and the *Centennial* newspapers were beside him.

Eustis looked at Sam from his place in the prime window-gazing chair. He was somewhat distracted by Sam's collection of preserved embryos in jars lining the back of the table being used as a desk. Wondering if he should do more with his own room, he looked over and asked, "What are you suggesting? We have no hope of finding ordinary clues such as weapons or footprints or written notes. Everything has been washed away by the ocean. I only have that scarf and the cigar stub."

"Don't you see? That is just it," Sam countered. "It is all about the waterfront. Everyone involved is there as well as the bodies of the two dead men you have seen. We need to think more about life there. Granted that you have found out about where many seafarers live in the boardinghouses and the taverns some of them visit, but that is barely a dent. How actually are they making a living? What do they specifically do?"

"Don't be obtuse. They go out to sea or work unloading or loading at the docks."

"Yes, but what does that mean, they go out to sea? Is that work as crew, officers, or captains of boats or ships? And where do they go? And what is the relation between these crewmembers? All good friends?"

"Fishing can cover anything from bottom fishing with a hook and line to deep ocean expeditions to harpooning those enormous whales," Eustis reasoned. "It can involve one day or months. They also take our produce down the coast and trade for other produce there and then bring back rice or wood from live oak trees. You do know that the best wood is live oak? They get it from the Carolinas."

"But what about supervision, Bill? Surely that must be part of it? Who owns these ships? Who are the leaders, the ones with money? And then there is the social aspect. Are there fights or injuries?"

"Uh-huh. I am beginning to see what you mean," Eustis agreed. "We have no idea of the infinite number of contacts or dangers encountered in those numerous jobs. And the money or especially the business dealings involved."

"Now you are seeing what concerns me. It is a prodigious problem!"

"Indeed. I wonder if I had best start to observe at the wharves and talk more with all those workers, just to see what they will tell me. But I have patients, Sam!"

"I know, I know. But we need to figure out the lives of the two dead men. We need better ideas, more specifically about what they did. And to do that we need to know who they knew and, may I remind you, their names! Impatience is creeping in for me as well. Do you have any specific ideas?"

"If I go now to check on Tommy, I may get a chance with his mother, Mrs. Sommers. I give you my oath, Sam, that I will pry all that is possible or probable or even potentially interesting from her that I can. Surely she knows more than she is telling."

"As you know, I'll be waiting," Sam promised. "Now off with you, and I'll take the window seat."

Eustis helped his friend get up from the bed and into his chair, made sure he was comfortable, and took his leave, waving to Surry on the way out. Sam was right, he thought, as he headed in the direction of the Sommers house. He needed to understand, to find out more.

Luck followed him. Mrs. Sommers greeted him at her door more relaxed with him than on any prior visit. She seemed extraordinarily happy. Her clothes and hair were cleaner than before. He wondered how the situation had changed

"Good day and my compliments, Mrs. Sommers."

Her reply stunned him. "We have such good news, Dr. Eustis. Bert is back!" Eyes alight, she smiled with delight.

"What? What a surprise! Joy to you, Mrs. Sommers. But I do not understand. Where was our wayward friend?"

"Come in and let me tell you. 'Tis a long story. He wrote a letter from France, many long weeks ago, of course, and it arrived here only late yesterday. His tale is astounding. I can hardly believe it. But he is alive, and he is back here!"

"This is excellent news! I do wish to hear it all."

She ushered him into their parlor, indicating a seat, then took one herself, smoothing her ample skirts. He noticed that the pinky finger on her left hand had been broken and had not healed well. It persisted in holding its curve rather than being fully straight.

"Well," she began. "This is what he told me. His ship had come into Boston in late August after two months whaling up north. The crew had a successful voyage up around Greenland and the Davis Straits and brought back an admirable amount of oil from those blackfish or small whales. They first chase 'em ashore, then haul 'em up on the beach to extract the oil, then load the filled barrels. When they got back home and to the Bird-in-Hand, they were paid off and felt the need to celebrate their success.

"As they were raising their tankards, a man came into the tavern recruiting a crew for immediate departure to take a shipment down south to the Carolinas. Trading our dried cod and apples for a full hold of rice for the return voyage. They were desperate for another crewmember and offered good wages. As soon as they heard that Bert was an experienced sailor, he was in demand. He decided on the spot to go, transferred from one ship to the other ship, and he never thought to come home to check in." She shook her head and grimaced.

Eustis was amazed she was so calm about it. Maybe Bert had brought home money.

"In the excitement of the moment, my Bert decided to send me a note instead and head out with them. No thought of seeing his children or me. It was his idea of bringing home substantial wages by the tail end of summer to make up for past years, and this trip would not take more than a month. Well, that is what he thought. I never got that note. The boy he gave it to never delivered it or lost it."

155

"I can understand your husband's interest," said Eustis, "but why go immediately?"

"Seems the ship was about to weigh anchor, and he reckoned he was carrying a good deal of luck and should take advantage. We had been through such trying hard times I truly can't blame him although I would like to. And me trying to get the family fed without any money, running up a tab everywhere. But let me tell you what happened next."

There was more? Eustis looked at her in amazement. The story seemed genuine and at the same time – outrageous.

"They went south, no problem, and Bert liked the captain," she related. "The cargo got sold promptly in Charleston just as planned, and they set out to come back north. But this is when they got into trouble. A French frigate appeared and sent a shot over their bow, hailing them to heave to. I cannot believe it, but Bert said they thought there might be some emergency, so they did. They actually stopped. A boat came over with a French officer and crew who demanded to interview the captain. Then when the officers returned from the captain's cabin, they informed the crew that those with whaling experience must come with them. They were being pressed into the French crew to become whalers for the French, sailing out of a port in France! The captain had agreed to this arrangement to save his ship."

"What? He gave up some of his crew to the French? How could he do that?"

"According to Bert, there seemed no choice. They would have damaged or sunk the ship. You remember how the British also impressed men during the war? Well, three of these men were put into the longboat and rowed across to the French ship where they were interviewed by the captain and signed on to his crew. The rest, once released, got underway and headed north as fast as they could, leaving the others behind."

"That is unconscionable!" said Eustis. "And I also do not understand why the captain did not relay this news to you and the other families here."

"They would have, but they did not get the chance. Seems they soon ran into a fierce storm along the coast 'bout at the opening to Chesapeake Bay. They ran aground on a sandbar and sank. Three crew members survived, but one expired ashore. I am not sure what became of the remaining two. They never returned here. So," she shrugged her shoulders, "no news for us."

Eustis was reminded of the vague reports of the Bonhams' son missing at sea. It might be more common than he thought. "And Bert is now in France?"

"No, no, no. He's here! I told you. He managed to get along and coach the French apprentice whalers. They are eager to develop a whaling industry of their own out of French ports. But it only took about a month before Bert managed to escape. He found an American ship, signed on as a crewmember, and made it back home."

"Ah yes," said Eustis, thinking. "I have heard of the French eagerness to develop their whaling industry and build success in the world. Their people are building toward revolution. They want to totally change their government. Get rid of royalty. And the generals are outrageously ambitious, including increasing the army. But, by God, this is a lot to take in. When might I talk to Bert?"

"He's presently at the harbor, probably renewing his contacts. He is wondering about ways to recoup his losses to get us through the winter. Ought to be back here this afternoon. You could come by later, perhaps at two, and I can tell him to expect you."

"That would work well. How is Tommy doing?"

"All seems good. I have high hopes." She smiled. "High hopes all around."

* * *

Reality hit him as he was walking down to the harbor. By God! That family had to begin all over again. How are they going to manage that? It was good to get Bert Sommers removed from their list of the dead, but who was the man in the tomb awaiting spring burial or the one already buried? He was back where he began.

He kicked a stone on the road and startled a horse, setting off the driver into loud cursing. It was somehow satisfying.

Stopping in at Jacob's office and finding everything calm, Eustis briefed Jacob and Nathaniel on the amazing story of Sommers's adventures. Jacob had also heard that the French were trying to convince whalers to establish their own settlement on the French coast. As they passed back by the watchman's shed, McAllister waved, cheerily calling out that he'd heard Bert Sommers was back. If Eustis had been Aggie, he might have snarled in return. All that wasted time and those dead men! He waved but kept walking.

But the question remained, who were the drowned men? A shadow of an idea hovered in his mind. He could not quite get it in his grasp and would have to let it smolder until some flame developed. The whole thing was frustrating. Sam could be right that it all had to do with the men around the harbor and, in turn, what secrets they harbored.

CHAPTER 23

About midday, returning from several medical calls, Eustis stopped at the pump in the yard, rinsing his hands and face briefly before going into the house. He was stopped by Cath demanding he hold out his hands.

"Bill," she said. "That is disgusting. You have black around your fingernails! Is that blood? How long has it been since you really scrubbed your hands?"

Meekly, he conceded and went into the back workroom, got a bar of lye soap, went back out to the pump, and scrubbed again. Sometimes it was just like when he was growing up and his mother sent him back to wash his face and hands. Sisters!

The family, gathered for midday dinner at the kitchen table, wondered about the shocking update on Bertram Sommers's arrival home and speculated on the state of a marriage that could survive through that long and unexplained absence. And that brought up the concern for their friend Norah.

"I do want to go over and check on her, but I must attend to a patient first. Probably dysentery," said Eustis. "I hope to get to Norah by this afternoon, not too late."

"I'll go," said Prudence, "and I can tell you about it when I get back."

"Me too," said Anne. "I have not been there yet. May I go with you?"

* * *

"Stupid, frigid pig!" Albert Lindholm crashed out of his boardinghouse room, slamming the door. In a blind rage, he could hardly see to negotiate the stairs, pounding the walls, not clear on exactly where he was going, then automatically storming downhill toward the harbor.

John McAllister was talking with Constable Enoch Cobb just outside his watchman shed when Albert came steaming toward them, red-faced and seething. He elbowed McAllister aside. "Out of my way, you misbegotten son of a whore!"

"Whoa! Stop now!" shouted the constable, putting out an arm.

"Why should I?" Albert growled and gave him a shove.

McAllister and the constable moved to restrain the man, clearly deranged, probably dangerous. He needed to quiet down before being turned loose on their roads.

Lindholm wanted a fight and did not care with whom. He hit out, catching the constable across the jaw, causing him to stumble and fall to the dirt road. Finishing his attack with several kicks to the ribs, Albert turned and, despite McAllister's whistle blowing and shouts, lurched on toward the harbor.

"Are you all right, sir?" McAllister asked Cobb.

"Aargh! That cockwomble!" He started to move. "Bollocks. He may have broken some of my ribs. Get after him – quick!"

McAllister helped the constable to a stool in the shed and called for a boy to fetch Dr. Eustis or another doctor if he could not find Eustis. "There is a penny in it for you!"

He did not want to leave the constable alone and blew his whistle again, beginning to draw a crowd. Among those going by was indeed Dr. Eustis, returning from his house call.

Seeing Eustis, McAllister called out: "Doctor! Quick! Do you know where that bloody dungbeetle Lindholm might go? He's injured the constable! He is off his head, an' I think he's headin' to your brother's wharf."

Not bothering to ask or say anything more, Eustis began running toward the wharf and Jacob's office. Filled with anxiety, he remembered how sympathetic Jacob was about the difficult life these dockworkers led. But what was Lindholm thinking? And why go after Jacob? He could look out on the wharf, and he spotted Lindholm entering Jacob's office.

Jacob looked up as the door flew open and Albert Lindholm surged in, red in the face and muttering dire threats. He approached the counter, banged on it, and leaned over, glaring at Jacob.

Barely coherent, he said, "Gimme work. I need it now." He hit the countertop again. "There's got to be something! Get me a job, Eustis! Or you will be sorry you did not!" He started to grab Jacob by his neck cloth when Dr. Eustis, out of breath, ran into the office.

"Stop it!" he bellowed.

Several men crowded in behind him followed by McAllister who pushed them aside, yelling, "You are under arrest, Lindholm!"

McAllister grabbed Lindholm around his arms and struggled to hold him. Two of the men who had followed him helped restrain this obvious madman. They got him down on the wooden floor and two sat on him. Within minutes, Lindholm was wrapped in rope, and they were trying to clamp iron cuffs around his wrists despite his thrashing. Once he found he could do nothing, he collapsed, hissing and muttering about getting back at them later.

"Aw, ye stupid eejit," charged McAllister, "we will talk after you've seen the judge, an' he will not be in town until days from now, so into the cell with ye. After that, it may be over to Castle Island."

"But you cannot lock me up! I have a family!"

"Should have thought of 'em before you got into this rage. What set you off anyway?"

"Ah, 'tis me wife. She is so stupid. Slow to get it right. I tell her again and again what I want. But she cannot understand." His anger was rising again. "I teach her to do it right, and she still doesn't listen."

Another watchman, startled at the mess in the office, hastened to report that Constable Cobb had been taken to his home where a doctor was looking after him. They were very concerned about the possible broken ribs and what other internal damage might have been done. And, of course, there was infection to anticipate. He shook his head. "Beatin' a constable! He will be in for it now! Are those prison ships still down there in New York Harbor? I remember how truly awful they were. People were dyin' in there ever' day. Starvin' too. Hardly came out alive."

"Yeth, but he's prob'ly crathy, so they'll just lock 'im up for the retht of his life," said a shabby fellow with a bandana and a large gap in his remaining brown teeth. "Heeth for it now." He and several other onlookers had crowded in to see what there was to see.

161

"Hope so," commented the watchman as he ushered everyone out of the office. "Move along now. All of you. Nothing for you here. Get on out."

Eustis left Jacob's office and watched McAllister, helped by three others, coax and drag the still-struggling Lindholm away from the wharf and toward the center of town. He'd best get home quickly and find out what the sisters knew. They were going to the Lindholms earlier, and he was concerned at what they might have found. Would Norah and little Annie be all right, not injured? Just one more medical stop before he could get there.

As Eustis arrived back home after tending to the case of dysentery, Anne ran up to him, her eyes filled with tears, and she wrapped her arms around him. "Oh, Bill, it was awful. They are both hurt. We just got back."

Catherine held the door as they entered, looking at her brother with great concern. They were in the middle of dipping candles, more winter preparations.

"How can this go on, Bill? Can you do anything?" Cath asked.

"What? You are referring to Norah and Annie Lindholm, I collect." said Eustis. "First of all, are there immediate plans here? Do I have time to go to Norah? And I will need Prudence along too. It worked well last time."

"You should go now, but first come in and I'll get you some coffee," said Cath. "Then I'll put together a basket of supplies to take with you. Anne? Perhaps you could call Prue. Sally, where's our good basket?"

Cath handed him a mug of coffee.

"It's bad down on the wharf, Cath," he said. "They hauled Lindholm away after a struggle and the constable was hurt, probably broken ribs. A doctor's with him now."

The women quickly went about their immediate tasks, soon gathering again at the kitchen table.

"How could that man do something so awful?" asked Prue. "I don't understand it. Has he lost his mind? Ah, what a hateful man!"

"We'll have to see what we can do for Norah and Annie immediately," said Cath. "Bill, do you know if we have any rights or if she does? Can she not leave him? I want to get her away!"

"All I can say is that we'll do everything we can. And I'll talk to anyone who might make a difference. First, I have to go see Norah's injuries. Would we have room for her here if I brought her back? Or mayhap we can go get her tomorrow."

"Just go see her," said Cath. "Then once we know the situation we can plan what is best. If you have to stay, send Prue back."

Eustis with his medical bag in hand left immediately accompanied by his sister carrying a full basket covered with a cloth. They walked quickly. Eustis thought that perhaps they should have brought the wagon. But we can come back for it if necessary, he reasoned.

They hurried up the stairs in the boardinghouse, found the door locked, and knocked. There was no answer, not even a voice of inquiry. Prue spoke into the silence in as persuading a tone as she could. Nothing. She turned to her brother. "We may have to get the landlady to unlock it for us. But I'll try again. Annie, Annie," she cooed. "Come open the door for me. I brought you some good things to eat."

There were sounds of movement inside. "No. Daren't," whispered Annie through the keyhole.

"But it is your friend Prue here."

"No. Mama's in bed. Sick."

"I am so sorry that Mama's sick. I can help her. Ask her."

A small wail. "No, no, no. Mama's not talkin'."

Prue continued her persuasion, and Eustis went downstairs to find Mrs. Flanagan.

"Mistress. Please open the door to the top room. Mrs. Lindholm is injured and needs help. I could bring the constable, but he has been injured by the same person."

"Ah, the saints preserve us," Mrs. Flanagan replied. "I knew he was a bad 'un right after they rented that room. He started carryin' on af'er that. Let me get my keys. I will come with you." Eustis sensed that Mrs.

Flanagan was also concerned about what she might find.

Prue was still talking into the door when they arrived at the top of the stairs. The landlady unlocked and opened the door, moving aside as Eustis and Prue hurried in to see Norah wrapped in blankets on the bed and Annie looking fearfully at them from beside her mother.

"C'n you he'p her?" the child whispered.

Eustis assumed his doctor mode and, talking softly to Norah, began carefully unwrapping her coverings. He nodded at Prue, gesturing toward the table, and she encouraged Annie to come to the table so they could unpack the basket.

Horrified, he gently lifted the bloody linens, realizing immediately that Norah had been severely beaten. God rot that man! He would need to determine what bones were broken and what cuts needed stitching, what splints, what surgery. But the reality was that he also needed Annie out of the room and some skilled help. He had not done this kind of detailed surgery in years. Sam had been a very adept surgeon. Could he consult?

He turned to Prue. Trying to be even and steady, he said, "Prue, I need a few more things. Perhaps you can take Annie back to our house and let Sam know I need him here if at all possible to consult. You or someone could bring him back in the wagon." He looked at her earnestly, and she realized the message to Sam was a call for help and to bring the wagon.

"Certainly, Bill," she said with false cheer. "I'll go get the other things you want. Annie can come along to help too."

Annie had no objections, having enjoyed adventuring with Prue once before. After she was dressed appropriately, they hurried out the door. The landlady was still there, hovering, and, after thanking her, Eustis sent her away as well.

He turned back to Norah. It appeared she had fallen on the bed and pulled everything she could on top. Or perhaps Annie had. "All right, my dear. I am here, and I am going to look you over so that we can tend to your injuries. You needn't worry about Annie. She will go home to my sisters."

Norah started to fret and, grateful for the sign of life, Eustis again soothed her, saying she just needed to take this small potion he had for her as he gave her a teaspoon of laudanum. As she relaxed, he proceeded to further unwrap her coverings. The blood had started to dry, so the linen stuck to the wounds, making it a painful exercise to see exactly what he had to deal with.

Once he had sponged her off, he could see the staggering bruises and marks of more than one beating including teeth marks on one breast. And little Annie had been a witness to it all. He wanted to weep for his friend, but he maintained his doctor mode of neutrality, inwardly raging and knowing he could easily kill that man.

"Well, my dear," he said, "let us begin at the top and work down."

And so he did, assessing each injury, then sewing, applying soothing ointment, and bandaging. Sometime later, about halfway through the process, he heard footsteps on the stairs and hastily covered Norah with a quilt. Looking over his shoulder, he saw Sam enter, leaning on Nathaniel.

"Thanks be to God. You came, Sam. This is a serious collection of injuries, and I need your experience and astute observations. I can explain more later, but right now I am looking at this wrist. I think it has been broken in several places."

"You know I am happy to help anytime, Bill, after all you've done for me. Show me what you have here." His eyes grew wider. "God help us! Looks like what we saw with survivors after a battle."

"Yes, that is why I need you and your knowledge. I'll get you a stool."

The two surgeons examined the most serious wounds that had not yet been tended and formed a plan of treatment.

"Let's do this right wrist first, then the left arm," Eustis suggested.

More laudanum and several hours later, Norah was thoroughly wrapped and bandaged. The doctors knew it would be days before they would know if their careful surgeries and stitches would heal and allow their patient to even survive, much less thrive. They expected they would

165

need to treat the inevitable infection and perhaps gangrene as well.

They also knew it would be best if Norah and Annie were taken to the Eustis home.

Nathaniel had brought their wagon. Their sisters were waiting and had prepared a bed for Norah. The final task was to get her down the two flights of boardinghouse stairs and into the wagon. Gratefully, Eustis acknowledged Nathaniel's presence.

But why were stairwells so narrow? Why so steep and curving? No room for two men across. Carrying Norah proved possibly more onerous than the surgery and bandaging. It was a relief that she was unconscious. Otherwise, Eustis knew she would have refused to go through with it. And Sam could not attempt it. Fortunately, Nathaniel was a strong and able helper. The landlady hovered throughout.

Norah, well wrapped up, was laid carefully in the wagon on a makeshift stretcher. Once Sam was settled on a seat, the exhausted friends started back to the Eustis home. Nathaniel drove so that the doctors could observe Norah throughout the journey.

There was a warm and caring welcome at Sudbury Street. Their patient was unloaded and gently carried into the first-floor bedroom where Cath and Prue fussed and fixed everything to their satisfaction. Meanwhile, Eustis drove Sam back to the Adams house, finding Sam's father in a state of worry, nervous for the welfare of his son who was out, most likely, on his final medical call. But he also realized it was just what Sam would want during his last year of life. They got him, exhausted but elated, tucked into his bed, and Surry brought tea.

"Sam, I am more grateful than I can say that you could come help." praised Eustis. "The bit about tying off that artery. I could not have done it without your suggestion. I didn't see it at all."

"And I am grateful to have been of help, even if I could only observe," Sam answered. "Not a likely occurrence in my life now to get out and feel useful."

"You know what I mean, Sam," Eustis replied, placing his hand on his friend's arm. Looking at his drawn face, he said: "Without your assistance, your knowledge, and ideas, I would have had a much more difficult time. You have to know how I feel and how much I appreciate the help, my friend."

CHAPTER 24

Driving the wagon back home, Eustis thought about all the things he needed to accomplish. It would help if he could put them into some sort of order. He passed the spot where he had run into Elijah and Noah. By God, he hoped they were doing well. Perhaps the lack of a recent letter from them meant that they were exceedingly busy setting up their business in South Reading. Surely they would tell him if they had moved on to another town.

That led to thoughts of Norah and her close association with Elijah. The Lindholm situation needed his attention. If Eli were here now, there would be a huge disturbance, a near earthquake, volcanic explosions even over Norah's treatment. Lindholm would not be safe.

Eustis had to figure out the activities in the busy harbor, all those wharves and their galloping businesses, and who was in control. Owners of the businesses or the ships? The men worked in gangs or groups. Did those groups stay together? How could he find out? His tired mind reminded him that if wishes were horses, beggars would ride. Wonderful! He chided himself for resorting to old Scottish sayings.

But the sun was setting in a rosy glow, and here was Aggie to welcome him. Supper was laid out on the table, fresh bread and soup made from some of their winter squash ladled into a bowl for him. Perhaps he could discuss the next steps regarding the Lindholms with Jacob and Nathaniel later. Meanwhile, feeling depleted, he spooned up his soup and hoped for a restful evening.

As it happened, Nathaniel suggested they go down to the Bell in Hand by the harbor for a short time, taking lanterns to light their way home. Eustis reluctantly agreed, knowing he did need to get a more thorough sense of the people and place when it was fully occupied.

"Only for an hour. I do not think my brain is working effectively now. I'm completely drained of energy from the afternoon."

"Oh! I am sorry, brother," said Jacob. "I just did not think. Nat and I can go and do a preliminary reconnoiter. Then you come with us tomorrow."

"Well, in that case, you youngsters can go enjoy. But I'll expect a report with breakfast."

* * *

They were as good as their word. The next morning, standing at attention before their older brother, they pretended to be schoolboys reporting on an assignment. "Our compliments, sir. We are here to report about our evening visit to the Bell in Hand."

As the conversations around them had developed, they had overheard an assortment of dockworkers and others, men who worked in the area, confiding their upset about odd behaviors and anger around the wharves. Jacob and Nat had managed to get into several conversations that helped them realize that the general population was uneasy.

"I am not sure what they were unsettled about," said Jacob. "Mayhap it was a single ship and her management, but I thought it seemed to be more complaints about the harbor itself and the men who worked there. But they were not explaining.

"And we seemed like strangers too, so there was no particular eagerness to talk to us. I hoped we got that earlier upset settled when we told them about the Society's members getting ready for the Springfield expedition. I guess you needed to be there to hear it."

"I think you are right," Eustis agreed. "All rumors, Nat! Anything seems to set this town off. I've got to get back to figuring out what or who killed those two men. What could be the motive behind it? Let's do a repeat later this afternoon, see what we can find out. But first," he grimaced, "and not the least is checking on Norah right now."

He found her tucked in securely with Annie snuggled under her arm. She peered at him through blackened eyes that were turning assorted shades of purple, green, and yellow, then whispered that Annie could try to find Sally. Annie cheerfully left to go in search of her marvelous new friend.

Eustis, his hand on her forehead, verified his suspicion that she was

169

running a fever. It was to be expected, and he meant to alert his sisters and suggest that they try to tempt her with a lot of liquid, including willow bark tea. That was the best he knew for fever. And perhaps cool damp cloths. Their next few days would be critical, trying to keep infection and fever at bay. Memories flooded in of the last time he had cared for Norah. It had been touch and go then.

"We will have success this time too," he assured her. "You just rest under my sisters' care. They know what to do."

He went back into the kitchen, took Sally aside, and assigned her the special duty of watching out for Annie, explaining that her mother, Norah, was seriously ill and needed a great deal of attention from the other sisters. "You must make sure she is cared for and does not bother her mother."

A final sip drained his coffee cup, and he was out the door. The morning clouds were giving way to small patches of blue as he hurried toward the Town House. Passing McAllister on the way, he asked about the whereabouts of the constable on duty. McAllister said that whoever was in charge would be found at the Town House every morning. There were four constables in all to cover the town, and they were now down to three. The injured Enoch Cobb was still recovering at home.

"That was certainly a disturbance I wasna' expectin', doc." McAllister recalled. "Will you be helping Lindholm or not? The chief constable is not a happy man, and I can tell you that is not a good thing."

"I can well understand that. Pray, what is the usual procedure? Do they hold Mr. Lindholm until the court arrives back in town?"

"My guess is that he'll be sent out to Castle William in the harbor. They call it Fort Adams now. And 'tis the most secure spot. There are those who would like to settle him for good – and underground too, I expect. Know what I mean?"

"I do, but I'll still go find the constable. A good day to you," Eustis said as he departed.

Chief Constable Samuel Winter was in his small office, sorting out paperwork. On being asked about Constable Cobb's condition, he sighed. "That Enoch Cobb was a good man, doctor. His ribs are going to have to heal, and he is all bandaged up. I hear it will be some time. Nothing much else I can tell you. That ill-begotten Lindholm had a nasty habit of beating his crew, and they all would like a piece of him now. As would I if I were honest. We'll keep him locked up for a week or so and then put him up in front of the judge. He'll set things in train. Just do not get one of those fancy lawyers like John Adams."

"Adams is a good man, a very astute lawyer, and just who I would want in my corner, Mr. Winter, but he is in England now. If you could keep me informed, I would much appreciate it. I have Lindholm's wife and child at my home. His wife is in a very bad way, near death, from his beatings, so he went well beyond those he assaulted on his job, attacking his family as well as the constable. I am hoping I can keep her alive. Can anything be done about that? Can we get him committed or locked up as insane?"

"'Twill all be up to the judge, doc. You may want to testify."

"Indeed, I will. Her injuries need to be addressed. As I asked before, pray keep me informed."

Being in the Town Hall brought Governor Hancock to mind, and Eustis wondered if he might be of help. Or it might be better to talk to the senior Sam Adams first. He had probably already heard about the whole thing from his son.

Making the Adams house his next stop, he retraced his steps and was delighted as Surry brought him coffee in Sam's room. God bless her! He might propose marriage next.

Sam seemed shockingly pale and drawn, still completely exhausted. Eustis realized immediately that he had demanded way too much from his friend, and now Sam would need bedrest to recover. He felt for Sam's pulse to find it racing as Sam exerted himself to greet his friend.

"No, no, my friend," Eustis cautioned. "Do not make any effort, please. No sitting up. I am just dropping by to report that all is well so far. I'll be back tomorrow, and I hope to see you better rested then. I will bring a little digitalis with me. Please go to sleep now. You know as well as I do that it is what you need. I am going to ask your honored father for his ideas on how we handle Lindholm."

"Told him about it," whispered Sam.

"I expected you would. And now I will go talk with him. You rest. See you on the morrow."

Downstairs, Eustis found the senior Adams at his desk in his small library talking with three men, all Sons of Liberty. That group still gathered and, despite new governance, kept watch on the town. There seemed to be a number of projects underway if the papers spread across a table were any indication.

When the men left, Eustis sat down to talk, reviewing all that had happened. As expected, Mr. Adams knew about the entire range of incidents in the harbor and had already been thinking of how to keep Lindholm under control. He was saddened that it had gone this far and prayed that Mrs. Lindholm would recover from her injuries.

Did the doctor think the deaths of the two men found floating in the harbor were somehow connected? Eustis was momentarily stunned by the questions. He knew that Mr. Adams had knowledge of most that was happening in the town. But to also think about this? Amazing.

"They do seem oddly similar," Eustis observed. "But sir, what can I do? I am visiting several taverns hoping to gather more information. So far I have several theories but nothing secure."

"Let me think further on it, Bill. We cannot have this kind of behavior in our noble town.

This is not what we fought for. Nor died for. By tomorrow I may have a suggestion or two. The Sons could take care of it, but as Lindholm is now locked up, it will be more of a challenge. By the by, I hope you have been thinking about my suggestions about working in local governance. I am thinking particularly of forming that education committee."

"Yes, sir. I understand that. I have no answers yet. I do believe that the government may be a way for me to feel more effective in helping people. I do not always have the success rate I would wish for in medicine." Then, remembering his patients and his growing practice, he said, "But, I am not ready to quit at this time. Not yet. I have responsibilities. I'll come to check on Sam tomorrow and will also count on talking with you again."

* * *

Late that afternoon, Nathaniel and Jacob joined Eustis to visit the Bell in Hand. They had barely found a small back corner table when an argument broke out nearby. The brothers were instantly alert, wondering if this was usual behavior in this place. Was this becoming more common in the taverns? It appeared that the local dockworkers were angry, or at least uneasy, about the murders and the arrest of Lindholm. Voices rose.

"I ain't sayin' he was a decent cove, Jed. Just that he should get a right square treatment, then go to prison. I am thinkin' he should be in front of a judge. I'm sayin' 'tis important to do it right. By the law! We're a republic of laws now! No matter what you want to do!"

"Yeah? Well, I think he needs the rope." Brown hair tied in a queue, needing a shave, Jed stood abruptly, angry in his sailor's dingy white shirt and trousers. "I hear he just about beat his wife to death. That bedswerver does not deserve decent treatment, laws or no. He was as drunk as Davy's sow most of the time."

"You know," said another, "if you could get one of those Tollivers to understand, it could be fixed in a minute. They straighten things out all the time. Or some of those other big men. The ones with money like Captain Bonham. They can fix things."

Another man sitting at the table, mug in hand, joined in. "An' what about those other coves? The dead ones. I hear Lindholm beat one of them too."

"How do you know that?" Eustis interrupted, wanting to know also.

"I 'eard a fellow saw them together fighting out on the wharf. That Lindholm had a stick or somethin' and knocked the seven bells out of the other, pushed 'im into the 'arbor."

Eustis glanced at Jacob who gestured to sit down and be quiet.

A seaman ambled over to the table with his tankard. "Can anyone get into this fight?"

173

A third man stood up and walked away, saying over his shoulder, "You are welcome to my spot, mate, but it is truly useless. There is no resolution without proof."

The arriving seaman joined in. "What do you mean, no proof? I got a friend saw it all!"

"So, who is he? If you are so sure, prove it! Bring 'em by and let us talk to 'em."

Sure, and assertive just moments before, the newcomer seemed to back down when asked to show his proof. After a hesitation, he said, "Aye, you poltroon, I will prove it. When do you want to meet?"

Arrangements for the meeting could not have been more serious, more similar to arrangements for a duel. Everyone leaned forward to hear the answer.

"I'll bring 'im the night after tomorrow. I'll have to get him from his ship, but he has to get leave too."

"Indeed, then. Skipping tomorrow night, then the next one, right?"

"I will see you here then." And still angry at being questioned, he stomped out of the tavern followed by several supporters.

All three of the Eustis men exhaled, relieved that the dispute had not gotten physical and satisfied they had a potential date to find out more. An unexpected result. They huddled over their tankards of cider and ale.

Quieter gossip by men at another table addressed who could be coming to this meeting. Those surrounding them in the tavern room looked interested. A man at a neighboring table offered a light for their candle, blown out accidentally in the dispute. "That's the way, mate," one of the men raised his glass.

"Hey, Amos, are you looking to ship out soon?"

"Naw, still not a full cargo yet. Need the goods to go south. We're waitin' fer the dried cod."

Jacob signaled to his brothers that he was ready to leave, and they all rose to head for the door, stopped on the way by a voice calling out, "Doctor, have you heard any news?" Jacob and Nathaniel continued on, and Eustis turned to see Mistress Joyful Noyes with her basket.

He tipped his hat. "Good evening, Mistress Noyes. I trust I find you in good health? Is this not a distance from home for you? Would you care for some company if you are going in our direction? I would be happy to accompany you some of the way."

"Bless you, doctor. Indeed, I am well, but I surely would appreciate your company. I forgot the time talking with customers back there." She chuckled her rosy face crinkled. "It always seems to happen, and this neighborhood is no longer exactly a safe one. Also, I have something I wanted to talk about with you."

"I am delighted to hear whatever you wish to tell me."

"I was over by that table way in the back against the wall. Do you know where I mean? And I was thinking it was time to head home when several men started talking about how life around the harbor is unstable, the anger going around from man to man. Saying it is no longer safe around here. That some want to take the law into their own hands."

"That does not sound good, Mrs. Noyes. Would you care to sit here and tell me about it?"

"No, doctor, thank you. I am grateful for this suggestion, but I would rather walk along toward my home, and we can talk on the way."

They left the tavern followed at a discrete distance by Jacob and Nathaniel.

"I feel most sensibly escorted," cried Mrs. Noyes with delight as they set out, lanterns lighting their way. "As I was saying, doctor, I do overhear all sorts of talk in taverns where I do my business. What I want to know is this. What is the truth to the story going around that Albert Lindholm killed those dockworkers? I know that he beat his crew severely, but it was to get the jobs done, and he was known to have a temper. But what really happened? It does not make sense to me that he would attack those two men. There must be something behind that behavior."

"I, too, am wondering, Mrs. Noyes. Something is lurking in the atmosphere around the harbor. Do you think it is a fear that more killings will happen – that they or their families are not secure?"

"I am not sure it is a question of security. I have also heard that one of the seamen on his work crew slandered Lindholm's wife, saying she had been flirting with other sailors and offering her body for a price."

"Indeed, that would set him off. Do you know which of the dockworkers might have said that, and if he is still around on the wharves?"

"I do not. And then there is the question of Bert Sommers's sudden departure on another coastal trader just after he got into the harbor from two months away whaling."

"Yes, it seemed odd to me too," Eustis acknowledged. "But I have received an explanation from Mrs. Sommers, although I am not sure if it is the truth – or if she even believes it. Does Bert Sommers frequently come to the Bell? Or is he mainly at the White Horse? I can see that I may do a great deal more sampling of cider."

Taking her arm, he helped her up a slope and several cobblestone steps as they approached Copp's Hill.

"Ah, there it is! My home is in sight," she panted, out of breath. "I can take note of where and when Bert Sommers is most often if that would help you. Shall I continue to listen in the taverns? I know you have that poor, hurt Mrs. Lindholm at your house and much to do. That brute. I can pass on anything I hear that might appear significant."

Eustis, surprised by how much she knew, thanked her for her interest and help. But then, he recalled, it was her business to know where people gathered, and what they talked about, to increase her sales of sundries. And she undoubtedly overheard a great deal.

After seeing her off toward her house, the brothers walked briskly back toward the Mill Pond and Sudbury Street, urged on by the deepening gloom and angry clouds.

CHAPTER 25

Brightening skies, strong coffee, a piece of cheese, and fresh bread, all followed by an encouraging interview with Norah, and Eustis was ready to begin his day. He would start at the Sommers house, just down the road, to see if he could find Bert. It was going to be a day of attempting to fill in the blanks after he had missed Bert yesterday.

The house seemed asleep, but Eustis was greeted at the door by Tommy. The boy appeared well on his way to good health. "Good day, Tommy. My compliments to your mother and father. Would they be able to receive me?"

The boy ran back through the house calling for his mother, and Mrs. Sommers soon appeared at the door. "Good morning, doctor. To what do I owe the pleasure of this visit?"

"The joy of the day to you, Mrs. Sommers. I am still hoping to talk with your husband. Is Bert about?"

"Oh dear. I am so sorry, but you have just missed him. He is off to the harbor to look for more work. I cannot keep him back!"

Mrs. Sommers was exceedingly cheerful about her husband's labors, and Eustis continued to wonder about it all. How was he to find out more about the man's travels and activities?

"Is there a good time when I may call to talk with him?"

"I am not sure of his plan for the day, doctor. Could I send a boy to fetch you when he returns?"

Realizing that was the best he could do, and having no legal authority, Eustis agreed. It was necessary to talk to Bert to get the dates straight. He doubted the Sommers boys would know what was going on. Might try a conversation with them, however. The Bell or the White Horse would be important sources too. And Mrs. Noyes.

Sam Adams chortled at the sight of his friend Bill entering his room. "Joy to you this morning. I can see the antennae at the top of your head. You must be seeking clues or have ideas churning in your brain."

For himself, Sam was nearly his own self after two days of bedrest and had progressed to sitting in his chair by the window. His surgical adventure had given him an inspirational lift.

Eustis, delighted at the change, sat down and began his report of the more recent investigations. "This man Sommers is invisible! I know he is at home now, but I cannot get a meeting with him. If I were sure of my premise of his involvement, I could go to the constable and get help. But as it is, we need to find out more. I just want to nail down exactly when Sommers was in and out of Boston."

"Can Jacob's shipping records help?"

"Jacob does not have the records of all the harbor's shipping traffic, and they may not even list the crews. But I suspect I am being put off in some circumstances. Could it be that Bert will not talk with me on purpose?"

"Well, my friend," Sam said, "it does seem strange. My father has several ideas to try on you."

"Yes. He said yesterday he would be thinking about it."

At that point, the elder Adams entered the room carrying a coffee pot followed by Surry dragging a chair and holding mugs. "Aha! Conference central!" he said with delight. Setting the pot on Sam's desk and taking the chair from Surry, he sat down and placed his hands on his knees. "How shall we begin?"

Eustis quickly glanced at Sam and said, "Sir, I am delighted that you have joined us. I was telling Sam that I am frustrated by my lack of ability to get a meeting or clear answers from Bertram Sommers on his travels and the dates associated with them. I want to find out if he was in town when the murders were committed. I want his actual activities over the past four or five months."

"Yes, yes," said Adams. "I can see that. It would give us a good start if we could set up a timeline of who was where when."

Us? Eustis looked quizzically at Sam. Did this mean his father was into the investigation?

Sam raised his eyebrows and shrugged. Who knew? They would find out soon enough. For now, they would speculate and decide where to follow up.

* * *

Later, walking to the Bell in Hand with Jacob, Eustis mused on the possibilities of too many stories circulating around the town. He wondered about the Sommers family. Indeed, how had Mrs. Sommers survived for that length of time without her husband. Usually there were accounts set up by husbands who were leaving for any length of time. Would it all be credit? Or could there be another source of funds?

He arrived at the door of the tavern, automatically ducked his head beneath the low lintel, and headed for a table with stools. Jacob, known to most of the customers from his work with consigning and shipping various cargos, was greeted from all sides. Patrons wanted to know when the constable would be sending Albert Lindholm to Fort Adams. Or would he be held in town? Their eagerness to learn specifics made Eustis momentarily wonder if they might be planning something.

Then, suddenly, there was Bertram Sommers. He seemed unusually friendly for a person who could never be available to the doctor for a meeting of any length. There was an aura about him that oddly seemed to keep some of the men at a distance. He was dressed in worn dockworkers clothes with his sheath knife in his belt. But what else was he doing? Bert appeared reluctant to sit or talk with them even though Jacob waved to him. And Mrs. Noyes must be on another sales run, another tavern, as she was not in sight.

The evening proved less than fruitful, and Bert avoided them. They wandered outside as the sun was setting. The remaining light streaming across the harbor illuminated ships at anchor, small boats hurrying to or from shore, and the outer islands. Eustis, followed by Jacob, strolled to the nearest wharf and out along the weathered pier, passing a large coastal trading ship tied alongside. Raised voices came from the darkness on the ship's deck when they passed. He looked down at the water as it lapped at the pilings. It was dark and deep. How easy it would be to push someone over. Even without a malicious incentive, it would not be

179

difficult. Was that how those drownings happened?

Jacob leaned over and said, "I know what you are thinking about. How easy it would be to push someone over."

Eustis smiled. "You always were a clever one. And I was thinking of the cigar stub I found. Could have lured someone into a conversation right here where we are standing."

A man came down the boarding ramp from the ship, putting something in his waistcoat pocket, perhaps his watch, and nodded as he went past. Silence reigned on the ship's deck.

Looking across the water to the adjoining wharf, Eustis could see other men gathered, standing, and sitting on a few barrels. They had either bottles or mugs with them. Across the water came the sound of singing.

"Active this evening," he commented to Jacob.

"Indeed, this and every night. You are just not here to see it."

"Then someone might well have seen something untoward happening if those men were murdered here on a wharf and then pushed into the harbor."

"It would seem possible. Unless it was in the wee hours of the morning and all were in their beds or asleep. There is usually a crewman on each of the vessels who is awake, although he may be in the cabin." Eustis remembered Sally saying she had slept near the wharf in between boxes.

"Jacob, would you know which vessels were moored here on any given night? We might find those that were nearby and someone who might have seen or heard anything."

"Possible. I can look through my ledgers tomorrow. But I still think that Sommers fellow is not telling all he could."

"I agree. But until we get a break, we are staggering around in the dark."

The Eustis women were well aware of their brothers' inquiries, and, finishing their candle making, speculated about what they could do. In particular, the Sommers household interested them. How could Mrs.

Sommers have managed without any assistance during the past winter, all on her own? Perhaps they could find out more – but someone would have to gain her confidence or, even better, be in her house.

"Would it be possible for me to befriend her?" asked Catherine. "Most women are busy during the daytime. I wonder if she needs help with her boys or their schooling?"

"Interesting idea," said Anne. "I might suggest to her that I am teaching our two youngest girls, and her boys could join them. It would give us a point of entry. And the boys may know much more than we realize."

"Clever girl! Try stopping by on the way to the market. Ask her!"

Eben and Nathaniel were consulted. And when Jacob and Eustis came in, they were told of the newest idea. Although apprehensive, Eustis thought it worth a try.

* * *

"March winds blow or is it the north wind, Cath? It seems brisk enough today," said Prudence to her sister as they hung out quilts. They were starting their enormous annual project of cleaning their house top to bottom, starting with the bed hangings. Later, they would wash all remains of winter smoke and ash from the bedroom walls, renewing whitewash and scrubbing floors. Then they would start on the first floor.

"Mrs. Sommers is hanging her washing too," said Cath, "and it might be a good time to stop by. She is probably starting her spring cleaning also."

Not much later, Anne strolled by the Sommers house. That was hard to do as it was set back from the road on a side alley. But she managed to make it look fairly inobtrusive. "Good day to you, Mrs. Sommers," she called. "I have an idea to suggest to you."

Being neighborly, Mrs. Sommers came to her fence to wish her a good day and ask how she did. Anne explained that she was beginning to teach their two "wards," or at least Sally Edwards and one guest, Annie Lindholm, their reading and sums. She led up to having the Sommers boys join them if their mother wished. Mrs. Sommers said she

181

would consult with her husband, and that it was a very generous offer.

"How long would this be for?" she asked.

Anne said it was indefinite at this point but certainly two or three months at least. "They need to write their names and do basic reading, and the boys need their arithmetic."

She returned home to report that Mrs. Sommers might be a new customer for what was becoming her new dame school. And she must send a message to remind the mother to send chalk and slates with the boys.

At their supper that evening, Jacob reported that he had the names of a number of vessels that had come into the harbor, including that earlier one in which Eustis had been interested, the one flying the quarantine flag from which the man had jumped. And the dates. They would have to spread it all out after their supper and go over it.

As soon as Cath brought out the basin to wash their pewter plates and tableware, the men retired to their other large table and arranged Jacob's ledgers across the top.

"Is there any paper? Ink?" asked Eustis. "We'll need to make lists to cross reference the ships in the harbor with dates." He reached for a quill and his penknife.

Before calling an end to the day, they found several possible ships and dates of interest. Jacob needed one more date, and he thought he could propose a possible scenario. As he said to Eustis, what if Bert Sommers's appearances coincided with the two murders near the wharves? We really have to get him to talk to us.

"And," offered Eustis, "our sister will be helping teach the children in that household. She may have a perspective for us. I think Mrs. Sommers may be involved. There must be some reason for it. We can all confer tomorrow. There will be a great deal to clarify if we are on the right track."

Carrying their clay mugs to the kitchen, they found Sally laboriously working on a sampler, huddled over it as close to a candle as she could get.

"Sally, my dear girl," said Eustis. "Past time for you to be in bed. Did someone not tell you?"

"Yes, sor. Mistress Cath did. But I wanted to get more done to show you."

"Well, your health is the most important to me, so you get along." He gave her a squeeze and a little push toward the back stairs leading from the kitchen.

The house was at last at rest, and Eustis retreated to his own bedroom, the one he had since he was a boy. He had to wonder how it offered such a sense of security for him whereas those who ended up as wanderers likely never experienced that feeling. He thought of Sally and then Elijah, Noah, and Maria. He understood the desire for security – maybe a castle or fort guarding his family. He certainly wanted to protect them all.

CHAPTER 26

"It is hardly likely I will need the constable with me! Pray do not overthink a simple visit, Prudence!"

Eustis finished his coffee and rose to don his coat, pick up his medical bag, and go out. He planned to stop at the Sommers house on the way to several other medical calls, with luck finding Sommers or his wife at home. And later a visit to the Bell in Hand and the proof of his assertions made by that fellow at the tavern. He had said he would bring another man to back up his story on this day.

Turning up the alley and approaching the Sommers house, he noticed that the curtains were all drawn. Were they still abed? He knocked again.

The door opened revealing a sleepy Tommy Sommers rubbing his eyes. "'Mornin', doctor."

"Good day to you, Tommy. I take it that you have had a late night? Perhaps your father is at home? I would like to meet with him."

"He's not here. Left with my mother."

Eustis was startled. "What do you mean, left?"

"Yes, sir." Tommy was waking up. "He went to the harbor with my mother sometime in the night. Mebbe you can find him there."

"Well, do you have any idea where he or they were going?"

"No, sir. We was to stay here and wait for our aunt to come along an' tell us what to do. Like when we came here to Boston."

"What do you mean, when you came to Boston?"

"My mother took us from that house and brought us here to this one."

"When was that?"

"A long time ago. When we came here."

"Listen to me, Tommy. Is your mother or father coming back soon?"

"I dunno. They said to stay here and wait for Aunt Louise. And we got beds here. An' food."

"Was Anne going to come today to teach you? Or were you coming to our house?"

"No, sir. My mother said we would stop."

* * *

Eustis rushed into the family kitchen calling out, "Cath, Prue. The Sommers are not there! They left. But the boys are still there, waiting for an aunt to come for them."

The sisters were clearing away breakfast. Anne, having heard, hurried into the kitchen. "Yes! Mrs. Sommers said the boys would not be in today because they had other things they were doing. I thought it was just for a day, not that they were leaving Boston. What about the boys?"

"It may be that both Sommers are just down at the harbor. I am going there directly, but I wanted you to know."

Then learning that Jacob had left for his office, Eustis hurried back out and to the harbor where he found his brother with a pile of paperwork and several waiting customers. He looked around the area as he approached and did not see anyone of interest.

"Excuse the intrusion please! Jacob, I must speak with you briefly."

Jacob gestured to the waiting men that he would be back shortly. "I'll just step outside with you, brother. What is happening?"

"Have you seen Bert Sommers or his wife? They left their home last night or early this morning. The boys are still there. Is there a ship leaving right now? And where is it?"

Jacob pointed toward the outer harbor where they could see the sails of a trading schooner being lowered and adjusted as it lined up with the channel, moving toward the outer islands.

"Is that it? Are any others leaving?"

"Only one that I know of today," said Jacob.

"How can I catch up to see if the Sommers are on board? Anything fast and light?"

Jacob immediately hailed a passing, swiftly-moving launch rowed by eight men.

"Hello! Can you help? Quickly?"

They slowed and came into the nearest floating dock off the wharf. Jacob and Eustis ran to them, climbing down the ladder. "Please can you

185

help us? We need to catch that schooner just now leaving," Jacob stressed.

"Aw, mate, I'm terribly sorry, but she is too far along for us to get to her in time," said one man beside the bow. "Do you have an emergency? We can send a signal to one of the islands. We have a semaphore station out there and can send a message. Here, come get in."

Jacob, with business underway, elected to stay, but Eustis climbed aboard, and the men rowed rapidly to the harbormaster's office where there was a system of signals to indicate what shipping was entering or leaving the harbor.

"Perhaps you know their destination?" he asked.

The harbormaster could find out. They went into the office and consulted, finding that the ship was off to New York City. An experienced rider with a relay of fast, fresh horses might get there first. Someone like Revere might do it. Realistically, however, it was not possible, and Eustis would have to accept that both Sommers may have left. But were they running away? This would take some unraveling. And he was not even sure that they were on the ship.

* * *

Consulting with Sam over Surry's coffee, Eustis sat at his friend's desk. "This is not making sense, Sam. If they left, in effect running away, it seems to proclaim guilt of some kind. But I am still back to why and what motive anyone would have for murdering or beating those men? Any ideas? This makes it look as though maybe Bert did it."

"How many Sommers children are there, Bill? Just the two boys, or are there more? Because the one thing that would drive a man mad would be if his children were threatened. Do you think those boys are protected?"

"They said their aunt was coming for them. And knew who she was. Said they had a similar experience before. And that doesn't make sense either."

"You know how I like to ask 'what if' questions," Sam countered. "In this case, what would threaten that family?"

186

"I cannot think of anything," Eustis answered. "They had housing, and Mrs. Sommers was able to care for and feed them. But how did she do that if her husband was away all the time? What about money?"

"She probably ran a tab at several markets, the way whaling families do," Sam surmised. "Or someone was helping her. Maybe there was another source of income. Let me ponder here. I know you have several medical calls to make. Come back after that. We may have another idea."

"Hmm. You are right. I probably better go. I do have a tricky surgery I am not looking forward to. They are getting him ready now down at the Bell. He got his arm tangled in the line feeding out during a whale chase, and it has gotten horribly mangled. They wrapped him up and brought him in, but I doubt I can save his arm. Days have gone by, so I hope I can at least save his life. Fortunately, the Bell is being very sympathetic and is loaning their back meeting room."

"Best get on it, Bill, and quickly."

* * *

Toward the end of the afternoon, Dr. Eustis emerged from the tavern feeling quite confident. The amputation actually had gone better than expected. He had managed to make a clean cut above the damage on the arm resulting in two very good and healthy flaps to stitch securely over the wound. Could not wish for more. He paused to savor the accomplishment, then realized he was running out of daylight to check the Sommers house.

To his surprise, his knock was answered by his sister, Anne, who quickly addressed him. "Good afternoon, Dr. Eustis. I am so glad you could find the time to come check on Tommy." She looked at him intently and then crossed her eyes.

He rallied. "As indeed I have. And I apologize for being late. It was due to a difficult surgery. How is he doing?"

Eustis could see into the parlor beyond Anne's shoulder. A woman of about middle age sat on the sofa holding a cup and saucer, probably tea. Her hand trembled. The cup rattled. She appeared impatient, mildly irritated, seemingly suppressing her anger.

Anne continued. "Do come in, and you know the way to Tommy's bedroom. Shall I accompany you?"

"Thank you, but it is not necessary as this is just a quick visit to make sure all is healing properly. Is his mother here?"

There was something like a poof of exasperation from the woman in the parlor.

"I will take over now, Miss Eustis, as I am their guardian," she said, rising.

Anne looked quickly at her brother.

"Not necessary. I will check on him first," he hastily assured Anne. "I would appreciate talking with you as soon as I return, if you can stay that long."

She reluctantly agreed, and he hastened upstairs to the boys' room without appearing to rush.

There he found Eddie, the younger boy, huddled on the bed with his brother. Tommy's lip quivered at the sight of the doctor.

"It is all right now," said Eustis softly as he sat on the edge of the bed. "Perhaps I can help. Tell me what is happening."

Tommy whispered, "We do not want to be taken away by her. She might be bad to us."

"Why would she be bad?" asked Eustis. "Tell me as much as you can."

"She is not our aunty. She might hit us or lock us in the cellar."

The younger boy, Eddie, hiccupped and sniffed, but Tommy earnestly nodded his head.

"Listen to me, boys," said the doctor. "You must stay together here on this bed. I will go talk to the woman and say that you are still sick. We can fix this." He turned to leave to the sound of sobs from the younger boy. "Not now, boys, not now. You must stop crying, be strong, and give me time. I will send Anne to stay with you."

Encountering Anne outside the parlor, he signaled her to go to the boys, then, entering the room, he approached the frowning woman, a small purse in her hand, standing in the middle of the floor. It appeared that she suspected something was going on.

"Good day, mistress. I am afraid I have not had the pleasure of meeting you. I am Dr. William Eustis, and I have been treating Tommy for a grievous wound he received recently. I can relate the good news that it seems to be healing as it should, and in a few more days he will be released from his bedroom and able to practice walking and getting his strength back. And you are?"

"I am their new guardian, and I have come to take them to my residence. I assure you that it is completely respectable, doctor, and I will be supervising Tommy's further recovery."

"Their parents are no longer in residence here, I collect?"

"They have been called away and made arrangements with me. Now I will just go gather a few of their clothes." She started to push past him.

"I beg pardon, madam, but I must see some letter of assurance from their parents before I can accept their leaving the house. Would it help straighten out the arrangement if I called the constable? He may have helpful suggestions."

The woman veered suddenly and went to the door. "I will be back tomorrow with the authorities, doctor, I assure you. Those children are now my responsibility." She angrily strode out the door, slamming it shut behind her.

Eustis put the bar across the door so as not to be surprised and went back up the stairs. Anne was sitting on the bed, an arm around Eddie with Tommy nervously huddling against her. Eustis joined them. "It'll be fine. We will make new plans now. No need to worry anymore." Then, after a slight pause, "Now, let's get serious here. Who is this woman, and is she the Aunt Louise you told me would come get you?"

All their fears tumbled out. Their parents awakened them during the night and, after telling them that someone would come stay with them, said they would return very soon. Their father just had one more thing to do before they would all go away together. But when this strange person knocked on the door, they did not know what to do. Eddie had run for Anne, and Tommy hid, keeping the door locked. She was not let in until Anne arrived.

"We seem to have become a great haven for the homeless," said Eustis, "but we'll take them with us, Anne, and I can alert the watchman."

"I agree," said Anne. She began gathering their clothing for a short stay away. "We should go along quickly."

Eustis inwardly praised his efficient sisters. When he and Anne arrived at the kitchen door with two additional children, the two other sisters immediately agreed to take them in, at least for the night. Cath mentally sifted through where she could find sleeping space, and Prudence considered their supper plans.

"We may need to install them with Norah, just for the night," said Cath. "That is the room with the most floor space at the moment. Let's just hope no more of your dependents or patients need space tonight."

Norah was sitting up in bed when the doctor entered her room. He explained the entire situation to her and suggested she might manage with two more roommates. If the Eustis house had been a public inn, it would have been common practice to move people in together so that everyone had floor space. The same system would have to apply here.

Norah explained it to Annie who soon realized that she had the advantage because it was her mother who had the bed, and she would have a place in it. While the sisters made sure the pile of bedding in Norah's room would work for the boys, Eustis hurried to tell the watchman the most interesting and surprising story of missing parents and deserted children. McAllister concurred with Eustis that something was wrong with whatever the arrangement was and assured him that he would remain alert and be ready to respond whenever Eustis needed him.

The situation still required some clarity, maybe in the morning.

CHAPTER 27

Just the words "spring morning" were enough to cast a spell on the day. Dawn had broken across the harbor, bathing the islands and rippling water with pale pink and peach shades. No fog. No gray. The sisters, inspired, spoke longingly of the time when they could sow their early lettuce in the garden. They hoped for dandelion greens soon.

At breakfast, Eustis talked with Jacob about their present situation and any further information they needed and where they could get it. It seemed a good idea for them to try to spend part of the coming evening sitting or walking near the wharves to see what activity went on after dark. It was highly possible one of the people around the area had seen or knew something that would be useful. The Sommers boys' arrival and the previous night's activities had negated any plans to visit the tavern.

Unless they had rented horses yesterday, or boarded a ship, the Sommers might still be in the area. Eustis still felt they had unfinished business here. And the situation with the boys puzzled him. He planned to go over to their house again to see if anyone was there. If he could get in, he might find a few helpful clues. And who was this Aunt Louise? That stern, rather severe looking woman was certainly not recognized as a relative. Or maybe she was one, but unknown to the boys. Hmm. Doubtful.

Anne was conducting her dame school for four children as well as an adoring Annie. She had arranged two benches in the keeping room and promptly had her new students working on their slates, carefully drawing the alphabet. Cath's youngest was back upstairs in his cradle, and Ben was again tied by his leading strings to the table leg in the kitchen. He could voice opinions from there, which he did. The only one eager to go outside was Aggie, earnestly directing pleading looks at Eustis and walking back and forth to the door.

After letting the dog out, the doctor went to check on Norah. He was pleased with her progress. Although hopeful, it had not been guaranteed.

Now, unwrapping the linen strips from her hand and wrist, he was pleased to see that the infection, although not unexpected, was subsiding. The addition of an herbal poultice with onions under clean wrappings should help it along even more. And two other bandages could come off so that the air could help with the healing. It would still take weeks for her hand to heal. She was strictly instructed to remain in bed for another day.

"But I feel such a burden to your sisters!" Norah objected.

"That you are not," said the doctor. "You are caring for a multitude of children in your room."

* * *

McAllister could give him no news when he stopped at the watchmen's shed, so Eustis went on to the Town House looking for the constable. Had they found Mr. and Mrs. Sommers? If not, was there a plan?

Later, walking back, still steaming mad, he acknowledged that it was unfortunate he had gotten so angry at the constable's noncommittal answers as to suggest that he should call out the Society of Cincinnati members.

"Look what they accomplished just a month ago with the rebellion of Daniel Shays and friends. We have missing parents and deserted children! How hard could that be? What was the constabulary's purpose anyway?"

I have to move on, he thought, and the Sons of Liberty came to his mind as did a possible idea. Self-discipline is necessary, he scolded himself. He would focus on walking to the Adams house without hitting the walls and fences along the way.

Although the senior Adams was out, he was expected soon. Sam Jr. was in his room with a mug of coffee. Surry immediately brought another one as well. Bliss! And although it was tempting to just relax, Eustis told Sam all about his recent experiences, some anger mounting as he told of his visit to the constable.

"Honestly, Sam! I have always believed they had the interest of the families and maintaining the peace in this town foremost in their minds. Yet they have done nothing about this situation to suggest it."

"Did you wait for their reasons?" Sam queried. "And what did you find about this mysterious woman who came to take the children? Mayhap they knew who she was."

"Argh, Sam! I just wanted them to rise up and present answers to the mess, solving everything with a blaze of glory."

"Not likely, my friend. But tell me more about the woman who came to get them. How do you know she is not a relative?"

"Erm. I do not. It is just that those boys were so upset. They did not seem to know her and did not want to go with her."

"I understand. But let us go over this and bring something like order to this chaos. And if it still seems a good idea, we can talk to my father about the Sons investigating. I heard him come in. Would that do for you?"

And so they began, Eustis explaining all that he knew and Sam questioning what he did not understand.

Sam then summed up the circumstances. "It would seem a family arrived in our town with something they wanted to accomplish, and the father went on several sea voyages that took him away for extended periods of time. We are not sure what the family survived on while he was gone, and his wife appeared only mildly disturbed at being left. You know, she must have known what this mysterious plan was all along if she was not frantic, or she was staying steady for her children. The family or the father probably had a reason for all that they were doing."

"But he could not have had a reason or wanted to be pressed into service for the French," Eustis reasoned.

"I agree. Let's try some other suppositions," Sam suggested.

"Hmm. What plan could separate a family like that, unless it was not really a family, and those boys had been picked up along the way to be useful in how the Sommers presented themselves?" Eustis wondered. He rubbed the side of his nose, glancing back at Sam with his finger covering his mouth, considering.

"But Mrs. Sommers was really concerned about those children. If,"

Eustis repeated, "if they did have a plan, what could drive a family to behave this way? Bribery? Money?"

"I know, I know," Sam shrugged his shoulders and put a hand on the small of his back. He coughed, and Eustis could see he was getting tired.

"I think I am almost there, Sam. If I could find out more from the boys, and Norah might be a help there, then see what happens on the waterfront, I may be able to reach some conclusion. I can also try to talk with this new relative who has shown up, at least get her correct name. It must be the Adams sensibility inherited from your honored father, Sam. You do calm me down, and I will go poking around just as you suggested. It is getting close to our dinner hour, and I cannot leave the sisters to handle that alone. Five small children with one injured mother as well as a missing mother."

Eustis passed the senior Adams as he was leaving the house. "Good day, Mr. Adams. I salute your son. He has the astounding ability to get my mind back into focus."

"Greetings of the day to you, Bill. I am glad that Sam is able to help you. He is a good lad." Eustis could see that Adams was moved by the memories of his son's previous abilities. Thoughtfully, he continued on his way back to his home.

All kinds of marvelous aromas were filling the kitchen as he entered. It seemed probable that a chicken was in the Dutch oven. He could see it sitting above a pile of coals at the side of the hearth with another scoop of coals piled on its lid. Anne's school must have let out for the midday repast as there seemed to be small children everywhere.

Saluting his sisters, he went in to see Norah. "How was your morning?"

Before she had a chance to respond, there was a loud, determined knocking at the kitchen door which carried into the bedroom.

Ebenezer was home for his dinner and was holding their youngest, so Cath opened the door to find the woman Eustis had described on their doorstep, the one who was supposed to be the boys' relative. "Good day, mistress. May I be of help to you?"

The woman frowned. "I am here for those two boys taken from me yesterday."

"Do you wish to come in?" asked Cath, setting aside her apron. "I will call my brother, the doctor. May I have your name?"

"I hardly think it is necessary," said the woman, "but if you must, I am Mrs. Gifford, Mrs. Abigail Gifford. I have a reason for being here." She raised her hand, shaking her finger at Catherine. "The children, right now, if you please!" Her eyes bored into Cath. "I insist!"

Fortunately, the doctor arrived at just that minute, moving to support his sister. "Madam, he said, "we are a family, and you are interrupting our midday dinner. It is important that the children get fed. If you could wait in the parlor, we can spend time together later."

The woman sputtered. Being met with what appeared to be a refusal preceded by a delay was not what she expected or desired. Eustis wondered briefly if she would attack him or in the least fling something at him. Luckily, she had no parasol.

"Now, Mrs. Gifford," he said after eating, thankful that he had notified the officials, "the constable and the watchman already know about these additional children. If you will be patient, I can send for one or both of them."

"Indeed! I am shocked. Do you understand? These children are my responsibility. Send for the constable immediately, and I will tell him how you have absconded with my children. I am Mrs. Abigail Gifford, and I expect to be treated with respect."

The children by this time were well aware that something was happening, and it did not sound appealing. They had quietly crept into Norah's room and onto her bed, huddling silently, wide-eyed. Anne went in and quietly closed the door behind her. She and Norah looked at each other with mutual understanding.

Prudence went outside and found a boy eager to earn a penny by running for the constable. He was worth the money, returning with both watchman and constable in a brief fifteen minutes. Meanwhile, Cath had talked Mrs. Gifford into the parlor and had her seated with a cup of tea.

Watchman McAllister and Chief Constable Winters filled the space and brought a sense of order and civility. They stood in front of the parlor fireplace and looked attentively at Mrs. Gifford. They had heard from Eustis about this woman's activity the day before and now wanted to see her for themselves.

"Do you have any letters indicating your right to these boys, mistress?" Winters tersely asked. "Or have you any way of proving who you are?"

As this questioning began, Eustis backed out of the room and went silently into Norah's room. There he gathered Tommy, leading him to peek into the parlor. Spotted by the watchman, Tommy was invited to come into the room to identify the woman in the chair. Clinging to Eustis's hand, he reluctantly advanced.

In a small voice, he said, "That is my mama's friend. She used to live near us in another place." Then he started to sob and turned his face into Eustis's side.

"And how do you answer that, mistress? The boy says you were a friend of his mother, not his aunt? Why the deception?" The constable straightened his shoulders and looked sternly at the woman.

Surprisingly, Mrs. Gifford seemed to back down and become smaller. "I just promised their mother I would look after them."

"This was not a particularly good way to go about it. Perhaps you had better explain. And why did you want to remove them from their home?"

According to her, the boys' mother had abruptly been called away and needed someone to look after her sons, saying she would be back for them soon. She explained that if she posed as a relative, she was sure it would work smoothly. She had no other information but thought the father was involved somehow. Besides it was more convenient for her to remove them to her house.

McAllister suggested that he talk to the boys privately. Followed by Eustis, he went to Norah's room, finding them clinging to her on the bed. He spoke reassuringly and asked what the boys knew, discovering that

Tommy's mother had indeed left quickly and told the boys to wait, that their aunt would come to care for them.

"We will need to find the parents and will alert the wards and the watchmen to keep their eyes open," McAllister promised. "I doubt they have left town, as we have had no ships leaving within the right timing. Unless they went inland."

The constable moved toward the door after McAllister joined him. Turning, he said, "The boys will stay here until all is clear and we have found and talked with their parents. And you, mistress, do not bother this family. You will behave or I will file a complaint and bring you before the magistrate."

McAllister followed Winters out the kitchen door, nodding to Eustis and muttering, "I will keep you informed."

There was a stunned silence. Cath turned and asked, "Will you join us for dinner or do you wish to leave, Mrs. Gifford?" Not waiting for an answer, she moved toward the kitchen, snatching up, then tying her apron back on. As far as she was concerned, normalcy would return with food.

Mrs. Gifford slowly rose to her feet, nodding to the doctor and, finding her manners, said, "Good day. I believe I have something I must do now. Thank you for the tea."

Prudence opened their front door, and she carefully walked out. Prue closed the door behind her, heaving a sigh of relief.

CHAPTER 28

After the children were seated at the kitchen table, served with chicken, carrots, and rice, the adults settled down to their midday repast in the keeping room.

The others were all talking, but Eustis's mind was spinning. Mrs. Sommers really puzzled him. He certainly must talk with Tommy, but how to approach all this? Walking helped when he wanted to talk with Sally. Perhaps it would work here too. He had two medical stops to make and then there was the harbor visit tonight.

Tommy Sommers was happy to walk with the doctor on an errand to the apothecary. He liked that place. It had those very big bottles and jars. Some of the largest bottles were made from dark green glass and were protected in wooden boxes and came off ships. There were all kinds of things in the bottles, and they smelled different, of far away places.

"Now, Tommy, you need to tell me everything," said Eustis as they strolled along the cobbled road. "You know I have always helped you and your family. Now tell me what is happening."

"I dunno, doctor. My mama just said to stay home and wait. I think she was worried about my father. They had a plan, and I heard them talking about it. It had something to do with my big sister."

"What?" Eustis stopped walking. "Tommy! You have a sister?"

"Not now. She died." The boy sighed. "I think those men killed her. Something like that. It made my father get very mad."

"When did she die?"

"It was back when we lived in New York."

Eustis crouched down in front of the boy. "How was it that she died, Tommy? Can you tell me?"

Tommy frowned and paused. "There were some very bad men. Mama said my father would kill them for what they did to Elizabeth. Mama was crying in her bed all the time."

Eustis was shocked. This sounded like a nasty situation, and he was immediately alarmed while trying to reassure the boy. "Can you tell me anything more? Maybe I can help."

"No. Nobody can. My mama was crying so much, and my father looked so mad. And sad too. He just kept walking up and down, hitting on things. He wanted to kill them."

"Well, let's think about something else. Come along, Tommy. We will complete our errands and then I will look for your mother to find out how to help her."

Arriving back home after visiting the apothecary and following a brief visit to a patient, they found Prudence passing out cookies to anyone who wandered into the kitchen, mainly children, and the kettle was boiling. Aggie was lying on the floor, tongue hanging out, obviously happy about being patted by some of the cookie eaters. Eustis grimaced and nodded at Prue saying, "We'll all talk later."

At the end of the afternoon, Jacob, Nathaniel, and Eustis headed down to the wharves and the Bell in Hand tavern. They told the sisters they were not sure how late they would be. Nathaniel was concerned to talk over his developing plans for going south to Virginia and joining his brother, Abraham, in the wine brokerage business.

The air had mellowed during the day. After a brilliant sunset, there were tiny sparkles on the harbor, giving the illusion of black satin sprinkled with diamonds. The waves wallowed under the wharves. Later, the moon's rise would add more illumination.

"Quiet compared to the daytime bustle of activity," said Eustis. "I want to find a place to settle in for an hour or so, watch what happens around here."

"No cider?" questioned Jacob." "Do you not want to find that fellow who was going to bring to the tavern that other cove with that evidence?"

"I will later, but you could go see what is happening there now. If the fellow is there, I will come in, but meanwhile I will stay here." Eustis indicated a substantial coil of heavy rope beside one of the pilings. As the two walked off, he settled down on the rope to observe anything that happened.

There was less activity than he had seen during the other visit. Most men were at home or in the taverns for their suppers. They would probably come later. Bread, brews, and stews, he thought. After a while, he decided to change his position for one less exposed, more in the shadow of one of the warehouses. Walking slowly toward the Bell in Hand, he was startled to see another person in the darkness of the doorway of a building he passed. Wondering if it could be one of the dockworkers, he almost went nearer but thought better of it, walking past without looking directly at the individual. Was it really Mrs. Sommers? What could she be doing? Surely not looking for customers! Several ladies of the evening were making their business arrangements, but they were farther from the tavern.

He continued past, veering to go into the Bell in Hand. So much for lurking. He would check on Jacob and Nathaniel and see if anyone had seen Bert Sommers.

He promptly discovered his brothers settled at a table near the door, tankards in hand, with three other shipbrokers, men with whom Jacob was frequently in friendly competition. It seemed that the man bringing the witness had not arrived yet. At Jacob's hail, Eustis waved and gestured that he would approach the publican behind the long bar in search of his own cider.

Spotting Mistress Noyes in the back of the large busy room, he mentally added her to his list of people who could be helpful.

A low, hoarse voice, oddly familiar, spoke in his ear. "Do not turn around. I have a knife. Come toward the door and go outside. Tell those coves anything, but just come outdoors. You can do that."

Eustis barely resisted the temptation to turn around, smelling the onions and tobacco on the speaker's breath, who then added, "You will do this if you value the life of your sisters." As indeed he would.

Easing his way back toward the door, he realized it would be difficult with Jacob expecting him to come there. "My brother expects me," he muttered.

"Make it short with him if you value your family. Then get outside. I'll be waiting."

Eustis headed for Jacob sensing that his escort had disappeared into the crowd. He wondered if it was Sommers. Nothing for it but to cooperate and go see.

"Jacob," he called out as he approached the table. "I have to duck back outside for a few minutes. Be right back." When he got close enough to put down his mug he whispered to Jacob, "Did you see who was behind me?"

"No. Sorry, brother. Someone I should know?"

"I am not sure. But he is threatening enough that I will go outside to talk to him."

"Shall I come?"

"No. I think it better that you stay here. If I am not back within a short time, about ten minutes, come running."

"Will do. I'll be watching."

Once outside, he could see several small clusters of men, all seemingly congenial. Who was it he must speak with? Again, he was approached from behind and urged to walk out along the nearest large wharf. After a short distance, Eustis stopped and said, "This is far enough. Tell me what this is about or I shall go back."

The man behind him hesitated, then said, "I have a knife, but you can turn."

It was Bert Sommers, large sheath knife in hand. Eustis had been trying to get time with him, but not this way.

"Mr. Sommers, what are you trying to do?" he asked. "I expect you know that threatening a man or his family is not the way to get good results. Can we just talk? What is going on here?"

"It is really bad for us, doctor," said Sommers desperately. "You must get my family out of Boston. Surely you know how to do that. I reckon you know a lot of folks who can get us on a ship." He paused, thought, then added, "And I am going to continue to threaten your family until you do."

"You will need to explain more about this. Are you being sought for a crime? What is happening? And now you want me to help you get away? Have you forgotten your two sons?"

"No, God help me!" The man's face crumpled. "I do this for them, but I did not do some of those other things, doc, you have to believe me. I know it looks bad, but I was out to sea because I had to bring home some money for my family. They promised me money too. I still am truly desperate. I owe so much. The constable is after me. But my wife and the boys cannot survive without some money to pay everything that we owe."

Eustis was taken aback. This was a total change in demeanor.

"But your family is with me, Mr. Sommers, and your boys are frightened. They cry for you. Neither you nor your wife have helped them at all. And where is she, their mother?"

"We had to get away quickly. You have got to help us. They have sent people to threaten me. I have been hiding because they are after me. Please!"

"Yes, yes. I know the constable is looking for you. Surely, he is not threatening you."

"No! You've got it wrong. Not him. It's those others. The ones that want me to do a job for them. I can't tell you or they will kill me."

Finally, Eustis got Bert Sommers to explain, although in a confused fashion, that he and his wife were being threatened by several men who wanted Sommers to attack a man on the wharf. Just as other men had been killed. If Bert hit the targeted man hard enough to knock him out, he could be pushed off the wharf and drowned. No one would know how or why it happened. It was the ideal murder, and Bert was told he could not be blamed because he did not actually kill the man nor have any connection to him. It had worked for them before. Sommers said there was a leader who gave the orders, but he had never seen him. Sommers got messages through dockworkers who were part of a group of some kind. Not many of them. Four or five. Sommers did not know who they were and begged for the doctor's help. And please, he was so sorry to have threatened Eustis, but he did not know what else to do.

"You could have just told me." said Eustis. "And who was that woman you sent to pick up the boys? She said she was a relative."

"What woman?"

Eustis realized this was getting much more complicated than he had ever imagined. Had Bert lost his mind? Was he in some other insane world? He could not be thinking clearly with this behavior.

Eustis's own orderly mind took over, making a list of priorities. First, he had better get his brothers. Then find Mrs. Sommers. Next, get the Sommers family in one room together where they could truly find out what the threat is. And this without alerting anyone who might be watching them. He looked around him. There was a surprising increase in the number of people hovering around the front of the tavern and then down by the waterfront. Someone might well be watching.

"Now listen to me, Mr. Sommers. Listen! Here is what you must do. You will walk quietly, without drawing any attention, up to that pile of barrels. Do you see them? And you will wait for me there. I will go get my brothers and be right back. Do not do anything else. Just wait."

Trying to appear calm when he desperately wanted to run, Eustis walked back to the tavern and got Jacob and Nat. Neither listening to nor joining in any conversation, he just said, "Come now." They quickly followed him out.

When they reached the pile of barrels, Eustis looked all around. Sommers was not there.

"God's teeth! Drat that man."

CHAPTER 29

Mail for the Eustis residence could often be picked up at the Green Dragon. That morning, as part of her shopping, Prudence stopped by the tavern. Letters now waited enticingly on top of the pie safe in the kitchen.

After a glance at Bill coming in the door, Cath immediately pointed at it. "Take a look, brother. You will feel better."

She was right. A letter from Elijah was on top of the several that lay there. He broke the seal and unfolded it quickly. What? It seemed incredible! All three of them were on the outskirts of Boston and intended to go directly to the area of boarding houses that Eustis had recommended to find a good place to live. The adventures were wearing on them, and they had come to the realization that Boston or New Bedford would be more flexible and accepting of them. Boston became the choice. They had even heard that a Black church had gathered, now organized on Beacon Hill.

But when was the letter sent? When would they arrive? Also, a surprise for him was implied. Eustis looked at his sisters who were standing in anticipation, hoping for the news as well. "They are coming to Boston! Elijah and Noah!"

"Oh, bless us," said Cath. "Where will we put them?"

"No, no. Please. Let me finish. They will be moving into a boarding house in the area up at Copp's Hill. How wonderful to see them all again. And they have a surprise for us. What could that be?"

Prudence looked at Cath. They could make a good guess but would say nothing and wait to see. "When do you suppose they will arrive?"

"Could even have been yesterday. They will contact us I am sure," Eustis said, smiling. Having them here would be a huge solace to him as well as a help in clearing up this mess on the waterfront. A second letter, official looking, revealed that the justice of the peace had arrived and Albert Lindholm would be put on trial during the next week for assaulting an officer of the law.

That notice was amended by Chief Constable Samuel Winters to say that Eustis might also like to come to his office within two days to meet a new coroner, recently appointed to make the job of the constables easier.

He looked around, appreciating the aromas of the kitchen, the hanging herbs, the drying apples. Here he was back at home in the middle of a normal day's business.

But last night! He still was constructing it in his mind. Upon finding Bert Sommers missing, and being joined by Nat and Jacob, he had quickly begun a search around the area. Remembering where he had seen Tabitha Sommers, he found her still there, huddled, seated on the stoop of a closed business.

Before she could rise and start to run away, he called out to her as he approached. "Where is Bert? Did he leave?" That gave her pause, and she waited for them. Eustis suggested they find a place to sit, indicating a collection of benches and barrels.

"Mrs. Sommers," he began, "I talked to Bert and he told me some of the difficulties you are in. I was expecting to meet with him just after I went for my brothers in the tavern, but he has gone. Did he come here?"

"Oh, no! God help me! They have gotten him. I know it! Please help me. I have to go to him."

"But where has he gone?"

Saying "We have to find him," she rose to start toward the waterfront, running toward the wharves, calling over her shoulder. "Where did you see him?"

"Stop," Eustis called out. "Listen to what I am trying to tell you. He is missing. Do you know where he could have gone?"

"Oh God, oh dear lord, help me! There is only one place where we would meet, but he has never been missing."

And she breathlessly told him about being chased by several questionable men who still were after Bert to do a job for them. She suspected that it was a murder, and they were threatening to tell the constable that he had committed other murders if he did not cooperate.

And no one would believe them. This is why they had to escape. But they needed help because of the additional threat to their boys, so Bert was hoping to find passage on a ship for all of them.

Eustis told her he wanted to understand better what she and Bert had been doing and why they were in such trouble. Tabitha quickly told her story revealing that Bert Sommers had been under the control of a small gang in New York during the British occupation but had escaped. Now they had been found, so Bert was trying to get enough money to get away again. His wife supported his efforts. She also knew that it all began after their daughter had been attacked on the street outside their boarding house in New York City. She thought it likely her daughter had been killed because she had refused sexual favors, or it could have been to get Bert to do work for these people. And now they wanted him to do a job for them saying they would reward him later. But it did not make sense.

And why had they left the boys? wondered Eustis. There is more to this.

For now, Bert would be hiding if he saw the men he was trying to avoid. They needed to search thoroughly. Jacob said he would look around the areas behind the tavern. Eustis and Nathaniel would take the dock area. Mrs. Sommers was to check spots where she and Bert had hidden before. And they were all to meet at the back door of the tavern in an hour.

It was Jacob who found him – even though he had not met the man. A crouched figure hiding under an old sail thrown over several large bins looked about right, so he had approached. "Bert?"

Once together again, it seemed imperative to get everyone to safety. For Eustis, any further talk with Mrs. Noyes would have to wait. The five hurried, keeping to shadows, back to the Eustis home and into the barn in the rear.

"We have no room in our house, but we can make you comfortable here for the night," Eustis explained. "I doubt you will be discovered. We can bring you blankets and quilts, and the cows will lend heat. The boys are inside."

As Bert and his wife, Tabitha, turned to go into the house, he stopped them. "Wait. Before you go to your children, you must tell me more of this scheme."

The story was surprising and somehow still did not explain it all. It seemed a new group had come to Boston with information from the gang in New York. According to Bert, this gang knew him and had tried to get him to join a small number of people presenting themselves as ardent patriots. They had a patron who decided how everything should be done. Bert had been told that they wanted to improve the way the states were governed and thought they could do much better without being controlled by an unnecessary central government. Paying taxes seemed wrong if they lived in freedom, and they admired the efforts of the farmers closing the courthouses in Springfield. Thomas Jefferson was right about states' rights, but this group went further in their thinking. They wanted the states to govern themselves without any central supervision. Everyone, separate but equal. True liberty.

And it had to start with removing those people who were backing a strong central government, the ones called Federalists, particularly here in Massachusetts. People like John Hancock, John Adams, Elbridge Gerry, and Benjamin Lincoln. Even General Washington was one of them. They had the wrong ideas of building the new government. Something had to be done to remove them and then it would be redone better.

If anyone happened to die of natural causes or fell into the harbor, it could all be handled. And it had been decided that Bert Sommers was well placed to handle some of these necessary accidents. That Daniel Shays and the farmers' rebellion had not worked did not disturb them. They knew they would be more effective – with fewer leaders but not as a rioting mob. A more controlled takeover.

The revelations continued, including use of the small barn by the White Horse tavern for printing posters. Eustis remembered seeing about a half dozen men walking by the tavern one evening. Were those the men? He and Nathaniel had tried to look in the window, but it was too high. Bert had assured them they would not have seen anything – just a printing press. That was the source of the broadsides urging citizens to rebel. Although Eustis had heard about these broadsides, he had ignored them. Hardly seemed worth his attention when he had heard no particular alarm about them.

Now they were talking murder. He must find out more about this radical group and who controlled it. Was it all the same group or several? He wondered what else Bert could reveal. He noticed Mrs. Sommers was becoming restless and needed to see her boys. He asked quickly, "Who were the two men killed in the harbor? Do you know anything about that?"

"Ah, yes," said Bert. Reluctantly, he mumbled the story of trying to rescue one of them, an exhausted swimmer, a man unknown to him, from the harbor. It was between his two voyages when he was heading out to board the coastal schooner, having signed on to the crew. He had flung out his scarf to a struggling man they had discovered drowning in the harbor. He had grabbed the scarf but sank again before they could pull him in. Bert thought perhaps the swimmer had come off a ship, but it could have been a pier. They rowed around in their boat searching, but the man never returned to the surface. Presuming he had drowned, they continued on to the schooner which promptly sailed out of the harbor at dawn. He never found out about that swimmer – if he had made it or not. Did Dr. Eustis know anything?

"Alas, Mr. Sommers, if he is the one I think he is, he did not. A body was pulled out from under a wharf by a watchman. I am still without a sure identification, but I thought he might be trying to get ashore from a ship just arrived in the harbor."

Jacob went into the house and warned the sisters about additional guests. "Oh, God help him," sighed Prudence. "Bill will have to take on a place of his own just to house the people he brings home."

"How are we ever to feed everyone? We'll run out of food by April. And where will they sleep?" Catherine wailed. Aggie watched expectantly, tongue hanging out, as Prue and Anne looked at each other and said "potatoes!" and headed to the cellar door. Something good always came Aggie's way when they were cooking.

* * *

But now it was another bright, clear morning, all those hopeful spring signs, and the brewed coffee smelled enticing. Eustis sat in the kitchen with his newspaper and relaxed for the peaceful few minutes he had left. Wasn't there some quotation, French? – about *apres moi le deluge?* Something like that.

When the entire household awoke, they would have their own version of a deluge. And appropriately enough, he had just received a request to investigate a suspected case of smallpox. He would have to set aside time to organize more inoculations.

This meandering of his mind over coffee had to end. He must turn to the business at hand, figuring out what was going on with this unknown group of "patriots" and with the Sommers family.

CHAPTER 30

Mistress Joyful Noyes sat in her favorite chair, her tea beside her, and frowned. She had not been sleeping well at all, especially during the hours before dawn after she started thinking. And she knew why. She knew too much and would have to do something. It involved talking to that charming, young Dr. Eustis again. He was trying to come up with answers to the questions the constable found too bothersome. But she knew it could not be let go. If this recent business was ignored, it would encourage others to go against the law and do whatever they wanted.

Her eyes roamed about the room. She liked where she lived, her two rooms; one for a private bedroom with a corner in which to store and sort her sundries, and the other her living, dining, and cooking area. Perfect! Both were also on the first floor of the boarding house. The necessary was out back. Could not be better as far as she was concerned. Stairs were difficult, but she could still deal with them. She just preferred to avoid them.

But it was these other things she had found out or seen that really worried her. If anyone realized what she knew – or even that she knew anything – her life could be in danger. It was not that she knew who was taking advantage of the ladies of the evening or that a wife was making money on the side when her husband was out at work fishing. She did know. Being an older woman, she was generally ignored when she was not actively selling her sundries, and she consequently overheard or saw much more than anyone suspected.

This was the reality of life in an active seaport. Her role as the cheerful salesperson enabled her to sell articles, but it might end up not being a good thing. Even the possibility that she had confidential information could endanger all those other people she cared for. If any of her customers suspected the danger, they would run for the harbor islands or any place far away and unreachable.

She shifted in her chair and rubbed the back of her neck. Who would help her? But she had to get herself together, consider her laundry, and think no longer of this. 'Twas high time to get going around the coffee houses with her basket. Perhaps she should restock her collection of pins before going out. She heaved herself up and began to consider her supplies.

A noise in the hallway outside the door startled her. She froze but then relaxed. Only someone going to the stairs. Usually they were noisy coming down but not when going up. The noise came again, and she eased back into her living area to check if her door was bolted. It seemed foolish, but better safe than sorry as they said. And her precaution was justified. Hurrying across to her door, she slid the lock in place, cursing herself for being too careless, then resumed packing her basket before beginning her rounds.

If I act strangely, she said to herself, someone will think something is wrong. Walking along the road, Mrs. Noyes tightened her grasp on her basket, sternly put her worries aside, greeted others, and smiled to appear as cheerful as she was expected to be.

Before entering the White Horse, usually her first and last stops, she sat on the bench beside the door, greeting those who entered but watching the barn at the end of the short dirt lane. It appeared occupied as she could see the light of several lanterns from its high window. She watched as a woman carrying a basket quietly, stealthily passed along the other side of the lane and approached the barn to be admitted quickly.

Huh. Another recruit, she surmised, before rising and entering the tavern. Open all day, it was serving morning coffee and beer.

* * *

As it happened, the watchman John McAllister was thinking about the disquietude in the neighborhood when he opened up his small shed. He pulled out his stool and sat just outside his door. He enjoyed the sunshine on a fine morning such as this, but he saw clouds gathering, and as a knowledgeable New Englander, he thought how the weather, as usual, was not predictable. Certainly not in March.

God rot it! He wanted to restore the area to its quiet, normal behavior

211

instead of this evil business of violence and drownings. And murders. The doctor was right in trying to talk with anyone who might know something despite the chief constable's lack of interest. Of course, he could put that down to Enoch Cobb's injuries and Sam Winters's need to attend to his own neighborhoods. Covering for Cobb was doubling his work. There had to be answers. But what to do?

The watchman despaired of a solution. In his experience, someone likely knew something but was too afraid to talk to anyone about it. A conversation would have to be private and confidential, mayhap hidden or possibly very public with plenty of business going on around them so no one would notice or hear. A loaded wagon rolled past drawn by two hefty, chestnut horses with large, tufted hooves headed to a wharf. He nodded to the driver, got up, and decided to walk his rounds.

Keeping track of activity as he went along, he also made a mental list of people he probably should check on, including Dr. Eustis, the Sommers family, and several other friends down along the wharves.

* * *

Sam Adams Jr. sat in his window, having seen his father off to the Town House to perform his duties as the new lieutenant governor, joining recently reelected Governor John Hancock. He gazed out, taking note of Mrs. Noyes and her pursed lips as she rolled by. An experienced observer, Sam knew she was thinking of something, trying to solve some puzzle. But what could worry her?

Not much later the watchman McAllister passed, looking almost as determined.

How amusing! Two puzzled people going by within minutes. It reminded Sam of the problems he and Bill had been worrying over. If someone noticed me walk by, they would see the same expression, he mused as he chewed his lip. Bill was right. They had to get this town back to its busy and peaceful self. There were too many secrets. With his father's new duties, Sam did not want to distract him by asking for help. Meanwhile, he could do nothing but sit and watch the world march by.

But what did they need to know? If Bill came by later in the day, they could go over everything including whatever new tidbits he had discovered. By God, he hoped there was new information! The question they should consider, thought Sam, was *cui bono*. Who benefits from these murders in the harbor? And what gain did the murderer want to hide that these two dead men could expose? Was it information or money? They must have known something.

Usually, much of what people in Boston were talking about was in the *Boston Gazette*. Another paper, the *Centennial,* was better for its advertisements. The editors for both papers printed what was happening. If it was not in the paper, it was not a public issue. And the papers had been silent.

There must be some private benefit to these murders, the motives behind them. Who benefitted? Money and a guaranteed decent life, shelter, food. Those seemed to be the main things in life. It was all what his father worked for – but his father had also embraced the big picture. The way of life, the general welfare, the government. Could that be it? Our government?

Yet it was known that people were planning to gather in Philadelphia in May for that economic conference, the one which was now going to review their Articles of Confederation. Delegates would be charged with making their federal laws function better for all the states. Huh! Could it be something needs changing in their government?

That is crossing the Rubicon, he said to himself. You could go beyond the point of no return with that kind of thinking and get into totally new laws and major changes. He chuckled to himself and turned back to his window. It has to be simpler than that. At least he hoped so.

* * *

Set back from Sudbury Street in the small Eustis barn, Mrs. Sommers sang to Hazel and Hattie as she milked them, feeling she could at least contribute this chore to the household. A calico cat wandered in hoping for a sample. Bert Sommers shooed it away. "Bring me a mouse or a rat and I will think about it," he said. Ever hopeful, the cat retreated to a rafter to watch.

"What do you think?" he asked his wife. They had been discussing their options since waking up before dawn. They had not come up with many. It came down to Bert going to a watchman and turning in the men who had been harassing him. He told Tabitha that she and their children prevented him from taking that chance because it would put them in grave danger if he failed. His wife promptly reminded him that he had managed to leave them and go to sea without a lot of worry.

"This new idea of protecting your family is absurd, Bert Sommers. Tell me and I will go tell the watchman."

Bert would have described his situation to close friends at the tavern as being over his head in deep shite. He clearly had made a mess of everything, and his wife was not being sympathetic. She had her own ideas and was tired of helping him. He sat on a small barrel and held his head. At least their sons would be occupied with Anne Eustis learning the alphabet.

* * *

The young woman gripped the arms of her chair. Taking up his scalpel, Dr. Eustis carefully cut into her arm so that he might insert a thread saturated with smallpox effluvia. Withdrawing it, he wrapped the wound with a strip of linen to keep it clean.

"I will be back to check on you tomorrow, Hannah, and by then we hope you are showing some signs of infection," Eustis advised. "You know it will not be as bad as the disease itself, being a second level, but you certainly will not feel well at all."

Looking worried, her husband hovered anxiously nearby, his arm bandaged as well.

Dr. Eustis gathered up his scalpel and his quills carrying the infected threads and thrust them into his medical bag. Standing by the door, he was already thinking of the next stop on his list. "I wish you all a good day," he said as he went out.

Driven by a sense of urgency, he hurried to his next stop, the home of the sister of the woman he had just treated. She and her husband had also been purged with the milk diet, and now both were ready for their inoculations. Then he would hurry along to see Sam. He had so much to report, especially about the night on the wharf and the recent information from Bert Sommers.

He hoped to see Mrs. Noyes too. And he needed to get the Sommers family to resolve to talk to the constable or at least Mr. McAllister. Hmm. Maybe if he went with them to see the constable. He also must collect some of his own unpaid fees to contribute to the rapidly diminishing household funds. All those people! He could not quit, sit, and hold his head as he wanted. Well, they would eat more lobster, more oysters. They were simple enough and cost less than anything else. Aha! There was the door to the Gibson family's house and his next stop. He went up the two steps and knocked.

* * *

Prudence, with Sally as company, hurried to the market that morning and brought home the least expensive seafood she could find for all the mouths they now had at their table; lobsters, oysters, and clams. Some called the crawling things big bugs or spiders and would not eat them at all. But with the milk from the cows, potatoes and onions from their garden, possibly some fish, they could feed a crowd. Everyone usually was happy to indulge in a seafood chowder with bits of toasted bread topping it. Those large reddish-green crab-like creatures were indeed a huge nuisance because it took so long to get the meat out, and Prudence was somewhat ashamed because it was a meal usually eaten only by poor people. The lobsters could be easily found along the beaches or for just a few pence in the market. Cath told her to be sensible and if she could make a better suggestion with the money they had, please do. Their brothers would not be able to feed all these people for long.

Prue suggested that Cath had forgotten to factor in Bill's growing practice, beginning to treat clients and could bring in coins. Cath reminded her that their brother's fees were often paid late and in produce. But better than nothing.

"Does not help us today," said Cath. And that was it. They got busy peeling potatoes.

* * *

The sun was dipping lower in the sky when Harry Tolliver and several men arrived, quietly coming up the dirt lane by the White Horse tavern, two pushing a barrow filled with paper bundles. A very close look suggested they might be covering something else as well.

Once inside the small barn, they stacked their paper near their printing press and prepared to set the type for the next illustrated poster. The writer's theme was how much the country needed right-thinking people to reevaluate how governing the citizens should work. Should there be prisons or should rulebreakers just be evicted? Forced to leave the country. Perhaps allowed only one violation; then on the second, sent away over the borders into the Spanish lands to the south or north to the French in Quebec. They could also round up slackers who would not work. And check out newcomers, evicting those who did not possess the skills they knew were most needed. Or any that looked odd or dangerous.

The men in the barn read the new poster and murmured their approval. Maybe this would also help them gain a few more volunteers. Several men had considered public speaking and marches to advance their cause, but others thought they should wait until there were more people in their favor. Around the harbor, their numbers were growing steadily.

Tolliver, their motivator, prompted the men to call themselves the Freedom Thinkers. The group was also discussing the need for a flag of some kind that could be carried like the Sons of Liberty carried their red and white striped flag. Once they had increased their following, they might have just white stars circling a slogan "No Laws" or maybe "The People Rule." They would be the new Men of Liberty.

Right now, they had to stay focused on their printing while there was sufficient happening at the tavern to deflect attention. Usually there was enough local activity to cover comings and goings as well as any odd sounds from the barn that might otherwise be hard to explain. They had to work secretly until they were ready to proclaim their existence and exhibit their plans for a new world.

Tolliver leaned lazily against a post and, looking away from the press, motioned one of the men over to him.

"Just checking, Jack. Have you got enough boys to distribute this next round? It should be ready in the morning after the ink dries. You will want to get it out promptly."

"In place, Mr. Harry, sir. They will meet me here tomorrow evening at half past eight. It should be nice 'n dark by then."

"And the men should be given a packet each to take to their neighborhoods," Tolliver added.

The man called Jack gave his leader a mock salute and turned back to continue talking with the man preparing the press.

CHAPTER 31

With his practice growing, mornings for Dr. Eustis had become strictly business. If he paid sufficient attention to his calls, he could still benefit from discussing his problems with Sam during the afternoons. He planned to reverse the process this morning, however, and strode along thinking that talking things through might make sense.

Despite being in a fine fettle himself, his sisters appeared annoyed, although Eustis was not sure why. He thought they had no reason to be upset, although he was glad to be out of the house. Leave them to settle their concerns among themselves.

Sweeping his hat off to Surry when she answered the Adamses' door, he proceeded up the stairs to Sam's room, finding him watching the middling crowd coming back from scavenging the morning's market, one seen to be lucky enough to have secured a very large haddock. Turning to greet Eustis, Sam asked, "Come 'n see, Bill. Do you know that young man? See? The blond fellow carrying the ream or so of paper. He is one of Abbott Toliver's sons, Winfield. I usually see him coming through here with an armful of paperwork. Wonder where it all goes."

Eustis rubbed Sam's shoulder in greeting, and said, "I leave that to you. Meanwhile, I have several new ideas to work through."

He sat on the stool at Sam's desk and told of all he had gleaned from Bert Sommers and their adventures near the Bell in Hand.

"Seems to me you have some answers except for the big one," said Sam. "Why? What is the gain here, or is it all about revenge and nothing else? I realize there are some men threatening Bert to get him to do a job for them – possibly murder, although I do not think that is clear. What is behind all this? *Cui bono*, my friend. And have we uncovered any identities yet?"

"Yes. You are right about gain, Sam. Who benefits from these murders? I cannot see a personal gain for Bert except that he would be done with the threats, and that may be enough. Bert says those pursuing him wanted a person killed. What is behind that?

"And threatening Bert to get it done. I better try to get more from Bert. It got personal when the talk leaned to the death of his daughter a few years ago, but I have to say I am not sure how it is all connected, if it is. Could he be the murderer we seek? I might have a better chance if I got him alone." He sighed. "I appreciate talking it over with you. Helps my mind figure it out."

Sam mentioned how he had seen both Joyful Noyes and John McAllister looking very distracted on their way toward the market or possibly to Faneuil Hall. Eustis stayed another half hour while they considered different scenarios. Then he excused himself to go back to see if the watchman had discovered anything. "I'll go to the White Horse later this day. Might be something there too. Farewell and a good day to you, my friend."

McAllister was back at his post and happy to chat but did not seem to have found anything new to add to Eustis's information. He did say that Albert Lindholm would come before the judge within the next week. But he was sure there would be an official notice of the court date, and he would check to make sure the doctor knew. He had heard that Lindholm was being a difficult prisoner and had to be restrained much of the time.

After one medical stop, Eustis arrived in time for his midday dinner. The house was in its usual busy state with fish chowder ready. Later, the women would suspend the leftovers of their creation in a lidded pot down the well to keep cool until the next day.

The doctor checked on his patient. Norah was sitting up in bed, working at her knitting. Her wrist was getting better, not as painful but still needing to be wrapped securely. Seeing the doctor, she immediately asked if she could be released from bedrest. After demonstrating her ability to walk unaided, and after making sure her bandages were secure on her arm and wrist, Eustis relented and shooed her off to join the other women, to their mutual delight. He knew that her next issue within a week or so would be where she and Annie were to live. And he had no ideas.

The sound of voices and a knock at the door brought the exceedingly joyful sight of their old friends Elijah, Noah, and Maria recently arrived in Boston. The trio entered, bringing the news of their new rooms in the Copp's Hill area. They had looked just where Eustis had suggested with great success. Three rooms! This luxury allowed them two small bedrooms with the third room to use for cooking, leisure, and various tasks.

Norah's daughter, Annie, was introduced all around along with carefully-worded explanations about Norah's situation. Word of the injuries done to his oldest friend generated silent, seething anger within a stunned Elijah. The memories of their years together flooded over him. He had no thought that he would even see Norah in Boston. Nor was he aware of her condition. Overwhelmed, all of his old feelings surfaced. He had trouble being attentive to the conversation around him and yearned for a chance to actually talk privately with her.

Aware of the mild tensions brewing, Noah and Maria invited everyone to come inspect their new dwelling as soon as they could. Furthermore, they had located a space that could well be their apothecary shop. They wanted the doctor's opinion before making a deposit.

"I would be more than happy to be of assistance," said Eustis. "Let us all adjourn to the White Horse tavern to celebrate, and we can see your new living space at the same time."

Anticipating an exhausting walk, Norah chose to stay behind to mind the babies and small children. Elijah said he would catch up with them later. Eustis went to Norah's room, got permission, and brought in Elijah. He then left them staring at each other.

The rest walked in clusters to see the new boarding house, rather alarming the landlady and several of the other inhabitants. After assurances that this would not be a usual occurrence, the relieved landlady welcomed them in.

The following visit to the White Horse was equally satisfying. Tables were secured and pushed together, cider and ale brought, and everyone huddled close to hear every word. It was not long before Elijah joined them and asked for details about Norah and what had happened.

At that point, Mrs. Noyes entered the room and, leaving the explanation to the others, Eustis excused himself to go talk with her. "A good evening to you, Mistress Noyes!"

"Ah, doctor. How nice to see you here. I have been wanting to talk with you. May we sit?"

Both went to a table, and Eustis called for a mug of ale for Mrs. Noyes.

"Now," he said, "please tell me all that you know. I can see that you are about to burst."

"As I am, doctor. I have become increasingly anxious about the activity at that small barn down the alley. I have seen signs of secrecy in their entrances and exits, and I am worried. It does not make sense to me or why a Tolliver lad is involved. And yesterday, as I was sitting outside, a woman entered carrying a basket. She did not come out with it."

"There are no laws against people gathering together, as you know," Eustis observed. "It may be just about arranging storage for the winter. I do think it odd that the barn was locked, but whatever is it that has you alarmed?"

"Seems too secret to me," Mrs. Noyes frowned. "Why are those men and now a woman so interested in keeping something out of sight? They must have some suspicious plan or project. I just do not like it, doctor! What are they hiding? I remember that my boys, when they were about ten years old or so, would not meet my eyes and would keep their hands hidden in pockets or behind their backs. Then I would know they were up to no good, and I was right."

"I have heard only of paper being transported and that it was storage for a printer," Eustis offered.

"Except that is not much to store. And they carry those packages out again," she countered. "I tell you someone needs to get a look inside."

Then, lowering her voice even more, she leaned forward. "And you should look into the Tolliver family, up there on Beacon Hill. Something is going on there. I have seen both sons around that barn, and I have heard of other nasty practices."

221

"You surprise me, Mrs. Noyes! But I should remember that you are everywhere and people talk to you. I'll ask Mr. McAllister his thoughts about the barn, and I will think about the other, perhaps discuss it with another." replied Eustis. "But I should join my family now. We are celebrating the arrival of friends who have traveled as far as Ohio and back. And I hope to talk with you again soon, in a more private place."

"Bless me! Please keep everything to yourself, sir, and you do need to join them. I am sorry to interrupt such well-deserved festivities. But you will see the watchman?"

"Indeed, I will."

Eustis went back to his cider and discovered that the secret the women said they of course suspected had been disclosed. Maria and Noah were expecting an addition to their family in about six months, a late summer baby. There were more hugs and congratulations. Such good news! The celebration went on for another hour until Elijah thought he should go back and keep Norah company. That caused the group to move toward home.

Following the family, Eustis wandered back toward Sudbury Street thinking about a slice of cheese with some bread before calling it a day and retiring to his room to go over his medical notes and think through or outline what he could about his present puzzle. Also, the attention Elijah was paying to Norah both delighted and alarmed him.

And what was Mrs. Noyes's additional concern about Abbott Tolliver's family? He knew they were involved in a great many business ventures around the town. Both the sons as well as the father. They were businessmen focused on making as much money as possible, much like others in Boston. Was it investments and shipping? He could think of other families equally involved in such businesses, starting with Captain Augustus Bonham, and of course, Governor Hancock. But then the governor had inherited his money. Many of the others had not.

As he thought about it, where had Tolliver gotten his money? Perhaps there were business schemes that were unknown to the average Bostonian. Foreign investments? Would people speculate on cargo shipments? What kind of cargo? There was still much more he did not know about the shipping trade, or other business practices for that matter. And he needed more time with Mrs. Noyes. He realized that she knew much more about what was going on around the town.

CHAPTER 32

As Eustis was thinking about him, Abbott Toliver was thinking over his own plans. A shrewd businessman, he was not above sly maneuvers or enlisting others to invest in his schemes. Monetary success was everything to him. He was not worried about ethics or legality as long as he could see a profit coming his way. Although he had no regrets about what might have been called his cruel ventures, the slave trade for instance, he stopped at outright murder. He had some standards and would not openly break the law. Something accidental was one thing, but outright murder, that was not for him.

Tolliver suspected his sons did not regard any of this behavior as out of bounds. They seemed to be developing contacts in many businesses but so far had been careful not to have anything questionable become public or embarrassing to their father. And they had been urging him to continue with his transportation of captured slaves or, if he was not interested, they would take it over. Although it was illegal in Massachusetts, it was not elsewhere.

Slavery was actively practiced in the South. For southerners, it was just business and necessary to keep the large plantations in operation. The estates operated as agricultural businesses, and a substantial number of people were essential to run them. None of the southern states would willingly give up their best livelihood. For them, enslaved workers were necessary. How else, they asked, would they grow their huge crops of indigo, rice, and tobacco? Production equaled income to maintain their style of living.

Tolliver sat in his library, decorated in the latest European style with decor and books imported by the lot from England. At heart a Loyalist, he had rather hoped they would win the recent conflict and end this stupid effort for "liberty," although he always supported it verbally. His home was here in the colonies, although he had a plantation in the Caribbean as did others in the town, and he had set up his businesses to his benefit in the more remote areas. And after all, he thought, others including his neighbor Hancock smuggled goods too.

The skill was in knowing where the lines were drawn. Questionable activities needed to be covered carefully. These latest plans of his sons had him worried. He was not sure who their contacts were or what they had promised. He probably should look into them. But he was pleased with his own achievements. He had respect and the admiration of the commonwealth. That was important to a man.

At his evening meal with both sons, after the cloth had been cleared and the port was served, the three lit their imported cigars and settled in to talk business. Harrison had some complaints, and each son hoped for his father's support against his brother.

"Do you remember that ship, the *Annie B*?" Harry asked his father. "We picked her up off Long Island. It was blown on shore in that winter storm. You remember? We still have some of the cargo and have got to get it out of here."

"Yes, that was a sorry disaster," his father acknowledged. "I think that the Bonham son was on her. Are those the people you have been keeping in that barn?"

"Well, yes. Many had died due to that nor'easter that tossed the ship around so much. They got tangled in their chains in the hold and unfortunately drowned. Lucky that they were not all damaged however. We were able to sort out the stronger ones and are getting them healthy again. More food makes a difference, as I am sure you will agree."

Winfield interrupted. "But slavery is against the law here now. The real issue, father, is if anyone has seen us. We want to make sure no one knows."

"Is there someone you know of?" asked Harry.

"No, but I feel nervous," said Winfield. "That doctor keeps going around and trying to identify who the dead men are. He is becoming a problem. And the man we had for the earlier jobs is refusing this time."

"Well, surely you can take care of that. Find someone else," reasoned Harry. "That doctor would not be missed for long. After all, is he not the weak one who has been recovering for the past three years or so? The only problem there is old Sam Adams. He still knows too much about everything. Maybe he should disappear."

Their father interrupted. "Now boys. Let us not sink to a ridiculous level where people disappear. That is not the Tolliver way. We can be smarter than that."

Quickly changing the subject, Harry smiled proudly. "Well, sir, I have a growing business in Charlestown. The Three Cranes tavern. More than Winfield has done."

"I have not heard about that. Is it a new venture?" asked their father. "I thought the Three Cranes was destroyed by the fire in Charlestown ten or so years ago during the battle there on Breed's Hill."

"No concern to you, father. I put money into its redevelopment some time ago. The tavern has been rebuilt into an excellent establishment featuring Mrs. Southfield and her ladies. Because I am an investor, I get special rates." Harry smiled again.

"That is beyond the pale, Harry. Surely you do not actually frequent it," chided his father. "What if you are seen over there?"

Winfield motioned to caution his brother. "Let's change the subject, father. Let Harry have his fun. Back to our problems here. We cannot threaten the senior Adams. That is absurd. Do not even think of it, Harry. He is the lieutenant governor and well-connected in the town. Think of his Sons of Liberty."

"How are we coming on recruiting our investors?" asked the senior Tolliver. "Money in yet for that project? That incoming ship is scheduled to disappear soon or sink. A news report should arrive just before delivery of cargo, I collect? Our profits will come from investors, insurance, and private sales. Have you got those instructions out, Harry?"

"Yes, sir. That captain is wholly reliable."

"Investors?"

"Getting them in," said Winfield. "I think it should go as smoothly as the others. But I am still concerned about getting that other stored cargo from the barn back aboard another ship. It may not have been wise to bring them ashore."

"Easiest way to fatten them up," said Harry. "And we have the excuse of printing posters in that barn. It can cover a lot of things."

"What did I hear about Eleanor stopping by, Harry?" asked Winfield.

"Not a problem. She was just interested in the idea of the broadsides, the protesting. I do not think she is suspicious. She brought us cookies and a cake."

"Well, you know what you will have to do if she begins asking questions," said Winfield. "Yes, yes," said Harry. "I understand. Either she disappears or gets seriously injured so

she cannot talk. I will watch for that. And I will not let her in the barn again. She is a very pleasant woman. I think she is just in love with me," said Harry, grinning.

"Balderdash, ignorant little bog-rat! You, my boy, had best keep alert," the senior Tolliver warned him, growing alarmed at the callousness.

"Father, do you hear what he has been saying?" asked Winfield. "He does not respect me and keeps trying to take the credit."

Their father sighed. He then talked at length of their ambitions and what they were trying to achieve. "We can build a huge operation here, and no one will cross us once we get big enough. You both should understand this. I thought we or rather you could at least handle some of the tasks without spreading trouble. That way we have total control within the family, make more on our investments, and no one is the wiser."

Trying to instruct his sons on their proximity to crossing a dangerous line, Abbott continued urging them to be careful. They must stay within the law. It was getting too dangerous if they mutually became competitive or took risks. He insisted they must not just do what they wished nor freely murder anyone who got in their way. Sinking that low was far too dangerous. Inwardly, he worried greatly that he had unleashed a duo that would not or could not be controlled. Besides, recalling when he was young, he had done just what he was cautioning them against.

* * *

Evening in the Eustis household provided much entertainment as they all continued to discuss, plan, and play. Cards, books, and games. Eustis was able to reminisce with Elijah about the news of the Hudson Highlands area where they had lived for those long war years and the people they had known. He reminded Eli that he still had the coffee mug he had bought from Mrs. Tobey, the trader at Robinson House. Eli said his grandmother, Mrs. Eldredge, was doing well and still caring for those in the original settlement, now growing into a small village as several of the families elected to remain and new ones arrived. They were even talking about adopting an actual name for their settlement. After all, the place where the ferry tied up had a name, and was now called Garrison.

Eustis said he would like to look at the small building the young people were thinking of turning into an apothecary shop. Morning would be a good time. He also cautioned them about being sensible with their expenses.

"You sound just like Gran," observed Elijah.

Talk later turned to Norah's future. They had received notice that her husband's appearance before the judge would occur within days.

"You know she is still legally bound to Albert," pointed out Nathaniel. "She cannot divorce or leave him without special dispensation from the governor's council or the legislature."

Indeed, Elijah did know all that. But his grandmother had suggested some time ago that he could move and live with her in the state of New York, and he could not get it out of his head. Of course, that was before they knew as much as they do now. Elijah admitted that he and Norah had even talked briefly about leaving but would wait to see what the commonwealth's decision about her husband would be. Unhappily, moving meant giving up the idea of his apothecary shop in Boston.

"I will go to the trial to be available to testify," vowed Eustis. "And I will do whatever I can to see a solution. We cannot predict anything. And I still need to deal with those men murdered on the waterfront."

CHAPTER 33

The day arrived. Judge John Ruddock, with jurisdiction over crimes of assault, battery, and affray, arrived in Boston to call the Court of General Sessions of the Peace to order. Criminal cases requiring decisions would begin precisely at nine o'clock in Faneuil Hall. The lawyers gathered, and the public was welcomed. Prosecuting were Samuel Quincy and Robert Treat Paine. Jurors, picked from the voting freemen of the town, were ready. Women, being considered too delicate, could not serve.

They began by defining Lindholm's crime as unprovoked malice with assault. Arguments disputed whether the crime was punishable by death. If so, the case would be referred to the supreme judicial court. Of course, the public, if sufficiently offended, might take matters into its own hands.

Eustis sat in a pew and, when called forward, offered his opinion. The jailors testified to Lindholm's uncontrolled behavior. The prosecutors seemed particularly eloquent with the end result being that Albert Lindholm was judged mentally unsound and a danger to the inhabitants of the town. He was remanded to a facility for the insane in Charlestown, to be locked up until further notice. There was neither a mention nor a decision about his marriage. Eustis knew that was a separate issue and would have to be brought before the legislature to be settled legally.

After a long day, relieved that the Lindholm case was resolved, Eustis headed home. Familiarity with the grim facility Albert would go into made him pause, but just a little. It was a dreadful and desperate place. Later, relaxing with his brothers over a tankard of cider, he relayed his depressing experience. Noah and Maria would get the update from Elijah who now spent much of his time visiting with Norah.

The women gathered in the keeping room to hear their brother's views and experiences with one question foremost: What can Norah do? She has no support and a child. And the workhouse is not the answer for a decent woman.

All chimed in with ideas, but nothing could be resolved. Everyone would seek outside advice. Eustis decided to talk privately with Norah to see what she wanted. She would have needs and desires and should have some say in this kind of momentous decision about her future. Neither she nor Elijah had voiced any opinion during the family discussion.

That's how the matter was left when everyone retired, cheered by Cath's promise of biscuits and gravy for their breakfast.

* * *

Sam had been thinking about the same trial and had discussed the possibilities with his father. He, too, was concerned about the life ahead for Norah. Sam was enough of a romantic to anticipate a future together for Elijah and Norah, but he knew well that Noah and Maria could be seriously affected if Elijah moved away. As he was sitting in his window glumly considering the possibilities, he saw Eustis approaching. He had not seen his friend for several days and anticipated a stimulating morning of what-ifs.

Preceded by Surry with a tray laden with steaming coffee mugs and cake, Eustis came into the room looking more concerned than Sam had expected. "Hail, fellow!" he called out.

"Fine for you to say," answered Eustis. "I am now in the midst of figuring out what to do or suggest to resolve Norah's and Annie's problems. We cannot keep them with us indefinitely. We already have Sally, and they need a place of their own. And do not just suggest they go off to live with Elijah and Noah. I am not sure that is quite the right resolution. Any ideas?"

"Ahh, Bill. I was thinking about that. Has there been any discussion with Norah?"

"Thank you for the coffee, by the way. It may help. I have been thinking of talking with Norah since I woke up this morning. But what to say?"

"What is Norah skilled in? Do you know? Could she open a shop? Teach? Make hats? Perhaps cook for a large family? Maybe a governess?"

230

"It takes money to get her set up, Sam. You know that. And where do we come up with those resources? Noah and Elijah want to have an apothecary shop together, and they are skilled in those healing herbs. I will be looking at a location they have found later this morning. But that does not resolve Norah's situation nor her money issues. I thought I would explore possibilities with her this afternoon. We may all have our opinions, may rush to decide, but after all it is her future. Some time ago, Nathaniel took the wagon and removed all of her belongings from the rooms she had occupied to our barn."

"I think you are right, Bill. Explore with them first. Look at Elijah's possible shop, and talk more with Norah. Then let us see what we can put together. You also have various people you can talk to around the town. I always think that before making a life-changing decision or even any big decision like this, you should first investigate and get as much information as possible. Then an answer may become obvious or we will wrestle with it until it does."

"You are right," Eustis agreed. "I do not know enough about all the possibilities. It is too soon to rush into decisions even if I want it all resolved." He frowned. "And hopefully soon. In fact, right now would be good."

"Keep in mind the resolution of living in the same building as the shop. That may help several of them," Sam reminded his friend.

The two men talked further and aired possibilities until Eustis realized he had better get back to look over the potential shop. The young men were waiting, eager to take him to the place close to the Green Dragon, to show what they had found.

The building was entered directly from the street and had two windows on one side of the door. Noah had the key and let them in, serving as an enthusiastic guide. "We can set up the shop in this room here," he said, gesturing to the space on the right with the two windows. Straight ahead was a staircase.

"What is upstairs?" asked Eustis. He was eager to get an idea if the site would also be livable. "Is there room to live here?"

The second floor had two small back rooms and a larger one across the front duplicating the first-floor layout. The walls were not plastered and were dark wood. It all was in need of industrious cleaning, perhaps whitewash.

The location was good, Eustis thought. But what about the cost? And was there a shed or barn? The young men explained that with the second floor they could either live there or rent it out to gain income to offset the cost of their present rent. They had to carefully consider their outlay for supplies and any improvements that might be necessary. Building a counter and having a sign painted were essential.

Elijah offered an idea that he had overheard in the coffee house nearest to where they lived. Two men were advocating for loans from a new firm interested in investing in new projects. They were sure it was sound because it had the backing of Abbott Tolliver's sons. And look where they lived in that big mansion on Beacon Hill near Governor Hancock. Elijah was eager to pursue the idea but wondered what Eustis thought.

As they walked back to Sudbury Street, Eustis explained his doubts about the Tollivers and that he would inquire as to what anyone else had heard about having an arrangement with an investor. He had questions. What was involved in this investment business? Why would they put money into an apothecary shop? How was an investor to make money on that? Had to be interest and what interest was he charging? Who had rights to what? Eustis did not understand the wisdom of accepting a loan without knowing what obligations went with it. Perhaps there were monthly payments? It would be taking a big risk if this investor ever decided to call in his loan when the young men were unprepared to pay.

There was a lot they did not know. That evening, the men sat with their heads together, going over the prospects with Eli and Noah. Jacob was consulted for his business sense as was Nathaniel.

And Eustis cautioned against being taken in by a display of wealth. "Let's look into this further. What other investments has that business made, and how are they to be paid off? And remember the interest is like rent and must be paid too. It seems almost too good to be true, and when that is the case, it often is not true. Let us all do our research tomorrow."

He thought he would talk to Bert Sommers. He may know or have heard of these people.

The Sommers family had moved back into their nearby house. Bert appeared determined to protect his family. He went about making sure his house was secure and vowed he would sleep, musket in hand, near the door. His wife was thrilled to go home to her own place as were the boys. She would sleep in the boys' room with the doors locked.

While Tabitha carried their few remaining belongings out of the Eustis barn and back to their house, Eustis talked with Bert, asking if he could share anything he knew about the Tolliver family. What had he heard about people investing in new businesses? Anything circulating in the taverns or coffee houses?

Bert was not absolutely sure it was the Tollivers running the investment scheme. But being in a vaguely knowledgeable position and being asked to give the doctor any information boosted his self-esteem. He was thrilled to hold forth on investors.

"Happy to talk, doc, happy to. What do you want in particular? Where do they live or who they have helped? Because I can tell you that I have not heard of anythin' like that yet. Only about some poor people signin' away parts of their businesses to 'em. They think they will get real big money. Mebbe 'tis too soon to tell and it may work out . . . but those Tolliver boys are doin' a real hard job of sellin' it, an' that always makes me suspicious. I am just not sure about those Tollivers anyway."

* * *

"Good morning, Mr. McAllister. May I quickly ask a question?"

Dark clouds with the threatening rainstorm made a farce of the new morning. Grimly going out to attend to a patient, Eustis passed John McAllister watching activities from his guardhouse and envied the watchman being under cover.

"Absolutely, doctor. I am pleased to be able to help if I can."

"What do you know about any activity around the Tolliver family? I hear they are starting to invest in new businesses. Is it legitimate?"

"As far as I know, it is. I have had no complaints. Funny thing. Just when I expect one, a complaint I mean, it quiets right down. Something always takes care of it, or it disappears."

After thanking the watchman, head down and trying to avoid puddles, Eustis hurried on to his appointment, thinking how grand it would be to have a carriage. Perhaps this moneylending idea was a good one, although he doubted it. But it was tempting to think he might get a carriage. Ah, well. A fellow can dream.

He headed home several hours later, immensely cheered by the successful delivery of a very large baby boy. The doctor's arrival and skill with forceps resulted in a thrilled family and a relieved midwife. In this case, the rain was just what was needed and brought good luck. All along Eustis had thought rain was only considered good luck for farmers and newlyweds. Tying the knot in the rain made it tighter, people said. Maybe something else could be said for rain and babies.

Midday dinner brought a smaller family to the table. Elijah had taken the wagon with Norah to see the possible new store, promising they would be back soon. That left only eight for Catherine to feed. Annie, of course, was glued to Sally when her mother was away. Until the garden came in, there would be a great deal of seafood in their diet. They would dream of dandelion greens, anything green. How marvelous it would be to have peas!

The sun started to break through, making the prospect of revisiting the waterfront so much brighter. By four that afternoon, Eustis was sitting with Elijah in the Philadelphia Coffee House, not far from the warehouses near the Long Wharf. Each nursed a clay mug of hot coffee. Eustis had encouraged Elijah to join him so they could consider his new ideas about an apothecary business and discuss his renewed acquaintance with Norah. He realized that he had been giving Elijah short shift because he was distracted by the activities and discussions around him, and he needed to explain. He talked about the several puzzles he was trying to figure out.

"My first question is how can there be murdered men floating in Boston Harbor just off here and no one notices or cares who they are? And second, I cannot understand why any person would offer investment money without some plan of repayment required. Also on my mind is your renewed acquaintance with Norah Lindholm and if you have plans there."

"Yes, I know, doctor. I, too, have a mind that is churning. It has been the highlight of my life to find Norah again. It feels like a lightning bolt entered my body, and I am stunned every time I see her. We have not yet decided if we will do anything about it. It has barely been two weeks, and she is healing rapidly. But I do know I hate being apart from her, and we have begun talking.

"As regards the business, it is as my gran always said. Do not trust anyone who will give you something for free. But may we please go outside along the waterfront? It is turning into a nice evening, and we could walk out on the wharf. I have yet to do that."

Finishing their coffee, they ventured out on Long Wharf, so named because it was indeed the longest. Several groups gathered, chatting and watching for the sunset over the town. As they strolled by two men, Eustis was startled to overhear what sounded like a threat. He walked slower and paused, looking out over the harbor while concentrating on the conversation.

The larger of the two men, black haired and bearded, clothed in the usual dockyard slops, leaned in close to the other and said, "Listen to me and mark my words, ye stupid eejit. Those men are not kidding, and they want you to cooperate. There is no changing your mind and backing out now."

"But I am not killin' anyone."

"You will if you are told to. The brothers got plans for you."

The men moved farther back toward shore and away from Eustis and Elijah who looked at one another. "What was that?" Eustis wondered.

Then the boats, the water, and the sunset distracted them for a few minutes.

235

Later, walking back toward Sudbury Street, they reviewed the issues about opening the apothecary: the cost of renting just the shop or renting the entire building or keeping their present rooms where the landlady included a midday meal. Then there was the question of where Norah wanted to live. Eli assured Eustis that she would likely want to live with them. She could help Maria with the coming baby as well as the shop. They all got on very well together, he said. But financing remained an issue. Their savings would only go so far.

With no clear solutions, they arrived at the kitchen door to find Noah just coming out. Norah and Annie followed. "We are off to our boarding house to make plans and get our supper. Maria is already there," Noah explained.

Eustis considered the time. He could just make it to the watchman's little house before McAllister's day was over. Or he could wait and go to the Town House and find a constable tomorrow. Opting for the more immediate, taking his lantern, he set out.

CHAPTER 34

John McAllister watched Dr. Eustis approach. There always seemed to be interesting dilemmas involving that man. Could he be some kind of trouble magnet? But in truth, a day was usually made all the better by a conversation with the doctor, and this would be a good end to what had been an unusually quiet afternoon.

"Dr. Eustis! Will you sit for a moment?"

"Happy to, Mr. McAllister. I have several thoughts I want to discuss with you."

And why am I not surprised, thought McAllister.

Once seated, Eustis told him about all the odd occurrences and the part of the conversation he had overheard.

"Are the Tollivers really so impervious to investigation? Does the senior Tolliver truly control the town? Is he that powerful? I am also wondering where his riches came from. For instance, we all know John Hancock's came from his grandfather, but where did Tolliver get his money?"

"You have certainly been thinking it over," said McAllister. "But I would caution you. Although Tolliver does control a great deal around this town, there are others who do as well. Hancock, as you mentioned, and other owners of shipping companies. I wonder about Captain Bonham myself. Even the Sons of Liberty. I have not heard of a successful direct dispute with any of those people."

"Hmm," Eustis frowned. "Tell me, Mr. McAllister, do you know what is happening in the barn down the lane from the White Horse Tavern? I have received information that questionable activities may be going on."

McAllister had heard nothing about anything going on there. Did anyone in the area know? It could just be local storage. He suggested that perhaps the doctor should go ask people in the area rather than deal with rumors. That did make sense and, somewhat disappointed, Eustis headed for home while thinking about his plans for the following day.

Children were following their families' cows along the lanes to make sure they did not wander off, although most knew the way to their own barns. Pigs and chickens were settling down after spending the day searching out things to eat, and the evening quietly descended.

The doctor's arrival in the barnyard inspired even more angst and upset in the Eustis household. "Is Sally with you?" The sisters and brothers surrounded him. They had hoped he had her. As it happened, their cows had come home without her, and now no one knew where she was. Where could that girl have gone?

He suggested they all go indoors and try to get their information together. Had she gone to get the cows to begin with? When had she last been seen? He would organize search parties to look in the areas where she might have wandered. Someone should try to reach the watchman before he leaves. And when exactly had the cows arrived?

The chaos settled a bit, and several in the family wanted to start searching. Eustis himself would go back to the Common where Sally had lived for a time on her own. Mayhap she had the idea to look it over again. She had been fascinated by the stylish houses there. He took Anne with him, and several others set off with lanterns in different directions, Nat and Jacob to the waterfront. The evening's darkness was growing, and they were anxious about losing what little light was left.

Reaching the Common, Eustis led Anne directly toward the clump of bushes where he had first found the young girl. The grass had grown back, and the shrubbery seemed undisturbed. He and Anne stood looking around them. A number of houses surrounded the Common. The lanterns and candles in the big houses were already being lit by servants, and the smaller brick houses lining the few lanes crossing Beacon Hill beyond the Common were starting to show the same sparkle.

Two carriages were approaching the Hancock mansion. Nearby, the Tolliver household seemed surprisingly dark. What could be going on there? Even servants needed lights to perform their evening duties. But wait. A few lights were slowly appearing toward the back. Recalling the attraction that Sally felt for the houses, Eustis walked in their direction.

"Bill, why go up here?" asked Anne.

"I know that Sally has watched and wondered about these houses as places where her mother might be employed. She talked to me about it, and she may have just gotten it into her head to visit them this afternoon."

"Do we go ask? At each door?"

"Might as well. I have no better idea."

"I think we should go home and see if she has been found," Anne offered. "This place gives me nightmares at night. Bad memories. She may have come back."

"Do you not think someone would have come to tell us? Ah well, you could be right. We will go back, although I have a feeling about those houses."

Sally was not at home. At Catherine's urging, they came in to have some bread and cheese before they headed out again with their lanterns. Anne was despondent. She now thought her brother had been right and that they should have searched around the big houses along the top and on the north side of the hill. They split into twos and went in different directions. Cath was left to mind her babies, make coffee, hold the fort, and generally keep track of where they had been and where they would go. Norah would go tell Elijah, Noah, and Maria. And what about the watchmen? Someone needed to go alert them.

With plans to meet back at Sudbury Street within an hour, they all set off. As the night progressed, the discouraged family gathered, regrouped, and continued to set out yet again. To no avail. They finally agreed they would have to give up the search until daylight and get some sleep. At least for a few hours. Eli, Noah, and Maria decided to stay and settled under quilts on the keeping room floor. They were all thinking about the young girl and how she had become such a part of their lives.

* * *

The sun had barely distinguished itself when, out at the pump in the barnyard, Eustis splashed water on his face. He needed to pull himself together to undertake more searching, and he certainly wanted to return to Beacon Hill.

239

Two of his brothers, looking equally haggard, joined him. They went in for their coffee and floated more ideas. Could Sally have gotten into the harbor? Did anyone know if she could swim? Has someone taken advantage of her? She was not particularly knowledgeable about men or town ways. They needed more answers.

Leaving the others talking, Eustis tied back his hair, grabbed his jacket, jammed on his tricorn hat, and stalked out the door. He would go house to house on the hill.

Approaching, he started first with the Tolliver house, in line before Hancock's pasture at the crest of the hill. Its curtains were drawn, and it looked unoccupied.

Rousing a sleepy servant, he was told that no one was at home, the family having left to visit relatives the afternoon before. But that was not right! He had seen activity here last night. Had servants been told not to answer questions and to say the Tollivers were not in residence? He asked to see the head staff person, presumably the butler.

As Eustis was waiting outside the door, the watchman approached. "Any luck finding the girl?" McAllister said he knew that the butler's name was Eastman, and he would try a little more persuasion.

Just then the butler came to the door, nodded to McAllister, and said, "I am sorry, doctor, but the family is not at home. I am sure they would have been pleased to greet you, but it will have to wait several days."

"But I was walking past here last night and saw lights and activity within the house. Can you not inquire again. We are searching for a lost child and cannot leave it for days."

"If you care to wait, I can inquire again."

The two men paced the hall and waited, hearing some noises in the back reaches of the house. Someone was home, but they must not want to see either the doctor or the watchman.

The butler returned and stood solemnly by the door. "Mr. Harrison has just risen and acknowledges that this is a serious problem. He will see you as soon as he is dressed. Meanwhile, please come in and take a seat."

Young Mr. Tolliver appeared about a half hour later, just when Eustis and McAllister were about to demand some attention or an explanation. He stood leaning against the door jam, one hand in his jacket pocket, and wearily asked: "Yes? What is it you want?"

Eustis was struck by his insolence and attitude. He stood and earnestly explained they were searching for a young woman who may have been walking nearby after dark the night before. As he said it, Eustis realized their inquiry was amusing Harry Tolliver. He seemingly believed he was untouchable.

"Well, Eustis," he drawled, smiling. "I guess someone got to her before you did. You lose. Too bad." And he turned to leave.

"Just one minute," said Eustis, his anger rising. "I resent your implications, sir. This girl is my ward and a resident in my house. You have no reason to cast slurs on her. If this continues, I will have to call you out. It is totally unacceptable!" Eustis was red in the face and fuming.

McAllister intervened. Even Harry realized he had overstepped his bounds. He turned back and reluctantly offered an unfelt apology. Eustis was still seething but realized he had better solicit any help or information he could get.

"Where were you last night, sir?" McAllister asked.

Harry smiled. "I was in Charlestown at my usual place in the Three Cranes. It is now my establishment, if you inquire. And it would seem that you should take advantage of some of our services."

"There were candles ablaze here last night. What was going on in this house?"

"This is really a private matter, and I resent your inquiries, no matter how concerned you are with the missing girl. As far as I know, my brother, Winfield, was hosting several friends here. And now I will bid you good day." Turning, he left the room.

Eustis looked at McAllister. "Winfield Tolliver?"

As the butler came to usher them out, McAllister asked, "Eastman, where is Mr. Winfield Tolliver today?"

Eastman was stony faced and declined to answer. "I cannot say. It is not my place, Mr. McAllister."

Eustis intervened and asked if there was a cook, a coachman, or some other staff member to whom they might talk? "Someone who might have seen anything last night. Anyone who was a daily employee? Please. This is a young girl who is in trouble, injured, or lost. Do you not understand?"

It may have been his desperate plea or anguish, but the butler suggested they speak to the coachman and said he could be found out in the back near the carriage house. Then he opened the front door and suggested they walk around. They could not stay in the house.

Circling to the back of the mansion and entering the carriage yard, they approached a man in high boots and an elaborate black uniform with gold braid on the collar, shoulders, and sleeves. He was a substantial, older man with creases around his eyes and mouth and stood watching as a groom brushed down a lively, brown horse which tossed its head and would not hold still. McAllister stepped forward and held the horse's head, immediately reassuring and quieting the animal.

"Nice work. May I offer you a job?" said the man in black livery.

McAllister, amused, introduced himself and Dr. Eustis and explained their purpose in seeking his help.

The coachman, introducing himself as McSherry, told them that Mr. Winfield had been at the house all night with several of his male friends. Mr. Harry had hired a small carriage to take him to Charlestown, as he usually did. Then McSherry did not have to wait there overnight. One thing was curious though. He thought Mr. Harry had another person with him. He had not gotten a good look as both quickly hustled into the carriage, which had its curtains drawn, using the door on the off side.

Eustis looked at McAllister and then back at McSherry. "Can you tell us this address? Where Mr. Harry Tolliver regularly goes?"

"Certainly, sir. It is the Three Cranes in Charlestown. It has been rebuilt after the battle and Charlestown fires and is now reestablished as a tavern with other pleasures for men in the evenings. You understand, I am sure."

After expressing their gratitude and shaking hands with McSherry, McAllister and Eustis quickly returned to Sudbury Street to regroup and get their own conveyance. They would go to the Three Cranes in Charlestown.

CHAPTER 35

Deciding to cross the river, Eustis sent a message to Chief Constable Winters and enrolled McAllister in joining him. Then, telling his brothers of his destination, he saddled Nelson and rode with McAllister to the ferry, the most efficient way to access Charlestown. It brought back memories of crossing the Hudson River when he was stationed in New York during the war.

Even after ten years of rebuilding, Charlestown still wore the scars of fighting and the conflagration of the battle on Breed's and Bunker's hill above the town. The ferry carried them to its usual landing place on the opposite shore, and they ascertained the direction to the Three Cranes, receiving curious glances.

"You know they do not open until a good deal later in the day," said one.

Eustis acknowledged that and, once mounted, both men moved quickly.

The Three Cranes was not far and had room to tie the horses in its barnyard. A bent elderly man approached from the barn. "What're you doin' here? We be closed 'til four this afternoon."

"All the better to get our business handled before," answered Eustis, walking toward the back of the main building and to what he presumed was the kitchen door. Rapping on the door, he persisted despite the old man urging him to stop, even reaching for his arm. McAllister stepped in, introduced himself, and explained they were there on legal matters. The man quietly retreated.

It took nearly fifteen minutes, but the persistent banging brought a squint-eyed older woman to the door. Her lower lip protruded in an exaggerated pout. She looked to be in her early fifties, gray-haired under her cap, and clearly irritated. "Cease that feckin' noise immediately, you ill-begotten gibberlumps! My ladies are trying to sleep. What do yer want?"

McAllister stepped forward, introduced himself again, and asked to speak with whoever was in charge. Perhaps Madam Springfield? Eustis also stated his credentials, and they both waited while the woman, muttering about her mistress, withdrew and shut the door. Both men hoped someone else would appear. Perhaps a person who knew what was going on or who could let them in. They waited, trading glances, pacing.

Drawing their immediate attention, the door opened and an attractive, middle-aged woman with a tightly corseted gown, her carefully curled hair verging on blonde, and a delightfully pleasant voice invited them in.

"Perhaps some coffee, gentlemen?" She led the way into a large room and asked them to be seated, promising she would bring coffee immediately.

Looking around, Eustis saw that the room was elegantly furnished with a variety of chairs and sofas with small tables. Several Persian rugs covered the floor. Having removed his tricorn, he stood again when, an appetizing aroma preceding her, the woman reentered carrying a tempting tray.

"Now," she said, after they were seated again and she was pouring the coffee into delicate cups, "please tell me what this is all about. And have one of those muffins."

McAllister nodded at Eustis to indicate the doctor should state their mission.

"We are searching for a young girl, about twelve years of age, who was taken from her home in the North End of Boston last night. She is my ward and responsibility. We must find her without harm as soon as possible."

"Alas, Dr. Eustis, we do not have young girls coming into this establishment. I am sorry that I cannot help you. Though I can see that you are most concerned."

McAllister shifted in his chair, balancing the dainty china cup in his large hand. He much preferred a mug. "You must understand that if we do not find this child we will return with other help, most likely the local constables, and search this place despite any owners' objections. We think she may have been brought here by Mr. Harry Tolliver. I am not sure yet of your name, madam. Are you Mrs. Springfield?"

"Yes, indeed. I own this establishment and have several investors. Mr. Tolliver is one of them. We do not want any trouble with the law. Would it ease your mind if I asked some of my ladies to talk to you?"

"I appreciate your help. Thank you," said Eustis. "While it could be informative to speak with several of your ladies, it would not prove that this young girl was not concealed somewhere under this roof. We really must be able to look for ourselves. And in every possible hiding place. Shall we bring back others?"

"I wish we might avoid that, Dr. Eustis. Let me just alert the ladies that, sadly, their privacy will be invaded, and then I will take you around myself."

She rose and left the room. The two men conferred to make sure they were in agreement. They must see every part of the establishment from cellars to attics. And then the barn and outbuildings.

"If you wait a little, doctor, I can call on a few of my associates here in Charlestown to help," McAllister offered. "But I see you are eager to start now."

"You are right, Mr. McAllister. We may call them later if we need the reinforcement. I hate to leave time for some person to escape or hide elsewhere."

That said, he noticed from the window a man wrapped in a cloak walking rapidly away from the house. "Wait! Who is that?"

McAllister glanced out the window and, rising to his feet, left running for the door to go in chase.

Mrs. Springfield reentered the room, surprised by the absence of the watchman. He appeared behind her with a discouraged looking gaunt man of about forty years in his grip, the other hand holding his baton. "Here 'e is, doctor. Caught him just as he was startin' to pick up speed."

"Good work, Mr. McAllister. You should receive a commendation for such rapid response. I have a few questions for him. And for you, Mrs. Springfield. But first let's get introductions. Who is this man?"

With greasy brown hair tied back in a queue and dressed in well-worn clothes, the man looked at the floor, saying nothing. He kept peeking at Mrs. Springfield. Perhaps looking for instructions if he worked for her. McAllister assured him that he could go to the local constable for questioning, they could handle it there, or he could come with them to Boston. It took a little while, but soon the man revealed that he was trying to get away because of his fear of punishment. "Af'er what we did. An' Mr. Tolliver too."

At that remark, Eustis knew he was on the right track.

It all came out shortly. The residents at the Three Cranes were fearful, worried about the influence and power of the senior Mr. Tolliver. His son Harry had promised severe retribution if they hesitated in obeying him.

McAllister cautioned everyone not to leave the premises and sent a sleepy boy who usually worked in the kitchen for the local constable. Then he suggested that the doctor take a look around with Mrs. Springfield while he watched their informer. "You know what we want," he cautioned Mrs. Springfield.

After walking through the kitchens, the pantries, the entire first floor, Eustis was getting discouraged. On the second floor, the smell of perfumes and scented body lotions pervaded the air. He followed Mrs. Springfield as she opened each door, apologizing to the occupant, who often woke at the sound of the door.

"Where are Mr. Harry Tolliver's private quarters?" he asked and discovered that they were in a side wing with its own entrance, storage areas, and attic.

McAllister's local help arrived. They took over the search of the upper levels and cellars of the tavern, leaving the doctor to explore the private wing. "You can stay with these men, Mrs. Springfield," said McAllister. "I will continue with the doctor."

Both outside and inside doors were locked between the tavern and Tolliver's wing. No one had keys. However, the resourceful Mr. McAllister had a lock pick and used it quickly. As they entered, Eustis thought he heard a slight whimper. Sally? He listened again. It came from upstairs. They found her, hands and feet tied, on the floor in a small room connecting to the second-floor bedroom.

Eustis gathered her up in his arms, and McAllister untied her restraints. She clung to the doctor and whimpered into his neck, "I wanna go home."

Holding her tightly, Eustis descended the stairs and went through the tavern then directly out the front door. He said to McAllister, "I am leaving everything to you and taking her home with me."

And he did.

CHAPTER 36

Alerted by the sound of a horse's hooves, the family poured out of the kitchen door to greet Eustis holding Sally in front of him on the saddle. Catherine's welcoming arms gathered her in and helped her into the warm house.

In the kitchen, Eustis quickly related what had happened, their venture to Charlestown, and Sally's discovery. "Norah should take Sally to her room to recover a bit," he advised. "I got here as fast as I could. I think she is unhurt."

Norah held Sally around the shoulders, guiding her into her room while they brought in the bathtub. Being tied up overnight had left the girl damp and smelly. Later, bathed and in clean clothes, she was tucked into bed with little Annie and Norah sitting on the edge, patting and reassuring her. Anne ran to the harbor, carrying the news to her brothers at the waterfront.

* * *

McAllister joined them two hours later to report to the family in the kitchen. "We have a warrant to arrest Harry Tolliver if we can find him. I suspect he is in hiding and waiting for his father to take care of everything."

Cath worried. "I am not sure how we can prevent his father taking over. I certainly do not want Harry to escape giving an accounting for what he has done. He should not be allowed to prey on other young girls. We must find him."

"Let me talk with Sam," Eustis said. "After all, his father will have some say as will Governor Hancock. If nothing else, Hancock surely will not care for this behavior by someone in his social circle being exposed. They will alert the constables, turn out everybody, and we will find him before words gets out." He thought this might be the breakthrough he had hoped for to explain all the nefarious activities going on around the harbor.

249

The men left on various missions, and before they returned the women would talk with Sally and ascertain if she was really unharmed. They could not let men do the necessary examinations but would call in Mrs. Fisher, the midwife. Even Dr. Eustis was excluded, and he waited outside.

Cath, Prudence, and Anne carried stools into Norah's bedroom and sat around the bed. By now, Norah had Sally calmed down and sitting up, wrapped warmly in a quilt.

"Oh, Sally," said Cath, "We were so worried. You have no idea of all the searching we did to get you back. But it was all worth it. We would do it again in a minute." She paused. "But now we have to ask you about everything."

"You may not want to talk about it," explained Prue, "but we have to know what happened to you."

Sally looked at them. "I can tell you." And she related a long story of talking to a very nice man near the Boston Common where she had gone to get their two cows. He had offered her a ride home in his carriage. It was such a beautiful carriage and she really, really wanted to ride in it. So she sent Hazel and Hattie on their way and got in, but they went someplace else. When she wanted to go home, the man covered her eyes and mouth with a scarf. She thought they had gone over a bridge and then had come to a house where she was carried in. There were all sorts of sounds, people crying out, laughing and talking, and she could smell food and other nice things like perfume. But she was put on the floor in a small room, her hands and feet tied, her mouth covered. Then she heard the click of the door being locked. At some point in the night, the man brought two other men to look at her. He was talking to them about what he called a "special arrangement" he could make for them if they gave him enough money. She had become really scared, thinking he might be selling her.

"Did they look at your clothes or under your skirt or at your legs?" asked Cath. Sally thought they were going to, but they heard a loud noise and left quickly. She thought they would come back. But they did not.

The sisters looked at each other. It seemed that Sally was telling them all she knew. She should be fine unless she had some flashbacks or bad dreams. Looking at each other, they breathed a mutual sigh of relief, thankful they did not need the midwife after all.

Catherine left the room to talk with her brother. "Bill! That horrid Harry Tolliver was trying to make a deal to sell her to other men. Somehow, they changed their minds, but I am sure he would have succeeded by tonight. God be praised that she was rescued in time."

"I can tell you, Cath, I was truly worried. I am going now to tell Sam the whole story and see what can be done from there." Eustis grabbed his hat and overcoat and left.

He found Sam wrapped up by the hearth downstairs in the Adamses' keeping room.

"Good day, my friend!" Eustis greeted. "Good to see you have ventured down from the nether regions to check on us common working folk."

"And good day to you too, Bill. I found that I was feeling well enough, so why not venture from my room. What is new in your world?"

"Not what we would wish, I am sorry to say. We were frantically searching well into last night trying to find Sally. She had been stolen from us."

Horrified, Sam stared at him. "What? This cannot be a joke."

"Mr. McAllister and I finally found her this morning across the Charles River in a brothel in Charlestown. You will not believe it, Sam. The infamous Harry Tolliver had found her at the Common and talked her into his carriage. He was trying to make an arrangement to either rent her out for deflowering or sell her. Fortunately, we arrived in time. And my sisters have since ascertained that she was not molested."

"God's teeth! Our Sally? How did that scoundrel ever get her? Please sit and tell me."

"More than that Sam, I want you and your father to help prevent this scoundrel, as you rightly call him, from continuing in his practices. That girl could have been seriously injured or worse. I left the Charlestown

251

constables searching the Three Cranes brothel with our Mr. McAllister and Constables Cobb and Winters. Seems Tolliver has disappeared. But I want him in court and answering for this."

"What do you need, Bill?"

"Could your father get us in to see Governor Hancock? He needs to be warned that he will undoubtedly be approached by the senior Tolliver to ease any accusations."

"Absolutely. My father is not going to be sympathetic to Harry no matter what anyone might think. He was charmed by Sally when he met her. And wait 'til Surry hears."

"Thank you, Sam. I will head back now and be back tomorrow to see what has developed. Perhaps your father could get the Sons involved to also find this menace."

"I am sure he will. He should be back soon. If nothing else, the news around town will ruin the Tolliver reputation. Are you sure you won't wait?"

"No, my friend. I will leave it to you. Now I need to be back home." Eustis shrugged his coat onto his shoulders, waved, and left quickly. And Sam settled in to wait for his father.

It is said that the wheels of justice turn slowly but grind exceedingly fine. The Greeks knew what they were talking about thought Eustis as he hurried back to Sudbury Street. In this case we may find it too slow for our taste, but we will more than succeed in the end. It was a good time for thinking, and he remembered he had not been able to talk with Mrs. Noyes as he had planned. Perhaps they could get to that this evening. And she might know of possible places Tolliver would hide.

* * *

Prudence was modeling the new shawl she had made for spring's chilly weather when Eustis entered the keeping room. The shawl was a soft olive green color that Prue had achieved by skillfully dying the wool. The younger girls, including Sally, were all admirers. Sally seemed to have recovered from her adventure now that she felt safe at home. Eustis suspected, however, that it would be unlikely she would want to immediately bring home the cows from the Common.

He briefly told Cath and Prudence about his brief visit with Sam and asked if anyone had given Elijah, Noah, and Maria the latest information about the search and outcome?

"I am ready to relax and try to get my own anxieties under control, but we might go to the tavern for a short time." He looked at his brothers with eyebrows lifted, a question in his mind. They agreed it would be good to get out to walk and talk.

"White Horse or Green Dragon?" asked Nathaniel.

They arrived at the White Horse within the hour and, seeing the barn at the end of the lane, Eustis recalled that he still wanted to look inside. Perhaps when they left. They selected their table anticipating a quiet chat, and large mugs of coffee were promptly brought by the same waiter with whom they had first talked some weeks before. It all seemed very familiar and comfortable.

Eustis had advised the brothers that he wanted to talk with Mrs. Noyes when she came in, so they were prepared when he left their table to join her at another.

"I am glad to see you, doctor," said Mrs. Noyes. "Seems it has been too long."

"I agree. Unfortunately, I have news and questions to ask. I cannot just visit."

"You look like you are tired and have had a hard time recently."

How did she know? Eustis went on to tell her all about the recent situation with Sally being captured and potentially sold to several men in Charlestown.

"Oh, my dear, that poor child!" said Mrs. Noyes. "I am so sorry to hear about it. Is there a way we can catch the men involved? This is just not right. We must find them."

They talked about what might be done, and Eustis urged her to listen around during her travels for hints of the whereabouts of Harry Tolliver, telling her how grateful he would be for her help.

She agreed but asked in exchange if he would try to find out what was going on in the nearby barn. This was probably the third time she had raised the question. Tolliver had seemed to be in charge there. They came to what might be called a "joyful" understanding, each agreeing to help the other, and Eustis returned to his brothers.

The day waned and they agreed they had better go back home. After all, they had a mid-day dinner celebrating Sally's return to look forward to. Leaving the tavern, Eustis looked again at the barn. "What would it take to get a look inside?"

"I doubt it would be a problem. Should not take long," said Nathaniel. "I bet you that I could climb up enough to see in that window or go around behind and get in. Want to place a bet?"

Eustis said he would take Nathaniel on. The winner would get a tankard of ale or cider, his choice.

Nathaniel left them to go snoop around the barn, and Jacob and Eustis enjoyed the clear, crisp spring afternoon outside the tavern while they waited to see what would happen next. As it happened, it was the arrival of two men heading for the barn. Jacob quickly moved out to hail them, asking if they knew if the barn was for rent. "My brothers could use more storage space," he added.

The men seemed slightly nervous about being stopped and hastened to say they just worked for some people who wanted broadsides printed. They were not even sure these people owned the barn, or the printing press, saying perhaps it all belonged to someone else.

Jacob made an effort to continue the conversation, hoping to give Nathaniel more time to get away if necessary.

"Could we see inside?" asked Eustis, walking over to them. "I saw that it was locked. Do you have the key? Indeed, if we could just have a look for future reference."

The two men looked at each other.

"'Tis possible just a peek in the door," offered one. "But I am sure we cannot let you inside. Nobody said anything about that or having visitors."

They followed the men and waited while the lock was opened. The men went in, and one turned to let them peer through the door. Nothing looked suspicious. Just a table with what looked like a printing press on it. There was a stack of paper beside it. All of this took up the area just inside the door.

"What is in back?" asked Jacob who was in front.

"Dunno. We never looked back there or up in the loft. No idea. Storage?"

At that point there was a faint thumping or bumping from above. Nathaniel on the roof? Eustis and Jacob glanced at each other, decided to ignore it if possible, as did the two men. They thanked the men loudly and withdrew, hoping their brother got away safely.

Afterwards, standing farther down the lane back by the tavern, they waited hopefully for Nathaniel to appear. It seemed to take too long, and Eustis was about ready to go back when Nat quietly appeared from around the far side of the tavern. They signaled to each other to leave quickly and went out to the road before stopping to talk.

"What of your adventure, brother?" asked Eustis. He felt amused, but looking at Nathaniel's expression he quickly grew serious. "Nat! What happened?"

"I think there are people in there!"

"Well, of course. We went and looked in the door with the two that walked up. They were going to print some broadsides."

"No, you idiot! I mean others, people, perhaps as prisoners in the loft."

"What! Are you playing with us?"

Nathaniel in turn explained that as he eased his way up onto the back of the roof, using the help of the fence bordering the back of the property, he heard faint sounds from within the barn. Had the brothers heard anything out of place? And they remembered the odd sound that both they and the men in the doorway chose to ignore.

"I thought it was you making a soft thump," said Jacob. "We heard it. Right?"

Eustis suddenly felt very concerned. Whatever was going on?

Tolliver could be in there. The three talked it over while walking back to their home. They had better return with both watchman and constable on the morrow. If those Tolliver sons were involved, it could mean their father was as well. Winfield could be hiding in the loft. But who else could be there?

CHAPTER 37

The Eustis household was back to its usual, bustling morning routine. The family had had its dinner celebrating Sally's return the afternoon before, and all were eager to get started on the day. The doctor had three medical calls to make, and his brothers were off to the harbor on their own business. The women were on to their numerous tasks of housekeeping that now included spring cleaning.

Stopping at the watchman's shed, Eustis gave McAllister a quick update, explaining their possible discovery. They arranged for a visit to the barn in question. McAllister would alert the constable. Enoch Cobb was not yet on fulltime duty, so they expected Samuel Winters instead. Planning to meet at three o'clock outside the White Horse Tavern allowed the doctor to hurry on with his rounds so he could be there.

* * *

In midafternoon, Constable Winters arrived at the meeting spot at the end of the lane to find the three Eustis brothers and McAllister who was carrying a large blacksmith tool for cutting metal. Winters had acquired paperwork for a legal search if it was demanded.

"I hope it works out," he muttered to Eustis. "Shall we?" And he led the way up the lane to the barn door, locked as usual. It took only a minute, and the heavy hasp was freed so the door could be opened. The men entered and paused to let their eyes adjust to the dim light. The dirty small window high up on the wall did little to illuminate the interior. The constable walked around the front of the barn surveying the printing equipment, the paper stacks, and several samples of the work. Then he started toward the back of the barn. The others followed. No one spoke. They could see a ladder mounted on the wall at the rear. Above was a hatch.

McAllister motioned that he would climb up through the hatch. He pushed it open then disappeared inside. They next heard his shocked exclamation. "Oh my God! This is dreadful! Constable, you better come see this." Winters, followed immediately by Eustis and then Jacob, took turns climbing up.

The loft was lit only by a tiny window set in the rear wall. In the dim light, Eustis could see what looked like five people wrapped in rags and lying on straw on the floor. They appeared to be chained hand and foot to the walls. The odor of urine was pervasive.

"Hey! What are you doing here?" Angry voices below challenged Nathaniel.

They overheard some sort of scuffle, and the constable and watchman descended as quickly as they could only to be grabbed at the foot of the ladder. Five men had entered the barn led by Winfield Tolliver. Those remaining, the two Eustises and five others in chains in the upper loft, stayed still, silently apprehensive, hardly daring to breathe.

Nathaniel kept his head and said, "We were just looking over the place and wondered if you know the owner. Wondered about the attic too. I would like to talk about a purchase. What are you doing here, Tolliver?"

Winfield Tolliver, pushing his way forward, glared at Nathaniel. "None of you have any right to be in here, and I intend to make you sorry that you ever thought of it. I'll file charges. As for you two officers, let me be clear. You have no rights here or over me, and you better remember that! Your jobs are seriously in doubt. If my father decides you will lose your jobs, you can bet you will. Now get out and do not come near this place again! You better be careful if you want to continue working in this town. We have ways to make you wish you were far away. But you probably will not be walking by then."

The men behind him glared in support of their leader. One, swaying from one foot to the other, smacked his fist into the palm of his hand. "Let me give 'em a sample, boss."

"No, Jason. They are not stupid. They know enough to stay out of our way now. Right?"

The three visitors nodded in agreement. They would do nothing to draw Tolliver's attention to the others in the loft. Instead, they would get themselves out, regroup, and get more help. There had been no sound from above.

"Dr. Eustis, Dr. Eustis!" a small boy ran in the door. "Where is he? My mother needs him. She said he was here!"

Recognizing Tommy Sommers, Nathaniel moved to grab and hold him tight. He assured Tommy that he would take him to Dr. Eustis but that the doctor was not here. "As soon as Mr. Tolliver says that I may go, I will take you to him."

He turned, looked at Winfield. "May we leave?"

Tolliver, pleased with this subservience, agreed. He had not really thought through what he would do with his prisoners. Nathaniel quickly ushered the boy out the door and down the lane where no one could hear his protests. "Shh, Tommy. I will tell you where Dr. Eustis is and all about it as soon as we get out to the road."

Jacob and Eustis, crouching in the attic, waited to hear what might happen next. Eustis hoped that Nathaniel would run to the Adams household and alert Sam and his father to call out the Sons of Liberty. Tolliver would be really stupid if he did not release the two policemen. And, of course, Eustis would have to find out what was bothering Mrs. Sommers. But first they had to wait for a while.

Tolliver decided they had better release the officers. There was no place to put them anyway, and he could not risk arrest or the fury of his father. Surely they had no idea about anyone being in the attic. He and his men had better secure the barn and leave to rethink what they should do. Yet he had to retain leadership. He swaggered about a bit, insulting the officers, then dismissed them as being of no importance anyway, feeling secretly relieved when they did hurry away.

"Let's secure this place and go have something to drink. The White Horse. It is all on me," Winfield said. The men with him were pleased, not wanting any confrontation, except for Jason who always enjoyed it. What the others enjoyed was the idea of the tavern.

"And we need to get another lock for the door. This one was cut," Winfield added.

One fellow was designated to go get a lock, the rest repairing to the White Horse, noisily taking a large table.

After they left, Eustis could move among the chained Black prisoners, checking their injuries. Slavery had ended in Massachusetts just a few years before in 1781 based on the Mum Bett case. He could not be sure about these people's stories or even if they spoke English. He should get Noah and Maria here. But these people who were illegally confined needed to get out too. The Eustis wagon?

He turned to Jacob who, having had the same thought, said, "I should run to get our wagon. Then we need to get them out as quickly as we can. Will you stay with them or come too?"

"Someone should stay, but I lack my medical bag. I need some supplies. If they come back before we are ready, it could be a disaster. Right now, Tolliver does not know that we know. I say we both get out and do our errands then come back with reinforcements, prepared to get these people out."

Just then one of the men spoke. Apparently, some knew sufficient English to understand the discussion and concerns. "Go fast, now. We wait," he whispered, knowing full well he had no other choice.

"Good," said Jacob. "We will be back as soon as possible. Come, Bill, now!"

The lock had not yet been replaced on the barn door. They went out, closed the door, and walked quickly away.

Once on the road, the brothers parted. Eustis to go to the Adams House and then to brief the watchman, and Jacob to run to their own home to get the wagon, the medical supplies and, if he could, Maria and Noah.

* * *

It was growing dark when nearly thirty men gathered at the end of the lane leading to the White Horse Tavern. The crowd included the Eustis men, McAllister, and the two constables, Cobb and Winters, with Elijah, Noah, and Maria. Most of the rest were Sons of Liberty including at least a dozen dockworkers, some men of color. Others were just indebted to Dr. Eustis or one of his brothers. They had all heard of this affront to the laws of their commonwealth and had personal reasons to be there. Some may have just hated the Tollivers. Chief Constable Winters wielded a large bolt cutter.

The vigilantes, for such they were, marched down the lane to the barn, noted the new bolt that had been placed on the door, promptly cut it, and opened the barn. The doctor led the way to the ladder in the back, going up first, followed by Noah then Elijah.

McAllister called out. "Get them out carefully. We are ready with the wagon." More men gathered at the base of the ladder waiting to be directed, to help in the loft, or to carry people out.

The assumptions were right. The prisoners could not walk well after their confinement. Four men and one young woman were gingerly lowered from the loft and taken out to the waiting wagon where an interested crowd from the tavern had gathered. Maria had blankets and quilts to wrap around the prisoners' shoulders. But where to take them? If there was an attack by the Tollivers, their new site had to be defensible but not obvious.

Bless Sam and his father, thought Eustis. The senior Adams had arranged for a waterfront warehouse to be opened for them, and they moved quickly to the North End, placing guards around the building. Once settled inside, Noah and Maria reassured the rescued, and Dr. Eustis looked them over, bandaging areas scraped raw by their restraints.

The Sons of Liberty were proud of rescuing the imprisoned people. Their connections around the town were broad, and women had been cooking. Enormous amounts of steaming chowder were brought in pots with bowls and spoons to the warehouse. To their astonishment, Mr. Adams, the lieutenant governor, came in to check the situation. He would keep the governor informed, he said, and they would help find decent housing as soon as possible. Meanwhile, the Tollivers, father and sons, would be prosecuted.

Eustis went to the senior Adams to thank him for his assistance. "I wish Sam could have been here."

"I know," said Adams, momentarily clenching his lips, "but you will come tell him about it tomorrow." He turned at the sounds of a commotion and hoofbeats outside the door. The senior Tolliver arrived in his elegant carriage. How had he found them?

CHAPTER 38

In elegant formal dress, wig and cane, Mr. Tolliver stepped down from his carriage and approached with an aloof expression. "Adams, how can you associate with these ruffians?"

"No problem, Tolliver. They are my ruffians. And should you wish for a display of their superiority, I will be happy to demonstrate. Are you ready to turn yourself in to the authorities? Or will you wait for the subpoena? We are a country of laws now."

Tolliver looked startled at this unexpected response. He immediately turned and went directly back to his carriage. There he turned back and said, "This is unconscionable. You will pay for this, Adams. And you too, Eustis."

"Our pleasure, sir," replied Mr. Adams with a bow and a smile.

* * *

The March evening proved to be verging on warm, a sure sign that New England might be joining the rest of the country in welcoming spring. His late supper over, Eustis decided to take a break and walk to the Bell in Hand to have a peaceful tankard of ale. They brewed the tastiest kind as far as he was concerned. He did not know if it was a homebrew or from some rural village. Otherwise, it was usually cider for him. Jacob said he would catch up to him after finishing some paperwork.

Ambling more than walking, Eustis took his time going toward the waterfront. Oddly, he felt that someone was behind him. But in glancing around, he could discern no one there. Very strange. He quickened his steps toward the tavern and heard steps move more quickly behind him.

Turning the second time, he caught a glimpse of a man turning into an alley between two warehouses. And beyond him one or more people seemed to be lurking in the shadows. What was going on?

"Hello there. Are you looking for me?" he called out. There was no response.

Then an oddly familiar voice growled in his ear. "You guessed it. Now turn around quietly and prepare to do what I tell you." It was not Bert Sommers, but the voice sounded very familiar.

Eustis turned slowly. The man with the muffled voice turned with him, staying behind him, coming close and pushing him back up the road, away from the docks. "Just keep going where I tell you."

As they passed an alley, Eustis looked out of the corner of his eye. It seemed like something was moving. Who was in there? It did not seem right. He slowed down only to be pushed forward. "Keep going." He felt something pointed pressed into his back. A knife? A flintlock?

"But where are you directing me? How can I go where you want if you do not tell me?"

"Just do as I say, and keep your mouth shut." Another push on his shoulder.

They passed a large deserted and closed ropewalk and were almost out of the area of barns and warehouses. There was no sign of anyone around. Piles of barrels, bins, and boxes but no people.

Something made him look up. One of the piles of barrels started to tip. With a great roar it all came tumbling toward them. Eustis just managed to move, crouch, and cover his head with his arms. He was slammed to the ground, stunned.

People shouted, and he slowly became more aware of where he was. People converged around him. He saw Jacob, Elijah, and Noah and another Black man. The man who had threatened him had been hit squarely by a falling barrel and was sprawled face down on the dirt lane. He was unconscious, wearing a head scarf, an old black hat, and dirty dockworkers clothes. Oddly, his stockings and shoes seemed remarkably fashionable. Eustis slowly sat up. Others were approaching, drawn by the noise. Elijah had grabbed a piece of rope, part of a coil that was lying by the barrels, and began to tie the hands of the unknown cove. They turned him over to an audible gasp.

Harry Tolliver lay sprawled on the ground bleeding profusely from a substantial gash on his forehead. Noah stood by to help Elijah if necessary. Eustis was still baffled. He bent and pressed two fingers against the side of Tolliver's neck to ascertain that there was a heartbeat. Tolliver? What had happened? Did he attack Eustis because of the incident at the barn?

Whistles shrilled as someone, a constable, ran toward them followed by several men, one carrying a lantern. They all circled the group, and Constable Cobb took control. Eustis, almost recovered and feeling more stable, was pleased to see Cobb was back on the job and immediately stated that he had been threatened and the others had come to rescue him. Cobb directed two of the approaching watchmen to secure the bleeding man on the ground and take him to the jail.

Eustis still felt breathless, a delayed reaction he thought. He would need to follow them to the jail, determine what had happened, and try to focus. Bert? What was Bert doing there by the warehouse wall? Too much was still moving around him. He needed a few more minutes to recover.

Noah approached, introduced his new friend, Cuff Peckham. Cuff, a Black man, had experiences similar to Noah's in the recent war, being with the First Rhode Island Regiment, and the two had immediately bonded. Cuff lived near Copp's Hill and the White Horse Tavern where they had met. He had eagerly offered to help the five freed people, finding housing for them through the African church on Beacon Hill.

* * *

The following day, fully recovered after sisterly attentions, Eustis planned to check in at the jail after making several medical stops. The first to report his news to Sam.

"It was really satisfying. Those poor people were rescued and will have some choice in their lives. It seems one of the captives speaks the same language in which Maria was brought up. They do not all speak the same language, so we were lucky to discover this connection and that most already knew a smattering of English."

Sam reminded him of the activities within a community of color developing on the back side of Beacon Hill. "They have that African church, and many people are building houses there."

"It was a good resolution for the captives, for everyone, but Sam, it is not over. We still have more mysteries to unravel. For one, the arrest of Harry Tolliver and why he was there. And we still have those murders in the harbor. I hear they also have brought Bert Sommers in. He was just standing there watching when I was nearly killed, and it seemed he would know something or why else was he there? I do not think there is a Tolliver connection with Bert. There has to be something else. Did he push the barrels? I have been mulling over what we know, and I keep wondering what those poor drowned souls did or did not do that made them a target. Were they given orders they did not carry out and suffered death as punishment? Or was it some vendetta among the neighborhoods?"

"If hired killers were involved in the drownings, they require resources to disappear," Sam reasoned. "They must be paid. And why did Harry Tolliver attack you? He usually has others do his dirty work."

"I am getting the idea that the brothers were concerned about my inquiries around town and invading Winfield's safe place in that barn. But then we have Bert. Why was he there? I will have to talk with McAllister. I need a bit more information. Thanks, Sam. You have set me on another path."

"But what path is that, Bill?"

Eustis stared out the window. Suddenly he turned. "I've got it, Sam. I've got a possible solution! I will be back tomorrow. Have a good day. I have to get on my way right now."

Eustis grabbed his coat, left Sam with a quizzical look on his face, and hurried back to his home where he gathered his brothers into the barn as the women were busy in the keeping room. Evicting them would not result in a good supper.

As the men settled down on hay, Eustis asked his key question. Who has been controlling the trade in the harbor? Tolliver? Or someone else?

Jacob suggested that it was not necessarily the senior Tolliver. He would more likely take advantage of business schemes. But his sons were beginning to branch out. Another person who would be very involved in the shipping trade was Captain Augustus Bonham. But there were other competitors as well.

"What about Bonham? Is he also in investments?" Eustis pressed.

"The captain has two large merchant ships and at least three other smaller ships in the coastal merchant trades," Jacob related. "Actually, I am wrong. He lost one very recently when it was caught in a gale off Long Island. Ran ashore coming back from the Caribbean. I hear it was a slaver headed for Rhode Island named the *Annie B* and considered a total loss. I have not heard if anyone survived. Bonham's son drowned in that wreck. Wait! Do you suppose those people we rescued from the barn came from that? But then how did they get here?"

Eustis was puzzled. The Bonhams? What had they to do with Abbott Tolliver? Were they in some kind of competition? But he had just found five wretched survivors of slavery in the barn that Tolliver rented or owned. Winfield Tolliver implied they were his. What of Bonham's loss of a ship that carried slaves? How did that connect? Did Tolliver steal the slaves? Could it be part of a two-family rivalry or a vendetta?

"I thought I had it, but I probably need to take a walk," he announced. "It helps me to think."

He still had the afternoon. He had not gotten back to Mrs. Sommers to find out what had gone wrong there. Bert Sommers had been found lurking near the wharf last night when he was supposed to be home protecting his family, and then he told the constable he had pushed the barrels. Now both he and Harry were in jail.

Eustis left to talk to the constable and check the jail. The short-term holding facility was in the basement of the Town House where the constables' office was located. It would fit in with the two calls he had to make.

* * *

Eustis and Nathaniel followed the watchman on duty down the stairs into the cellar under the Town House where three cells with iron bars held those needing to get sober, awaiting trial, or expecting a judge's decision. Harry Tolliver, head bandaged, was yelling threats from one cell, and Bert Sommers was sitting on the cot in the other. He seemed a little uneasy about the situation he found himself in.

"Doctor! You came! How is Tabby, my wife? She is going to be upset that I admitted I did this to Harry – pushed the barrels over."

"Just wait until my father hears of this," shouted Harry.

The others ignored him in favor of listening to Bert.

"Your wife is with my sisters, Bert, as are your boys," Eustis reported. "She will likely leave town and is halfway packed up now. I have never seen a woman so angry. She would happily kill you."

"Well, she just does not understand, doctor. She will be fine once I explain it to her."

"I would not bet on it, Bert. Now will you tell me what happened?"

"One of Captain Bonham's crew grabbed me when I was walking down at the harbor. I think it was his bosun, and he took me to the captain. He explained to me about my daughter and his daughter, and how Harry Tolliver had taken advantage of both of them in New York. Killed 'em both too. You know I have been looking for the cove who killed my daughter. It really set me off, and I said I would kill Harry if I found him. Sort of my revenge. Bonham agreed and said he understood. He gave me some more of those cigars he has to set the deal. An' I did. Went after Tolliver. Just like Captain Bonham suggested. Then I had the idea to push the barrels over on 'im. 'Tis all good now."

"Another question, Bert. Captain Bonham had asked you to kill people for him before. Am I right? And probably said he would tell you about your daughter if you did. What exactly did you do for him before this?"

"Uh-huh. Well, there was some other ones. Got one cove down at the harbor on the wharf. But then I decided I did not want to do any more work like that for him. But the captain really understood about my daughter. He was sorry for me not being able to get my revenge on Tolliver. It was personal. He used to give me cigars to use to get the bad 'uns to come to the wharf. And he said he would look out for me."

"Tell me about Monty Thurman."

"Was not me that actually killed Monty. He drowned. Captain Bonham thought Monty knew something bad and would make trouble. I offered him some cigars, and he came down to the wharf. That other one jumped off the ship to get away from the captain's bosun."

"Oh, Bert, are you sure about all this? It is possible Bonham may have ordered his bosun, but he used you. It was his revenge killing, not yours."

"No, doctor. I am sure you have it wrong. You will see."

"Yes, I am afraid I will."

CHAPTER 39

Eustis and Nathaniel returned to the constable's office and asked if there had been any inquiries about Bert from Captain Bonham. The constable assured them that the captain had nothing to do with Bert's story. He had already been in and cleared himself of any connection with Bert.

Now the doctor could see the entire plot and why Bert had been followed and what was behind it all. It was Bonham's strike back. The attempt on Harry Tolliver's life for Tolliver's theft of Bonham property, the slaves in the wreck. The death of Bonham's son might be involved as well. He would talk with the chief constable and then go to see Sam. It was about harbor feuds.

When Sam heard the story, he responded: "The fault, dear Brutus, lies not in our stars but in ourselves that we are underlings."

"And that we, not only Sommers, are gullible," added Eustis

"Actually, it is an unbelievable story," Sam observed. "Remember, you found that end of a cigar on the wharf, and it probably was from one that had been used as a bribe. Bert must have offered cigars as a lure to get a man out on the wharf."

"Just what I was thinking a while ago, if you remember. Did I not suggest it, Sam?"

Eustis had just thought through the past six months of rivalries and intense competition among Mr. Tolliver, Captain Bonham, and other likely investors and captains with their growing businesses. A vast number of warehouses along the waterfront were filled with imports and exports as the harbor grew more prosperous. In a town of rich businessmen and entitled strongmen, several had become engaged in full-fledged, all-out war. But it had all been kept under wraps unless it served any of them. No one stopped at insults, dirty deeds, or, in this case, murder.

It was Eustis's surmise, as he explained to Sam, that the initial drowning in Boston Harbor was probably an accident. "That man who jumped off one of Captain Bonham's ships probably gave the captain the idea for dealing with some of his other problems. Or he was indeed chased by Bonham's bosun. He was trying to escape from some threat aboard the ship and chose to attempt to get to shore. It could be that he intended to report something, talk with somebody. Unfortunately, no help arrived for him. Maybe his connection was only that Bert tried to rescue him.

"The second victim, Monty Thurman, worked for Captain Bonham, making deliveries or carrying messages. He must have overheard something, and they thought he was going to expose them."

And then there were the Tolliver brothers, Eustis offered. As disagreeable a pair of young men as could ever attempt to go into business in Boston. Each felt he was justified in doing whatever he wanted to do; each somehow convinced that he alone was above the law. They certainly had ranged well beyond any area their father would have approved. And it had started years before in New York. Throughout their childhood they had been assured of their brilliance and superiority. Their father had then moved to Boston to escape any suspicions of wrongdoing in New York. Then it devolved into the sons' competition, that each grew more important, better than his brother, by making more money. Money was the ultimate goal. Morals, if either had any, disappeared.

"But Bert is the greatest loser," Eustis concluded. "Stupidly convinced to murder Thurman, perhaps others, then deciding to eliminate Harry. All this was really Bonham's attempt at revenge, or at exerting power against the Tollivers. Ah, Sam. Why do we ever believe these self-declared strongmen and their promises? People seem very impressed if they are so rich they can maneuver beyond the law.

"Somehow we believe we will gain by it, and that blinds us to the reality of what they are doing. It is all about money for them. They do not care who they step on or the lies they tell. They just want to have the most money, and that makes them feel like king of the hill. And poor, stupid fools, those who believe in the myth of another's superiority, are the ones who suffer."

271

* * *

It would seem that as soon as the news of his sons' activities and arrest reached the senior Tolliver, he immediately left the country on one of his ships without waiting for a full cargo. His servants would again be enslaved in Barbados. Left behind in Boston were his sons, and other men who had worked for them, to face any prosecution. Tolliver did, however, send money for their defense.

When investigating Captain and Mrs. Bonham, the constabulary discovered that their son had indeed disappeared earlier in the year, possibly drowned in the wreck of that Bonham ship. The Bonhams decided they had better move out of state and left promptly for Rhode Island before a constable could build the case to connect them to Sommers and arrest them.

And Bert Sommers never understood what he had done wrong but was given a prison sentence anyway. His wife left with her sons, moving to Connecticut to live with relatives.

* * *

Invitations were sent to everyone who had helped with the investigation including Mr. McAllister, the constables, and Mrs. Joyful Noyes. They all cheerfully crowded together in the Eustis keeping room, kitchen, and parlor. A toast was raised to the rescuers and the rescued by the doctor's father, Benjamin Eustis. He had followed the adventures of his son with intense interest and was proud to have suggested looking at the Tollivers and Bonhams several months earlier when he noticed some oddly favorable arrangements leaning their way.

Holding his tankard aloft, Eustis said, "Here's to a successful solution, and to persistence in reaching it. In Massachusetts, we do seem to start activities that have repercussions across the country. Just look at what we did out there in Springfield. It is still influencing the government. I believe the conference in Philadelphia will result in good things."

He was interrupted by Anne entering and holding aloft a fresh apple pie. And when he could, the senior Eustis added: "As the Bard said, 'All's well that ends well.'"

272

EPILOGUE

A convention of delegates from the states gathered that May in Philadelphia. Based on a motion by James Madison, they soon disposed of the original Articles of Confederation that had ineffectively guided the United States. Three and a half months in Philadelphia's summer heat found the delegates negotiating a new form of government to be explained in a new Constitution, sent to the various states for ratification. Governor Hancock presented it to the Massachusetts General Court for deliberation and acceptance in October 1787, and a ratification conference was called for the following January in Boston.

Despite the widespread interest, William Eustis did not attend that conference. He sat with Sam, his dying friend. Announced in the Boston *Gazette* on January 18, 1788, Sam Adams Jr. died in his home on Winter Street. His father, the lieutenant governor, and the rest of the town were thrown into mourning, and Boston's ratification convention adjourned so that members could join the funeral procession.

ACKNOWLEDGEMENTS

Much of the research that provided the background for this story was done for my earlier non-fiction book, *Allegiance: The Life and Times of William Eustis*. Dr. Eustis's life seemed such a remarkable adventure that I wanted to make it into a fictional series using some of the highlights.

A great deal of appreciation goes to those initial readers who were willing to go over, at best, a confused plot and characters including Holly Hobart and Jay Evans. I am grateful for friends who seem to enjoy discussing murder and difficulties in plot or location, and who consistently offer encouragement.

My gratitude goes out to countless people who made suggestions and inadvertently gave me other ideas. And special thanks to the Falmouth Historical Society and its executive director, Rachel Lovett for letting me photograph inside their federal gem, the Francis Wicks House, as well as their archivist Meg Costello who is always helpful with tricky questions.

Special kudos to Bob Haskell, the king of removing extra commas and putting them in the right places. As always, his hours of work made this book better by far, miles beyond my early beginnings. And many thanks to Stephanie Blackman and Riverhaven Books for being so patient with me.

HISTORICAL NOTES

I have based the characters in this story on actual persons who lived in Boston in 1786. When the Revolutionary War ended in 1783, Dr. William Eustis finished eight years of service as a surgeon in the Hudson Highlands area. Under General Washington's direction, Sam Adams Jr., a fellow surgeon, helped him close the last hospital at West Point. They returned to Boston together, each needing substantial time to recover from the post-traumatic deprivations of the war. Sadly, young Dr. Adams had contracted tuberculosis, called consumption at the time, and would die from it in 1788. His father, Samuel Adams Sr., had been and would remain a part of Dr. Eustis's life for decades.

Eustis moved into his Boston home occupied by his large family. His father had remarried after the death of the mother of his children and moved to his new wife's house nearby. The household accurately included six siblings and Ebenezer Wells, the husband of William's eldest sister, Catherine. They would add a son in 1785 and another in 1787.

The only person I added to the household was young Sally Edwards. She was a real person known to Dr. Eustis when he was an apprentice to Dr. Joseph Warren. Eustis paid Dr. Nathaniel Ames for her board and care after Warren's death at Bunker Hill. Sally disappeared from the official records when she was put out in an indenture by Dr. Ames – also a real person. The Dedham Historical Society has Dr. Ames' account book that includes Sally's birth, but Sally has not been found in subsequent records.

John Hancock did live in a big house as described at the top of Beacon Hill. John Ruddock was a real Justice of the Peace, and Samuel Quincy and Robert Treat Paine were prosecutors for the Court of General Sessions of the Peace in Boston. And Paul Revere, besides riding to alert the countryside that "the Regulars are coming" in April 1775, was an enterprising silversmith and merchant who built a foundry in the North

275

End of Boston in 1787 to cast bells among other things. He also had a copper mill and made sheets to cover the bottoms of ships.

Farmers rebelling in the western part of the state fomented what became Shays' Rebellion. The Commonwealth of Massachusetts had to solve its problem of the farmers' revolt because the Confederation Congress had neither the money nor the means to do so. Dr. Eustis, as vice president of the Commonwealth's Society of the Cincinnati, went on the expedition to Springfield to quell the revolt and participated in a raid.

The Bell in Hand, the White Horse, and the Green Dragon were actual taverns and their locations in Boston are close to accurate. The Three Cranes Tavern in Charlestown actually burned down during the Battle of Bunker Hill.

Loosely united under the Articles of Confederation, the thirteen American states met to rework their alliance in Philadelphia in 1787, resulting in our Constitution. Sam Adams Jr. died of tuberculosis, Dr. Eustis at his side, during the ratification conference for this new Constitution in Boston in 1788.

William Eustis continued to practice medicine in Boston where he went into state politics in 1790, urged and supported by Samuel Adams Sr. In 1800, Eustis was elected as a representative to Congress, traveling to the brand-new capital of Washington City for the 1801 inauguration of the third president, Thomas Jefferson.

More adventures awaited him in Washington.

Tamsen George